Seasons:
Carol of the Bells

Seasons:
Carol of the Bells

Written by Kahner C. Calloway

Edited by Miranda Hale-Phillips

Copyright © 2018 by Kahner C. Calloway

Edited by Miranda Hale-Phillips

Cover design by Hannah Ellis

Book layout by https://daverphillips.com

ISBN 978-1-7329789-0-4

FIRST EDITION

https://kahnerccalloway.com

For my mother, Nadine.

You always showed me that it was important
to never lose my wonder.

Table of Contents

CHAPTER ONE

The Son of Winter

Heat rose from the several mugs scattered throughout the little inn as smells of cider and chocolate rose in a comforting mist. It was late November and workers had made their way into the little building nestled in the outskirts of the city. Sounds of laughter and sharing of daily tales rang outside of the brick building as children ran by heading to their homes.

Several circular tables laid inside the common room, each filled with eager customers, awaiting the waitresses to bring them their beverages or meals. The main room took up most of the bottom floor along with the kitchen tucked into the back. A staircase was built on the back side of the building, giving the owners access to a smaller home located upstairs. A fireplace was built high, giving the room a warming glow. Music came from a bard sitting in a corner by the entrance, stroking up seasonal songs upon request. A game of chess was being played in the other corner by an older gentleman who made his daily visits to the tavern to enjoy his free time with the innkeeper, a large man, who would look up from their game on occasion and answer questions from his employees. It was growing closer to December, and everyone was getting rested for the final rush of the year where they would all have to work together to finish their quotas.

The windows were dark with the night sky despite it being the start of the evening. Time was not kept by the coming and going of the sun, because in certain parts of the year it would not go down for days. Other days, it would not rise, such as today. The cheerful sound of merry-making continued as the time for rest crept through the city. The innkeeper had finished his game of chess, losing to the gentle old man. He gave him a curt bow before heading for the kitchen to check on his wife who must have had the ovens going full force. He was stopped half way through the joyous crowd when the bell from the front door rang.

The owner turned to greet the newcomers, but he had an instant feeling that these visitors had something strange about them. Sticking to his duties, despite his qualms, he walked to the front so he could meet the three new guests. In a warm voice that hid his unease he said, "Good evening, gentlemen, and welcome to the Lake of Frost. My name is Borian Mugsteeve. Is there anything I can interest you in while you warm up from the cold? Some hot cider, or some of our original snow cakes, best in the city?" he finished, smiling into the hoods of the mysterious people.

They wore deep brown cloaks that wrapped fully around them, concealing everything about their features. It was odd that they still had their hoods up, because the fire had the place toasty. The one on the left was a foot shorter than Borian, who was an average size man himself. The other two were easily a foot taller. The ones on the outside looked through the crowd, possibly scanning it for empty seats. The one facing Borian leaned in slightly and said in almost a whisper, "We would just like one of your tables for a little while." He stretched out a gloved hand to the innkeeper, who accepted five of the city's gold coins.

Looking at the coins questioningly for a moment, Borian nodded at the men and led them to an empty table next to the old chess player, who was now reading a newspaper and awaiting the next challenger. "I hope this is fine. We're slightly packed tonight with the coming of December and all." The three looked at each other, then took their seats, pulling them close to one another. Borian took this as an answer and walked away from the men. He told one of his trusted employees to keep an eye on them before heading to the kitchen.

Walking through the double-wide doors, Borian found that his earlier guesses were accurate. His employees went to and fro, cooking or filling glasses to take to the guests. The three ovens located on the back wall glowed red as the bread inside them baked. His wife, touched gently by age, stood in all her radiance he had seen from her since the day they met. She had her trademark apron on and held a wooden spoon in her hand, using it to give commands to her cooks. She was a caring woman who held an iron grip when it came to the kitchen. Even though Borian was the owner, he would never try to cross her in here. He walked up to her and she greeted him with a smile, leaning in and kissing her before telling her of the newcomers.

"They could just be shy," she assured him, after Borian confessed his unease. "They could have just moved here and want to get to know the place."

"You're probably right," he nodded. His wife always had a logical answer for everything. A yell came from the front room, causing the workers in the kitchen to freeze at the sound, unsure of how to react. Borian ran to the swinging door and pushed it open. The customers around the room held the same stupor as the kitchen workers, with the musician's silence adding to the effect. Their expressions were no longer joyous, but fixed in expression of disbelief. All eyes fixed on the three strangers whom he had seated minutes before.

They stood together, facing the corner, so close that their robes looked like solid drapes. One had its arm stretched upward, with a decrepit hand clenched around the throat of the chess player. The old man was limp, eyes closed. Borian ran at the intruders, not knowing what made him so courageous, yelling as he lowered his shoulder to tackle the one holding up his friend. Instead he came into contact of the hand of the shorter one, which sent him back across the room, slamming into a table. Pain ripped through his back and head as drinks spilled on top of him, and his vision swam as hands reached down and picked him off the floor. He grabbed one of the men's shoulders who helped him up and focused back on the creature. It could not be human, because no one had that unnatural strength.

The one holding the old man dropped him, where he crumpled to the floor. In unison, they all turned toward the crowd. Everyone backed away from them, frightened of their next action, which was to move towards the unfortunate Borian. A scream came from Borian's left as his wife jumped in front of him. He knew there was no time, so he grabbed his love and pulled her down, protecting her with his back to the intruders. Borian waited for the pain but all that came was the bell from the front door. His eyes widened as he looked over his shoulder, realizing that it was not the front bell of the inn. It was another bell—one known throughout the entire city. When rung, it gave the individual who heard it an overwhelming feeling of hope.

The one who had killed the old man had drawn a weapon from his cloak: a curved dagger with a dark green blade. The lethal looking weapon was stopped mid-stroke by a long, straight, soot-grey blade with a simple guard that looked as if it were made from glass with a handle wrapped in white fabric. It was wielded by the person who had just saved their lives.

He stood facing the innkeeper and his wife, his sword casually over his back blocking the dagger. He wore a forest green shirt under a hooded white jacket, with two pockets along the front breast. His pants were slightly baggy, white, and held in place with a black leather belt. The fabric appeared light on his frame, yet it was woven in a sturdy manner. His black boots matched his gloves, which were both made for combat. What shocked Borian the most was how young this person was.

Though he wore his hood over a white winter hat stitched with a black pattern, Borian could still see enough of his face to distinguish an age. He had to be in his late teens, with brown hair stopping just past the top of his ears. His eyes were dark blue and held a look of concern as they surveyed Borian. After confirming the innkeeper was well, a smile came across the young man's face as he said in a low voice, "You might want to watch who you let into your home."

Borian opened his mouth to reply something, but all he could manage was, "Look out!"

The other two shrouded men had pulled their blades as well, both the same sickening green. In unison, they swung for both the young man's sides. Without so much as looking at his attackers, the young man in white turned on the spot, parrying the first sword and stepping away from the range of the other two. His speed caught the dark hooded figures off guard, long enough for the young man to kick the one to his right in the chest, sending him flying through the opened front door that some of the guests had escaped through. He was strong, Borian thought, probably stronger than the enemy seeing how the one now outside flew with more force than the unsuspecting innkeeper had.

The other two brought their swords in front of them, guarding themselves. The young man, however, took his blade and slid it through a sheath hanging white on his belt. This caused more confusion, but the green sword wielders took only a second to recover before the smaller one lunged forward, sword ready to run its prey through. Right before the sword pierced the white coat, the young man stepped sideways, and in one graceful movement took the arm of his adversary, kicked the legs out from under him and threw him into his partner at the front door, who had recovered enough to try and re-enter the inn. Both disappeared into the night and seconds later were joined by their third comrade, who had waited too long to attack and had paid for it by another quick throw of the young man in white.

With all three attackers outside the savior turned back to the innkeeper, his smile gone and replaced by a hard look and a voice that demanded attention, "Take care of him. He's not dead, but he does need the hospital. The rest of you," he looked around at the silent guests, "wait five minutes, then get home." With his last command, he turned to leave.

Borian's wife spoke up right before he exited the door, "Wait, you saved our lives."

The young man didn't turn back as he said, "Not yet, but I will."

"What's your name?" Borian at least wanted to know the name of the man who had just given him and his wife a gift they could never repay.

The young man turned his head and smiled before telling them, "Kol." And with that he vanished into the winter night.

******

Kol stepped from the inn and searched the ground. The hooded figures were no longer there, and he wanted to catch them for questioning. He searched the ground and found footprints different from the others around it. Bare feet, not shoed. Kol determined their path, then sped left after them.

The road was illuminated by street lamps, light from the surrounding buildings, and the light of the full moon. The trail Kol was following turned down an alley then back up the adjacent street. He continued this pattern of street hopping until he went down another alley where the footprints ended. Looking around, he saw no more trace of the creatures. Snow fell in front of him, and Kol instantly turned his gaze to the roofs of the buildings on either side of him. A dark figure jerked back at his gaze and shuffled faintly backwards. The buildings were three stories high, but Kol bent his legs and pushed from the ground, leaping into the air. He then pushed off a window on the second floor before rolling onto the roof. Back on his feet, he sprinted for the three attackers, glad to be gaining on them.

Their speed was unnatural, but so was Kol's as his hood fell from his head. Gap after gap he leapt, but he was not gaining on them fast enough. If he didn't do something soon, they would hit the end of the buildings, leap onto the city wall, and disappear into the tundra. Thinking to himself, Kol reached into a case attached to his belt. Grabbing the silvery object in his hands, Kol waited until he felt he was close enough and shook it once.

The three offenders came to a stop as the tiny bell tolled. The shadows in the hoods looked up at Kol who now stood in front of them. A hiss started and the brown robes came off the three beings. Kol was slightly surprised to find humans standing in front of him, but the flesh of these "humans" appeared to be rotting. Festers and boils covered them completely and the red and black of their skin barely stood out in the moonlight. The exposed bone did, appearing randomly on their body from what looked like bite marks. The greenish weapons from earlier must have fallen with the robes, because only rags hung from exposed bone. Their eyes were bright yellow, and their posture was slouched as they cracked their fingers.

"So tell me," Kol locked his eyes on the middle one, assuming him to be the leader. "What are ghouls doing this far North?" Their rotting flesh gave him all the clues he needed to know what they were from the brief description he had read in one of his books.

"We do not answer to you, Son of Winter," the one on the left spat out.

"Oh? then who do you answer to?" Kol said, raising his eyebrows.

The three then answered one after the other, speaking quickly, "He will have you all."

"The set is placed."

"All will be broken."

"Decisions."

"Make one."

"To save few or all."

"Or None."

"What do you mean?" Kol reached to his belt and pulled his sword. "Stop speaking in riddles and answer me!" The three of them looked at the sword and smiled at its wielder. Before Kol could stop them, they turned towards one another and began to attack. Limbs came away with a ripping noise and teeth sank into flesh. "Stop!" Kol demanded, but it had no effect as the ghouls destroyed each other, laughing their way to the grave.

******

The city had grown quiet with the night's aging. Kol had stopped back by the Lake of Frost to make sure no one else had been hurt. After he had left, the Cadence had been called to investigate the commotion. Finding everyone was in good health with only shaken spirits, they had finished their investigation and departed. The innkeeper, Borian, greeted him with more thanks, wanting to bring him in and get him something to eat, but Kol declined politely. He only asked if the hooded figures left anything behind. The innkeeper looked for their payment when the Cadence came, but could not find it anywhere. Kol told the apologetic man it was all right. He asked after the old man, making sure he had been taken to the hospital before leaving. Once Kol had his answers, he departed from the inn to begin his journey home. He walked amongst the quiet buildings, fortifications built to channel his thoughts down one street or another.

The whole situation made no sense to him. Why would ghouls be here when they preferred cool climates, not freezing? Kol's breath misted in front of him as if to prove his point. And how did they even know where here was? This place was too strongly guarded for them to be able to enter, at least without alerting someone. Then once inside randomly attacking someone, and within a crowded place? Could hunger drive them to do that? There was also the fact of their numbers. From what he had read, ghouls were very territorial, regardless of their gender, and they wouldn't hesitate to attack any living thing around them. Always searching for nourishment, which was flesh to them, they saw nearby ghouls as a threat to their food supply. The final part of this confusion was the fact that not only could they speak, but they knew who he was. Could it be possible that they were after him all along? That idea was just as ridiculous as any of the others he could come up with, but he made a mental note to do further research on the creatures the next time he visited *Ve'rema*.

Kol examined the buildings around him more closely to give his mind some rest on the matter. They soared higher and higher the closer to the center he went. If the city was seen from afar they would look like glacial peaks reaching into the sky. On closer inspection, it would become clear that it was not glaciers that you perceived, but beautiful stone and glass crafted into wondrous architecture. The large buildings meant for the people of the city to work within were made of a white-blue stone and square at their base with rounded corners at the top. The buildings grew smaller as they grew higher and rounded off into a ledge. On top of each building was a large glass dome that would shine when the lights inside were on. Gold and silver cross beams held the glass in place, and the dancing lights that reflected off the material helped the tops of the buildings glow.

Once this place had been nothing but a small town, but now it was a metropolis of individuals who had needed a place to go. Decorations of tinsel, wreaths, and ornaments of all different shapes, sizes, and variety hung along each one's base. Down the side of the roadways, trees stood against the barren cold, themselves dressed in the elegant suit of the season. In between each tree were simple lamp posts with red and gold tassels, mounted into the wide sidewalks. The fire inside did not burn from fuels, but from enchantments placed there.

The walkways were vacant of ice, and crews made sure to keep them clean, but the road was a war the workers decided not to fight. No vehicles were parked here, since the inhabitants of the city used the underground trains for long journeys. If the destination was too far to walk, however, or if the people preferred to not travel below, large carriages could be found striding along the street. Vehicles such as snowmobiles, weather adapted trucks, aerial vessels, and other engines were reserved for emergency use only. Kol took the time to admire his familiar surroundings because the excitement of the decorations could still be felt even this late. Christmas was once again upon them, and there was nowhere else on earth that it was more celebrated.

Continuing his journey to the center of the city, Kol stepped from the streets onto the carefully placed stone paths of the ring-like, forested park. The park stretched close to ninety meters inward, the paths illuminated still by the enchanted lamps. Not far from the paths, the people of the city could find stone tables and benches to relax should they wish to stay off the ground. Kol enjoyed the lack of the usual commotion and eventually exited the park into the central plaza. This place was known for taking one's breath away, especially on that special night.

Kol stood in a huge circular area large enough to fit thousands of people—the entire population of the city, in fact. The stone tile surface blazed in a multitude of colors, depicting images of the history of the city. In the center of the plaza stood a massive Douglas fern which created a legend upon first sight. The trunk was so thick a comfortable home could be carved inside it with room to spare. The branches above were wide and strong and the tree reached high into the night, even above the tallest buildings. The tree was also decorated in the classic design of a Christmas tree like all those throughout the city. Hanging bulbs of golds, reds, and greens glittered above Kol, taller than he was. Ornaments of snowflakes shimmered and looked to be made of diamonds. Tinsel wound amongst the branches so thickly that children could climb on it without fear of it breaking. Lights were wrapped around it as well, but they would not be turned on until the first of the month. With the darkened buildings built at a distance and the trees that circled the plaza left dark, save for the faint lamps, the full power of the stars and Aurora Borealis fell over him.

This very spot that Kol walked across was the site of the original village that had stood here. As the mosaic depicted beneath him, it had been destroyed and the occupants decided that it was time for a change, all thanks to one man who had planted this very tree to signify the unification of life here. Kol was well past the tree by now, making his way to the only building that had not been destroyed so many years ago. In fact, it had begun as a workshop, and additions had been made over time. The home was made of white stone stacked expertly upon one another with a clay roof. Brick chimneys were built along the outside so that the rooms were well warmed. The lowest two floors were the largest, with the two floors above built in a smaller size. If someone wanted to exit the third floor they would be able to walk atop the second as a wraparound porch. The front doors twinned one another and arched into a soft point. They were of a darker stained wood and held large stained-glass windows. All the windows on the first floor were stained glass, and those on the other floors were simply transparent, but all matched with dark stained frames.

Several lights were lit along the building. The one that interested Kol the most was a circular window at the top of the fourth floor. It was dark, which meant those inside were hopefully asleep. Kol climbed the wooden stairs that cascaded into the plaza: the house's front was made flush with the ring of smaller trees. He could have climbed back through the window he had left, but with it being so late he decided the front door would not hurt. Kol removed his glove as he approached and reached for the iron handle. He left it there for a moment while the house recognized who he was. Once the enchantment was satisfied, a soft click emanated into the night as Kol went quietly inside and closed the door softly behind him.

The entrance room was massive, decorated in seasonal appeal, and was of wood carved by hand to express a forest of pines during winter. From here anyone could take the door to the right to enter the kitchen, which was even larger than this room. The door on the left led to the main common room for visitors to meet with the owner. From these rooms and scattered staircases, a visitor could gain access to the library, guest bedrooms, and other expansions. Two staircases began on both walls and climbed to meet on the third floor. Those were the master's quarters for the owner and family. The bottom floors were mainly used for work, while the top two were meant to be private. Centered across from the entrance, beneath the staircases, were two large doors that led to the largest area in the house, the workshop.

Kol headed toward the left staircase, hoping to escape into his room before anyone noticed he had left. He made it halfway up the flight of stairs when a voice came from behind him, sounding slightly high pitched. "Master Nicholas, we are glad to see you have returned. Your father would like to speak with you whenever you have a moment." Kol froze at the voice. He made little noise when he moved, needing stealth for his work, but it seemed that no matter how hard he tried he could not sneak past those ears. Turning slowly, he found the elf looking at him with a smile.

"Slee, how many times do I have to tell you not to call me that. You know I hate it."

The elf rocked back on the heels of his feet with his hands behind his back, still smiling. His shoes and pants both shone black, and his shirt was a button up crimson. He stood slightly shorter than Kol, and to truly define him, his ears came to a point out from his golden hair. "Oh, you don't have to tell me anymore, I know you don't like it. That's why I'll continue to say it to you."

Kol couldn't help but smile at Slee. He was a very close family friend, after all. "He's still up?"

"He figured he would get a head start on the list," Slee said, still gleefully. "And…also waiting on you to return."

Kol gave a soft laugh at this. "Okay, lead the way." Slee nodded rapidly and started down the stairs for the doors to the workshop. Kol caught up and together they pushed open the double doors.

The area inside was vast, challenging the main room of a cathedral. Dozens of work benches lined the floor to each side and made of a dark varnished wood. Each work station had its own assortment of tools for the trade. Along the left and right walls were raw materials of wood, metals, wires, and cloth, all ready to be crafted. An upper deck could be ascended by golden ladders where the gifts would be wrapped and stamped. A multitude of paper was attached to the walls in every color and pattern, some attuned to the season and some not. The room was lit by more enchanted lamps, but that did not hinder the moonlight coming in from the stained-glass windows of the back wall on the second floor. This alone would stop visitors, with its intricate design of Christmas color.

The workshop was usually alive with elves and humans alike, walking back and forth between the work benches, tables, and wrapping stations. Given the hour of the night, however, it stood empty and quiet. Two staircases were centered on the left and right walls and spiraled downwards into the basement. With the increase in work over time, the workshop had needed to expand. Instead of expanding outwards, it grew downwards into the ice and rock below. Only the most masterful of workers labored here; they were the leaders of the workforce below. Craftsmen who came to their jobs could be checked in below after leaving the transit system. This helped keep the house secure from anyone trying to get inside through any means other than the front door.

Kol and Slee crossed the workshop and made it to the center staircase which took them up to another set of double doors. These were also red, and engraved on them was nothing more than a simple snowflake. Slee stepped out of the way and held his hand out in a butler-like fashion for Kol to enter. Kol pushed him aside playfully, and Slee laughed before jumping over the wooden handrail and disappearing. Never a dull moment with Slee. Turning his attention back to the doors, Kol took the right doorknob in his hand and entered.

If the city was the embodiment of Christmas, this very room was its heart. It was a circular room with shelves lining every wall with books and trinkets, all editions dedicated to the stories ever read to children before they slipped into peaceful sleep. Other objects joined the books as well. A blue wooden horse sat next to

T'was the Night Before Christmas. A red train with two freights behind it and a small golden-haired doll rested cheerfully next to *A Christmas Carol.* Right next to *How the Grinch Stole Christmas* was a teddy bear, with an uncomplicated design of golden fur. It was meant to protect those who held it dear from the monsters lurking under the bed and in the closet. It had protected Kol well, and he only knew of this room as a rightful place of retirement. These were some of the first toys ever created here.

The carpet was stitched with images of eight reindeer leaping into the air towards the desk that sat in the middle of the room. The desk was carved by the owner of this home, with mistletoe and other symbols of the holidays engraved in it. Stacked on top of the polished wood desk were scrolls, all inscribed with the names of various children. The room was lit by a chandelier of candles hanging from a gold chain connected to the center of the dome-like ceiling. The ceiling looked like snow, ready to fall to the floor. The man sitting behind the desk looked up at Kol through his square spectacles as he entered the room.

His hair flowed sliver from his head, merging with his beard down the front of his chest. He had slight wrinkles in his face, but all the age was wiped away with his smile which spoke of nothing but youth. His red long-sleeved shirt came over his notorious belly with black suspenders stretching over either shoulder. The most noticeable part about him was his shocking dark blue eyes, the encasement of winter, that seemed to bore into someone's soul, searching for who they were.

He went by many names: Kris Kringle, Saint Nicholas, but most called him simply Santa Claus. A legend of the highest level, he was known to deliver toys to boys and girls round the world, and all in a single night on Christmas Eve. His eight-magical reindeer pulled a sleigh filled with gifts created by the very elves and men in the city. Down the chimney he would go and take delight in the cookies and milk left for him. Though he had the title of Father of Christmas, Kol simply called him dad.

"You know it's a new generation, Father. We have computers now," Kol said, stepping more into the light. "Would make it a lot easier to read that list."

"Ho ho ho." His trademark chuckle vibrated off the surrounding walls as Kol's father, Nicholas, said, "Well, I'm not one to break tradition. What kind of song would that make?"

"A great one, of course." Kol took a seat casually on the carpet. He could pick a chair, but ever since he was little this had been his favorite spot. "So, why did you want to see me?" Kol wanted to tell his father about the ghouls, but would rather know why he had been summoned first.

"Well, I wanted to talk to you about the coming month and your escapades through the city," his father said, his tone becoming more serious. His gaze lingered on Kol's sword.

Kol felt an old irritation perk its head up from deep within him and completely forgot about the ghouls. "My escapades keep the city safe."

"That is the job of the Cadence," Nicholas told Kol calmly.

"Which I plan on joining after Christmas."

"As you know," his dad said, ignoring his son's last comment, "this will be your eighteenth birthday, and I believe it's time we discussed your future again."

Kol felt a little uneasy at these words, adding to the other negative emotion. "What do you mean?"

"I mean, I think it's time we started ushering your studies back into our original direction," he continued, seeming to choose his words carefully. "You see, even though I am who I am, I may not be able to continue my duties one day. I may need someone else to take the reins."

Kol studied his father closely. He could find no information hidden behind his father's eyes. What was he getting at? He knew Kol couldn't be Santa: only the man sitting in front of him had the capability to achieve that task. He felt his case on his belt grow heavy. There was no way he could ever gain that level of ability. He had come to terms with this when he was younger and was tired of it coming up. "You know I can't."

"Yes, you can, Nicholas," his father said his name with a powerful force of emotion. The passion that continued behind his words could not be ignored when he said, "I know that if you just believe in yourself you could surpass me one day."

"I can't hold onto the Sound like you, nor can I grasp the Studies," Kol said softly. He appreciated his father trying to motivate him, but all this did was create a feeling of hope that ended with failure. "Look, I know what I am and what I want to become." He was standing now, voice slightly rising. All this talk was bringing up old memories that he did not want to revisit.

His father looked up at Kol and his eyes seemed to gaze through Kol in a way that spoke of the bond between father and son. It baffled Kol how his dad could not get angry, or even sad at his son's disregard of his chosen path. "As do I, son," was all he said. Kol knew the conversation was over, so he turned and left the room before any more thoughts came up. Kol walked quickly across the workshop, threw open the doors, then sprinted for the front door. He passed these too, and continued across the plaza to the giant tree. At the base he jumped hard and grasped a branch, easily swinging up to land on it. He walked up the branch closer to the trunk. Once there he began to jump from branch to branch, where the branches were large enough for him to be able to place his feet. Higher and higher he climbed, even higher than most of the larger buildings. He didn't stop until he reached a few branches below the top of the tree. Finding his usual spot, Kol took his sword off his belt and placed it across his lap as he sat with his legs folded under him. Here he could take in the sleeping city in all its glory. The North Pole stretched from his eyes and ended in the icy plains of the north. Kol could hear a train's faint whistle, signaling its departure. All of this was created because of his father, Saint Nicholas Claus.

When Kol was born, his father could not have been happier. A person who gave his entire existence to bringing happiness to others finally received his own special gift, and the one he had always dreamed of. As Kol grew he started to understand just how important his father was, and how much he was needed in the hearts of children everywhere. Kol was not jealous of this, but proud. So proud that he hoped to one day do the same. That day would never come, however, and he had to reevaluate his life. Instead of following in his father's footsteps, he started down his own path. Kol's "escapades" through the city were a result of all his arduous work. His father had forbidden him from joining the Cadence, so Kol had taken the matter into his own hands.

The North Pole continued to gleam brightly around where Kol sat. Wanting to think on another matter, Kol returned his thoughts to the ghouls. He meant to tell his father of what happened, but had forgotten due to the nature of the conversation. He decided to do so first thing in the morning when he saw his dad again. It was not unusual for creatures of the dark to enter the city, just extremely rare. The city was well protected, but sometimes those wandering outside could catch a strand of luck. During these rare occasions, the Cadence would know the moment they entered the city or came close to the wall.

Kol had searched the ghoul's robes for any more information, but he had found nothing. Even the weapons they had used were gone, and he still could not locate them when he retraced their steps. They had said someone was coming, which seemed like an attempt at theatrics. Still, Kol would have to figure out what they meant, as this could be linked to something far more important. He may need to inform the Cadence to add evidence to a case they already had. Of course, that would either put him in a dark perspective with the Cadence or a better one.

It was also an alarming thought that they would know who he was. The city knew that Santa had a son also named Nicholas, but very few knew what he looked like up close. Kol liked it better that way. He still wore his hat and hood up to keep his late trips into the city separate from his daily life. It was the minor changes in character that kept those who spotted or spoke with him unaware that they stood before, as they saw it, royalty. It was an unnerving idea that the ghouls recognized him, the son of Father Winter, and the thought would not leave him. Someone had to have told them. The someone who had sent them.

Kol shook his head to clear his clustered thoughts. The moon was turning again, meaning he had been up here far too long. Standing on the branch, he replaced his sword in his belt. His home was safe for another night, its people tucked away to gain some much-needed rest. Kol gazed across the only city in the world that slept. Starting down the branches, he figured he needed to get some sleep, too. The morning was going to be a busy one.

CHAPTER TWO

Making a List

Kol was awakened by intense knocking at his door. He had only been asleep for a few hours. Grabbing his pillow, he rolled over, covering his face. As if the person behind the door knew his reaction, the beats came harder, along with the strong voice of a woman that could only belong to one person. "Nicholas, it's morning," his mother said, entering his room. She reached towards the end of the bed and tickled his feet, forcing Kol to quickly pull them under his blanket. She had done that all his life and Kol had always hated it. "You said you would help me today, and here it is an hour past the time you said you would be there. I honestly don't understand why you sleep so much."

Kol took his pillow from his face and threw it at her. She knocked it to the floor easily and smiled at him. His mother held far more youth than his father did. She stood a head shorter than Kol, with curly brown hair down to her shoulders and green eyes of a deep forest. Though she was shorter, to Kol she always stood taller and strong. No matter how hard he had trained Kol didn't think he was any match for his mother.

"I sleep because it's good for you," Kol told her, stretching out his arms. The only ones who knew about his late-night runs were his father, and in a fashion, Slee.

"Well, so is being awake," she continued firmly. "Now I want you dressed and downstairs in ten minutes. If you take any longer I will send up Leosh, and you know her methods." With that she left, slamming the door behind her.

Kol fell back onto his bed and sighed. He had forgotten about his promise to help his mom. If Kol wasn't so sure of her threat he would just go back to sleep. The last time Leosh came to wake him he ended up running for his life down the halls wearing only his underwear, covered in brown sugar and honey. The elves around here always wanted something new to laugh at.

Rolling to the left of his bed, Kol stood and stretched again. His room was rather simple compared to the rest of the house. His bed, made neatly with a grey duvet, was centered between two doors, one to his bathroom and the other to his closet. A brown blanket he slept under was left crumpled on top. His mom didn't like the fact that he never slept under his duvet, but it stopped him from having to make the bed. In front of his bed was his desk, carved from a dark maple and displaying images of mountains, which was given to him by his dad one Christmas. He had spent plenty of time studying there. On top of his desk was his computer along with other trinkets he had collected. A bookshelf had been placed above his computer, holding all his favorite fictions and nonfictions. Some had been gifts, others he had bought.

That was another thing he was proud of with his upbringing. If people outside of the city knew that Santa Claus had a son, they would probably think he was spoiled as a child. A toymaker for a father? Yet this had not been the case. Instead, he received one gift a year from his father, just like all the others around the world. Of course, it also depended on whether he had been naughty or nice that year. This taught Kol about others less fortunate than he, and how everyone should be treated fairly.

Kol went to his closet and changed out of his pajamas into a simple pair of blue jeans, black shirt, and his second favorite running shoes. A black trunk was nestled under his hanging pants, hidden from his mother. Inside held his gear from last night, including his sword and bell. Checking the chest was still locked, Kol left his room, turning off the light behind him.

The hall was empty, which was strange because usually an elf could be found walking the halls. With December starting tomorrow, he figured everyone was preparing for the festivities.

Kol made his way down the hall to a small stairway. He took the carpeted staircase down to the first floor, making the kitchens his destinations. On his way he passed a few extra bedrooms, a media room, and finally Slee wearing his white work uniform, who walked past him then turned to rejoin him.

"Why, Master Nicholas, you look well-rested. Did we turn in early last night?" Slee's smile showed every bit of his sarcasm. Kol answered by swinging his forearm at the elf's head. Slee ducked under it effortlessly, then laughed while punching Kol hard in the side of the knee. This caused Kol to freeze up mid stride, but he grinned at Slee as they continued. The doors of the kitchen were located at the end of the wing. The smell hit Kol's nose before he pushed the door open, Slee right behind him. Both doors were made from golden wood and showed depictions of a feast. The imagery and smell combined to trick Kol into thinking it had been ages since before he had had anything to eat.

The room was massive: not as large as the workshop, but probably the second largest in the house. Five rows ran the room parallel to each other. Each row held all the appliances of ten kitchens, meaning fifty basic kitchens in all. Each was full of color from red, green, white, and blue to match the coming month tomorrow. At the far end of the room stood a raised platform, which was the master kitchen. From there a person could control the rest of the room's appliances in preparing mass meals or use the range of ingredients and books behind it to create something completely new.

Elves and humans ran up and down the aisles, cooking various amounts of food. Music played through the room: not a holiday tune, but one from when his mother was his age. The life in the room was energetic as the occupants danced back and forth in their work, joking and talking about tomorrow's festival. The walls held towering windows to the outside, the top half composed of stained glass that slowly cleared showing the view outside. Curtains of green and red hung next to the windows. Stepping into the room, Kol could immediately feel a shift in pressure, which meant the magic being used in here was in full use and strong. The pressure was not unbearable, and to the untrained mind would easily go unnoticed or dismissed. To the trained mind, it was a light nudge to one's senses that power was near and should be noted.

Kol scanned the crowd for his mother and found her walking up the third row toward the master kitchen. He followed her, Slee behind him. Kol was still unsure why the elf would choose to journey with him on his coming task, but he had nothing against sharing his burden with his eager friend. When he ascended the stairs, however, he found that Slee had once again disappeared. Looking over his shoulder, Slee was nowhere to be seen, which was something he liked to do often.

"Took you long enough." His mother grabbed his attention from the rest of the room, where she was standing in front of him with hands on her hips. Kol was a good foot taller than Lilian Claus, but he still felt his inner child looking up to her. Her hair was brown and curled wildly when set free, but it was tied back for now in a bushy bun so that she could work without fighting it. Her eyes were a deep green and held a mixture of sternness and caring in them. Her white apron was already covered in several different ingredients, and some were even on the boots she wore under her blue dress.

"I came down as soon as you left," he replied.

"Should have come down before I left. Or at least made it back. Now you're no longer in my good graces," she said to him, face stern.

Kol cracked a smile before saying, "Have I ever been in them."

"Only when you actually listen."

"So, never, then. You know you don't have to sugarcoat it with me." His mom smiled at him after this. Many would say they were mean towards each other, but it was really all in playful fun. He respected his mother more than anyone else because she demanded it, and, truthfully, deserved it. "So, what do you need?"

His mother walked over to a large red pot, grabbing one of her large spoons as she began to stir it. "Start chopping up these vegetables please: I'll need them in just a minute." She pointed to a cutting board next to her, with a large variety of vegetables stacked behind it. There were so many they were stacked higher than Kol.

"You're kidding, right?" he asked, but all she did was snap her fingers at the board. Kol heard Slee's soft laugh from somewhere behind him; Kol's embarrassment was the reason he had tagged along. This irritated him a little, but he decided to do it anyway. Kol usually would like to butt heads with his mother, but he knew she needed his help. Plus, he got to play with knives. To enthuse himself more, he walked over to a counter and pulled out four silver handled knives. He then washed his hands and prepared for his work. With his new toys in hand he got to it, plowing through the stacked field of crops. His mother took what he finished and placed them into the pot, moving to other stations in between cuts. When he wasn't cutting he was washing more vegetables, the pile never growing smaller.

They continued this pace for a little over an hour, his mother giving him side commands while she went about her own tasks. They made a wonderful team, just the two of them on the platform. His mother had sent her personal help down to the floor to fill in the missing personnel who were busy in the warehouse. All had to be prepared for the grand feast tomorrow. The first day of Christmas was one that would be celebrated throughout the city, where many would come to the plaza tomorrow for the festivities and food. They would all sit around the tree, getting the final bit of celebration before the rush started.

It had now been two hours, and Kol had just finished his last carrot. He was then instructed to cut up chicken, which again he did not mind. He rewashed his hands and started on the first one with a clean knife. While he cut the whole meat into its different pieces, his mother decided they had caught up enough to have a conversation. "So, did you talk to your father last night?"

Kol took the meat from one of the poultry and tossed it into the clean pan next to him. "Yeah, we talked."

"And?" she asked, checking something in one of her five great ovens.

"And what?"

"What do you think about it?" Her voice was stern but still calm. She of all people knew it was a touchy subject.

"You know how it went. There is no reason for me trying again and failing," Kol said, focusing more on the meat. "My heart's just not in it."

His mother looked at him sideways, catching his lie. "You won't be able to do anything if you don't believe in yourself, Nicholas."

"It's not a matter of belief," Kol placed the next piece of chicken into the pan before stopping and turning towards his mother. "I am not my father; he was chosen for this."

"Lilian, I have a question about your instructions on this recipe." One of his mother's top chefs had approached the raised kitchen.

Kol's mother took a few moments to continue looking at her son before turning to the man. After they spoke, she returned to what she had been doing. "Get done with the chickens," she told Kol, pulling a book from the shelf. "I have an errand I need you to run."

Kol nodded and continued working, keeping his thoughts away from the topic. Looking up across the mass assortments of kitchen accessories, he could see the chefs, humans and elves alike, continuing their jobs gleefully. It was amazing how the two races could work in unison here, creating masterpieces in whatever they did. Whether it was gifts, food, or the glistening buildings outside, everything they crafted was a high standard of excellence. Kol figured it was because of how important they were to the world.

Kol finished the last chicken, filling at least ten pans with the meat. Taking each one, he placed them on a counter near the ramps up to the master kitchen. Here the cooks would come grab the ingredients as they need them. He washed his hands and the knives in one of the sinks. Finished, he turned to look for his mother, who was studying the large bookshelf of cookbooks.

She turned in his direction to see who was coming up. "Done already?" she asked, scanning the books again. "When I inspect your work, I expect it to be edible."

"Well, if it's not," he said, "blame your lessons."

"No, just my son," she smiled, grabbing a brownish book from the shelf. "I need you to run to the post office and pick up some ingredients I ordered."

Kol raised an eyebrow at this. "What kind of ingredients?" The last time he was sent for ingredients he had to fight with a bag of carrots. He believed he still had a scar.

"Not anything like that," she said, remembering as well. "The label didn't say they would bite."

"Maybe because you wouldn't expect carrots to bite."

"Well," his mom continued, walking back to the kitchen counters, "this one is a rare ingredient I wanted to use. If you leave now you should make it before they close."

Kol nodded and started down the ramps to walk across the room to the exit. Since this room was a corner of the building, there were only two doors leading out: the one he came through and the one that exited into the entrance hall, where he was currently headed. He had to duck and turn out of the way of the chefs, since they would not hesitate to run over anyone in their way. He was sure some of the elves would love to see him dressed in cake or some other form of food. After another close call with a bowl of pudding, Kol made it to the large doors and exited through them.

The entryway was clear, except for Slee who suddenly appeared beside him. If Kol had not grown up with this, it would have probably made him jump. "Off on another errand, are we?" Slee said happily.

"Yea," Kol told him. "Ingredients."

This caused Slee to giggle. "Well, hopefully it doesn't end up chasing you."

Kol thought about this comment for a moment, then swung his leg out to kick his friend. "That was you, wasn't it?" Slee somersaulted over his leg then began to run for the workshop door, laughing as he ran. Kol wished he could figure out a way to get him back. He may have to find something later, though he didn't know how he could top biting carrots. Kol sprinted up the stairs and into his room to retrieve a jacket and hat.

After Kol's preparations for the cold, he made his way back downstairs into the grand entrance way. Kol walked over to the front door and grabbed its crafted handle and pulled, letting in the chill from outside. Kol stepped out into the large plaza, the giant tree clear in his view. Since it was technically the middle of the day, the citizens of the North Pole walked across the plaza, heading to and from their jobs. The buildings surrounding the mansion and park all gleamed brightly now, their occupants working hard to finish monthly dues.

Kol started across the tiled area and joined in the mass of moving people. With his destination, slightly to his left, he slowly eased his way against the current of the crowd, careful not to draw attention. Everyone was dressed in an array of furs, their daily clothes hidden underneath. Making his way now through the ring of trees he found a street sign in front of him that read To Russia. Smiling at the joke, Kol started down the street on the shining side walk.

The street was less crowded than the plaza, and Kol could move more swiftly. He enjoyed examining the buildings as he went, looking carefully at the polished stone and watching his reflection in the shining windows. This would continue until he peered into an alley before the next building started. There was nothing unusual about it until he reached the tenth ally he would pass. As he passed he spotted an odd sight.

A man had been standing in shadow with another figure that turned out to be an elf. Kol stopped in his tracks as they vanished from his view, the new building in his way. Usually Kol would continue walking, wanting to finish his chores quickly. However, the feeling that came over him when he saw the two strangers was enough to set him on edge. Kol made a quick glance back into the suspicious alley to make sure the two inside were looking the other way before he lifted his hood to cover his face and silently stepped closer.

"So, what kinda metal is it made from?" The voice belonging to the human was deep and even.

"I'm not sure, but the color of it is what interested me." The elf's voice was a high pitched and slightly louder than the other.

"Just the color? The inscriptions on the blade are worth a look. I tell you what, how 'bout one hundred for it."

There was a moment's pause before the elf replied, "Make it a hundred and fifty and I'll hand it to you now. I won't barter any lower."

Kol was only a few meters from them before the elf's ears picked up his steps. The elf gave a small yelp as he turned to see him and Kol wished he had his field boots on instead. The man looked up at him and turned to run. The elf tried to do the same, but as soon as he turned Kol grabbed him by the back of his collar. He pulled his captive around and placed him against the wall, letting the man run free. The elf looked terrified in the small light that was allowed and was holding a bundle in his arms. All Kol could see were his brown eyes from underneath his knitted hat. "Please don't hurt me!" he pleaded.

"Relax," Kol said, letting go of the collar to show his intentions. "I don't want to hurt you. I just want to see the blade you were trying to sell."

"Of course, but he had it when you grabbed me." He opened the bundle in his arms to show there was nothing of interest there. The elf was frantic as he did so. "I didn't steal it, only found it in an alley near the edge of town."

"Were there any others?" Kol released him. He should have started after the other one, but he had questions that needed to be answered.

"No, none; just found this one behind some trash cans. Please, I meant no harm, I thought it would look good above someone's fireplace." The elf looked on the verge of tears.

"Where exactly did you find it?" Kol demanded.

"Out in the housing districts, near an inn."

Kol placed a hand on the elf's shoulder, "It's all right, friend. Go home and get some rest; tomorrow is a big day. If you find anything else like that again, I suggest you give it to the Cadence, agreed?"

"I was only trying to make some spare change."

"Like I said, it's okay, if you need help you know where to go to ask. I expect to see you at the celebration tomorrow." With that Kol started to sprint down the rest of the alley, not knowing where the blade must have gone.

Kol hit the new street and turned left, throwing his body into a full sprint. He was glad that the traffic of people was low because the frost made it easy to track. Kol cursed himself for not grabbing his belt before leaving the house. That along with not being in his gear brought him back to his normal speed. The man had crossed the street a few buildings away, then made his way down another alley. He passed a few citizens on the way who either did not notice him sprinting or gave him a brief glance before hurrying on their way. He continued this pattern for just a few more streets. Kol did not think the man was fit enough to make it that far; he must be wanting a rest sometime soon.

He was on another street now and the footprints vanished among a vast number of others belonging to both man and elf. This street was more crowded than the others, with workers heading back from lunch. This street was dedicated to keeping the people fueled, and restaurants lined either side. Kol glanced through the crowds, looking for any sign of confusion. Everyone had the same pace to them, with no abnormalities in walking patterns.

Kol decided to walk the street, just to be sure there wasn't anything he was missing. Smells of all kinds came across him as he made his way up the block. He passed one restaurant, which he was sure was themed Italian. Kol had not realized how hungry he was until then, having skipped breakfast. He continued walking, looking now for a place to stop, figuring he had time before the post office closed. A few minutes later he decided to stop at a restaurant concocting Japanese cuisine. He did not have anything to go on with the stranger now, and he would have to search more once the streets had cleared.

Kol pushed his way into the small eatery, sitting under the protection of the building above it. The place had eight tables lining the wall, four to each side. Three of them had occupants, a woman sitting at the far back to the left reading a newspaper and two elves closer to the front on his right. A bar ran along the back of the restaurant, for customers who did not plan to stay long. Kol decided to take a spot there, overlooking the walk path behind the counter, which led to the kitchen. The entire room was dark wood, polished to a high shine.

A woman came from the kitchen, door swinging shut behind her. Her complexion was pale and she had dark hair tied into a small bun on her head. She was probably in her late twenties. She smiled at Kol. "Welcome. What would you like to drink?"

Kol smiled back at her. "Nothing to drink, please. But could I order a bowl of noodles?"

"Make that two." The voice was a familiar one to Kol, so he did not need to turn around to see who had entered the restaurant when the door opened. He nodded at the waitress who nodded back and returned to the kitchen.

"It's been a while, Holly." Kol looked to the stool on his right as his old friend sat in it. Sitting she was still a head shorter than he was, with dirty blond hair that stopped just above her shoulders and flipped out, bangs tucked behind her right ear. Her eyes were blue, and she was smiling at Kol in a way he always found mischievous. She was wearing a dark green shirt labeled with one of her favorite rock bands, blue jeans, and a pair of white running shoes. Her brown jacket lay in the stool beside her.

"Only a few months, but who's counting." Her voice was in tune with her smile, with a gleeful charm mixed into it.

"Done with the academy already?"

"Not even close, but they let us go for December." She reached across the counter and grabbed a bottle of soy sauce, examining the label. "We're due back at the first of the year."

Kol continued watching her as she read the ingredients. Holly was never one to stay focused on one thing for too long. "Training hard?"

Holly nodded, "Yeah, and they're just getting us in shape. I enjoy it, though I'm just ready for the more exciting stuff."

"What about your drum?" Kol handed her a menu to go through next. She had replaced the soy sauce and had been looking for something else.

"They give them to us on the first day. It's part of the 'in shape' part." Her gaze settled on the variety of sushi she could order. "But you would know that already if you had joined when I did."

"Well, you know that's difficult right now."

"He still against it?" Kol saw her looking at him from the corner of his eye.

"You know he is." Kol looked down at the table while he talked. "He still wants me to continue with the family business." Holly was one of the few to know who he really was.

Holly squinted slightly then smiled. "Well, I think it would suit you, all dressed up in red."

Kol couldn't help but smile back at her. He had met Holly a few years back, when her family moved here from the States. Kol had been personally educated at home by tutors while growing up. Along with that it was either his mother had him in books or he learned workmanship from his father or his uncle when he stayed with him. By the time Kol was old enough to attended secondary school he had asked his parents if he could be enrolled with the other kids in the city. His father thought this would be a great idea and even agreed to Kol's other request, that he go without anyone knowing who his father was so that he would not be treated any differently. His mother had told him not to be ashamed of who he was, but his father understood Kol's perspective and agreed. It was easy enough once the headmaster had been brought in on it, and Kol was a common enough name when others could assume the spelling. That had been when he met Holly.

He had noticed her on the first day of school during his second year enrolled. She had been sitting a few seats away from him in their history class, head down, drawing pictures in her notebook. Kol could see that she felt awkward in the unfamiliar environment, not sure of what to think of it all. They had two classes they shared and lunch together. One day after school Kol found her being picked on by a few individuals, who thought it was appropriate for newcomers. Kol came to her aid after she had given one of the three a bloody nose. After that they slowly became close friends. Kol eventually told her who he really was, which was hard for her to take in at first, until he introduced Holly to his father. They had graduated together, this year in fact, and had both planned to attend the academy together. He unfortunately could not sign up due to his father stopping him, and she left for the Island to begin her training.

"You don't think I'm too young for a white beard?" That was one part of the problem, though a subtle one.

Holly's bangs fell over her left eye as she shook her head. "Not at all; I think it would suit you."

"I'm sure you do." The waitress was back with their orders in each hand. They both thanked her as she placed the bowls in front of them. Kol handed Holly a pair of chopsticks and they both began on their meal, with little room to talk from the number of noodles they were consuming.

The Cadence Corps had been the career he had chosen for himself once his other dream became impossible. They were the military/police force that protected the North Pole. Whenever the rare monster would wander in, it was the Cadence's job to capture them before they caused any harm. Their job was of immense importance to the city: upholding the law and regulating civilian traffic to and from the city. This place was built with the ideas of Christmas, but it was still a city. The more people, the higher chance of crime. When he was younger, he felt that this was the best way to serve his city and make his father proud. He had been the one who convinced Holly to sign up this past May.

"So, what are you doing out in the city? I figured your mother would have you to the grindstone," Holly had come up from her bowl long enough to ask.

Kol placed his eating utensils in his bowl and slid them away. Feeling satisfied, he said, "She does; I'm running an errand for her as we speak. I have to pick up ingredients."

"Ones that don't bite, I hope?" Kol shot her a dirty look, and she laughed, returning to her bowl. "So, what brings you to this side of town? I thought it was strange for you to be here when I saw you outside."

"I was following somebody."

"Ah, so you're still up to your vigilante ways. You know, when I finish training, I'm going to have to stop you." She finished her bowl, pushing it away as Kol had. Kol had forgotten he had told her in a letter what he had been doing. "Why were you following him?"

"I'd like to see you try, Holly." Kol could trust Holly, so he decided to fill her in on what had happened the night before with the ghouls up to the elf with one of their blades. She listened carefully, waiting for him to finish.

"So that would explain the report that came in concerning the inn that I overheard at work. The Cadence came by as soon as you left. I had a feeling you would have something to do with it. Did you tell that to them?" she asked when he had finished.

"I haven't had time to. Nor have I had a chance to tell my dad. I planned on seeing him when I returned home." Kol reached into his pocket and pulled out his wallet. Holly started to do the same, but he went ahead and placed the coins for both their meals on the counter. "I wanted to get that weapon when I heard about it, though. If I could get hold of it I could discover where it came from."

Holly glared at the money then at him. "It's still dangerous, Kol. Go tell the Corps about it; maybe they have some of their own information to go on. It's their job to do it, not yours."

"I know that, but if I didn't intervene, someone was going to get hurt." Kol stood and started for the door, Holly walking beside him throwing her jacket on. "Plus, I would like more than just my word to give them."

"What about the ghoul's bodies?"

"Dust. Once they finished killing each other they dissolved into the wind. Only things left were just their clothes." This was also unusual, even for a ghoul. "Come on, I should get to the post office before it closes. That is if you didn't have anything better to do."

"Sure, I have nothing but time now."

"Makes two of us." He smiled at his own inside joke, avoiding Holly's curious look.

The streets outside had emptied now, the final hours of today's work ticking by. He retraced his steps back To Russia, talking with Holly about the festivities tomorrow.

"So, what all is your mother making this time?" Holly asked, and he remembered that she was fond of his mother's cooking.

"You know, everything she can. Really, there's nothing that is left out with her on these occasions," Kol said as they made it back to the main street.

"What about your dad? Do you know what he's up to?" When Holly said this is sounded like a second thought. Looking over his shoulder, Kol saw she was considering the buildings they were passing.

Without even giving it a thought, Kol said, "Making a list."

"Checking it twice?" Holly couldn't resist, the tune slipping in.

"Going to find out who's naughty or nice!" They sang together. Kol was glad his friend had come home, giving him someone else he could talk to.

They had made it to the post office. It looked different than the other buildings, nestled in the smaller buildings of the city. Shining red brick with a tin roof and giant windows stretched between floors. On top of the building was a giant hanger that would receive the bundles of floating letters or the mail deliverers. It was true that the city had very few vehicles on the road, and the same could be said of the air if not for the Cadence Corps during emergencies and the post office delivery system. Humans and elves who worked here would deliver the mail in the city while riding on small enchanted gliders. It was incredible to see the red wings zipping by. As if to prove his point, one went whizzing by overhead and landed within the port to deliver his payload.

"I still find this city amazing," Holly laughed and started up the stairs to the front door.

"You will the rest of your life," Kol said and followed.

The front doors slid back as they approached, engulfing them in warmth. The lobby was furnished in dark leather couches for the waiting customers and were placed around a curved welcome desk that a young woman sat behind. She wore a white uniform shirt with the name "Candace" stitched across it. She looked up with brown eyes and smiled at the two of them as they approached. "Welcome to the Post Office. How may I help you?"

Holly made it to the front desk first. Leaning on it, Kol stopped short. "I'm here to receive a package for the Workshop."

"That's a nice hat you have there." Holly always focused on the oddest things. Though the hat Candace was wearing was different, with a green box shape to it.

The woman smiled at her. "Thanks." She tapped on the keyboard in front of her. "Yes, it arrived this morning. Take the elevator to the eleventh floor. You can pick it up there."

Kol started around the desk, pulling Holly had with him who had started on the pamphlets on proper wrapping procedure. "Thank you," he said, and walked around the desk to the glass elevator at the back. The door slid open and they entered. As Holly went to the back of the cart to peer outside, Kol pressed the appropriate button then leaned against the panel, hiding it from his friend. A soft hum started in the box and they slowly ascended the shaft.

Parts of the city came into view as they rose higher. The post office was sitting on the border between the commercial and business part of the city of and the smaller outer ring dedicated to homes, small inns, and mom and pop shops. Kol thought of that area as old Christmas. All the small buildings were made of wood, carved elegantly, and just felt traditional to the old songs. The larger part of the city represented the modern part of the holiday, which was needed to balance the other out.

The elevator made a soft ding as they made it to their floor. Holly and Kol exited into a barrage of chaos. Elves went by with carts of mail, two of them pushing it and one sitting on top yelling out directions. They were still in the lower floors of the building so the room was circular, but a lot of the space was taken up by boxes and letters. Kol made his way across the counters on the other side, ducking and dodging carts. He was alone on his excursion because Holly decided to inspect a nearby cart. Four elves sat behind the desk filtering through papers. Behind them Kol glimpsed twenty cylindrical tubes of assorted sizes running from floor to ceiling, used to distribute and sort mail.

"Excuse me." The elf in front of him didn't look up at first, so Kol had to repeat himself louder to get his attention.

The elf gave a start as he looked up from his work, his eyes barely leaving the documents. "Can I help you?"

"Yeah, I'm here to pick up a package for the Workshop."

"Do you have your ticket?" He was back at his work, checking off packages that must have arrived.

Kol reached into his pocket, pulling out the small piece of paper his mom gave him. Unfolding it, he handed it to the elf who held his hand out. "Ready for the rush, I see."

"The rush began yesterday at two," the elf said shortly as he snapped his fingers. The piece of paper became engulfed in purple flame. Kol scanned the room quickly and had just enough time to duck as the small box flew past his head and landed gently in the worker's hand. "Thank you for using the Postal Service. Have a lovely day."

"Thanks. Don't work too hard." The four elves snorted at his comment, still focused on their paperwork. Kol made it back to the elevator door in one piece, pulling Holly along with him. They made it to the lobby and exited. Kol nodded at the receptionist before they reentered the frigid air, the package easily held in his right hand. Holly skipped along beside him as they walked towards the center of the city, humming songs of the season.

Kol listened to her carry on, so much energy in one person. He was half tempted to join in but decided to just enjoy his friend's company. Most of the crowd they walked in was headed in the opposite direction, since it was time for everyone to go home. He didn't think there would be much sleep due to the anticipation. Someone bumped into Kol's shoulder, and hurried on without an apology. He almost let the motion slide if not for the way the stranger held his hand in his cloak.

Kol was following him a second later, weaving through the crowd. He had left Holly to continue walking, not having the time to grab her too. He saw that the man was balding with brown hair, a hunch in his brown cloak as he hurried on, not even apologizing to the people he bumped into. Kol followed in his wake, easily gaining ground on the older man. He was only a few meters away when the man looked back and saw Kol. This caused him to panic and surge harder through the people. Kol increased his haste, not wanting to lose him again.

The man pushed across the crowd, heading for another alley. Kol had to step over one of the elves the stranger had pushed to the ground, with no time to help him back up. The alley was a mistake for the old man: Kol now had space to move. Kol tossed his package on the ground and was on the old man in seconds, grabbing his arm to turn him around. He had to release him immediately, however, to retain his own. The sickly green blade cut through the air then back again as the man took another slash at Kol. He had no choice but to step out of the way each time, but it wasn't without effort. The old man could move quickly: more so than any human should be capable of.

Kol glanced around looking for anything to fight with, but the walkway was completely empty. He would have to take his chance. The man aimed for Kol's head, but Kol ducked just in time and grabbed the man's wrist. He had to hold on tight, his grip almost breaking from the bizarre strength. Kol blocked a wild kick. He needed to act fast before the man became wilder. Pushing the man's hand upward, Kol hit him hard in the gut. The man's reaction to this was for him to swing with his spare hand. Kol blocked the punch with his own free hand, then kicked the sword holder hard in the chest, sending him backwards. The man lost his footing and fell on his back. Kol lunged at him, but the man was already back on his feet, swinging even more wildly. Kol readied to disarm him this time but the attacker never got close.

Something flew past Kol's ear, centimeters from his head. The object hit the man directly in the forehead, stopping him in his tracks. More objects followed, hitting its target hard enough to knock him back down, and this time he stayed. Kol saw the four wooden drumsticks, intricate designs climbing them, lying on the ground, and knew the owner. He turned and nodded at Holly who held two more sticks in each hand. Her voice was stern as she walked up, his cheerful friend gone and replaced by someone serious. "You could have grabbed me."

"I didn't have time."

"Make time." She stepped past Kol and stood over the body. Taking both the man's hands she placed them in a pair of handcuffs she pulled from her back pocket.

"So you carry your gear with you?" Kol couldn't help but find this version of Holly interesting.

"Never leave home without it." She collected her sticks and tucked them into her jacket.

Kol reached down and gingerly picked up the curved blade. He examined it while Holly propped the old man up on the wall. The blade was light, even more than his own. The handle was wrapped in a linen fabric, very basic. The dagger was all one piece, the guard and handle merged with the blade—a crude design, but effective. He was having trouble with the material it was made from, as it was nothing like he had ever seen. This alone intrigued him. He looked closely at the blade now, and saw that there was an inscription running the hilt.

"Put it down, Kol." Holly was next to him now, examining the blade as well. "It could be cursed."

"I think you're right." He laid the dagger on the ground, and looked at the old man. "I don't think this guy knew what he was doing."

"How so?" Holly knelt in front of the man and began looking for identification.

"No one that age should be able to move like that. For a human, at least. He was almost too fast for me. And he could take a punch directly in the sternum, which usually causes people to stop. He didn't, though." Kol went back to the blade. He didn't know why but when he looked at it a bad feeling swept over him. "He had this wild look in his eye."

"Plus, he works at the library." Holly was holding up the man's identification card. "I'm going to call the Cadence and let them examine him."

"And the blade?" Kol asked.

She looked at him sideways. "Evidence. So, leave it."

Kol thought over this for a moment, then nodded in agreement. He wanted to take the blade back with him and do some research, even ask his father. But he would be busy now, and this was the job of the Corps. "Be sure to leave me out of it."

"Of course. I'll just say he attacked me." Her grin was back now. "It will look good at the academy anyway. I'm also going to tell them this may have something to do with the attack at that inn."

Kol smiled back at her, anything to help a friend. A sizzling noise grabbed his attention away from Holly, and he turned to look at the blade. The metal no longer was solid but was quickly eroding. Kol wanted to grab it and stop whatever was happening but he knew better. Holly looked on, amazed, as the blade continued to deteriorate until nothing was left. "Well, there goes the evidence."

CHAPTER THREE

A Chilling Presence

Kol had run straight for his father's office the moment he returned home from the post office. Unfortunately, one of the workers told him his father had left the city for the night. Being forced to wait, Kol had retired to his room to attempt some research on the weapon with the books he had there. Judging by the man's enhanced abilities and unsettling demeanor, Kol had no doubt the weapon was cursed. Struggling through his research, Kol was at his wits end when he received a message from Holly. It had stated that the man from the alley had woken up and had no memory of what had happened. The last thing he did remember was looking for a gift for his son.

This pushed Kol back into action. Quickly donning the gear from his trunk, he made his way back out into the city to continue his investigation and look for the two remaining weapons. The more information he could have for his father when he returned, the quicker the situation could be handled. Thankfully most of the city's denizens had found their beds by now, leaving Kol enough room to run at his max speed thanks to his enchanted gear. The stone walls of the surrounding buildings became blurs as he past.

After about twenty minutes of running, Kol was in the Hearth district now. It was the traditional part of the city now, with the log and brick houses lit by fireplaces. Kol turned down between two homes and leaped into the air. Placing one foot on a windowsill he pushed himself upwards, catching the roof with his hands and pulling himself up with one smooth motion. Kol was heading across the roofs now with hardly any momentum lost.

Leaping onto another roof, he put on an extra bit of speed to clear the next gap, heading toward the Lake of Frost. Someone gasped from the road he was next to, and without even looking Kol switched to the other side of the slanted roof. He wanted as little attention as possible, since the last thing he needed was the Corps after him. He went over the events that had occurred today again. The blade had only been in possession of the librarian for a little more than an hour. He had not acted aggressive until Kol moved to stop him. The elf who originally had the blade had seemed unaffected, meaning any spells placed on the object seemed to only affect humans. That was when the librarian had lashed out, and continued to until he lost the dagger. Or until Holly took him out.

Kol stopped on a roof located behind the Lake of Frost, his foot sliding slightly on the snow. The bottom lights were still on in the kitchens, meaning someone was still up either cleaning or cooking. The back door opened, and the innkeeper came out carrying two trash bags. Kol watched as the man walked to the trash bin located down in the little alley behind his house. Kol rose to his feet as the man lifted the aluminum lid, then stepped from the roof, landing softly on the snow. "Mr. Mugsteeve," Kol said, not wanting to startle the man any more than he was going to.

The man was indeed made of something solid, because he only looked up at his name being called in the night. When Mr. Mugsteeve found who had said it, he smiled. "Ah, Kol, glad to see you again, and so soon. Would you like to come inside? I'm sure my wife would love to fix you something up. Margaret makes this roast that brings in the whole city. That or her desserts."

"No, thank you, but I promise one day I'll come in to try it out for myself," Kol told him. "I'm here to ask if you had found anything else left behind after the incident yesterday."

Mr. Mugsteeve finished with his chore then scratched his head. "Nah, like I said: nothing at all was left. Besides the damaged furniture, that is." He gave a quiet laugh.

"Has anyone found a weapon of theirs, maybe?"

"Not that I've seen. And they would think twice about bringing it into my home." Mr. Mugsteeve crossed his arms.

"All right, I was just checking one more time. Didn't want anyone else to get hurt." Kol turned to leave, heading for the small walk space leading back to the street.

"Yeah, besides ole Shane Hargon, who's still in the hospital."

Kol stopped, turning back. "Is your friend doing any better?"

"He's awake now, and the wife and I were going to see him in a few days if he has to stay in there." Mr. Mugsteeve placed his hands inside his apron pockets, a thoughtful look on his face.

"Who is he anyway?" Kol asked. He hoped he did not sound rude, but an idea had formed in his head.

"Just a tired old man. Comes in every other night for the past year now. Plays people at chess for coin. Far as I've seen he never lost. Not to me, anyway." This brought on another small laugh.

"Well, let's hope he continues to play." With this Kol nodded and started moving towards the closest building.

"Don't be a stranger now!" the innkeeper boomed. Kol heard someone yell Mr. Mugsteeve's name and he took his chance to ascend to the roof again. Once on top Kol saw the inn owners standing in the doorway, light forming their silhouettes. Kol watched them kiss and turned away awkwardly, not wanting to intrude. That was a moment meant for postcards. Making his way back across the roofs, Kol turned back toward the center of the city.

Kol's path to the hospital was slightly longer than his journey out to the inn. He had to follow the village roofs around to the opposite side of the city before entering back into the Reciprocity District. If Kol tried to move in a straight line to his destination, he would be captive to the whims of the streets, losing his momentum to constantly change directions. The buildings there were far too high and spaced too far apart to make use of their roofs. Here in the Hearth District, however, it was just a small hop to the next house and he could keep his swift pace.

The night was late, but interrogating the old man could yield some results. If not, he would return to continue looking. The houses started to become the small buildings, and Kol dropped from the last roof in his path and started up the street. He passed a line of chariots, gleaming white and decorated for Christmas, ready for the morning. The horses would be in the stables, resting up for their big day. Similar chariots would be sitting on several other streets. They would be used to bring people to and from the plaza, a way of exciting the crowd.

He slowed his pace as he approached the hospital. The glass windows were dark on the bottom floor, since visiting hours were over. The floors above, however, were lit for the night shift for doctors and nurses who walked between the rooms checking on their patients. Kol walked to the door and pulled on the handle. It did not move, of course, and no one was going to allow someone with a sword into a hospital. Kol walked around the large building looking for a back door, which were all locked as well.

Kol stood in the shadows of the building located near a loading dock. He would have to wait until the morning to see the old man. He could break in, but what kind of person would he be then? The only thing Kol could do now was return to his search. Before he could move, a soft click came from the rear door and an employee wearing a pair of blue scrubs walked out. He must have wanted some fresh air, and to wake himself up, apparently, indicated by his wide-armed stretch and yawn. The nurse stood there for a few minutes, looking at the sky. He rolled his neck a few times before turning to go back inside. Punching in a number pattern on the keyboard, the soft click came again, and he disappeared inside. The door swung shut a bit more slowly than usual, thanks to Kol, leaving a few seconds for him to dart into the briefly open doorway.

He was in a long hallway stretching the length of the building. Kol pressed up against an indentation in the wall, flattening his body so the employee who looked at the door in mild confusion didn't notice him. The nurse in scrubs looked for a little longer, then figured it was fatigue teasing his mind. He disappeared through another door labeled "cafeteria." Checking for anyone else, Kol started down the hall.

He passed several more labeled doors before finding the one he needed. Remaining stealthy, he opened the door to the stairwell and disappeared into it, closing the door softly behind him. He had seven floors to cover, the first floor not included. He decided to start with the third, which was his lucky number. Kol eased into the dim hallway carefully, glad for the quiet building. The only light came from the middle of the hall where the desk was located for whoever was on watch. Patient rooms lined both sides of the area, their charts hanging on the doors.

It was impressive the way the area shone, with no sign of dirt anywhere, so much so that Kol checked his boots, not wanting to leave tracks. Cleanliness considered, Kol pondered how to best find his quarry. He could go from door to door, but that would take too much time. Carefully he eased into the light, looking for whoever was manning the desk. The seat was empty, which meant the nurse was making her nightly rounds or just getting something to eat. Kol quickly shifted through the paperwork looking for the documents that would tell him which patients were where. He found it attached to a clipboard under a magazine.

Kol's first guess had been wrong. There was no Shane Hargon on this floor. He was actually located on the eighth floor. Of course, it would be difficult. Placing the clipboard back in its place, Kol headed for the stairs. He made it just in time, because somewhere behind him another door opened. He climbed the stairs carefully, ready to dart through one of the exits if someone decided not to use the elevator. It seemed he had regained some luck because no one else appeared.

He exited on the top floor, the design like the floors below it. Another day, during the visiting hours, he wanted to come and see the rest of the place. Despite his mishaps, Kol had done his best to avoid needing the hospital's services, and had rarely stepped foot into the place. Kol moved slowly again, not wanting to take any chances. The desk on this floor was occupied by an elf in a set of green scrubs. The chair she sat in was turned away from the hall, and her mind was set on the paperwork in front of her. Kol eased by: it was difficult to go unnoticed by elves. He managed, though, and made it to the end of the hall and turned down another corridor. This hallway only had rooms on his left, with the right wall completely transparent, allowing anyone to see into the middle of the hospital, all the way down into the lobby.

Kol had to stop and enjoy the sight for a moment. A Christmas tree stood in the center, stretching from the first floor to the eighth. The tree in Tannenbaum Plaza was of course far larger, but the sight of this one was pleasant as well. Moonlight illuminated the tree from the glass dome above, and some of the elves had enchanted the roof to snow on it. He could see across the open space to the rooms on the other side of the building and the floors under it. This got him moving again; the last thing he needed was a chance for more people to see him. The door he was looking for was just a little further. Grabbing the door handle he easily let himself into the room, locking the door behind him.

The room was a small one. It had a simple area with a door to a bathroom and a window that looked out over the building next door. The bed was next to it, with the occupant asleep under the covers. A couch was placed next the bed for any family that wanted to visit. The last thing was the painting which hung on the wall: polar bears in front of the city. When Kol locked the door, the man sat up to see who had entered his room.

"Who are you?" he asked, his voice ragged, and Kol could clearly hear the fear underneath it.

"Relax," Kol said, trying to make his voice soothing. "I'm not here to hurt you, just wanted to ask you a few questions."

The old man squinted into the darkness, and Kol stepped into the moonlight so he would be seen. The man's eyes widened. "I remember you, from the inn. You stopped those creatures."

Kol nodded. "Yeah, that was me, and they are gone now. But I haven't stopped them yet, and they may have left something dangerous behind, so I need to ask you a few questions. After that I'll leave you back to your rest."

"I've already talked with the Cadence, and I don't see what help I could be of...." the old man tried to finish.

"What happened to you? I mean, why did they decide to attack you?"

Shane's expression seemed to harden as he squinted at the shadowy young man at the foot of his bed. Kol believed he was concentrating on the memory, and hoped that maybe the memory would recall that he had saved the man's life, and would perhaps convince him to tell his story, despite the strangeness of the visit and lateness of the hour. Shane appeared to make up his mind and cleared his throat, rubbing his forehead. "It's hard to recall. It all happened so fast."

"Please, anything will help." Kol moved to the front of his bed. "They could still be a danger."

"I remember when they came in," the old man said, taking another breath. "I remember Borian greeting them, saw it over my newspaper. He brought them over to sit at the table next to mine. They seemed shy, so I tried to strike up a conversation with the one closest to me. Asked him if he wanted to play a game. They ignored me, though: seemed determined to keep to themselves. So, I went back to my reading."

"Were you able to hear any of their conversation?" Kol asked.

"Not much, no. I try not to stick my nose where it doesn't belong. Might lose it," Shane ran his fingers through his grey hair with a soft smile. "I did catch bits and pieces of it." Shane sat more upright, shaking off his grogginess. "They said that they should leave something more towards the center of the city. It would be easier for someone to find."

"Leave what?" Kol already thought he knew the answer.

"They didn't say, only if they didn't figure it out then the punishment would be severe. Said the instructions from someone named Wenn were very specific." Shane took a deep breath before continuing, "Well, I got nosy then, and asked what they were about. The response placed me in this bed."

"And that was all true?" Kol asked and the man nodded, "Well, I appreciate you taking the time to talk with me. I'll leave you be then. Be sure to rest up; this coming month is going to be a tough one." Kol gave him a soft smile, trying to cheer him up after the rude awakening.

"Who are you? I just realized that I have no idea. You're obviously not one of the Cadence."

Kol stopped at the door and looked back, "My name is Kol, and I'm just a protector." Kol turned the lock on the door and exited the room.

The hallway was in the same state he had left it. With luck he could make it outside without raising any form of alarm. He was nowhere closer to finding the other blades. He had a name, which was the only plus, but it was not very helpful for the current situation. He would do research on the name Wenn, hoping it was not a common one. By research he meant to ask his father. If anyone knows a name, it's Santa Claus.

Kol was now passing the windows, with the Christmas tree continuing to sleep at its resting spot. Tomorrow it would join many others, illuminating the path for the city to follow. The mission of everyone who came here was to bring joy to the world. Kol could not help his smile, and even though this had always been his life it never lost its luster. He would even go as far to say his dedication rivaled his father's. Or at least came close to it.

Kol reached his turning point to make his way back to the staircase, but halted abruptly. Just before he turned his gaze from the tree he swore one of the branches had moved. Kol stepped close to the wall, the furthest point from the window. Using the shadows to conceal his presence, Kol waited. It could have just been his mind playing tricks on him, signs that fatigue was finally catching up to him. His mind had nothing to do with his instincts which warned him of danger.

Moments passed, and still no more signs of movement. The enchanted snow continued to fall on the branches from above. Maybe it was just a large mass of the ice falling to a branch below it that caught Kol's attention. Shaking his head and smiling, Kol dismissed his paranoia as fatigue born from his evening jaunt. It was therefore a surprise when in the next second he watched the snow resting atop the branches begin to lift back into the air.

The flakes had started to float against their brothers coming from above. Kol heard no wind, but the ice started to swirl around the top of the tree, swarming thicker with each passing second. Kol stepped closer to the glass watching the phenomenon, amazed at the sight, though he had seen it multiple times before. The fact that it was here, in the city, was the shocking part. Snow had become so thick that Kol could no longer see through it to the hallway across from him. Kol's senses tingled in the eerie silence, and he was proven right as he had only a few seconds to leap to the side before the ice came crashing through the glass, plowing into the hall.

Kol regained his stance from his jump, his expression curious. The snow mixed in with the shattered glass across the floor, moonlight illuminating it. The crash was bound to raise an alarm, which would intensify with what they found. But by the time anyone arrived they would no longer find a mound of snow. Not where it landed, anyway.

The snow began to move again, but this time the movement was subtle. Kol stepped closer when a small part of the frost pushed towards the sky, a hand reaching for salvation. The description was not far from the truth, as the hand's features quickly became more apparent. Another hand of ice rose next and then together they pushed from the ground, pulling the rest of the mass along with it. The snow folded on itself, over and over, compacting together and shaping. Moments later the ice was no longer a mound but now formed the model of a person or, more accurately, a man.

Kol knew immediately what the being was. A Snowman, standing at least three meters tall and right below the ceiling, body carved in strong muscles mimicking one of an athlete. There were no organs or bone beneath the white skin, only harder packed snow. Kol stood behind the Snowman, but he knew that the face he could not see was featureless except for two black eyes of coal that would be gazing down the hall towards the room that held the injured old man. Kol tensed along with this thought, hoping that the two events had nothing in common with one another.

A scream came from behind Kol, and he did not need to turn to see the nurse running for the alarm. The Snowman, however, did, looking over his left shoulder to find the source of the noise. Kol continued to watch the creature's actions. Kol looked for his eyes, but did not find them. Was it possible he was blind? Something laid over where his mouth should be, but Snow People did not have visual mouths. What added to the eeriness was not just the absence of his eyes but the striking lack of an article of clothing. Did he hide it inside him to protect it or was that thing on his mouth some form of clothing? "Why are you here, Snowman? You know what can come of this?"

The Snowman responded but not with words. Sweeping his left arm back, Kol was hit in the chest hard, the packed ice as hard as steel. The strike lifted him from the ground, flinging him backward before he landed hard and continued to slide until a wall stopped his momentum. The air left his lungs as pain shot through his body from his spine. Kol's vision doubled, and he quickly shook his head, getting back onto his feet slowly. An alarm sounded through the building, lights flaring and movement erupting on every floor. He focused on the Snowman who had turned back away from him and started down the hall, each step a deep thud.

After picking himself up, Kol placed his left foot against the wall that had halted him. He took a sprinter's stance, then exploded down the hall full speed at the colossus. Doors opened beside him as he flew by, the sick and injured looking for the emergency. Half a meter from the moving ice, Kol drew his sword with his left hand and dropped, sliding between the Snowman's legs. He swung the blade swiftly, cutting where a kneecap would be if the snow were flesh. The effect was close to the same because the Snowman took another step and found his support missing. Kol rolled over and was back on his feet as the Snowman, body expressing surprise, fell to the ground.

The Snowman fell apart into a sheet of white along the hall. This would only slow it down, and the hands reached into existence again. Kol gripped his sword in both hands in front of him. "I'm not going to be ignored. I'll give you one more chance to explain yourself." Nurses stood among the floors, everyone looking up and toward them, having found the danger. Patients who could walk were there as well, everyone looking on with expressions of surprise, awe, and worse—fear. "What are you doing, get them to safety!" Kol shouted, as the Snowman was close to regaining his form. It took a few seconds, but Kol was able to start movement again as evacuation was now in full force. The Snowman, standing at full height now, cast a shadow over Kol from the overhead lights. The Snowman again swept his arm back to attack Kol, but this time Kol was ready.

It was the right arm this time, its movement stiff and slow. Kol stepped to the side, avoiding the extension of ice that shot with the force of a cannonball past him. Sword held high from his movement, Kol brought his blade though the arm. The arm continued to soar down the hall before falling and shattering. Kol was expecting the Snowman to roar in frustration or show any sign of emotion, but it emitted no sound, staying consistent in the calm that reflected the ice his body was made from. Kol had to ponder that later as he dodged the left arm now, the glass behind him shattering and sending ice to the lobby below. Kol thought for a moment of the people down there trying to safely move the patients to the exit.

The situation was only barely staying within his control. Nothing but force seemed necessary to end this, and Kol would need to find the article of clothing and take it for his own, or worse, destroy it. He would need to aim for the mouth. Rolling to his feet he swung his sword horizontally, striking for the knee again, hoping to bring the head closer. The same effect from a moment ago was lost, however, because the Snowman had stopped his movement to avoid collapse. The leg just healed, molding back together instantly. Kol knew this because it came up with a kick, making him flip backwards narrowly avoiding what would have sent him to the roof. Landing on his feet, right hand in front to catch his balance, he was met by another blast of snow, sending him down the hall.

Kol landed on his back, sliding again to a stop. He tasted metal in his mouth and knew he was bleeding from the force to his head. The Snowman was moving towards him again, slow steps like thunder. One of his legs touched what was his right arm before Kol had severed it. Like a sponge it absorbed into his appendage. Kol could see the body readjust, arm regenerated, no harm apparent any longer. Hands reached down and grabbed his jacket: someone was trying to pull him to his feet. Kol accepted the help regaining his balance. Looking to his helper, he found Shane Hargon staring at him.

"Are you all right?" Shane voice sounded weak but alert.

Kol felt guilty for having disturbed his rest again, along with all the other sick trying to get better for the holiday. "I'm fine: you need to evacuate the building." Kol turned from him and started toward the Snowman. The best he could do was continue to slow it down until everyone was safe and the Cadence arrived. Fire was the proper weapon in this situation, but he had none and using any of the gases in the building could result in an explosion.

Another jet of snow followed a jab. Kol brought his blade before him, splitting the jet of ice along the middle. He nearly lost his ground from the force of the ice, but once it was gone Kol turned his blade sideways and cut the arm in a quick clockwise sweep. The next arm came, which he ducked under, bringing the blade over his head, causing his enemy to lose both arms. Kol looked up at its face again and found what had caught his interest before. Where a mouth would be on a human, and not be on a Snowman, was what looked like a strip of paper. Scrawled across it were characters that Kol did not recognize. He had no more time to examine it as he dodged another kick.

The Snowman readjusted from its lack of snow, and was now standing at a shorter height. This brought its arm strikes quicker, but with less force. Kol had to move back from its reach, which allowed the Snowman to collect the snow it lost and regrow to its full height. Snowmen could build themselves from the moisture in the air, but at a much slower rate than reclaiming from what was already made. This was going nowhere fast, and the heat within the building was not going to help at all. The temperature of Snowmen could be self-contained in low heat.

The alarm he had been ignoring shut off, and the high-pitched wail that followed meant the building was clear. New sirens could be heard outside: The Cadence was fast approaching. This would have to be his debut to them, followed by arrest. The fight continued down the hall and Kol was starting to grow tired. Judging from the sirens he had five more minutes to hold out. A kick came he wasn't ready for, swiping into his side. He collided with the wall where he was pinned by the Snowman's right arm. His sword slipped from his grip, and he could not reach his back pouch on his belt. He watched the left arm rise and move to crush him. Kol braced for impact, ready for the blow.

Heat erupted all around Kol, so intense that sweat appeared on his exposed face instantly. The Snowman released him from the wall and fell to the ground on all fours. Kol stared muzzily at the fire raking across the white back of the Snowman. Still no screams of agony came, just a slow crawl down the hall. Kol moved away quickly, wanting to avoid the blaze. In a matter of seconds, the movement stopped, and the snow became water, then steam, vanishing into the air. The flames extinguished, leaving no signs of burn damage anywhere on the walls.

Confused, Kol looked back up the hall from where they came and found Shane Hargon standing in his hospital clothes holding a wand. His face was stern as he looked from the now vacant spot to Kol. His gaze softened when his eyes met Kol's, a smile cracking as he shrugged.

"So, you're one of the Learned?" Kol asked, standing and retrieving his sword. Wiping the water on the blade with his jacket, he slid it home across his back.

Shane laughed slightly. "I am indeed, but not a very good one, I'm afraid. Took me a moment to conjure that."

"So why couldn't you stop the attackers?" Kol questioned further, his own smile coming now. "Surely a wizard could have handled them."

"Well, I wasn't expecting to be attacked at my favorite pub in a city that is supposed to be warded from the likes of them."

Kol nodded in agreement feeling foolish. "Understandable." He looked to the ground, looking for any clues left behind, but found none.

"Looking for something?" Shane said beside him.

"Any signs of his clothing." Shane let him determine the fire had left nothing. "I don't understand why one of the Snow People would come here with violence in mind, either." Kol shook his head. "They should know how much tension exists between them and the city."

Shane was searching the ground now, his eyes contemplative. "Did you see anything strange about him?"

"He had no eyes or an article of clothing." Kol was glad to see that Shane saw the Snowmen as beings of life. Others in the city did not. "Unless you count whatever that was over where a mouth would be. "

Shane nodded as if confirming his thoughts. "Could you tell what it was made of?"

"No, I did not have a chance to get that close, unfortunately." Kol looked at the old wizard quizzically. "Why do you think he came here?"

"Who knows, could have just been on a friendly stroll, breaking glass along the way." Shane chuckled at his own joke. Kol shook his head, but smiled anyway. He thought about telling him that the Snowman had been heading for his room. Kol decided to keep that information to himself to not worry Master Shane. Perhaps when he was back at full strength.

"Well, if this news gets out it will only spell trouble for the city." Kol looked around at the opened rooms. "But that can't be helped now."

Footsteps could be heard down the hall, dozens of them ascending the stairs. The Cadence was in the building now, moments from their location. Kol looked over at Shane. "Well, that's my cue. Will you be all right?"

"Continue to baby me and someone will be asking you the same thing when you wake up," the wizard replied, the smile still on his face. Kol chuckled softly at that. He would not worry about the old wizard anymore.

Kol nodded at him and turned for the hall, away from the marching steps. He found a staircase empty of the Corps. Within minutes he was back on the first floor. Finding an emergency exit, he pushed it open and stepped into the chilly night air, emerging into the alley beside the building. Lights of blue and red flickered sporadically down one side, the snowmobiles and other means of transportation sitting there. Kol could see a few patients, too, wrapped snugly in thick blankets, cups of hot chocolate in their hands. Thankfully they did not catch him in person, but Kol suspected they would see him from the security cameras. They could finally have proof that this "ghost" people had spoken of actually existed.

Kol was glad no one had been hurt, besides himself. Moving his neck, he could feel where it would be sore in the morning. Some unexplained stains on his clothing could be avoided if he could get to the laundry first, but at least his wounds seemed minor. Turning from the lights, he headed toward the back of the building. A clock built into the side of one of the buildings showed the time in bright green letters and hands. Kol smiled at it, knowing his mother would be pounding at his door two hours from then.

CHAPTER FOUR

On the First Day of Christmas

The pounding on his door came as hard as Kol knew it would, his mother's words soon following. "Nicholas, it's time to get up! We have a big day ahead of us."

Rolling his eyes, Kol shouted back, "All right, I just got out of the shower, so I'll be a few more minutes."

"I'll give you three," was her reply before she started down the hall. "And that's three to get to the kitchen!" Her voice grew smaller as she walked further down the hall. Kol knew she was in a good mood, the smile clear in her voice. Why wouldn't she be? It was December first.

Kol stepped from his bathroom, steam billowing out behind him. He made his way around his bed, entering his closet to find clothes for the day. Looking down, Kol found his chest still open with his gear tossed lazily inside. Kol kicked it shut and started to get dressed, finding a clean pair of black pants and a white t-shirt he would wear under his white button-up dress shirt. His pair of dress shoes were behind a few pairs of his tennis shoes, an even coat of dust applied to their surface. Knowing what would happen if he didn't clean them up, he walked back to the bathroom to make them shine. Grabbing a clean washcloth, he held it under the sink.

After he was done with one shoe he had to stifle a yawn, his hours awake surpassing the twenty-four-hour mark. After the hospital, he had continued to search the city looking for the other blades. Kol knew the Snowman had been after Master Hargon even though it was only his direction of travel. The question was why? A vendetta against the old wizard was out of the question, as he didn't see the old wizard as the type to insult a Snowman. No, the Snowman had been sent, and possibly by the same person who sent the ghouls. Yet Kol did not know of anything that could use the People of Ice as puppets. His father would not be able to do it, though he would never try. The Snow People race was far too proud. Kol needed to get to his father soon, hopefully before the festivities started. This Wenn person was either behind it or at least connected to it.

The workshop office had been the first place Kol had gone once he had arrived home an hour ago. The office was still empty, with no sign of anyone since last he checked. What his father was doing so close to the festival outside the city he did not know, but whatever it was could hardly come at a worse time. He would get reports of what occurred in the city, since the Corps made sure of it if anything of interest came up. A Snowman was always a thing of interest.

Shoes properly applied and a jacket collected from a hanger, Kol exited his room and headed for the kitchen. He passed several elves and humans along the way, all hurrying to apply the finishing touches. In a few hours, the house would be empty: everyone would be needed in Tannenbaum Plaza. Kol made it to the double staircase in the entrance room and slid down the banister, shouting apologies as he slid past helpers. Pushing off the end, he landed with ease on the bottom floor, dodging more helpers on his way to the kitchen.

Where the rest of the house seemed like ants going about their labors in an orderly fashion, the kitchen was controlled chaos. The multiple counters held all the food that had been prepared from the previous day. Hundreds of turkeys, far larger than usual, lined the first row. Side dishes of many sorts covered the second and third row, dishes hailing from all over the world meant for special occasions. The fourth row was the home to the many breads finished baking, resting in an array of crisp browns.

Finally, dessert was laid upon the furthest counter, the prize of the kitchen itself. The chefs scurried about adding finishing touches to the presentations. Kol looked to the master kitchen and found his mother. She stood on the stage, wooden spoon in hand shouting orders throughout the room. No music played, so her voice went unchallenged. Carefully he made his way to her. "Army in full swing, I see."

"Be sure that the barrels are carefully filled as well." His mother's command sent three helpers out of the room heading for the cellar. Turning to Kol, she said, "Yes, but it would go smoother with my trusted lieutenant beside me."

"I am but a humble soldier," Kol bowed, smiling. This was a mistake, because he bolted upright after the wooden spoon cracked him on the back of the head.

"Who can never seem to get out of bed on his own. Why do I have to come get you every time?" her look was stern, meaning that Kol should not cross her.

So he did. "Every time? Isn't this place about tradition?" he said, rubbing his head.

His mom couldn't hold it back then, a small smile appearing on her face. "Well, all the food's done, so I didn't really need you. You'd sleep through the whole day if I hadn't come to wake you."

"Hard to argue with that." Kol agreed, following his mother to the cutting table. "Is Dad back yet?"

"He returned a few hours ago; I believe he is in his office," she said, not looking up from the table, chopping the last potato to add to a big pot of stew.

"Thanks. I'll see you at the feast."

Kol's exit from the kitchen was easier than his entrance. When he made it to the workshop he found it was surprisingly empty except for a few scattered carpenters among the benches. A few of them smiled and waved as he walked past them. He returned the gesture and hurried on. Bounding up the stairs, he pushed through the carved door. Kol's father was wearing a bright red sweater and silver suspenders over his shoulders holding his dark green pants. He smiled at Kol's entrance, looking through his square spectacles. Though his expression was joyous, Kol knew the eyes of someone who had been a while without sleep.

"Nicholas, I thought you would be in the kitchen with your mother." Saint Nicholas was tired, and had possibly been awake more than a day.

"I was, but she said that everything was ready." Kol walked up and took his spot in the middle of the carpet. "I was hoping that I could talk to you before the festival."

His father gave him a long look, then gathered his papers in a bundle and stacked them neatly in the corner of his desk. Taking his comfy chair, he sat down, removing his glasses and rubbing his eyes. "Well, of course you can."

"Where have you been?" Though it wasn't a part of what he needed to say, he couldn't help but ask.

It took a moment before Saint Nicholas replied. "I made a trip out to the Island. Doing a routine checkup."

Kol shrugged at the explanation. "Were the Flakes a part of your journey, as well?"

Saint Nicholas sighed to himself. "It was, and he still holds firm. Doesn't feel it's safe to send anyone."

"Maybe I could talk to him. Things will only be getting worse after what happened at the hospital last night."

"So I heard, and I was right in guessing that you were somehow involved." Kol's father had grown stern. It was no surprise that he would know.

Kol shifted his weight slightly, and explained, "Yes, I was there checking on someone. The fact that it was a Snowman who attacked the hospital will be troubling."

"It will. I'm afraid we'll be set back on the matter for quite some time because of that." His father removed his glasses and began to clean them. "He said that he had no knowledge of this attack and will begin to sweep his family to find who is responsible."

"It's what I feared too when the Snowman attacked. All our progress will now be tarnished. Other than that, Dad, there's something I need to talk with you about that has happened over the last couple of days." Taking a deep breath Kol started from the beginning. "As you know, the last time we talked I had been out in the city again. Ghouls had somehow entered the city and attacked one of the inns, so I intervened and chased them towards the city wall."

This cast a brief dark look across his father's face. "That's impossible. How did they even get into the city?"

While Saint Nicholas turned this over in his mind, Kol provided the rest of the story so that his father could have all the details. "The ghouls were not normal, at least not from what I had read about them. Besides the oddity of them being so far north, they also worked together when they are supposed to be independent. They could speak and knew who I was. They spoke of someone coming for us all, which makes me believe that someone plans to attack the North Pole just like so many years ago. They also wielded weapons when they attacked the inn. That's where the problem becomes worse." His father listened without comment. "The weapons they had were discarded during the chase and I was not able to find them when I retraced my steps."

"Besides the obvious, did these weapons appear dangerous in any way?"

"No, not on first sight, but because of what I believe is simply luck I was able to find one of the blades in the city the next day. Holly and I found one carried by a citizen while I went to the post office for Mom. I followed him, and once I came close enough to speak with him he attacked me. What's worse is that it was like he was possessed. After Holly took care of him, I went to study the blade, but it dissolved into thin air, and I had nothing to go on or show you once I returned home. We think they could be cursed, and two more are still out there. The man couldn't remember anything that had happened after getting the weapon."

"So the report about the librarian is linked to this as well. Thankfully you two were not hurt. Holly seems to be coming along nicely with her training. She informed the Cadence of these blades and the possibility of there more being in the city. What about the hospital?"

Kol was glad to hear his father's calm voice. He was taking in every word Kol said and was deciphering it. "I went there to talk with Master Shane, a wizard the ghouls attacked, and that was when the Snowman attacked. I am sure he was heading for the wizard's room."

His father stroked his beard. "Did the Snowman say anything to you?"

"No, he did not make a sound, and to add to that he had no eyes or an article of clothing. The only thing on him was some small dark fabric over his mouth."

If his father understood any of this, he did not say or show it in his face. "So what did Master Shane hear the ghouls say?"

"That they needed to find a place to finish Wenn's instructions. So maybe this Wenn who sent the ghouls also sent this rogue Snowman. Does the name sound familiar to you?"

Saint Nicholas stood and walked over to one of his shelves. Kol knew he was searching his mind for the name. After a few minutes he shook his head and turned back to Kol. "It does; thousands, actually. None of them had an outstanding in negative aura. So it's little use to me, though I have the locations. I will have to check into them later, though. The fact that these ghouls were able to enter the city without so much as an alarm is very disturbing. It would take advanced magic to even break the barrier, and usually monsters are detected far outside the walls. The barrier was never made for the Snow People, but I fear I may need to ask *Ve'rema* to change that. This is all very troubling, indeed." Kol's father walked around the desk and sat with his son on the carpet, one leg tucked under the other, hands resting on top of his knee. "Son, I appreciate what you have done these last few days. Thanks to you, the people of the inn were safe, and so were the people at the hospital. I will speak with the Section Leaders and Major and inform them of the whole scenario. With this information I believe that we can find these other two blades swiftly. Your uncle and aunt had good intentions, but you cannot continue to act as a vigilante. It is against the law and even though you are my son, I will not stop the Cadence from acting accordingly if they catch you."

"But you won't let..." Kol went quiet immediately as his father's hand shot up to stop Kol by laying on his shoulder.

"Even though I'm against it I want to give you an early Christmas present. I went to the Island to talk with Smithson. She will be expecting you at the beginning of the year." His father leaned back slightly, waiting for Kol's reaction.

"Are you serious?"

"Ho ho ho, of course I am." Kol was glad to hear the joy in his father's laugh. "Your mother and I talked and I can't force anything on you. But I have one request."

"What is it?"

"That you start training with me again during your breaks."

Kol thought about what his father offered for a moment. He was going to join the Cadence, regardless of his father's wishes. Now he had a blessing from his parents, which he was glad to finally hear. To start training again sounded useless, though; the last fourteen years showed that. He had no choice now, however, and maybe a miracle could happen. "All right, it's a deal."

They both rose to their feet, hearing one of the helpers coming to the door to summon Santa Claus to the festival. Kol was almost level with his father's gaze, who placed a firm hand on Kol and said, "Just know that I'm proud of you, no matter what happens. I want you to stop your investigation, though. I will look into the matter myself later and you can help, but no more running through the night." Kol knew that promise would be hard to keep, but he nodded.

A knock came at the door and Slee entered the room, smiling as usual. "It's almost time: everyone has gathered outside."

"Thank you, Slee. You two go on: I will be behind you in a moment. I need one last thing."

Kol nodded again, smiling, and he and his friend exited the office to journey across the now completely vacant workshop. The entrance halls echoed with the cheerful cacophony of voices, yet it too was empty, which meant all the helpers were now outside where the forming crowd would be carrying on in merry tones.

The deafening sound exploded over him as he pushed through the front doors. Everyone was in jubilation, the crowd in the plaza so thick you could not see the colorful stone that lay underneath their feet. They could feel the stone, however, because there was an enchantment on the plaza to give off warmth during occasions such as this. All the people were decked in their festive clothes which included long hats of blue, red, and green, trimmed with fur. Clothing was dyed in these colors and featured silver and gold buttons that reflected the light. Where the people were not standing there were beautiful dark wood tables and benches. The furniture started from the central tree and spiraled out into the surrounding park. A stage had been constructed beside the grand tree where Kol's parents would sit with other officials of the city.

The northern lights danced beneath the stars. Enchanted toy planes and helicopters zoomed over the crowds, showering them in colored snow of red and green that glowed and provided light. Vendors lined the walls, handing out gifts of sweets and toys for the children who lived here. Despite the festivities, Kol still had a sad thought while watching the humans and elves mingle and wishing their equality could go beyond the boundaries of the city. As he descended the stairs he heard the topic of the Snow People more than once while making his way through the crowd.

Kol looked over his shoulder and found that Slee had once again vanished, possibly off to his next duties. He decided to find his mother if he could and see what he needed to do. Still moving at a slow pace, he pushed to the center to look for her, having to lift his leg out of the way as three small children with knitted hats dashed beneath him, all holding wooden planes. Laughing at them, Kol was barely able to catch his balance. "Thought you were more graceful than that." Kol looked up at his friend's voice.

Holly stood in front of him, her smile bright on her face. Kol had to look a little harder at her so he was sure exactly what he saw. Holly was always the type of person to wear jeans and Converses along with her trademark jacket. She would much rather knock the boys in the dirt than play with dolls, which eventually led to her joining the Cadence. Today she looked different. Instead of jeans, she wore a green skirt with a pair of green heeled shoes to match. Her hair was now held by a red ribbon tied in a bow.

"Well, look who got all wrapped up!" Kol laughed.

Holly responded by hitting him hard in the chest. She smirked at him as he doubled over. "Yeah, and it doesn't say 'to you' anywhere on me."

Kol straightened up, still smiling. "Well, who is it for?"

"So, where's your mom? I figured she be chewing someone's ear out by now."

Kol looked over the crowd towards the tree. "No idea. I was on my way to look for her. Which may be a bad idea."

"Good idea. Sit with me, then. I wanted to give my parents some room to breathe anyways." She grabbed his hand and started pulling him to a nearby table.

"You're not going to sit with anyone from the Corps?"

Holly shook her head. "No, everyone is on duty, if you can't already tell. And I'm not that close to anyone in my class. Well," she looked through the crowd hopefully, "not yet anyway."

Kol thought he heard a small longing in her voice, but knew she wouldn't say if he asked. Looking through the crowd, however, he saw that Holly was right. The Cadence moved among the crowd, watching everyone. Kol saw an elf sliding between a few people. All Cadence members wore the same uniform: red tactical pants and combat boots, along with a mesh green shirt.

The main piece of the uniform was a dark red jacket with white accents and buttons along with the Corps symbol etched on the back: a pair of crossed drum sticks over a wreath of silver music notes. If the jacket wasn't enough to show their authority, there was their weapon hanging from their belts: the single drum, a red shell with white top and Cadence coat-of-arms printed center, attached behind them. Kol knew that several drum sticks lined the inside of their coats, used for throwing, defending, or playing. The last was the worst for anyone who decided that being a criminal was an illustrious career. The Cadence used sound as effectively as any other weapon. He nodded at the elf when he scanned over them, the shaded protector in high honor in his thoughts. Then the elf was out of his vision as Holly pulled him further into the crowd.

"So how far have you come with the sound studies anyway?" Kol asked as they came to a halt in front of one of the tables. The important thing about joining the Cadence was that you did not have to be born with the gift to perform magic. The instruments were enchanted to work for anyone who played the proper melody. Holly took her seat and Kol joined her. The rest of the crowd around them started doing the same.

"It's actually the branch I excel at." Holly started to look up and down the table at the people who sat around them. "I don't know why, but it's really simple for me to grasp."

"Hopefully I can say the same when I go back to the island with you."

Holly's focus snapped back to him, her green eyes hard. Kol noted how rare it was for anyone to grab her full attention. "What do you mean?"

Kol looked across the table, smiling. "Dad says I can join at the end of the year."

"What!" her shout quieted a few people around them. Not caring, she continued, "But why the change of mind?"

"He said I couldn't force anything on him. But he wants me to train with him still whenever I go on break. I don't see the point, but I agreed."

"Kol, that's great, and extra training to boot."

"Yeah, but you know it's useless."

She eyed him keenly before her vision started to drift back around them. In a lazy voice she said, "I don't know, maybe this time will be different."

Kol just shook his head at the thought. He was going to reply back when another voice spoke, "Ah, Kol, mind if I join you? Seems everywhere else is filling up."

Kol looked across the table, and his vision filled with a shimmering gold cloak drifting around an old man. Kol smiled at Master Hargon as he sat down across from them. His cloak was covered in ancient symbols of white, a token that showed he was a member of the *Ve'rema*. "Of course you can; I don't see any reason not." Nudging Holly, he added, "Holly, this is Master Hargon, a Learned from the Halls of *Ve'rema*."

"Oh, you're the one who was attacked by the ghouls!" Kol tapped Holly with his elbow. She realized she had spoken loudly and started to blush with embarrassment. Kol scanned his vicinity quickly but it appeared no one had heard her.

Master Hargon only laughed at her outburst, placing his hands in front of him. "I'm afraid I am. Just out of the hospital this morning as it were. Glad I was able to make the celebration."

"How are things there?" Kol asked. Holly was back to her observations, focusing right now on someone's fur shoes.

"Well, everything there is fixed up now, though a lot of the patients are still shaken. The nurses, too, and word got through the city no doubt as well." he sighed.

"So you don't see them as monsters, then?" Kol was glad to meet someone who was not a part of the majority.

"A Snowman, in my eyes, is not. Though I'm not quite sure that he was a member of the Snow People that live a short distance from here," Master Shane stated.

"Because he wasn't wearing any clothes, right? I thought of that myself."

"Exactly, and that fabric over his mouth you told me about was something else that caught my interest. I have not been to the Hall yet, but when I do this evening, I will consult with my colleagues." Master Hargon sighed before continuing. "I tried explaining this to the Cadence and the other members of the hospital. But they are all so set on the idea that a Snowman was acting barbarically."

"It's true." Though Holly never seemed to be paying attention, Kol knew she was. "I went to the precinct yesterday. There's talk of action against the Snowmen. A few people want the Corps and the Learned to journey to the Flakes and take care of the whole situation."

Kol placed his head in his hands and closed his eyes. Taking a deep breath, he said, "I just can't see how a place that is dedicated to what we are is so fearful."

"Well," Master Hargon reached into his cloak, pulling out a pair of glasses and placing them on, "The Elves still remember the war, and they have told the people stories. It's difficult to move on from something like that. Imagine what it must be like for the people who move here from the world. Coming from what they saw as normal to this, then finding out that nightmares do exist along with their dreams. It's almost too much for anyone, really. Hopefully Santa will be able to sort it all out."

Kol nodded at him but kept his face blank. He glanced at Holly who never broke from her oblivious searches of interest.

Kol was going to start up on another topic when any attempt for his voice was lost when the voice of Gene Autry filled the city, playing from every speaker along the street. Kol turned to look toward the mansion, the doors opening slowly, and his father stepped out into the plaza. The crowd erupted in cheers, everyone yelling his name or singing along with the song. He waved to them, his people, the joy clear in his gaze. To these people, Santa Claus was more than a childhood figure: he gave them a reason to live, a gift far better than any that could be wrapped in paper and bow. He gave his people hope.

The eight reindeer for the chosen flight came over the house next, a trail of light following behind them as they soared through the air. Creating a show for their audience, the reindeer flew in synchronizing patterns, all at speeds that made their images blur. The crowd clapped and whistled at the cartwheeling and corkscrews. The only thing missing from the sleigh carriers were the trademark bells, but those were locked away in the house and would come out twenty-four days from now. The reindeer performed their last trick before seven of them darted down the streets simultaneously, the eighth one soaring upwards during the final maneuver before landing next to his father. Santa patted Vixen, then climbed onto her back. Vixen kicked hard, leaping over the crowd and landing on a high stage where his mother waited for him along with other figures of importance. Santa slid from Vixen's back, who took to the air again to rejoin her squad, and he walked over to Kol's mother and kissed her gently on the cheek.

The crowd went crazy again, clapping at the affection, and Kol's father scanned the crowd. Kol nodded at him when their eyes met. His father just smiled. His father and mother would want Kol eating with them, but Santa saw Holly and nodded back. He waited a few moments for the uproar to quiet down before lifting both hands in the air to quiet the city the rest of the way. Once everyone was listening he spoke.

"Greetings, everyone." His voice magically boomed and was heard clearly down every street, reverberating off the buildings. "And welcome to another December. This time each year we are called upon to bring hope and joy throughout world, to all those who truly believe in the goodness of others. I know now, as I knew when we began this great city, that I cannot do this alone. It takes the strength of everyone here, every hammer swung and every stroke of a brush, for the day twenty-five from now to become a true miracle to the world. " The crowd still held silent, but Kol could see the eagerness in their eyes. That lasting hope still burned bright. "Let us once again be the beacon of hope the rest of the world can look Northward and see." With these words, he turned to the Christmas tree.

Everyone held their breath for what was coming next. Kol's father slowly raised his hands to either side, his eyes closed in concentration. The lamps that had been keeping the plaza alight dimmed and extinguished. The animated toys finished the last of their illuminating snowfall and flew back to their makers. His hands came together with a sound like thunder, the shockwave passing across the people of the North Pole. Light flooded every crevice of the city as the Christmas lights came alive. The great tree at the center of the plaza blazed brighter than any sun could on top of the world. The lights ran down the tree and across the plaza, up the buildings and through the streets. Kol knew they ran all the way to the outskirts of the city, through the traditional villages, halting only at the wall.

The crowd once again erupted in cheers, and Kol thought they were the loudest yet. Santa turned to the crowd and took a playful bow. The Christmas spirit was in full swing now, the decorations dancing with the lights. Music slowly rose from the speakers hidden beneath the center stage. "Jingle Bells" was the selected song for the start. During the waking hours a Christmas song would play every hour, and humans and elves would dance and sing while walking down the streets.

"Now that the lights are on, I believe we can all see our food now." Another wave of his hands, green sparks flying from them, and the food that had been prepared began to fly from the opened doors of the house and onto the spiraling tables. Kol knew that what he saw in the kitchen was only a fifth of what was here now. "Help yourselves, everyone. Tomorrow we start: tonight, we feast!"

And they did. Everyone who had not settled in yet did, filling their plates with the food around them. People passed food to one another, turkey or bowls of stuffing. Kol started to fill his own plate, which he found already held turkey. He glared at Holly who shrugged as she reached for a plate of macaroni and cheese. Rolling his eyes, he started on some other entrees. Kol looked back to the stage where he found his father sitting next to his mother, beginning their meals. The two of them where engaged in pleasant chuckles over some topic his mother must have conjured up. The rest of the table had similar faces of joy, though not entirely the same feelings of matrimony.

To Saint Nicholas' right sat Jereme Survon, along with his wife Shelia. Both were in their late forties and had dark hair and copper skin. Jereme wore a golden colored shirt that was clasped with silver buttons beneath a short-trimmed beard, and she a delicate yet simple blue dress. On his mother's left sat another pair of individuals, both of whom were elves. Slovian Jains sat with her husband, Mova, in matching red tunics. The two of them were old, yet Kol knew their spirits were still young. Slovian's hair was grey and in neat curls and Mova was completely bald, his pointed ears taking up most of his head. Pinned to the shirts of both Slovian and Jereme were badges crafted into sliver and shaped in a four-sided diamond. Slovian's badge had a green "E" engraved upon it while Jereme's had a red "H." Both individuals were the elected officials of both the human and elf races and sat in respected seats on the Crafted Council.

Though his father did not truly accept the title, he was still seen in the eyes of his people as their king. Unable to sway them any differently he decided he had best act as rightfully as he could. He decided to create the Crafted Council to create camaraderie amongst his people. There were four other seats in the council other than his father's, and every five years the different races could vote for whom they wished to represent them on the council. There was a limit to the number of terms the individuals could serve, but there was also a vote each year to confirm that the races still agreed with whom they chose. The final two seats went to the two large factions. High Master Renshu was the leader of the Learned in *Ve'rema*, and as such represented them on the council. Though he was known to be a powerful wizard in his old age, he was also known to forget important events, always busy in his work. His seat on the stage was empty probably because of that very fact. The final seat was held by the youngest member for both of her positions. Drum Major Eileen Smithson was the head of the Cadence Corps and made her office on the Island, which was both the training grounds for the Cadence and the prison for criminals. Her seat was empty, as she also focused completely on her work. Whenever his father had to leave the city, they made decisions in his stead through a voting system. It was agreed that if there was a tie, his mother would cast the final vote. If she was not available, then it fell to Kol. Kol went to examine the other influential figures of the table before Holly brought his attention back to his own.

"So what is it you do, wizard man?" Master Shane smiled at Holly despite her crude remark, which he took no notice of or simply did not care.

"I play with sparkly things, of course; what else do you think we magic folk do?" Master Hargon laughed at his own joke.

Holly laughed with him before continuing, "I meant, what is your specialty?"

"Ah," the wizard swallowed some mashed potatoes before answering, "I specialize in illusions, actually." He pulled his wand from within his cloak and gave it a soft flick, muttering under his breath. A transparent white rabbit hopped into existence from the air, made a few jumps, then vanished. Holly giggled as Master Hargon continued, "I am also on the Conventicle of Learned who assist in translocation magic."

"Portals? That's rather advanced—or at least so I've heard." Holly started on a piece of turkey.

"Oh indeed," Master Hargon tucked his wand away while explaining. "It takes the lot of us along with a few powerful tools to perform them, so we do not deplete our stamina for the day. It's possible to do so on your own, but you'll be fatigued for the week after."

Holly swallowed another bite of food before asking, "Can the Learned leave the city, just like the Scribes?"

"Everyone can leave the city if they want to. Just so long as the secret is locked away." Master Shane examined a single green pea. "But tomorrow we will be sending the Scribes off on their duties. It will be a draining day, but we are all more than fine with doing our part."

Kol nodded, smiling. *Ve'rema*, or the Halls, was the building dedicated to the magical arts. Originally it was founded by the elves, but as humans came to live here they became interested in the Studies as well. The elves were cautious at first, but after some negotiations with his father, a master of the Studies himself, they allowed other human pupils. One of the jobs of *Ve'rema* was helping the Scribes who could not fit on the train to their assigned location. There were simply too many for the locomotive to handle, so the Learned were more than willing to lend a hand.

The Scribes were the ones who would dress in red and white attire and attend functions throughout the word in the name of the North Pole. This ranged anywhere from parades to school functions and shopping malls. Any child who sat on the lap of a mall Santa was not sitting on his father's lap, but a representative of the North Pole. That way their Christmas wishes could be heard if the children never placed it in a letter. The Scribes would live in their respective locations and send the children's information back home. His father did participate in a few parades, however. What a smile it would bring if the world knew that the Real Santa was sitting on the float they watched every American Thanksgiving in New York!

"So how do you know when to bring them home?" Kol asked, working on his second plate.

"Ah, we open up portals in the respective locations they are assigned. They must be sure to make it to the location or they will miss the trip back. Usually if it happens they write to us and we send another, followed of course by a very light scolding." The wizard laughed softly. "Can't always blame the eggnog."

Kol laughed too, then gave an apology to the middle-aged man next to him who was cutting his daughter's turkey. Holly had created a smiley face in her plate now, an elf, he thought because of the green bean ears. "So what about the safety and secret of the city? What if one of the Scribes told someone about the North Pole?"

"Well, we have precautions for that." Master Shane placed his fork on his plate, finished with his main course. He placed both hands together in front of him. "Like I said before, the secret must be locked up. We place a charm on all the Scribes, which they know about fully and agree to. Whenever they try to speak about the city, their memories of it vanish. A harsh rule, but it is needed."

"I don't think I like that idea too much," Holly frowned.

"Well, we don't either, but after the battle it was agreed upon. It's the only way to keep the city safe." Shane looked up the table towards another wizard wearing the same colored cloak. "We have to do the same to anyone who wants to leave the city. It's far too dangerous if someone on the outside knew that we actually existed. That is why we allow them to willingly choose."

"Well, that's understandable, but it still feels wrong."

"Agreed, little drummer, but necessary." The topic was lost as the food vanished and was replaced by dessert.

Kol grabbed his new clean plate and started to reach for a piece of strawberry pound cake. He next went for his favorite type of dessert, which was, humorously enough, cookies. He agreed with Holly when it came to the secret of the city. He did not like the idea of the men who went out to work in the North's name to be mentally chained as they were. The elves insisted on it; they all knew too well what the touch of man could do if the thoughts were of wickedness. Hopefully one day the world could know of their existence, and people could come freely to the North Pole. It was a day they would be a long time working toward.

As the evening continued, Holly and Master Hargon discussed other topics or joked with one another. Kol continued to eat, lost in his thoughts of the Snowman attack, the ghouls, missing swords, and his joining the Corps in January. He was so focused inwardly that Holly had to nudge him to bring him back to the surface. "Your dad's about to talk again." She pointed to the stage where indeed his father was now standing. The feast was almost over, everyone's bellies full. Thoughts of warm beds must have been shared now.

"I hope that everyone has taken their fill." His voice was once again amplified by his magic. "But before we scurry off to our pillows, I would like to say a few words to you all." He waited a few moments to make sure he held everyone's attention. "As you may have all heard, yesterday the hospital was attacked." Murmurs started, a soft hum that was quickly quieted by his father's voice. "And the rumors are true, it was indeed a Snowman. Why he attacked we do not know, but I have reason to believe he was not acting of his own accord. My Family," he said, addressing everyone here. "We are supposed to be a symbol to the world; one of peace, love and forgiveness. Let us remember this as we think of the Snow People. I know that long ago, hatred came to our doorsteps, bearing its teeth. But those of the Flakes have no need of hatred. So, I am asking you..."

What he was asking never came, however. Before he could finish, a disturbance occurred below the stage, bringing his father's attention. Kol stood to see and those around him followed suit, making Kol glad of his height. Kol could see what looked like a man in his seventies trying to climb onto the stage. He was wearing a brown cloak that appeared to be patched in some places. His cough, possibly from a cold, echoed over the now silent crowd, watching in puzzlement. Kol's father reached down and attempted to lift the man up to the stage, one hand gripping the person and the other shooing away the Corps members who had ran up to secure the problem. His father seemed to be saying something to him, his caring eyes searching for the cause of ailment. As Kol watched his eyes caught something beneath the man's cloak. He reacted instantly, leaping onto his table and sprinting towards with father in the center. He saw another man trying to climb onto the stage, those around seemingly assuming he was a family member of the sick man. Kol was not far from the stage when the unthinkable happened. The sick man brought up his arm and plunged the green blade into his father's ribs.

CHAPTER FIVE

Across the Shifting Ice

The crowd stood in shocked silence, and even the Cadence were frozen with uncertainty. Kol had not stopped, though. He leapt onto the stage, his eyes on the other man who had climbed up, his right hand holding the third blade. He held it high, charging at Kol's father, and in a growling voice he yelled, "FOR THE SNOW PEOPLE!"

Kol was in the man's path. Planting his footing, he brought up his leg and kicked the man in the chest hard, sending him sliding backward. The blade left his hand and flew through the air, vanishing into the crowd. The man coming to a stop was enough catalyst needed to break the shock. Someone screamed, and people began to scramble in fear. Kol turned from the man he had kicked and went to his father who was now laying on the ground. The sick man was restrained by three members of the Cadence. Two more hopped on the stage and passed him, heading for the other attacker. Kol knelt beside his father, cradling his head in his hands.

"My son," he said weakly.

"Don't." Kol looked down at the blade. The green metal was sunk halfway into his body. There was no blood coming from the wound.

"Kol, listen," his father grabbed his shoulder, pulling Kol's attention back to his face. "Whatever happens to me, they will need you."

"Nothing's going to happen to you." Kol's eyes were hot. His training had left him after taking care of the attacker. Now he felt hopeless.

"Kol, they will need someone to look to. Don't let the hate spread, Kol." His eyes closed slowly.

"No!" Kol's tears came from his anger. He looked at the blade and was horrified by what was happening. The blade had begun to liquefy just as the other one had. As its physics changed, it began to sink into the wound, and once the greenish substance was completely inside, the opening closed, leaving behind only a faint pink scar. Someone squatted down beside him, grabbing his hand. Kol looked up and found his mother watching him.

"Go inside, Kol; we will take care of him." His mother's voice was calm and gentle.

"No, I won't leave."

"He is not dead, Kol. Now go; the Corps will bring him inside." She brushed her fingers across her husband's cheek.

"What do you mean?" She did not answer because a sound of thunder became audible: a rolling steady beat that suppressed all shouts of panic. The Cadence Corps declared order, and everyone slowed in their panic. The melody used was meant to magically calm emotions. Looking up Kol could still see their frightened faces begin to lessen as the Corps moved everyone out of the plaza. Kol was then pulled away from his father by more members of the Corps. Slowly they placed their fallen king on a stretcher and picked him up into the air.

******

Kol swung his sword, cutting cleanly through the pillar of enchanted ice placed in front of him. He moved gracefully to the next target, his sword striking through that one as well. He was in the training room built within his father's house. The place was a large room covered in enchanted ice from the stone floor edges, through the columns that ran along the walls between the high windows, to the ceiling. It was a cavern of ice where Kol could place runic scrolls on the ground to create columns of additional ice that were similar to the height of a humanoid attacker. Training equipment lined the walls, and on raised wooden platforms were weights for lifting, pads for hand to hand practice, and melee weapons of all forms. Kol had spent most of his time here during the day so long as other matters did not call for him. It was his place of sanctuary.

It had been a week since they brought his father inside and the people were all safely home. His mother had brought in everyone who could possibly help. The doctors said that he showed no sign of poison or irregularity in his current state; he was simply asleep. The Learned came next, but none of their observations were useful. They could find no trace of curse nor spell on him. Even High Master Renshu could not help. Despite his delving failing him, he still believed a curse was present: he simply could not detect it. He promised Kol and his mother that he would continue researching into the matter. Since no one in the city was able to help Santa at the current moment, his father was left to lay in his bed comatose. Kol went to his side every night since the attack. It was almost unbearable. His father, an anchor strong enough to hold the most important people of the world together, lay silently, breathing as though asleep, yet unable to rise from his slumber. Kol's words could not break through.

The Crafted Council wasted no time in regaining order. The Drum Major had come from the island to complete the elected group while his mother and the rest of the Crafted Council had talked to the citizens after the attack, assuring them that his father was well and would recover shortly. The panic that had started to build was pacified, but only to a certain point. They asked for everyone to continue as they were, preparing for Christmas Eve. It was what their king would want, even in his weakened state. The people of the city stood together on the idea, so they took to the workshops with his mother at the head of the craftsmen army. Everyone wanted things to be right when Santa Claus walked into the plaza to mount his sleigh, a miracle everyone was hoping for. In a place such as this, it had more power to happen than anywhere else in the world simply because they believed.

Another cylinder of ice fell to the floor, shattering. That one was the last of them. He looked back at the fifteen crumpled sculptures he had left in his wake. There was another thought the people seemed unified on, and that was the call for blood, or in this case water of the Snow People. The man's shout was more present in the streets now and not just in the alleys. It was the final act needed. Of course, there was the logic that it was a human that made the attack and not one of the Flakes, but people feared what they did not understand. Many believe the man had been cursed and sent in from the Snow People. In a world full of magic, that was an easy conclusion. It was a logical enough inference, but Kol was convinced that the Snow People were framed. Kol threw his sword at the wall in frustration, remembering his father's words. How could a place built on the ideals of Christmas hold hate toward others who were not the same as they were?

The door to the training room opened slowly, the figure looking through the door to make sure the coast was clear. "It's okay, Holly, you can come in," Kol said, walking over to a rack holding dry towels. He took one and started to dry off where the ice had melted on his skin and mixed with his sweat.

"I don't see how you can stand it in here. It's freezing." She was wearing her usual clothes now, her trademark hoodie wrapped tight with the hood snug as she closed the door behind her.

Kol, lacking a jacket, shrugged. "What's the news?" Kol was hoping to hear something good.

"Well, I've been down at the station all day, and the two men still are in custody." She sighed and sat on a bench jetting from the wall. "Both have no recollection of what happened."

"I heard. Thankfully you and I know there is someone or something else there pushing all this along." Kol threw the towel back onto the rack. He had thought about telling the Drum Major all he knew but had decided not to. Not that Kol cared to be in trouble, but he figured it simply would not help. The Corps had made the connection to the ghouls and the blades from the report given by the people who were at the Lake of Frost during the attack. It was the rogue Snowman at the hospital that truly caused the most harm. If a Snow Person could get into the city undetected, then it does not take much fear for the average individual to assume that they could just as easily send other creatures, too. Harder evidence was needed to prove the lack of connection.

"But who, Kol? It does make a lot of sense that they would be able to make these weapons. Especially ones that the Halls have no written records of. It's not the first time they have created new forms of magic."

"They didn't do it, Holly!" Kol's voice rose slightly, then he brought it back down at the look on her face. "I'm sorry. Just so much has happened."

Her expression was sympathetic. "It's okay. You know I know the truth, but you have to admit it all looks suspicious. Thankfully, the Council has no intentions of going to war. Major has every intention of having solid evidence before sending an envoy to the Flakes. I fear that the people will act regardless and march on the Flakes despite the dangers. Even members of the Cadence have voiced this."

"Any attempt to go past the wall will send them right back. There is more than enough cold out there to calm the fire." Kol took a drink from his canteen. "If only I could find where the weapons came from."

"Well," Holly shifted uncomfortably where she sat, "That's why I came here." She reached under her jacket and pulled out a small bundle of blue cloth. She gently lowered it to the ground and unwrapped it. Inside laid one of the green blades, the one held by the man he had kicked and watched it fly into the crowd.

"Where did you get this?" Kol squatted down beside the blade, looking very closely at the marks on it, being careful not to touch it. He had searched the grounds looking for the thing but had found nothing, and had assumed someone in the Corps had already taken it in for evidence. When the Major had told Kol's mother it had not been found, he feared someone else would be affected by the blade.

"When you left I started to follow as usual. I was halfway towards you when you stopped the man who yelled. When he threw the blade away I grabbed it in this fabric." Holly gave a small smile of triumph.

"Why didn't you bring it to me afterwards?"

"I couldn't: The Corps wanted everyone home. I was no exception." Holly hesitated, being careful with her next words. "I didn't take it to you first. I went to the station to turn it in. It was only when I heard their accusations that some of the Cadence actually believed the Snow People were behind it that I thought better of it. Better to bring it directly to the council, but I never got the chance. Because of what happened, the Major has required all hands on deck. I got orders to travel with the rest of my class to the Island to assist in preparations in case the city comes under attack, so it was hidden at home until my return." Holly watched Kol's face carefully. "Best to be prepared, right? That's why it took so long to get this to you. We just now arrived back."

Kol looked at his friend and nodded. He had already been told the Major would begin defense preparations. Kol could not blame her for doing her job. "I'm not angry at you. It was the right thing to take it to them. In fact, Master Renshu should get this immediately. I would have just been afraid of the curse affecting you as well."

"I made sure not to touch it with my bare hands," Holly told him, touching the fabric the blade was wrapped in.

"I can always count on you. Before I take this to Master Renshu, I have to check with someone else first." Kol started to fold the fabric up around the blade, once more making sure not to touch the blade.

"Kol, who else are you going to ask about it?" Holly had both a knowing and concerned look in her eyes.

Kol knew only one person who could take this blade and tell him what it truly was without having to look over old books. "Holly, I have to go to the Flakes."

"Why?" the concern of Holly's eyes was now in her voice.

"Because I have to." Kol stood, placing the bundle under his arm. "Holly, I can't explain why. Not this time." Kol turned to his friend. "I have to go find answers and there is only one person I know who can help me. Don't tell my mother where I've gone: she has too much to worry about with everything that has happened. When I return, I'll give it to the Council and tell them I found it, so you don't get into trouble. That way if I find out nothing then Master Renshu and the rest of the Learned will still have a chance to come up with information."

Holly shook her head and laughed. "You're crazy going out there, you know that."

"Of course I am." Walking over to the wall, he pulled his sword from the ice where it had stuck. Holly looked at it, noticing it for the first time. Her eyebrows rose but she laughed. Kol turned and exited the room, leaving her smiling.

The training room was on the first floor of his home, but it only took him a few minutes to make it to his room. Kicking open his trunk, he dressed in his gear and made his way downstairs. Fingering his bell in its pouch, he felt the reassurance of what he was about to do. He didn't go through the front door; his destination was towards the back of the house. Walking through the empty, elegantly carved halls, Kol had to smile at the idea of his father crafting all of this when he rebuilt his home a second time. Kol finally made it to the door of the stable, carved with two magnificent deer, and pushed it open.

The room was long, with stalls for the animals running along the right side. There were fifteen stalls, and each held one of the magnificent deer that pulled his father's sleigh. The floor was covered in hay, and the harnesses, feed, brushes, and extra hay were against the left wall. He walked up to the nearest reindeer, Comet, and patted his head in between his antlers. The deer returned the kindness by nuzzling him in the face. "That was a great display all of you put on the other day." The deer in the stall next to Comet, Vixen, blew at him playfully. Kol smiled back, rubbing her head as well. He made his way down the row of dark wooden homes, talking to each of the deer as he passed.

Eight of the reindeer held the rank of Sleigh Puller, each named accordingly with the traditional titles. They were the distant descendants of the first reindeer to ever pull the sleigh. The other stalls were occupied by other offspring who hadn't made the cut. They were not simply placed aside, though; each one of the others had their own jobs to complete, either delivering messages or giving his father a ride when needed. He was looking for a particular one, however. He passed one labeled Maple, who was only a few years old. He smiled, patting the deer as she placed her front legs on her stall door. He made it to the last stall with a gold nameplate reading "Soar." Looking inside, he smiled at the reindeer sleeping in it. "Hey, sleepy, you up for a journey?"

The reaction was instant. The deer made cheery noise as it leaped up and out of its stall, landing on Kol. Pinned to the ground, Kol struggled to break free, Soar thoroughly licking his face. "Enough! Let me up. We have something to do." The deer stepped over him, toward the reins on the other wall. By the time Kol stood back up the deer had already pulled his straps from the wall and tossed them at Kol's feet. Even though the circumstances were dismal, he couldn't help but smile at his friend. Soar could sense his owner was in distress and was doing whatever he could to make it better.

Kol was ten when his father brought him down to the stables to witness Vixen giving birth to Soar. Afterward, while the tiny deer was learning to stand, he would not walk but would constantly leap from spot to spot. Kol told his father it looked like the tiny deer was eager to start flying as soon as possible. Laughing, his father asked him to name the little deer, and Kol named him for what the deer wanted to do most. Soar was from then on his reindeer.

Kol strapped Soar's saddle to him, which was more difficult than it should have been because the deer did not want to sit still. Once fitted, Kol returned to the stall and reached for a bundle of brown fur on the top shelf. He quickly untied the string that bound it and unfolded another pair of pants, gloves, and a jacket. The chill within the city was easily managed but the winter that waited beyond the walls would reach through someone's skin and stop their heart. Kol enjoyed the cold, but he would rather be safe in case his stubbornness caused the loss of his fingers. Fitting his legs through the thicker clothes and tying the bottoms over his boot, Kol secured the jacket and hood before pulling black goggles from his pocket and putting them on.

Soar eagerly led him to the door and out into the cool night. Kol looked at his friend. "It's a long journey. Are you going to be able to make it?" Soar's response was to head butt Kol hard. Kol rubbed his head in between the antlers and said, "All right, I won't underestimate you." He walked around the deer's side, placed his foot into the stirrup and climbed on. Soar turned his neck to look at Kol, a stern look in his eyes. Kol smiled and reached into his riding jacket and pulled the collar over his nose and mouth. Grabbing the reins, he held them firm: the first time he had done this he had fallen off. Luckily his father had been with him and had caught him before he hit the ground.

Soar planted his feet deep in the snow, and Kol knew he was concentrating on the air. Kol's father had told him that the reindeer could fly because they could walk on the wind. It was like being able to swim to others. Kol braced his feet as Soar crouched low and then leaped into the sky. He felt his heart jump as they moved upwards. Flying always gave him a rush, and Soar always made the best of it. They corkscrewed into the air, gliding higher and higher. Kol pulled on the reins, causing Soar to flip backwards before he positioned them to fly towards their destination. Soar flew between the buildings, then over the village, bouncing off a few roofs as he went. Kol knew it had been far too long since he was free of the house. At this rate they would be there in a few hours.

CHAPTER SIX

The Chief Beneath the Glacier

Kol reached up to his goggles and rubbed each lens. The night magically shone brighter through them, allowing him to see the last part of the city passing under him. Soar slowed as they passed over the border and they both felt the soft pull of protection, as if the city gave one last tug for them not to leave, before they sped away. Endless ice now lay in front of them, the mutable land constantly shifting from the sea water slamming sheets of ice together. Kol leaned onto Soar and they shot faster over the white landscape. The city was well protected, not just by the wards reinforced by *Ve'rema*, but by the endless waste that no creature could cross without difficulty. Besides, there were polar bears.

A long time ago, before Kol had even been thought of, the city of the North Pole was no bigger than a village. Small cottages housed the elves who had taken residence there to escape some form of turmoil they had endured. The only human who had been allowed to live with them had been his father, who, according to the elves, came to them pulling a broken sleigh behind him. He had been covered in furs, far thicker than what Kol now wore. The sleigh had held only a bundle of blankets that his father curled under to sleep and a few remaining scraps of food. When he finally made it to the village he had collapsed there, exhaustion taking him after months of travel. The elves nursed his father back to health, asking why he had made such a dangerous trek across a land as cold as this. His father had told them that he had been sent here, and that was his only explanation.

Not even Kol knew the real reason his father came to the top of the world. Once he was fully rested, he began a kinship with the elves. His father helped them build better homes and the elves taught him the ways of their magic, which they referred to as the Studies. Now, Saint Nicholas had always been a man of motivation and had a heart to always help others. While learning their magic, he came up with an idea to help the world as he knew it at the time. The plan seemed so simple when explained. The world was falling further and further into darkness. People used one another selfishly, bringing pain to the less fortunate. It could easily be said that this was always true, but something more was occurring. Monsters moved in vast numbers and preyed on the innocent. His plan was to affect the children of the world, and show them that there was more to the world than what they were shown. For one year of kindness the children would receive a gift, one that would show them that someone in this realm of existence whom they could not see believed in their good natures. Not only that, but all the gifts were enchanted to protect the children from more than just the shadows of their room. No longer could the innocent be preyed upon from under their beds. What about the naughty children? Were they not worthy of magical protection? According to his father, yes, they are. That is why he leaves a gift for every child, one that Saint Nicholas believes would best help the child's growth.

Years went by, and eventually the existence of the village was discovered by the wrong kind of beings. They came in hundreds, all wanting this spot for themselves so that they could use it for their own needs. Monsters, straight from nightmares that Santa Claus' gifts fought against, marched across the barren waste, all pushed by the greed of power they believed his father possessed. Their assault made it all the way to his father's doorstep before he was able to stop them. Using his knowledge of the Studies and his own devices, he and the elves crushed the enemy's final assault.

When the siege had finished, only the remains of the North Pole stood.

After that night, his father swore to work harder to protect his home. Using his newly acquired magical skills, he shielded the area. Anyone who had not been there before could not gain entry unless shown the way. The elves explained to his father that they had always been running from the monsters, yet were always somehow discovered and attacked. Saint Nicholas understood, and sheltered them. Many years later he began to bring people into the town, explaining they would need all the help they could find because the world as they knew it was growing exponentially. They agreed as long as they could tell the newcomers the history of the North Pole, and the importance of their safety. With their agreement, his father went out, looking for those who would want to leave behind their world and join him on his mission.

His father was tired of seeing orphans and the homeless wandering the world in agony and loneliness. It was these people he gave a chance for another life, bringing them to the city and giving them a place to live, a job, something to eat, and, most importantly, a reason to live. These people raised families here, passing on their loyalties and love of the idea of the North Pole to their children. But they also subtly passed on a fear. In becoming part of the legend here, they learned of the existence of monsters they thought only existed in fairy tales from the elves. This insidious fear slowly infected the newer population of the city. His father did not like the idea of his people living in fear—he wanted them to see the world in equality. He could not force this understanding on them, though; he could only lead by example. His example, however, had a drawback to it that his father did not anticipate.

Kol had no way to tell how much time had passed, but he would have gambled for close to an hour. The shifting ice had diminished in frequency as the ocean gained mass beneath him. He did not worry about where he was, for he saw his destination visualizing on the horizon. A pair of mountains crashed with the sea, a glacier splitting them both as it too struck the ocean. No vegetation grew on the grey, which led others to believe there were no animals as well. Solitude was the truest defining word Kol could ever create for it. He crossed the beginning of the glacier and scanned it, looking for the entrance. After some difficulty, he finally found the dark hole far to the right. Kol pulled Soar's reigns and landed softly on the shining ice. Dismounting, Kol patted his companion as a nuzzle of worry graced his shoulder. "Easy, my friend. I'll be fine. Wait for me here; I'll not take long." Soar whined softly but did as he was asked.

Stepping into the opening was difficult. His footing had to be correct or he would slip on the floor and end up stranded below the ice. It was dark for the first few minutes, but Kol kept his careful pace until the walls began to give off a faint light. The path was quiet but through the walls water could be heard rushing as the ice melted its way along the mountains before freezing again. For several moments Kol had to stop as the tunnel branched off into several different directions. He listened carefully as he had always been taught before selecting the correct path. He listened not for the rushing water, but for the soft hammering of metal. That would lead his way. For him these tunnels were an annoyance, but to others they would be confusing simply because they were mutable. The confusion was an understatement: these tunnels were meant for those unwelcome to become lost. Because the ice was constantly shifting, new tunnels were created frequently over time. Anyone who had been here before could not take the same way back, but Kol knew what to follow. His path became ever brighter and Kol was thankful that his feet connected with stone on his first attempt through the tunnels. He had made it safely.

The cave he stood in was large enough for him to move about freely and the ceiling stretched well out of his reach. The walls reflected the soft glow of the ice, as did the pointed, arched door that stood solidly before him. It too was made of ice, but anyone could tell this ice was different. Besides its glow, it was carved delicately in flowing art that represented an icy wind. It was also strong. No form of force would break it down. Anyone who did not heed the first warning of the door would find their weapon shattered the second time they struck. Stepping closer, Kol pulled his left hand free of his glove and placed it on the center of the beautiful work. It was cold at first, but after he was recognized the door began to melt away. He felt no guilt in destroying it, for when he stepped across the threshold the door froze back exactly how it had been.

The tunnel was now in the form of well-polished stone stairway leading down under the mountain. The path was lit by enchanted icicles that emitted a cool blue light. Kol felt nostalgia warming his blood as he stepped further into the cold. This place was just as much of his home as his father's workshop was. Kol ignored any more branches of tunnels and continued straight. The stairs emptied into a vast cavern of ice and stone. Every ice-covered stalactite glowed with the same power as the icicles before. The walls of this chamber consisted of elevated walkways and additional tunnel exits like Kol himself had just stepped from, though these tunnels were closed by more of the beautiful icy doors. Along the walkways large mounds of snow lay scattered about. The floor also had sporadic mounds of snow. Where the snow was not piled, the floor of cracked polished stone peeked through. Each of these cracks was been filled with the glowing ice and leveled out. The only object on the cavern floor was a large throne made of beautifully worked metal. The designs across it were made to look like glaciers. As Kol moved closer he could see placed in the center of the throne was a large black top hat with a red ribbon circling above the brim.

His footsteps echoed around him as he moved closer. With each sound, movement began to stir along the walls. The scattered icy doors melted away and the tunnels began to fill with figures of white and hints of several other colors. Curious eyes of coal watched him as he stepped along. Each of the Snow People that looked upon him wore articles of clothing: knitted hats of assorted styles, leather belts, sewn vest, shirts, or pants. Some even wore shoes. Out of all these clothes there was only one article of clothing among each Snow Person that was truly important. These clothes were what gave the Snowmen life, and they wore more than one to hide which one was their soul. As long as these clothes existed, they could form the ice around them into their bodies. Strangely, it was only ice they could do this with, perhaps because of the original Snowman. Kol smiled and gave a light wave at the titans, who only watched him silently as he moved closer to the throne. "Hello, Uncle. I need to speak with you."

A voice came, deep and rumbling. It seemed to be coming from beneath where Kol was standing and resonated off the cavern walls and ceiling. "It has been a long time, Nicholas. What is it you need from me?"

Kol pulled the covered blade from under his jacket and held it before him. "Can you give me advice on this? Something terrible has happened."

There was no quick answer to his question. The snow throughout the chamber began to stir. Softly at first, then growing to the likes of an avalanche, colliding into itself as it raced to the throne. The top hat vanished in the turmoil as the snow packed harder together. One limb at a time erupted from the mass. The body was the tallest of any of the others, Kol remembered, when it stood at its full height. The right arm reached into the chest and pulled forth the top hat that was then placed atop the now forming head. Positioned correctly, two eyes of coal emerged from his face and connected with Kol's. He looked back up into the eyes of Frostein—or Frosty, as his song stated—the Snowman, chieftain of the Snow People.

"Tell me, Nicholas, what has happened?" Frostein's voice held concern under the deep grumble.

Kol swallowed before starting. "My dad's been attacked. And the North Pole believes it is your doing."

"What nonsense is this?" Frostein's voice now held anger. "I have no reason whatsoever to raise a hand to your father. Something I have said for a long time." Many of the Snow People shouted in agreement.

"I know, but the people won't hear it." Kol had to yell slightly to make sure he was heard.

Frostein raised his hand to command silence. "Start from the beginning, Kol. Tell me what has happened." The concern was back in his voice, now mixed with confusion. Kol held back no secrets, knowing it would cause more harm than good. He started from the inn, telling how the ghouls had somehow made it into the city, followed by his trip to the post office and how one of the blades had affected the librarian. Then he talked about the hospital and about how a Snowman had smashed apart the eighth floor, though Kol knew his father had already told Frostein. Kol added his own information such as the lack of eyes and piece of clothing. He ended his narration at the festival where his father was attacked. Frostein never interrupted, but made slight motions to keep his people quiet. Kol finished his story, ending it where he now stood.

Frostein continued to sit, pondering over what he had just heard. Moments passed in silence before he finally spoke. "Starting with the Snowman that attacked the hospital. As I told your father, no one here is missing, and I know of all my people," Frostein said. Reaching down, he held his large hand in front of Kol. "Let me see the blade."

Kol did as instructed, placing the shrouded weapon into Frostein's hand. The Snowman brought the small item closer to his eyes to exam it. This was why Kol brought it. If anyone knew metal, it was the Snow People, and if there was one person Kol could truly trust outside of the city, it was his uncle. Frostein was sworn brother to Kol's father. Where his father was a master carpenter, Frostein was an excellent blacksmith. Every Snowman was able to follow the craft flawlessly if that was what they wished. They were masters of metallurgy, from basic materials to enchanted alloys. The Snow People crafted objects of the highest quality before their forges. They did not fear the fire, and in fact they viewed working with the one thing that could destroy them as a rite of passage. They placed their item of clothing within their bodies and donned leather fabrics enchanted to resist heat. This was where Kol had come to learn the art when he was much younger and finished with wood working. The people of the North had a lot to owe to the Snow People. It was scarcely known to the denizens of the main city, but the two inhabitants continued to trade with one another. Using the train to move goods, the Snow People would receive wool from the farms to make their clothes, since no animal could live within these caves. In return, the Snow People supplied steel and through hushed hammers they had a great hand in constructing the North into what it stood like today.

"This was not crafted by us." Frostein's voice was angry again.

"Then where did it come from?" Kol took a seat on the stone.

"It was made by Goblins, and the metal is rare. The curse that is placed on it was set by someone powerful in the dark arts."

"What does it do?" Kol was glad to finally have answers.

Frostein held up two glacial fingers. "It does two things, two curses, which shows the power of the crafter. Applying one curse is difficult, but two that do not conflict with one another is another level entirely. One is to take control of the holder's mind, sending him on a preset mission or thought. Safety precautions are set in place to ensure the mission is accomplished. The holder has no free will once the curse sets in. It will also destroy itself if in the wrong hands."

Kol thought of the man attacking him savagely. "That sounds right. The ones who wielded them acted strangely. Seeing as I'm fine, it must be through touch. What about the second?"

"That is the second curse." Frostein leaned down and held the metal close to Kol's eyes. "The one that grabs the mind is inscribed in blood along the handle. Which means it was applied after the forge. The first was during the forging process. The blade comes in a pair. They are called *Clauditis* blades."

Kol went through his metallurgy training, but nothing came to mind. "You've never taught me about those."

"Because the magic is dark, along with the metal. They originated around the same time Rome was created. The sorcerers of that city had invented them for the use of the powerful. The *Clauditis* blades are designed for preservations. The closing blade, the one I have here, is meant to enter the target and render them comatose. And multiple closing blades can be made. The only way that the victim can be woken is for them to be stabbed by the opening blade, which is kept with whomever sent the first. And there is always only one closing blade."

"That doesn't make sense. Why not just kill the person with the first blade instead of placing him in a coma? Why risk so much?"

"That is a good question. One reason is so that they could weaken the person they are after, wanting to question them. Another reason is that they could be after something the person that is cursed has."

"All right, but what could they want with my father?"

Frostein leaned down, bringing his head closer to Kol. "If you had the Father of Christmas at your disposal, who has knowledge that exceeds libraries long lost, could you find a way to use him for your own benefit?" Frostein straightened back into his throne.

Kol knew he was right. "So it has to be someone from the outside. But who?"

"That I don't know, but from all these events I only see that someone is after my brother, and I plan to use this aggressor as fuel for my fires if ever they are discovered." Frostein crossed his arms. Though he showed no emotion, Kol believed that Frostein was afraid for his father. "There is something that I noticed as well. The blood must be by the creator of the curse. No one else could make the sacrifice. A double curse is unheard of, so the

Crafted may overlooked this. As far as my eyes can tell there is no sign of a block to stop a trace back. It is a mistake they have made, likely because they think the blades are indistinguishable from each other."

"So someone from the Halls can determine its origin." Kol was feeling excited to discover this information.

"Yes. Go, Nicholas, and find the other blade. Only then can you save your father. No more time should be wasted." The Snowmen around Frostein began to disperse back into the frosted plane. "I will remain here and attempt a means to awaken my brother. This is hopeless, but I have done well in hopelessness before."

Kol turned to leave. "What of the North Pole? They still fear you and the others. I know the Snowman who attacked the hospital was not someone from here, but they believe he was. Nothing I can show them will change their mind."

"Don't worry about us, my nephew." Frostein began to slowly fall apart from himself. "We will not move against the city. But if they come, we will have to defend ourselves. Hurry back with the other *Clauditis* blade and wake your father. You shall find more proof than you'll need. NOW GO!" The ground shook with his final words, and Frostein became an avalanche that ushered Kol towards the exit before dispersing into the surrounding caves. Echoes filled the room as metal began to strike metal somewhere beneath his feet.

Kol dashed away from the throne room and back up the icy tunnels. Soar greeted him with an excited snort and gave little time for Kol to set himself in the saddle before the reindeer galloped once more into the sky. Back across the shifting ice they went, the swirling colors of the aurora borealis entertaining them with its dance. As his reindeer galloped, Kol begin to think more about how the tension of the North Pole and Snow People had started.

The origin of "Frosty the Snow Man" was true. But like all stories, it changes over time as it is continually told. The story of the

Snowman had been passed down through several generations, until an individual decided to turn it into a song for the people today to enjoy. The magic in Frostein's hat was ancient, the origins unknown to anyone in the North. When Frostein was born he learned from the children around him, and saw the joy that Winter brought. When the adults came for him, waving torches, Kol's father swooped down and offered him a place where he did not have to fear. Frostein accepted and came to live in what was then a large village.

Frostein also worked with his father in woodcraft. Wanting to better assist his friend, Frostein had the idea that metalwork was the best way to do so. Frostein took to metal quickly, learning everything he could about it. He would study for hours in his father's library, and he would spend even more hours before an anvil, slowly becoming the master of the craft. With Santa's help he also learned how to perform certain aspects of magic, specifically manipulating it into the metal he forged. This work alone was not enough for his uncle, however. Despite having a friend, Frostein was still lonely as the only one of his kind, and no amount of effort could drive away his empty feeling.

He asked for permission to enter the Halls of Ve'rema to study the origin of his hat. After many years of learning from Saint Nick and the books within the Halls, Frostein was able to bring to life the second Snow Person whose soul was woven into a green scarf. The process had almost cost him his own life, but from his labors he brought forth Iceana, who would eventually become his wife. Frostein then discovered the process of making another can be done more safely with two Snow People working together. Both he and Iceana could bring children of their own into life. The family built a small home for themselves next to his father's. Though the elves and humans were still hesitant, they lived peacefully enough.

The fear of the Snow People had begun after Frostein had started living among the people of the North Pole. When he first arrived, the citizens saw him as dangerous: another monster come to attack them. His father told them that Frostein was harmless and just wanted to help the rest in their shared dream. In the beginning, Frostein's ignorance of the world would cause him to become angry, and he often turned to breaking things. That and the fact that he still was not used to his body made him capable of causing a mess out of sheer clumsiness. That went away with age, but it was still a whispered question of concern. In time Saint Nicholas helped him find who he was in the world.

The fear grew worse once the Snowman had created another. One angry behemoth was a possible problem, but multiple could become a catastrophe. Frostein decided he would move his family from the city despite his brother's objections. He said that visits would be made to strengthen the fragile bond, but the elves and humans had a point. His children to come would need room to roam and come into themselves, and so would the children *they* would have. So they journeyed to this mountain and begun to construct the frigid cathedral Kol had just left.

With the distance came uncertainty as generations passed in the village. Stories of the Snow People slowly became warnings as their appearance was rarely found. They were great titans that spent their day making weapons and armor, brutes who only understood violent means. Though the Snow People were known for their physical engagements to establish dominance, they were far from monsters. The worse of the paranoia began when Kol had only been a small boy, though he hardly remembered any of it.

No one knew exactly what occurred that night. The people of the North only saw the aftermath. Frostein had come to the now city to see his father, since it had been too long since last they sat and bonded. The two of them had become too busy to find the time needed for one another. The North Pole population had awakened from their beds to find destruction that started at Saint Nicholas' house and ended in the residence area of the North Pole. Several buildings had been demolished, and so had a large part of Kol's house. The only person that could have caused this was his uncle, who they found at the end of a rage being consoled by his sworn brother.

After seeing this there was no stopping the erupting fear of what the Snow People could be capable of. His uncle and father had no choice, and from that day on no Snow Person ever entered the city again. Their hope was that a new bond could be remade in the far future. Unfortunately, Kol believed that they no longer had the time the two leaders had wanted.

CHAPTER SEVEN

Useful Gifts

The city gleamed among the ice and darkness like a fallen star. Anyone unattuned to the city would only see darkness, however—darkness and an endless stretch of ice. The only reason Kol could even see it was because he was allowed to. He snapped the reins, and Soar ducked his head in excitement, racing the wind itself. They passed through the barrier and felt the warmer air, as if the city welcomed them back with an inviting hug. The night was late, but not everyone had gone to bed. The underground exits still had a stream of people coming from them, heading home to their warm fires or off to the inns and taverns for some entertainment. Nudging Soar to the right, Kol aimed for the outskirts of the city, knowing where he should look first. He found what he was looking for instantly: the building was larger than the homes and stores around it.

The Lake of Frost was crowded tonight, with the shadows of the occupants inside moving about. Soar descended lightly, landing on the roof. "What is it with reindeer and roofs?" he asked his friend, patting Soar's neck. Soar gave a snort sounding close to laughter and hopped to the road, barely missing the sign that read the name of the inn. Dismounting, Kol asked Soar to wait there. Not wanting to cause any unrest, Kol untied his sword from his belt and hung it from Soar's saddle. "Protect this for me, will you?" Knowing Soar would, Kol made his way to the front door, pushing his way inside.

The atmosphere within was completely different than it had been before the ghouls attacked. A musician played Christmas carols with his flute, but that seemed to be the only merriment available. Elves and humans sat with their heads close together over some mugs of drink or plates of food. Most of their faces looked stern, the topic too easy to guess. He even heard the word "Snowman" a few times before a mass filled his vision. "Kol, back again so soon? Couldn't resist the offer, could you?" A few people sitting near them looked over briefly to see the commotion before turning back to their meals.

Kol looked up at the innkeeper, searching his memory for what he was talking about. Thankfully his stomach rumbled, giving him the answer. "Yeah, you said it brought in the whole city."

"And I wouldn't lie to you, my friend." Mr. Mugsteeve chuckled and patted Kol on the back. "Come. I'll get you a table."

"I was wondering if Shane was around." He left off the wizard's title in case he wanted his work private. Mr. Mugsteeve seemed to believe that Master Hargon was a retired old man, which made Kol assume as much.

"Oh, yes, need to speak with him, aye? He's in his usual spot." He pointed over to the area where his friend sat. "Go on over there. I'll bring your plate to you."

Kol started for the old man's table. "Thank you, Mr. Mugsteeve."

"Of course, Kol. Anytime. You're always welcome here," he called after, laughing. Kol saw him walk to the kitchen out of the corner of his eye.

Kol approached the table and looked down at Master Shane. He was thumbing through a small velvet booklet, looking puzzled. Kol took the wooden chair next to him. Master Shane looked up and gave a start. "Kol!" he laughed at the sight of him. "I hope this does not become a recurrence. You jumping out of nowhere in the middle of the night."

"Well, usually it wouldn't, but I need your help." Kol wanted to show Master Hargon the blade, but if his own blade could cause a stir, one exactly like the assassins' definitely would.

"Ah, well, I don't know what good I will do." Master Hargon closed the little book and placed it into his chestnut brown jacket. Kol wasn't going to ask but he figured the chess board had something to do with it.

Kol started to set the chess board in front of them before continuing, the figures expertly made of glass and wood. "It's about the attack on Santa." Kol didn't look up from the board. Master Hargon smiled down at it as if to accept the challenge.

"You mean your father?"

Kol almost knocked off his king piece when he looked up in surprise. He took a moment to let the surprise pass and let understanding take its place. "I guess it's not that difficult to figure out? I try my best not to be seen when I'm out at night. When this place was attacked, it was the first time."

Master Hargon chuckled while moving a pawn across the board to begin their tabletop battle. "Now, now, don't get disheartened about it. With that hat turned down low and your hood up, I'm sure no one else has picked up on it. You had my suspicions in the hospital, but when I finally got a good look at you in the plaza, it wasn't hard. Most of the city is used to seeing you in finer clothes and your hair brushed back without the warm hat you have. They wouldn't suspect that the prince would wander into a place like this for a nice drink. And of course you would appear to help your father, so no worry there either. I'd like to suggest a mask though, if you're going to keep this up."

Kol nodded in agreement, and moved his own pawn. "I guess that wouldn't be a bad idea. Please keep this secret. If the Major were to find out, it wouldn't go over well. Only my father and two others know about it." A waitress arrived to take a drink order from Kol, and he stopped speaking to avoid being overheard.

Master Hargon waited for her to leave for Kol's hot chocolate before speaking. "Oh, I imagine it would be quite the scandal." He smiled at the idea, and moved his queen, strangely enough. "But I get no joy from that. You have my word, Kol"

"All right. That is a relief to hear." Kol considered the odd move, and moved his next piece. "Are you any good at tracking spells?"

"Let me tell you a bit more about myself," Master Hargon chuckled again, his next piece sliding quietly. "I came to this city about twenty years ago. Before that, I had no home to call my own. Trash cans were my delicacy, like so many others. That's when your father's Scripters found me and brought me here. I was examined like everyone else, seeing where my qualities lay. I had a gift for magic, apparently, so to *Ve'rema* I went." He paused long enough for Kol to receive his beverage in a green mug and motioned for a refill of Master Hargon's ale. "Though I had the spark, it has always been a weak one."

"What do you mean?" The game seemed almost halfway through now. Kol had his opponent's queen and Master Hargon had a few of Kol's important pieces.

"Well, I'm not very good at magic, except for my illusions." Master Hargon took a swig from his mug.

Kol looked down at the board again to find that Master Hargon's queen had his king in check. Kol gave the old wizard an amused look, who smirked and put down his mug, waving the illusionary piece back into nothing. Kol laughed softly. "I bet that trick has won a few games for you."

"Oh, only when there is money on the table, and only after my opponent begins acting rude for one reason or another." Master Hargon scratched his chin while pondering future strategies. "Illusion magic seems to be the only thing that doesn't take a lot of energy out of me. That elemental act you witnessed put me in bed for a few more hours than I expected the next morning. I am also on the translocation team. Only as a support to the leaders of the magic, but the other masters believe that helping in one of the most advanced forms of magic would increase my strength. They are right, as I have improved over the last three years, but it is a slow process."

"So you can't help me with a tracking spell, then?" Kol did not want to go to the Halls right away. He wanted to avoid the unnecessary questions, and he feared that too much time would be wasted studying the blade. Even if Kol explained what his uncle said, they would still try to undo the curse by their own means and not by finding the twin of the object.

"I can; I'll just ask one of my colleagues. I already have one in mind." Master Hargon was thinking about his next move. "What is it you need to be tracked?"

"Some blood." He was not going to show Master Hargon the blade, not yet anyway. He would have to explain about Frostein and his trip to the Flakes. He was short on time as it was. "I think it may be from the one who sent the assassins."

The wizard looked up from the board, eyebrows raised. His opened his mouth to say something, but he shut it as Mr. Mugsteeve came over with a yellow plate of potatoes, green beans, and roast.

"Here you go, Kol; on the house," Mr. Mugsteeve said, handing him the plate.

"No, I'll pay," Kol objected. The sight was overwhelming. The roast had been crafted to perfection and was topped with carrots and mushrooms. Next to it were two golden pieces of garlic bread.

"Nonsense! I won't have it." Reaching behind him, Mr. Mugsteeve pulled up a chair to join them. Their game was on hold while Kol started to eat. He didn't realize how hungry he was until the spices hit his tongue. After his first bite, he knew he wouldn't stop till he was finished. This dish rivaled that of his mother's, but he would never utter any such world so long as she walked the city.

"Thank you," he managed.

"Anytime." Mr. Mugsteeve patted his belly and turned to his old friend. "Glad to have you back in good spirits, Shane. So, what's the talk of the streets now?"

"Same as usual. I went down into the workshop today. They're all tinkering away, smiles as they go. But if you so much as mention the name Snowman, the place goes quiet." To prove his point, a silent bubble rippled from where they sat. Kol took no notice, focused on keeping his fork out of the gravy. Every table was on the same subject regardless.

"Doesn't make much senses to me." Mr. Mugsteeve shook his head slightly. "Too much fear in this place. That's not why we come here."

"I agree with you, old friend." Master Hargon took a long swig from his mug. "But after what happened in the plaza, no one is willing to listen. With no leader to look to, it's only a matter of time before panic returns. The Crafted Council are managing the best they can, but with them unable to give answers, the masses have grown restless. It was bad enough when we all thought he was gone."

Kol choked on a carrot, causing Mugsteeve to pat him on the back. Taking a swallow from his hot chocolate, he breathed, "He's fine, though, I heard. Just healing and weak."

"Yes, we know, but it doesn't help now, does it." Mugsteeve hung his head and sighed. A server came up and whispered in his ear. This seemed to jumpstart him, and standing, he stretched. "I'll leave you be. Kol, you come back for dessert. I suspect you'll be on your way soon as you have done twice before. Shane, I'll play with you later on in the night if you are still here. The wife has summoned me. Gentlemen." He gave a slight bow to Kol's nod due to food in his mouth and Master Hargon's wave over his mug. Turning, Mr. Mugsteeve headed for the kitchen door.

Kol finished his plate and set it to the side. Master Hargon and Kol both returned to their game. "So, will you help me?"

Shane nodded. "Yes, I will. In the morning, though."

Kol looked at him quizzically. "Morning?" An elf stepped gracefully past, lifting Kol's finished plate onto others she held. She was gone before he could give his thanks.

"Yes, morning. My friend is more than likely asleep, and I will not wake her at this hour for anything. Quite the temper, that one." He moved another piece. "Check. And you also need to go home and get some rest. You look like you haven't been able to sleep, though I already understand why."

Kol looked at the board but was not focusing on it. He wanted to tell Shane how much of an emergency this was, but something in the way the man looked and spoke told him his decision would not be changed. And this was the only person within the Halls he could ask for help without raising too much suspicion. Reaching under his cloak he pulled out a small bottle with the dried blood from the weapon. He had scraped it off on the ride over with his knife. He handed it over to Shane who took it from his hand, wrapped it in a cloth from his robes, and tucked it back into the fabric. "When will you know?"

"Tomorrow. I will send you a message." Master Hargon looked down at the board. "Now hurry home."

Kol was not a fan of orders but he had no choice. Looking down, he moved his final piece. "Checkmate," Kol stated and got up to leave the table. He didn't look over his shoulder to see how Master Hargon looked when defeated. Kol thanked the server who had brought him his hot chocolate and placed a gold coin in her hand before exiting the building.

Soar was no longer in the street, but Kol knew how to get his attention. Bringing his fingers to his lips he gave a sharp whistle. Soar's head popped from a roof in front of him, his eyes heavy with sleep. Seeing Kol, he became instantly awake and was on the ground in seconds. Kol grabbed one of his antlers and pulled the reindeer's head down. Soar fought back playfully before turning for Kol to climb on. Feet in stirrups, they once again took to the air. Knowing his companion was tired, Kol headed for the house.

The tree showed them the way for them to travel. Soar erupted into the plaza, swinging wide and running along the buildings. Kol laughed from the thrill. Soar knew how to cheer him up. They lowered over the house and landed in the back, the stable doors slowly swinging open. Once inside, Kol unfastened the saddle, hanging it on the wall. He grabbed his sword and swung it on his back. The other reindeer were mostly asleep besides Maple, who once again propped her front legs over the stall door. Kol brushed Soar down and led him to his bedding, which Soar took to gladly. Kol rubbed his hand over Maple for a few minutes, telling her of their ride today before starting for his own room.

The halls of his home were once again quiet. Everyone was probably in their rooms, still mourning over the occurrence. Together they kept their spirits up, but who knew what happened when everyone was tucked under their blankets. Kol climbed the wooden staircase, touching the mistletoe engravings as he went. He made his way down the wing his room was in, vacant as well, and entered. Going to his closet, Kol took off his gear, placed it neatly inside the trunk, then closed it, putting only his favorite flannel pajama pants on before he fell across his bed.

The event of his father's attack had affected him greatly, more than he let anyone know. The sorrow he had felt when he thought his father was gone had quickly turned to anger. Anger that remained internal and turned him cold. Anyone who reached towards him would feel the sting of it, mistaking it for heat. But it had only lasted a little while, until the wizards and doctors had looked at him. His father's words had come back to him, to not let the hate spread. He had thought deeply about those words the night of the attack after looking for the other blade. The only way he would be able to stop the hate would be to save his father, no matter what the cost.

Yes, he had said they would need someone to look to, but he knew he wasn't the one for the job, despite what his mother said. He knew what he was meant for, and now it was more important than ever to find the person behind the attacks, no matter what. The worst part was that it had happened so close to Christmas. Not only was the whole city counting on Christmas, so were the millions of children all over the world. As cliché as it sounded, it was absolutely true. They all believed in his father, and Kol was not going to let that go to waste. Sighing in frustration, Kol rolled from his bed. He knew sleep would not come to him anytime soon, so he found it best to go find it. Quickly grabbing a white t-shirt from his closet, he pulled it on and exited his room.

With the hall still empty at this late hour, Kol made for the workshop, moving silently down the stairs with bare feet. The door opened for him quietly and he slipped inside. The massive room was in shadows. Little light fell through the windows set in the ceiling. Stepping down the few stairs in front of him he made his way down the aisle. A table was set with teddy bears of multiple colors piled upon it. Another was covered with small cars, tuned for the speed their owners could imagine. Kol smiled at the other simple toys. No matter how far technology advanced, his father never wanted to leave the originals behind. Kol turned down a row of tables, heading for one of the candy-cane-pattered staircases that led to the workshop below. Down there was where the more advanced toys were constructed.

The steps allowed him to descend to the first floor beneath the workshop. Kol entered the locked tunneled area with the use of his house key, following the brick path deeper into the ground. Light came from the crest of the tunnel in a narrow strip. Other tunnels would appear every few feet, wooden signs above them engraved with green color giving directions to the wrapping stations and bow tying. Other paths led further down into the work place. Kol found the one he was looking for.

The tunnel was short, and Kol emerged into one of the shipping areas. He was walking across a raised platform, still following the brick pattern of the tunnels. Conveyer belts covered the majority of the large room, starting from metal shoots to floors above. The belts carried the packages towards the bagging area. On the wall, opposite of Kol was another raised platform, home of the control panels that operated the place. Though he could not see it, there was a large claw suspended above him to help distribute the gifts. He made it to the end of the next path and entered another tunnel.

He passed a tunnel sloping downward towards electronics and another climbing upwards to clothes and accessories. The place he was looking for was at the end, where he now stood: a small dome of brick with a simple silver door in front of him. The sign above it told anyone that the experimental toys and gadgets were created inside. This was where the elves and people could tinker with both science and technology safely away from anyone else outside the room. Kol grabbed the small silver handle and opened it.

On the other side, he stood on a small catwalk, metal rails holding either side. The bridge connected to the large floating spear suspended from the roof above, within an even larger spherical room. The room he now occupied was huge, murals of swirling colors on every piece. Snow gently fell around him, the light gentle on the eyes, as if he were looking into the woods during a December night. The snow was an enchantment to buffer any escaping experiments, whether it was spell or matter. He walked slowly to the suspended room, finding an identical silver door which he opened and entered.

The room he stood in was a brilliant near-blinding white. There were only two couches, camouflaged with the rest of the room with only the black trim giving their features away. This room was usually used for waiting, but he knew the inside would be mostly empty. He found the white door across from him easily despite it too blending with the walls. He was glad this next room was basic, at least in a North Pole sense. Brown carpet matched the lighter brown walls and light ceiling. It was a hallway leading off to different departments of the office space. He passed the one he knew led to explosives, and entered the second one on his left. Here he found Slee's back to him, the elf concentrating on something Kol could not see.

The room was small, barely large enough for five people to stand without touching the other. A simple waiting chair stood by the door. Shelves to his left were full of small gadgets Kol had never seen before, and a large black safe was built into the wall on his right. The walls themselves were a polished wood, and a blue carpet lay under his feet. Slee sat in an adjustable chair, a white work table in front of him with tools hanging on the wall.

"Master Nicholas. Up late, I see," Slee said, not looking up from his work. Kol couldn't help but hear his missing smile, ready for some form of trickery.

"I couldn't sleep," Kol said simply. He took a seat on the carpeted floor.

Slee sighed, a noise Kol was not used to coming from him. The elf turned in his chair to stare at Kol. His face was smiling now, but it was a sad one. "I know the feeling all too well, it seems."

"What have you been working on?" Kol leaned slightly to glance at the table.

Slee picked up a small device, made of gears and springs, which gave no clues to Kol. It could be something to wear for all he knew; Slee made jokes like that. "Well, it's nothing now. But I have been searching for a way to wake your father."

This made Kol feel more awake than ever. Sitting up straighter, Kol watched the little device more closely. "Any luck?" The hope was clear in his voice.

Slee looked down at the device in his hand, a frown on his face. Another expression that was not common. "The machine won't work the way I want it to. I thought maybe sound would be the key for him." Kol nodded, understand where his theory came from. "But nothing I try seems to work, and I dare not tamper with the bells."

"Well, at least you're trying, Slee. But there's only one way to wake him." He told Slee what had occurred over the past week. He wanted to tell him, because he needed someone here who knew the truth besides Holly who could alert his mother should anything happen to him. Kol also knew how much Slee cared for his father. Unlike the other elves, Slee was not born in the North Pole. In fact, he was descended from a group of mountain elves. He wasn't sure how, but eventually his father found him stranded in an abandoned house. Slee was the last of his family, and had been attacked by humans. Santa told him that he was from a place where others of his kind lived. At first Slee didn't believe him, but having nothing left he decided to take a chance. Once at the North Pole he was welcomed by others like him, making him feel right at home. They explained to him what they did here in the North, and Slee was more than eager to help. He took an interest in the developmental science department. He designed many of the modern gadgets his father used on his sleigh, which kept him both safe and on schedule. Slee was very attached to his father, which was one of the reasons Kol had grown up with him there.

Slee listened to Kol's story intently, his face completely serious. Kol finished his story, stopping where he left the blood sample with Master Hargon. Once finished, Slee added a smirk to his face, gaze tilted to the side. "So, you plan on going after the other blade?"

Kol nodded again, leaning back on his hands behind him. "Yes, as soon as the tracking is finished. Which should be some time tomorrow."

"How interesting, but I guess it can't be helped." Slee slid from his work chair and started to spin the dial on the safe. "He would want you to take this with you."

"What are you talking about?"

The safe popped open, allowing Slee to reach inside. "Your father left this with me." Slee pulled out a small box, wrapped in white paper with a blue bow tied around it. "It's your Christmas present for this year. Wrapped early, and given to me to hide from you." He joined Kol on the floor, sitting cross legged in front of him. Gently he placed the box on the floor. "And I added my own gift, too. Who would have thought how useful it was going to be to you now?"

"Not supposed to open before Christmas."

Slee gave Kol a side long look, then laughed. "You know every day around here is Christmas. Now, open it."

Kol laughed with him and started on the package. Usually, one would tear the paper to shreds, eager to acquire the gift inside. Kol never was for that form of barbarianism. He tugged on the bow, loosening its binding, then unfolded the package from around it. With the paper folded to the side, Kol lifted the lid from the cardboard box. Slee could barely contain himself, rocking back and forth where he sat. Kol was glad to see his friend back to normal. Well, normal for Slee.

Kol looked inside, and saw it held two items. One looked like a square panel the size of his hand, black with a snowflake design on it. The other was a small pouch. To Kol's eyes it looked to be made from snow. Reaching in and pulling the pouch out, Kol noted that it was almost weightless and soft to the touch. The black panel was also lightweight and the screen dark.

"That is the only device like that. I designed it to connect to the North Pole database, meaning that the user can look up any-one in the world, their address, and their status on the Naughty or Nice list. Your father keeps it all in his head, but we elves aren't so vast in our memory." He laughed again, this time at a small joke to himself. "There are also other features you can figure out for yourself."

"That's a lot of responsibility." Kol pressed the small power button, and the screen came to life. The letters NPN slid across the screen, along with a small Christmas tree underneath. Kol turned the device back off and set it on the carpet in front of him. "I don't know if I'm able to accept it."

Slee shook his head. "You just don't get it, do you? Besides your father, you're the only other one that can be trusted with something like this. It is your birthright. Besides, I'll be sad if you leave it." Kol had the feeling that sadness was not what he had to worry about from his friend. His mischievous grin had more effect in the dim light.

Kol picked up the pouch now, once again examining the soft-ness. "That material is the same fabric that your father's bag is made of. Though the inside is nowhere near as vast as Santa's, it still can hold quite a large number of items."

"An Everstore? Where did he find the material?" Kol couldn't help the small feeling of excitement.

"From your father's own bag. He came down and cut the material just after the night you came in late and talked to him."

To Kol, this gift was extraordinary. The Everstore, or the original he should say, was used by his father to carry all the gifts created here in the North Pole. It was no bigger than his father's back, laying comfortably across it. Not only could it hold all the gifts of childhood, but it was as weightless as this bag was now. "I wish I could tell him how much this means to me."

"I'm sure he knows, Kol, and I'm also sure he knows you're doing your best to straighten all this out." Slee leaned forward to gather the empty box. "He is proud of you, which I'm sure you also know."

Kol's fathers voice echoed through his head. *They will need someone to look to.* No, he wasn't doing what his father asked, but it was the best he could do. If the people did know what he planned they may just look to him regardless. "Thanks, Slee. I think I'm going to try and get some rest." He felt like he was sinking within himself. This gift from his father was almost too much.

"I'll be right behind you shortly. Need to do a few more things." Kol nodded, knowing Slee's reason for staying was the same for him leaving. Taking the black device, or his List, he placed it in his pouch. The light fabric folded in his pocket. Kol turned and left Slee's office with a silent nod between them. Quickly he made his way over the small bridge, back through the tunnels, and across the sorting room. In just a few short minutes he was back in the original workroom, night still hanging softly in the room. Instead of heading for his room, he went to his father's office.

The room was no different despite his father's absence. He grabbed a piece of parchment and a fountain pen from the desk. If all went according to his plan, he didn't want to leave his mother in the shadows. His hand flowed across the paper, trying to combine his will with the ink. She would be upset, but it was time she knew what he did during the night. Hopefully she would understand, and continue to lead the workers in his father's stead with the Crafted Council beside her. Finishing the letter, he put it in a yellow envelope he found and wrote his mom's name across it. Placing it carefully on the desk, he left the room, one last look around for good memory. He did not know how long it would be until he saw it again.

CHAPTER EIGHT

An Unforeseen Detour on a New Path

The streets were busy early this morning, with everyone heading under the city preparing to make toys. "Jingle Bell Rock" played from the speakers, but no one sang along with the lyrics. Kol walked among them, blue jeans and white shirt with a gray jacket pulled on around him, his trusty beanie pulled low. The faces he saw were trying to express looks of joy, but their eyes showed sadness and fear. Would their leader return in time for Christmas Eve, and would the Snow People stay at bay? The further he walked the more his determination grew. Something must be done about these downcast eyes.

Kol had woken an hour ago, having barely slept. The worry he felt would not allow his mind to rest, so he showered, packed his pouch with his gear, spare clothes, and other essential items he figured he would need on this journey. It amazed him how easily the things he placed inside his father's gift vanished from existence. With his bag full, he gave his own room a last searching look and turned from it. He left the house quietly before anyone else had the chance to awaken or find his letter. He would find a place to eat in the city while waiting for Shane to contact him. He was not really hungry, but he knew he needed his strength up for whatever was to come. Kol decided on a small diner nestled in between two buildings, its silver cart gleaming from the Christmas lights surrounding it. It reminded Kol of a train cart, ready to slide from its foundation for its next journey.

The air inside was warm, the smell of breakfast strong. Kol was thankful for that because it slightly pulled his body from his numbness. He took a seat at the bar, the red, cushioned chair swiveling up under him. The place held only a few others. An elf sat at one corner eating a waffle and an older lady in a high-necked coat sipped her coffee while reading the newspaper. An elf walked over to him, asking what he would like, and Kol ordered the waffle with hot chocolate. She smiled at him and walked away to place the order.

The door to the diner opened again, allowing someone else shelter from the cold. Kol looked around, watching the man take the seat a stool away from him. He wore a blue suit and a white button-up shirt underneath with a black tie. He was an older gentleman, and he appeared tired but in good spirits. The waitress came back a few seconds later with Kol's plate, which he thanked her for graciously. He was applying syrup when the man turned to him and said, "Journey ahead, huh?"

Kol looked over at him, setting the syrup back down. "I'm sorry?"

"You're preparing for a trip. I can tell by the way you're sitting. Whole body ready to move, a new destination in mind." The man picked up his fresh cup of coffee from in front of him and took a swig. "I've seen my fair share to know what it looks like."

Kol nodded at him hesitantly, starting on his plate. He took small bites, each one followed with hot chocolate.

"So where is it you plan on going?" The man was still studying him sideways. "I hope you know it's not so easy getting back once you do go."

Kol nodded again. "I know, but I have to go. Plus I have a way back." Even if walking was his means. This man was acting more knowing than Kol intended, so best to let him think he was one of the Scribes.

"If you say so." The man stood and pulled his wallet from his back pocket. As he placed some money on the counter, something silver flashed out. Walking over to Kol, he sat it down next to his plate. "This is if the way is not true." With those last words he left, back into the streets.

Kol followed him with his gaze, feeling confused. He looked down at what looked like a silver ribbon sitting next to his plate. Setting down his fork he went to examine it, but his vision was blocked by a magical envelope falling on top of his hand. He quickly tore it open, reading the message from Shane. Placing money on the table he grabbed the letter along with the silver ribbon and put it in his pouch. He left his unfinished waffle behind as he pushed through the exit and started up the street. He quickly glanced around the now empty street and began to run. The spot he was supposed to meet Master Shane was close, just a few streets over.

He saw the building he was looking for where the people inside worked on the List. His destination was the alley next to it. Slowing, he stepped into the darker area, looking around for Master Hargon, who was not yet there. Master Hargon probably guessed that Kol would be coming from his house, so he had some time. Kol figured he would sit and wait, but before he could find a comfortable spot on the stone, Master Hargon's silhouette cut the Christmas lights coming from the entrance.

"Kol!" he exclaimed, striding towards him. "Here so soon?"

"Yeah, I was eating breakfast a few streets away." Kol looked closely at the man's eyes. "Did you get any sleep?"

Master Hargon realized Kol's searching gaze was examining the bags under his eyes, then laughed at himself. "Well, yes; I fell asleep while researching, actually."

"Too much to drink?" Kol smirked.

"Something like that," the wizard gave another small laugh before continuing. "I guess you're wondering why I asked you to meet me here of all places."

"It was a thought, but I figured you'd let me know." Kol crossed his arms.

"Well," he looked over Kol's shoulder then back over his own, making sure no one was there. "Me helping you like this isn't exactly legal, Kol."

"The only reason I'm asking is because I know if I go to the Cadence they would not listen to reason. Everyone is so terrified. Only the Drum Major would, and she went back to the Island this morning." Kol did not want his voice to sound pleading, but if Master Hargon was having second thoughts he didn't know what to do.

"Don't worry: I am going to help you." He laughed slightly to himself. "I haven't been up to any form of mischief like this since I was your age." He cackled a little more to himself, apparently losing his fear of being caught.

"So you found the location?" Kol asked hopefully.

"Oh yes, it was easy. Finding it, that is, not persuading my friend to perform the spell." He reached inside his jacket and pulled out a small map, its parchment wrinkled and stained, but still a perfect drawing of the earth. "It is odd, though."

"Where is it?"

Kneeling on the ground with Kol joining him, he pointed to the area. "It's in the United States, a small little city more towards the south. Its exact location could be anywhere in the surrounding area." He gestured to the red circle. "I'm afraid you'll have to search a bit."

Kol felt his small bag, hanging lightly on his belt and thought of the List that Slee had given him. "That's fine; it shouldn't take too long."

"That leads me to the first problem." Master Hargon straightened again, folding the map. From inside his robes he pulled out a large glass sphere. Inside a swirl of blue energy danced for freedom. "Now, Kol, magic that deals with space can be extremely taxing on the body's stamina. Because of this, it is usually better to have a team working together. But don't worry, I'll be able to do it with the stored energy I have here, but that will be it for me today. If I am to send you there, I will not be able to open a portal up to bring you back. At least not immediately. I'll have to 'catch my breath' and then also catch some breath in this here orb. It will take about a week to do so."

Kol nodded, "I understand. What you're doing for me far outweighs a few extra days."

Master Hargon nodded as well. "I'm glad you understand that and the risk I'm taking. Someone will be able to detect the portal from here and then they will investigate. I don't mind helping you, but I would rather not be caught. They will take my certification, and then you will be stranded there."

"That would be unfortunate," Kol replied. "So what do I do to return?"

"Take this with you." Master Hargon ran his fingers through his hair with a nervous laugh as he handed Kol what looked like an average small box wrapped in simple Christmas paper and bow. "This is a signal box. We give it to all the Scribes. When you are ready to go home, just open the box and a signal will be sent to the Halls and myself. If I'm unable, someone will open a portal for you at your location, thinking you to be a Scribe needing to return. You may have to do a bit of explaining when you are found to not be a Scribe, but I am sure you can manage that."

"What if they catch you after sending me on?"

"Don't worry; I'll simply say you were a Scribe who ran late. If there are to be punishments, I'll gladly accept. Reviving your father is the most important thing right now."

Kol nodded with him. "All right, it can't be helped. What about the spell placed on Scribes in order to keep the city an actual secret?"

"Yes, I thought of that too. I believe it is not necessary because if anyone knows of the importance of this place, it is you." The old wizard sighed to himself. "I'm sure you have all you need with you. Are you ready for this?"

"Yes." To be honest, Kol had never been away from the city before, besides the Flakes and once the Island. He was not going in completely blind, though; he had read all about the world from his father's library and the stories the families here would tell. Kol could feel his body growing excited even under the current circumstances. The rest of the world had so much to offer, and deep down he had always wanted to see it all. But now was not the time for sightseeing: he had a mission he had to complete. "Open the portal, Master Hargon; I'll be home before Christmas."

With a nervous chuckle, Master Hargon walked closer to him. "Don't touch the sides, or you'll be lost." Kol looked at the wizard, confused, but had no time to question him. The old man raised his wrinkled hand and held it in front of Kol's chest. The wizard muttered something to himself that Kol did not understand. Before Kol could ask he was distracted by the bright blue light of the orb. It was blinding for a few seconds before dying away, slowly moving from its container and into Master Hargon's palm that held it. Master Hargon's wand appeared in his other hand. The shocking blue energy danced along the instrument. A few more unrecognizable words and the wand touched the ground before Kol, causing a circle of magical runes to appear around where he stood.

A circling barrier of green light rose from the runes and came to a point above Kol's head. All sense of sound left Kol's ears, his vision blurring and turning a dark green. Kol realized that he was incased within a conjured barrier, a pod stretching from head to toe. Kol felt a moment of unease as his feet slowly left the ground, but he remained calm so as not to lose balance and touch the sides. Kol figured it was a good idea to heed his friend's advice.

Only seconds passed before Master Hargon lowered his hand again and smiled up at Kol. A portal of swirling color opened below him large enough for the encasement to fit through. He only had a moment to look back before his world beyond the pod vanished. He was moving through a void absent of light. At least, Kol believed he was moving, but his body felt no tug of inertia or ripping of air. The only light he had came from the dark green glow of his vessel. This was what the wizard meant when he said Kol could get lost. The area outside his protection appeared infinite, and it was not a place he wanted to remain long. Kol crossed his arms carefully just to be sure there wasn't an accident. He had just begun to wonder how long he would have to be like this when his vision found light again and he immediately squinted his eyes shut against the brightness.

Kol's feet made contact with the ground softly. There was a quiet pop with the dispersion of the barrier. He did not have time to catch his balance and his hands felt the ground in front of him. He realized he was shaking, the adrenalin pumping through his body from the trip. He felt a strange warmth across his back like someone had laid a warm blanket on him. He opened his eyes slowly to take in his surroundings.

Everything was brightly lit, not from the winding string of lights he was used to, but by another source he only saw half of the year. The sun illuminated everything from high above him. This was another strange phenomenon to him, because when he saw the sun it never rose further than a few meters from the horizon. The rays were hot to him, along with the climate around him. With his vision fully adjusted he sat back on his legs to examine the environment further.

Kol was sitting on pine straw, gifted to the ground from the several trees that surrounded him. He was in a small wood that cleared out a few yards from him. A sidewalk flowed there, twisting away from his vision, with another cluster of trees across it. Kol rose to his feet, brushing the straw from his jeans. The straw was another oddity to him. Sure, the agriculture buildings in the North had floors dedicated to orchards and crop growing, but the public was rarely allowed to enter there. Many buildings had small groves of trees, too, a place for people to take breaks during work and such. Flora was only something he read about, though these trees were not lush with life. The sleeping browns were a pleasant sight for him to admire.

A noise came to his ears of soft padding hitting pavement, reminding him that he could hear. The noise belonged to a jog-ger who appeared from behind the trees, black jumpsuit on and headphones in her ears. She did not even notice him as her blond ponytail disappeared with the pavement. Kol was glad he had gone unnoticed and he quickly moved toward the walkway, feet sounding softly. He casually started to walk in the opposite direction of the runner.

Kol quickly learned he had been delivered to a park: his few minutes of walking brought him to a large opening of playground equipment and benches. The area was vacant, except for an elderly lady wrapped in a long brown coat and red scarf resting on one of the benches with her cane across her knee. She smiled at Kol who smiled back at her, hurrying on. The path forked off and Kol followed the right to a small gate. The park was sitting within a dark brick wall standing just below eye level. The hair on the back of his neck rose as he opened the gate. Turning, he found why this feeling had come over him.

Someone had been watching him, sitting off in a patch of trees just like he had been when he arrived. It was a scrawny boy who looked close to his own age with copper colored skin. His clothes looked like rags, ripped blue jeans with no shoes poking out from under them, and his green jacket was splotched with dirt. His hair was black and sticking out at odd angles. But what made Kol feel unease was the deranged stare of his brown eyes. The boy was smiling slightly at him, head cocked to the side, but his eyes appeared both distant and focused at the same time. Amusement was there as well, and a gleam of knowing. A squirrel hopped up to him and started pulling at his jacket, which the boy ignored. Kol only gave him a moment's glance before hurrying on. Normally, Kol would want to ask if he was all right, but he had no doubt the person was fine. Possibly more than fine, and Kol did not want any attention if he could help it. He had a mission to complete, as soon as possible.

Kol was in a city, but one far larger than his home. Only one building stood tall at twenty stories, from what Kol could see. Other buildings surrounded it, but there was no symmetry to the layout, and most of the structures stood half as tall as the main building. The park was nestled in what he believed was a cluster of apartment buildings. Older buildings, with their brick facing crumbling from the strokes of time, stood across them. The first thing Kol wanted to do was to get on top of one of the larger buildings to examine the city better. He started to cross the street, but leaped back as a blast of a horn warned him. He had been seconds away from an old pickup truck plowing through him. He quickly stopped his shock and surprise and this time checked both ways before crossing.

At the North Pole all that moved down the streets were horses to ride, carriages, or snowmobiles. The larger vehicles that were used for travel in the surrounding wasteland were rare to be found in the city streets. He had to treat all this as if it were new, and even look at everything as though it were hostile until potential danger was negated on further examination.

The city was full of vehicles, some parked on the side and some moving slowly through the streets. People traveled along the sidewalks, but far fewer than he was used to. He figured everyone was driving or riding the buses that he had the pleasure of seeing pass by in a gust of wind. Everyone was bundled up against the wind. It was only a second of confusion before he understood that his tolerance from cold was far above the people who lived here. It was lucky for them, because he was feeling toasty. He had to roll up his sleeves to stop himself from sweating.

He passed a variety of businesses while heading for one of the larger buildings. A coffee shop was on one street and a musical instrument shop on another, and all the stores were no different from the aging of the city. The windows looked like they had not been wiped in a while, and the merchandise behind the windows looked cracked or faded from the constant beating of the sun. Still, Kol would find children looking in intently before being urged on by their parents. One of the buildings was an apartment with a rusted fire escape nestled in the alley. Without a second thought Kol started for the ladder, jumping off of the dumpster underneath it and catching the bottom rung in his hands. In another fluid motion he had pulled himself onto the first platform and started for the roof.

A blast of air met him as he climbed over the ledge and landed on hardened tar covered by rocks. Pigeons took to the sky when the new visitor came closer to them; Kol paid them no mind as he looked over the city. The tallest building he had seen from earlier was to the left of him, a simple rectangular shape complete with a steeple on top. Its roof was a light green, matching several other roofs surrounding it. Churches lay scattered throughout the blocky buildings, some of simple build and others of grandeur. A river cut the east side of the city, the buildings ebbing and flowing along the bank. That was where they ended because on the other side of the river was where a wood line started.

The building Kol was currently on was close to the outskirts of the city. Roads and highways paved throughout the surrounding woodland. Though the neglect was apparent, the city had a special feeling to it that Kol could not recognize. Reaching into his white bag on his belt, Kol pulled out the device that Slee had given him. He had just realized that he did not have a name for it, so after a brief thought and smile he decided to call it his List.

Opening up the device he viewed the words NPN on the screen. A search bar was across the top of the home screen and under that were three symbols. One looked like a present, complete with a bow, and the other looked like a small book. The third one was in the shape of a globe, which Kol took for a map and pushed it. Instantly his location appeared on top of the building. Kol found the scroll bar for zoom on the left side and he zoomed out to discover where he was in the world.

Kol was in one of the southern states of the United States, in one of its sprawling cities. That would explain why it was so hot during winter. For proof Kol had to wipe his brow on his sleeve. His discomfort would not last much longer, thankfully, because the sun was beginning to descend. Night would soon be upon him. Returning to the main screen he typed in the four letter name and waited for results. A soft chime came and the map appeared again. Five red dots were scattered throughout the city and four more in what appeared to be towns far from the buildings. Sighing, Kol placed the device back into his pouch and started for the fire escape. He had his work cut out for him with so much ground to cover and all on foot. He would have to find some way to move faster, and soon. Kol wished Soar were here, but that would have been hard to hide. For now, he was going to make his way to the closest dot.

Back on the ground Kol moved closer to the center of the city. He wanted to run, but he had to remind himself that these people were not used to someone moving at the speeds he could thanks to his boots. Kol passed another family, walking into the street to give them room. One of the children smiled up at him from under her hijab. Turning up another street he passed a food stand, which made Kol glad that his father had currency stored from all over the word just in case. Kol had wanted to only take what he needed, but who knew where this trip would take him. It had currently made him hungry, so he stopped at the food stand, curious to see what it had to offer.

Kol seated himself on the edge of a stone fountain, its white marble gleaming from the casual spray of water. He did not mind because it helped him with the heat. Starting on his hamburger, he was surprised at how good it was as he looked at the shops across from him. An odd feeling came over him as he focused on the shop window. Centered among Christmas decorations and fake snow stood a three-foot doll of his father, complete with the traditional red coat and hat. Well, it was the basic idea of his father; Kol thought that the image was nowhere close to the truth. In the North Pole, images of his father did not exist like that even though he was the world's symbol for Christmas. Kol figured it was because the people knew the truth behind the myth. He also figured his father did not want to appear as an idol or something along those lines.

Starting on his fries, Kol noticed the spurts of people were beginning to thin out. Pulling out his List, Kol checked the direction he needed to travel and started on his path again. He had made it a great distance when the night finally crept on him, and the streets were now deserted. Street lights flickered to life, but only the areas beneath them were truly illuminated. Now shrouded in the darkness, Kol could push himself to his full speed. He quickly ducked into an alley and switched into his field gear. This was much better, as his field clothes gave him the full enchantment. Stepping out of the alley, Kol was double-checking the route for the night with his List when a car turned on the street ahead of him. Kol was just able to dart back into the alley before a spotlight hit where he had just been standing.

A few crates were stacked near what Kol believed was an exit door for a restaurant. He hid himself behind the crates, positioning himself to see the invading light. Slowly it grew as the car came closer. The hood of a car, painted black and white, appeared at the mouth of the alley. He figured it was a police car, judging from his studies. He hoped they would move on soon so he could continue. To his horror, the noise of brakes came. Kol tucked himself deeper into the shadows, the spotlight now fully illuminating the entire alley. He heard two doors open then slam shut. Two silhouettes filled the light followed by soft clicks of flashlights turning on.

"Whoever it was must have went down here," one of them said. His voice was scratchy and held age.

"You sure? I didn't see anything." This voice was more even, and sounded bored.

"Yeah, 'cause you were too busy lookin' at your phone," the older snapped.

"Quit acting so paranoid. You know nothin' happens here," was the other's retort ending in a laugh.

The older man grunted out his next sentence. "Oh yeah? The missing persons' cases have increased in the last few weeks. You call that nothin'? Besides, 'nothin' happens here' is the typical phrase before...FREEZE!"

Kol did not listen as he darted from his hiding spot. The officers had been coming closer and he knew the flashlights would find him. In seconds he had jumped onto the top of the stacked crates, leaped over the two officers, vaulted over their car, and sprinted up the street. He heard one of the two men, probably the younger, sprinting after him. Kol darted into another alley to try to lose his pursuer. A siren echoed after him, which meant that the other cop was after him as well and was likely calling for backup. Kol exited the alley and turned left on the adjacent street just as the officer behind him entered, flashlight bouncing off the walls.

A parking garage was ahead of him on the right, and judging by the siren the way forward would be blocked soon. Running towards it, Kol leaped over the entrance gate and started up the ramp. He was impressed that the one on foot was still after him, though at the bottom of the parking garage. Kol made it to the top, ignoring more of the officer's commands. The garage was not full, with only a handful of cars on each level, but there was nothing he could use to hide. Kol heard tires sliding on pavement, and from the sound of it a second police car had joined the first. Sirens shut off, and the officers in them would find their younger partner slowing on the fourth floor.

Kol met a refreshing breeze as he jogged to a stop near a ledge on the final floor. Beneath him was the roof of an office building that was only three stories tall. Kol made a quick circuit around the top: two sides led to the road beneath and the last to a building consisting of five floors. The distance across was further than Kol was used to, but he would have to manage. Stepping a back from the ledge to get a running start, Kol took a deep breath, focused his thoughts, then sprinted for the ledge. Leaping, his feet landed on the concrete guard rail and he pushed with all his might, vaulting across the gap. As he flew, Kol believed that he was going to make the clearing smoothly, but second thoughts came as he slowly fell.

Flinging out his hand, Kol's fingers came in contact with the ledge, sending his body slamming into the side of the building. The air in his lungs left him, but he kept his mind focused, knowing what would happen if he lost his grip. Swinging his other arm up, Kol firmed his grip with both hands and pulled himself up. Safely on the roof, Kol made for a nearby air conditioning vent and hid behind it. His heart was pounding with adrenaline, and he needed to steady his breathing. He could hear the officers shouting to one another, looking under cars and inside the elevator. It should give him at least an hour to get away. A slow smile crept across his face as he stood and pushed the rubble from the roof off his pants. Regardless of his mission, the joy of his recklessness still coursed through him.

Looking over at the garage, making sure none of the officers saw him by chance, Kol made his way across the roof. Stepping around the sky windows, Kol was glad to see the building next to the one he was on was far closer and on the same level. He jogged to the edge and bounded over, landing lightly. This roof was like the other, and Kol believed the next one he would come to would be even lower to the ground. Kol leapt to this one as well, glad his assumptions were right. This would not slow him down too much, though the street would be faster. He also did not know if the buildings would be too far apart again, but walking down the street would risk him being seen again.

The architecture made up its mind as he ran out of buildings to walk on. Thankful to find another fire escape attached to this building, Kol descended it into the trashy alley beneath, then moved towards the exit to check for any law enforcement. Satisfied, Kol stepped out and started walking into what appeared to be an assortment of apartment buildings. Glancing around once more, Kol pulled out his List and checked for the location. The place he was looking for was only a few blocks away, which seemed a stroke of luck because he had not remembered the way he was supposed to go while being pursued by the cops. Kol kept an easy walk, thinking that being more cautious would be the best way to avoid unwanted attention.

The apartments were stacked two residences high, with about four per building, small spans of yard separating the dying grass in between. Each building held the same aged look as the rest of the city. Kol could see a television on through a few windows and heard the occasional bout of laughter. He hurried on, rechecking his list as he moved. The first dot would be the next building on his right, as long as the system in his hand was accurate. He would have to check every room, though, just to be sure. Kol couldn't help but wonder why someone who was making an attempt at his father's life would live here.

The two living areas on the first floor were completely dark, the blinds closed to the world. The only light he could find came from behind the building. Crossing the lawn, Kol went to the back to see that the second-floor window was illuminated. A large oak tree was nestled behind the building between the other apartment behind the one Kol was looking at. Bending his knees, Kol jumped and caught the branch closest to the ground. He slowly pulled himself up, trying to make as little noise as possible. After several minutes Kol became level with the window. Easing himself out to the farthest part of the branch, Kol peered inside.

The room that Kol saw held the same decay as the building outside, the walls a soft yellow, stained from some type of food or liquid thrown on them. The carpet was a dark brown, the soft shag tangled together sporadically. It was a child's room—seemingly a boy's—sparsely furnished with fading blue and green furniture: a small dresser, a night stand, and a small bed. The room was strangely clean for a child. Judging by the small lump under the checkerboard patterned quilt, someone was sleeping underneath.

This had not been what he had expected, which was not much of a letdown. He still had other rooms to check. His locater brought him to this building, so what he could be looking for could be the home adjacent to this one. Not wanting to cause any form of a disturbance or scare whoever was sleeping, Kol started to ease himself back towards the trunk so he could lower himself down. He had only progressed backward a second before he heard the soft click of the bedroom door. Kol froze as he saw the door slowly swing back.

It was another child, if his assumptions where right about the one under the covers. A small girl, no more than three or four with brown curly hair and eyes to match, huddled in the doorway. She was wearing obviously hand-me-down pink pajamas and a sweater that had probably been bought from a thrift store. Kol checked to make sure he was safe in the shadows because it seemed as though the girl was looking straight at him. He was even holding his breath: the last thing he wanted was to frighten her.

"Wenn?" she said in a fearful whisper. Kol tensed, unsure what to do next.

The small lump under the covers began to move, slowly rising until a curly haired boy's head poked out from underneath. This one must have been six or seven years old. He looked at the little girl, a tired questioning look in his eyes. "Sally, what's wrong?"

"I had a nightmare," she said tearfully, and Wenn pulled up his blanket, giving his sister room to leap under, which she gratefully did.

"It's okay, it was only a dream." Wenn put his arm around her as they both sat with their backs against the wall. "What was it about?"

"I don't know. It was all dark and I was being chased by something in the woods. I woke up right before it got me," she shuddered, and her brother squeezed her tighter.

"Well, nothing's going to get you in here. We're safe now."

"Is Mom home yet?"

Wenn looked at his door for a moment then shook his head, "No, she had to work late again, but she'll be here in time for us to get ready for school."

"I wish she didn't have to work so much." Sally put her head in her hands.

"I know, but with Dad gone she has no choice," Wenn said, then he added, "What do you want for Christmas?"

"For Mom to come home?" Sally sniffled, her voice starting to break, and Kol heard the soft sob that followed.

"Well, she will be, but if you could ask for one thing, what would you like?" Wenn pried a little more.

Sally looked up, a small smile on her face. "Well, I would like another doll, so that mine wouldn't be so lonely?"

"Well, ask Santa that when we go to the mall this weekend," Wenn smiled back.

"Are you even sure there is really a Santa, Wenn? I sometimes wonder."

Wenn looked down at his sister and thought carefully before answering, "If you believe in something, then it's real. For me, I'm sure he does, and he can't wait to hear what you would like."

"Well, what are you going to ask for?"

"That you get your doll," Wenn told her and hugged her again. "Come on; let's get you back to bed." Sally nodded as they both climbed out of the bed and exited the room.

Kol sat there for a moment more, his mind in wonder at the conversation he just heard. Slowly he eased back to the center of the tree and lowered himself down. Reaching into his bag he pulled out his List and activated it. He went through the map and found the small boy and his sister both there. Both were on the nice list, though Wenn's file seemed to be coming to a close soon. Looking back up at window he smiled. The boy was starting to question, but he was not going to ruin it for his sister. Kol went to Sally's file and added what she wanted, making sure to put importance on it. As for Wenn, he jotted down another gift, one the boy would never forget. Nodding to himself, Kol felt a wave of emotion come over him. Kol knew his father would be proud.

Starting for the street again, Kol continued to work with the device. He was not expecting the Wenn in this place to be young. In fact, all the other targets could be children, and Kol did not think any of them could send three ghouls to the North Pole to set up a plot and exploit it. Looking through the search screen he found an advanced search engine that gave him a selection to show age. When he had a moment he would look at this thing closely so he would know how to use it fully. Researching the name Wenn again, it popped up, this time with red numbers under their name. The ages varied. A few more were children, one in his late teens, and the others far older. These were the one he would look for next, hoping to end his search sooner. Kol would leave no stone unturned, and no one was out of the question; just more unlikely than others.

The next target was about ten kilometers away now, and Kol wanted to make it there before the night grew later. He had exited the apartment complex now and was once again among the buildings. He kept to the shadows, glad that his path led away from the parking garage. It had been at least an hour, but the town seemed to stay quiet, so something like someone vanishing in a parking lot would have the police on guard for the rest of the night. Kol would do them the honor of doing the same. He had turned down another alley before he heard a scream. It was a woman's, full of panic. Kol bolted, following where it seemed to have come from. His guess was right when another shriek came, louder this time, with the word help mixed in with it.

He turned at a building and crossed another street. Seconds later he was in another small park with a playset atop of sand. He could see two shadows among them, one standing over a crouched figure. Kol flew across the grass, hit the sand, and then lowered his shoulder into the standing form. Pain shot down his back as he collided with the person, who seemed as immoveable as a wall. The figure was not that resistant, however, as it took the force of Kol's impact and slid a foot away, falling on its face. Even with the lack of light, Kol could tell something was off with this person.

Slowly it rose with its back to Kol, and Kol realized from its body structure that the figure was male and clothed in a leather jacket. The woman sat frozen in place, either in fear or surprise by Kol's sudden appearance, but seemed unhurt judging from a quick glance. He was not going to take his eyes off the man in the leather jacket more than he had to. Once fully upright, the man brushed the sand off of himself and turned to face who had hit him.

Kol was right that something was off, and it was the stranger's skin. It was pale, far too pale for any human. Almost like granite, with a slight rigidness. These features would not cause any alarm at first glance, as the man's face was handsome but older, possibly mid-thirties. His short, sleek hair was spiked with some form of gel. The eyes are what made it inhuman. The entire eye was a solid dark red. Kol had never seen one before, but knew the creature for what it was.

The vampire slowly crouched, a smile crossing his face where a scowl had been from the interruption of his meal. He must have now thought that it had only gotten better. Kol would have to disappoint him as he reached into his bag, his hand finding the handle of his sword. A soft hiss came from the monster's mouth, and the fangs appeared, shining brightly and razor sharp. Kol waited, wanting his sword to come as a surprise; this time his foe would underestimate him.

Sirens came from a distance. Someone else must have heard the screams, too. The vampire's hiss stopped, and disappointment flickered across his face as he looked from Kol to the girl on the ground. Kol started towards him, but the vampire was already gone, his movement a blur as he crossed the ground in between a coffee shop and laundromat.

"What was that?"

Kol was surprised that the girl had found her voice, though shaking. "Are you all right?" He asked, looking over her torn white jacket and blue jeans. The vampire had been playing with his food. A bruise was rising on her left arm and right cheek.

She reached up to touch her injured face. "Yeah...but...." Kol did not hear the rest as he was already running after the monster. He knew the police would take care of her, but if he had not been close there would have been nothing left to take care of. He would return to his main mission once this situation was dealt with. No one else would fall victim.

CHAPTER NINE

As Thick as Blood

Kol moved swiftly, glad that his feet made no noise on the tar and graveled roofs. Another gap came that he leaped over, rolled, and was back up again without losing any momentum. Vaulting over the occasional duct work, Kol made sure to keep the darting blur that was only four or five buildings in front of him constantly in his sights. At the speeds the vampire was moving, he could drop back to the ground and vanish. The vampire seemed to be moving along easily, not knowing he was being pursued by someone, and Kol was keen on having the element of surprise. He did not know what vampires were truly capable of, and he had no intention of finding out the wrong way. Kol almost lost him initially, but the vampire dashed on top of a trailer truck after leaving the girl and leapt onto a nearby roof. Kol had just seen the blur of motion before it disappeared out of eyesight. Kol had caught back up to him, but was now staying a safe distance behind to remain undetected.

The chase continued for what felt like hours. Kol was feeling the ache in his legs. The vampire showed no signs of fatigue, and Kol believed he even heard a laugh or two coming from him. They had stayed on the outskirts of the city mostly, heading towards the north part of the river. The moon was creeping closer to the horizon; Kol expected the sun in only a couple of more hours. If legends were correct, Kol suspected his friend was heading for his bed. This would be the perfect time, if any, to make his move. Motivated by his last thought, Kol found his second wind and continued on.

The buildings stopped looking like offices spaces and started to take on the appearance of warehouses. Kol saw his quarry begin to slow, so he did as well. The vampire's blurred figure began to slow. Kol came to a stop right before the next ledge, and ducked behind in case the vampire looked back. He did not, though; he only came to a stop himself, looking over his own ledge onto the ground. He seemed to be examining something, possibly looking for something to eat or if the coast was clear. If it was the first Kol would drop on him quickly. The vampire glanced back towards him, but Kol dropped the moment he saw the head turn. A few minutes passed before he slowly rose himself back up to look.

The vampire was gone: there was no trace of him to the left or right. Kol leaped to his feet and crossed the distance with only a few seconds wasted. Coming to a stop where the vampire had been standing, Kol placed his foot on the edge and quickly scanned the ground. The river ran a good distance in front of him with the area between him and the water consisting of gravel with different construction vehicles parked on it. The machines were crammed into a chain link fence built between two apparently abandoned warehouses. Kol saw the vampire across the street walking towards the building to the right. He continued to watch as the dark figure gave the street another glance before turning and entering the though the front door.

Kol looked the street over again before stepping off the ledge. He landed lightly, placing his right hand on the ground to steady himself. Standing, Kol examined the building further. He could just simply walk through the front door, but that might give him away to the vampire. The windows all appeared to be boarded up on the front and right side. Maybe he would have more luck on the left. Kol's eye caught one window, on the second floor, that looked broken. Kol made his way to the locked gate carefully, wanting to make as little noise as possible. Easing his foot into one of the links, Kol reached for the top of the fence, made a firm grip, and then hoisted himself over easily.

Crouching, Kol made his way among the machines, watching for the open window towards the back. He found it between two dump trucks and was grateful to also find a shipping crate directly under the window. Kol climbed onto the hood of the dump truck, using his hands to crawl up the windshield and into the bucket of the vehicle. Getting a running start, Kol made it up the rear ramp of the bucket and stepped over onto the shipping crate. The window was indeed broken in, shards of glass sticking from the frame. The inside was completely dark, probably an office space. Careful not to impale himself, Kol slipped through the opening into the room.

His feet crunched on the broken glass that littered the carpet. He found his assumptions of an office were right after his vision cleared. It was complete with an old bookshelf, a couple of filing cabinets, desk, and chair. The place was a mess. It looked as if someone had brought in a sledgehammer and started breaking the drywall. A variety of colors complemented the wall in the form of graffiti. Kol walked across the room and studied the door, the outer layer shredded from years of mold. Grabbing the handle and lifting, Kol slowly eased it open and stepped out into the hall, ignoring the scent of decay that wafted from the groaning door.

Kol closed the door behind him carefully, taking away the small source of light he already had. No amount of adjustment was going to help him now, so he had to make his way down the hall, checking for any furniture along the way. He did not want to risk a flashlight and be discovered, but tripping over furniture would have the same effect. He was lucky to find the hall empty except for the wall telling him to turn right to continue. Faint moonlight outlined a door at the end of the hall. As he moved closer he could hear voices, though faint. It sounded as if one was laughing and the others were carrying along as well. Kol gripped the knob and turned it softly, waiting for the click that told him he could open it. He opened the door just enough to hear and see what was being said and to survey the area.

It was the main part of the warehouse: a vast room filled with stacks of cardboard boxes, piles of what looked like assorted metal, and a conveyer belt machine used for transport lined the far walls. The conveyer belts were nothing like the ones in his father's shop. These were old and rusted, the belts rotting from the mildew off the river, which clung to the boxes and rusted the metal. The grated catwalk in front of him lined the entire outer wall, and two more were on the third and fourth floor above him. The moonlight was coming from several skylights—Kol was surprised that they were all intact. The only form of movement came from the five figures standing around on the bottom floor. Kol knew they were not human.

"I still can't believe you let a human interrupt your meal." This was the one who had been laughing: a young-looking male with blonde spiky hair wearing blue jeans and a black shirt. He was sitting on a large wooden crate.

"I told you the cops were coming." Kol's quarry was standing closest to the front door in between two more vampires, a brown haired one with a pair of kakis and white button up shirt and the other one had blond hair as well, but with streaks of brown over his ears, and his face showed that he was several years younger than Kol. He wore a black shirt and blue jeans, and had his hands stuffed into his pockets. The other one present Kol could not see, but he could hear her laughing below him under the catwalk.

"Still, though, it's sad. I could have finished them both off and been gone before the cops got another mile." That was the spikey blond one.

The one Kol had chased shoved the spikey blond one. "I'll finish you off before you get another mile." The blonde jumped right back and the two began to wrestle on the ground. This carried on for a while, bringing on shouts from the others. The blonde one acquired the mount and began to slam his opponent's head into the ground, causing the concrete underneath to shatter. The playful banter was beginning to be replaced by anger as the two began to shriek at each other. The one on the ground was able push the other off of him, then grabbed a nearby piece of metal. As soon as his opponent was fully upright, he was sent flying several feet after the metal pipe collided with his head. The vampire then whirled the pipe around and threw it like a javelin. The blonde dove out of the way before the pipe could impale him and instead stuck into the concrete wall and remained there. The two sprinted towards each other in the same blurred speed and collided with a sound that echoed off the walls.

"ENOUGH!" A shout came from the door. A new vampire had entered, and as soon as he spoke the others immediately stopped yelling. The two that were fighting jumped away from each other and knelt to the floor with their heads down. "You think that this is some form of entertainment?" The newcomer's voice was deep and the commanding tone was hard to miss. This vampire stood taller than the others, and his body appeared to be chiseled stone. His hair was cut short to his scalp. He wore a suit, black jacket and pants with a red buttoned shirt and black tie. He led the room on his every word, even though he spoke with heavily accented English. "You are given this gift, and you lower yourself to that of animals?" His gaze was on the two kneeling. "Maybe I should just take it away from you if you do not cherish it?"

"We are sorry, master," the dark haired vampire said.

"We were only seeing how powerful we were, nothing more," the blond one added after.

"How powerful, you say?" The master walked over to the two and studied them. His glance looked to the pipe protruding from the concrete wall and the small crater that had been created from the constant head barrage. "Well, in that case." In a quick motion, the master had both the fighting vampires by the throat, one in each hand, and had lifted them into the air. "If I ever find any of you acting this way again, I will just have to show you what you can be fully capable of." With another burst of frightening speed he threw the two in opposite direction, one hitting the conveyer belt and the other a stack of boxes. Both collapsed in on themselves as the bodies collided with it. "Now for business."

He turned to the others, seeming to be basking in their obedience. "I am glad that you all made it here, and you've all done very well with hiding your movements. I must admit in the beginning I was skeptical you could." He must not have known about the girl in the park yet.

"We only want to do what's asked of us, Master." The woman beneath him finally spoke.

"I know you do, Samantha, I know." The hardness in his voice slipped into a soothing tone, which seemed to make Samantha gasp. "And you will continue to do so, but the process is not yet done." Kol could see him reach into his overcoat and retrieve a small white box. He tossed it out of Kol's sight, probably to Samantha. "Here is the week's dose: drink."

Smiles erupted through the small crowd as the box was passed around. "Thank you, master." The blond vampire had come out of the wreckage and so had the other one from the pile of boxes. The others nodded in agreement as they pulled out a small object from inside the gift. Samantha walked closer to the master vampire. Kol watched her closely, noting her red hair and blue dress. She held the small object up to the light. It was a vial with a black top sealing it. Samantha unscrewed it swiftly and dumped the contents into her mouth. She let out a refreshing gasp and then threw the bottle on the ground. The others did the same, though not so theatrically.

Once they were all finished they focused back on their leader. He nodded to them all, a small smile on his own face.

"Now," he stopped for only moment before continuing, "we need more recruits."

"More?" The spiky haired boy asked.

The older vampire gave him a quick glance that caused the boy to lower his head again. "Yes, Jim; more, many more before we can continue our plans."

"I'm sorry, Master, but if we could know what kind of plan it was we would have an idea about the certain types of people that you require." Samantha seemed to hold a certain appeal with the leader because he did not give her the cutting look like he gave Jim.

"Samantha, if you continue to ask me that I will consider it insubordination and tear your head off. If one of you were to fall in the wrong hands, all would be ruined." The master vampire turned his head slowly from side to side. "Besides, you are still young, not fully used to your senses. Which is why you've missed the sound of the heartbeat that is in this very building with us." The group became suddenly tense, a pride of lions surprised by prey coming so close.

"Where?" Samantha shrieked.

The leader smiled. "I'm not telling you. What better way for you to learn your skills? Meet at the next location in four days with new recruits. The one that brings me the intruder's head will reclaim great honor." The master vampire looked at Samantha before turning and exiting the building in a blur.

The ones remaining began to let out a low hiss, heads twitching from side to side, looking. Samantha stepped up to the spot where the larger vampire had been standing. "Split up," she commanded. "Find the human." The next instant they departed, leaving Samantha standing alone, glee clear on her face before sprinting off herself.

Adrenaline hit Kol the moment his position was known. He had his sword out now, gripped firmly in his left hand. He had been so careful with his movements, but he had no idea that his heart would betray him. He could hear them, moving quickly through the building, turning desks and chairs as they went. They had no idea where he was, and he was glad to hold that much surprise to himself. Someone was coming, though; Kol could hear new crashes echoing the hallway he was in. In his readiness, he felt his belt pouch that held his bell. He did not plan on using it, but he was still uncomfortable with the strength at which that pipe had entered the wall.

A chair flew into his line of sight, smashing apart as it collided with the end of the hall. The footsteps came next as the vampire stepped from around the corner. It was Jim. When he saw Kol he crouched, teeth bared and fingernails shaped into claws. The red eyes shone bright with hunger, disregarding the fact that his prey was armed. An unnatural shriek filled the air before he lunged.

The speed was expected. Kol moved to the side the moment the vampire sprung. He felt the wind of the vampire's arm as it made a swipe for him. A weakness had been given and Kol claimed it with his sword. The vampire slid to a halt in front of the door. He looked in disbelief at where his right arm should have been, and panic slid across his face followed by anger as he looked back at Kol, hatred dripping like saliva from his mouth. Kol did not give him the chance to act again. He kicked the severed arm on the floor at the vampire who grabbed it with his remaining hand. Kol then stepped on his outstretched boot, pivoted, then planted his other boot in the vampire's chest. Kol remembered what the one he ran into at the park felt like, so this time he applied more force.

The vampire knocked the door from its hinges and collided into the catwalk rail. Kol did not give him any chances. He stepped through the open door frame and stabbed with the point, aiming for the one point of weakness legends said would stop the undead creature. The vampire jumped back from the blade and fell over the rail to the hard floor. Kol followed, leaping over the rail and landing on top of the vampire with both feet. He gave a final shriek as Kol drove his sword where its heart was supposed to be. To Kol's surprise, the vampire dissolved into dust.

An ounce of guilt dripped into his bloodstream. The vampire had once been living, once had a family and a home. Kol did not know whether the vampire chose this or someone else had. Judging by the conversation it was a choice, but he did not know that for sure. This person had been missing from somewhere, and he had ended any chance for him to return from where he came. Doors broke above him on all levels. The four remaining vampires had heard the last shriek and came back to see what had happened. Kol knew he had no choice but to stop these monsters, despite the whispering instinct urging him to flee. If he did not stay and fight, others would fall to their hunt like he was about to.

Their shriek came, shaking Kol's bones as it reverberated through the open space. The four landed around him, knees barely bending. They were in a formation with three up front and Samantha standing behind them. Their faces were furious, and all concentrated on him. "It's you!" the vampire he had chased said.

"This the one who took you out, Ryan?" It was the dirty blonde-haired boy.

"Yeah, and this time he's not getting away." Ryan cracked his knuckles. "Looks like he took out Jim. Too bad: looks like there is more for us." The others murmured in agreement and Samantha cackled. Kol said nothing, readying his stance for the next attack. He turned his head slowly from left to right, making sure to keep them all in his sights. They all began to laugh at him, as if they believed they had already won.

"Look at him," the dirty blonde boy said. "Who carries a sword?"

"Let's just get this over with," the brown haired one bellowed.

They started to lunge for him, making swiping blows with their hands. Kol swung his sword to parry the attacks but found only air, making no contact. It was as if they were testing him out, looking for any form of weakness. He wasn't going to show it, though. Two came at him at the same time and Kol was able to cut the blonde one across the arm, a piece of clothing falling off. The vampire cursed and took a couple of steps back while the others held their ground. Kol took his sword in both hands now, wanting to make a cleaner cut next time. The remaining three came at him again. Kol was able to dodge the first two strikes but the final one finally found flesh.

Kol winced at the burning pain. He could feel warm blood trickling down his leg. The vampire who had clawed him was Ryan. He was currently licking his hand, a satisfied look on his face. This seemed to drive the others mad, as all of them were beginning to shriek. Kol stepped under one of them, attacking wildly, and had the two in front of him. He quickly looked around for the blond vampire and found him just as the flat piece of iron left his arm. Kol brought his sword up and deflected it, the power of the throw flowing though his own blade and into his grip. He held tightly so as not to lose it and deflected the other objects being hurled towards him.

He knocked a sawblade to the ground, followed by several pieces of rebar. The metal came so fast that he had a hard time keeping up with it. The other vampires waited for him to falter so that they could make their move. Kol blocked several more strikes but was not fast enough, and a jagged piece of iron sliced his arm deeply. He ignored this one too, forcing his mind to remain focused. All the events from the day were beginning to stack against him now and it seemed that he had no choice. He shifted to reach into his belt pouch when Samantha appeared inches from him.

Samantha swung at him making Kol duck under her fist. He came up with his blade, but she was already out of his range. The others were on him again, Ryan kicking out his leg from under him. Midair, another opponent grabbed a handful of Kol's shirt in his hands and slammed him to the ground. Kol felt his breath leave his lungs as the pavement underneath him cracked. Desperately he fanned his sword in hopes of taking off some of their legs. They leaped away from him before the blade touched. He could hear their shouts of excitement and Samantha's laughter.

"You think you could come into a basement of vampires with a sword and stop them?" Samantha's laughter was an annoying one. Kol was on one knee, now slowly raising himself up. "Look at you, not too bad looking, really. I'm going to enjoy draining you dry." She flashed her fangs to give more impact to her last remark. Kol ignored it. He was tired of this and now was as good as time as any. He reached behind his jacket and unclipped the pouch.

One of the skylights exploded, showering the vampires in glass. They looked up in surprise as something landed on top of the blond vampire. He had little time to act surprised as the object, which Kol took for a person, reached down and ripped the vampire's head from the body. The figure then struck its hand into the chest of the body he was on, turning it into dust. The others looked horrified as Samantha and the other boy started in on the new intruder. Kol was on his feet now and sprinting towards Ryan who was closer to him.

Ryan turned to meet him and dove out of the way of his blade. Kol kept up the assault, forcing him backward toward the wall. The vampire looked around for help, but found Samantha and his other companion fighting whomever had fallen from the roof. "Stop, please, I didn't want to cause any trouble." He hissed and swiped at the blade.

Kol continued his assault. "What about the girl in the park?"

Ryan's eyes scanned his face in panic then drew back in a snarl. He sprang, either for Kol or to escape. Either way, Kol swung his blade to take out his knee then curved it around to impale his heart. Kol stepped through the dust to help his ally finish off the other two, but found that everyone was gone. The stealth vampires could move in was eerie. Kol looked the room over again, confused as to where they had gone. No shutting doors or sounds of running—they were simply gone. He did not think that they would have fled, but if so, they would have gone for the street. Kol turned for the door and found a vampire's hand around his throat slamming him into a crate, his sword pulled from his hand. He heard it clatter to the floor somewhere next to him.

"What are you doing here?" his assailant's voice demanded, angrily. Kol grabbed the wrist of the vampire, but the grip was too firm to even budge. The vampire was not trying to cut off air flow, only hold him in place. Kol could see that this was who had fallen through the skylight. He was around the same height as Kol, but had a slimmer build and had black hair that fell just past his ears. The rest of his features were vampiric, with the granite skin and crimson eyes that glared at him with distaste. He wore a black jacket with several pockets on the front and a pair of blue jeans. He pulled Kol away from the wall and slammed him into it again. "Answer me!" Kol's tolerance faded into the wall behind him, and with his right hand he reached for his pouch. "You got in the way: there is no telling how far this will set us back."

The soft bell echoed from the walls, a faint sound that could be dismissed as the wind. Kol held his blade to the vampire's throat from behind him. He stood there with his hand still out-stretched, gasping air. "I do not think hostilities are needed. If you want to kill me say so now. I have no time for games." Kol could hear the fatigue in his voice. He did not care, as he would do what was necessary.

The vampire showed a look of brief surprise, but quickly stilled. He slowly turned to face Kol, ignoring the blade at his neck. "If I wanted to kill you, I would have when I grabbed you."

Kol ignored the comment and continued, "So why help me? Why not just join in with them and finish me off?"

The vampire slowly tilted his head to the side. "Because not all monsters want to go bump in the night." The vampire looked down at the blade in his neck then back to Kol. "No longer needed?"

Kol lowered his sword, having no place to sheath it now with its sheath somewhere in his pouch. Studying the pale-skinned figure in front of him, Kol remembered his father had always taught him that what you see on the outside may not be what is truly there. Did he let the others escape, though? Could he be trusted? "Where did they go?"

The ally vampire turned towards the front door. "The other one's name was Jonathan. He and Samantha bolted for it a few seconds after you finished that one off." He pointed to the pile of dust a few meters from him. "I had been tracking them for some time now."

"Until I got in the way," Kol said and the vampire nodded. "Why were you tracking them?"

The vampire made as if to answer but lost it in the shrieks that followed. Kol spun towards the rear of the building. The glass windows, eight in all, were shattering to the floor and in each one stood two to three vampires. All of their mouths were open, shouting angry yells at Kol and the other vampire. Samantha stood in one of the windows by herself, smiling down at them. "That's them: they are the ones who are threatening our plan!" The small army shrieked, ready for the command.

Kol raised his sword, other hand reaching for his bell. "Come on," the vampire behind him said calmly. "That trick of yours is not going to continue to work." He moved towards the door. Kol looked back at him knowing it was an underestimating remark, but it could not be truer. Kol turned and sprinted after him. He did not need to hear and see that the vampires were right behind them.

Kol leaped through the gaping double door into what looked like the front lobby. He did not stop to look but continued out the front door after the vampire running in front of him. The vampire peered behind him to see that Kol could keep up, and once assured they both pushed for their top speeds. He turned at a storage building, waving for Kol to hurry. Kol pushed his legs harder and made it to the corner just as the front of the warehouse exploded into the street with mounds of fighting bodies, all wanting the same thing. The vampire had come to a stop in front of a covered car. In one quick movement he ripped the tarp away and tossed it to the ground, revealing what was underneath.

Kol couldn't help but stare. Despite the mob coming behind him, he had to admire the vehicle. He never knew much about cars, since they were not needed to move through the city. The exterior was black; everything from the tint to the rims. "Get in." The vampire motioned for Kol to open the passenger door. The shriek came from behind him again, and Kol quickly shook his admiration aside to climb in. "Put your sword in the back and watch the blood on you."

Kol slammed the door behind him as the vampire pressed in a numbered sequence on the console. The interior was also black with blue stitching. The car came to life, a soft rumble that insinuated exactly what it was capable of. The gauges gave off the same color blue as the rest of the car. "Seatbelt," he said, looking at Kol.

Kol looked to him then down the street where the vampires were rounding the corner. "Are you serious?"

"They better not scratch my paint," his ally replied. Kol just shook his head and pulled on the seatbelt. It was not the regular type, but a harness strap. As soon as the click came, the vampire slammed the clutch and then shifted into first. Kol's head slammed against the headrest as they bolted down the street. The car was already in third gear before they made it to the end. It felt like Kol's heart stopped as they sped towards a building ending the street. The vampire smiled as he downshifted and pulled the emergency brake.

It felt like the car was sliding on ice as they rounded the turn. Kol was glad he had strapped in or he would have hit the car door. He got a glimpse of the vampires behind them, and he didn't like how close they were in the side mirror. The car straightened out and started down the new street. "They should be giving up soon."

Kol looked at the driver. "What makes you say that?"

"Sun's coming up."

He was right: Kol had not realized it yet. A soft orange could be seen moving across the horizon. Only a few stars stood out in the purple night. "What about you?"

The vampire laughed. "I'll be fine." Kol looked at him and gaped as the vampire reached up and pulled one of his fangs from his mouth. The vampire was changing: his skin no longer appeared pale, but was instead gaining a warm glow. The claw-like fingernails were receding back into his hands. The remaining fang that Kol could see from his grimace vanished as well, and the red eyes slowly slipped away, leaving white with a chilling blue at their center. He was turning human.

"How did you-"

"The same way you could appear behind me," the ex-vampire interrupted. Kol got the hint. If Kol was willing to tell the former vampire how he used his bell, he, in turn, would let him know how he turned back human. Placing the tooth into his jacket pocket, the once-vampire shifted into the final gear as they turned onto an interstate. "I'm Harvest, by the way."

"Kol," he said in return. "So, why were you tracking them?"

"Why were you there?" he returned.

"Following a vampire that attacked someone." Kol waited for his question to be answered. Harvest did not respond and continued to look out the window. "So, are you going to answer?"

"It's not my place to say. When we get back to the camp, she will decide if you can be trusted."

They drove on, winding through the city, the sun cresting over the horizon. Kol could already feel the warmth coming off it though it was still early. The night had been a long one, and he did not expect a vampire to get in the way of his mission, let alone an entire mob of them. He had already wasted enough time fighting the ones in the warehouse, though he did not regret it because it meant another life saved. He had always read that vampires were complete creatures of darkness, only seeking to quench their everlasting thirst. They acted human when they were not wanting to eat, well, humans, and worse, they were organized. Now he was riding with this person named Harvest who had saved him and now was taking him to some camp to be questioned. He knew he should have left Harvest and went his own way, but he wanted to know why this person had dropped in. He moved in the seat to look out of the window and was reminded of his wounds.

Looking at his leg he saw that it was not so bad. Three gashes across his thigh, shallow but still stinging. The blood had dried now, and it was attempting to heal so long as he kept it still. His arm was another matter: a deep cut that blood trickled from freely. He sighed to himself at the wounds. It had only been a day since he had come here and he was already hurt. He had no idea how to patch himself up; he had only been taught basic medical lessons. Kol thought he would learn more whenever he went to the Island. He could not let this slow him in finding out who Wenn was. "Don't worry," Harvest said to Kol, noticing Kol's self-examination. "Iris will fix you up." And he was back to watching the road.

Kol did not know who this Iris was, but he would probably take a pass on the help. He just wanted to see if he could gain any information and be gone. He wanted to check his List to see where the nearest location was, but decided against it with Harvest sitting next to him. He had a good feeling about this person, but still knew nothing about him, so it was best to stay on guard. Searching for something else to think about, Kol had to ask. "So what kind of car is this?"

Harvest's eyes seemed to light up at the mention of his ride. "It's a Subaru WRX STI Impreza, one of my favorite models." The way he said it sounded breathless with the excitement of talking about something he enjoyed.

All right, Kol liked the guy. "How fast can it go?"

"Better to show you." And with that he pushed the accelerator to the floor and hit a small red button on the dash. Music erupted in the car, mostly powered by the bass. They sped on, weaving in and out of traffic. No shame in having a little fun while he was out of the city.

Caravan of Consequences

The city was gone and Kol had no idea how far they'd come. The minutes spent on the road literally went by in a blur. The scattered buildings had been replaced by acres of forest, mostly pines with dead limbs and bushes littering the ground. They had left the interstate for a couple of kilometers now, and Harvest continued his speeding pace weaving back and forth around the upcoming turns. Kol was not afraid of the speed; in fact, he greatly enjoyed it. They were now entering a small town, passing a few gas stations and mom and pop shops before exiting again. He was unable to catch the name of it, though. Kol was starting to wonder how much further when the car began to slow. Harvest checked his mirrors before turning onto a dirt road.

A dust cloud billowed behind them as they went. Harvest used more speed than necessary, but nowhere near what Kol now knew the car could do. They made another turn and rode for a little longer before coming to a halt in a dead end of forest. Harvest turned the music off and rolled down his window. Kol waited, not questioning what they were doing. An explanation would come soon. Harvest reached into another of his pockets and pulled out a small tube, placing it in his mouth and blowing. The note that came from the little whistle was high pitched, and the sound would wake anyone up to a fresh morning. The tune reverberated off the trees before them, and if Kol was not mistaken a soft wind began. Kol felt the familiar pressure of magic rise, an old one of protection that was welcoming them in.

The trees in front of them began to pull away, hardened trunks flexing apart and crooked branches straightening and grasping one another. Roots rose from the dirt and laid out the course in front of them in a wooden road. The woods were expanding into a dense tunnel of trees, large enough for the car to fit. The eruption of lignin stopped as quickly as it began. Harvest was waiting for the stillness, because after it was done he put the car into gear and started forward. Once the rear bumper cleared the first line of trees, the trees began to shift back into their original spots. It was a protective ward allowing them safe passage to wherever they were going. The road in front of them was a straight shot, with no turns or twists needed, and despite being made of roots it was surprisingly smooth. Kol could see the small light that must have been the exit growing larger as they moved. He looked out from the window trying to examine the wooden tunnel more closely. Harvest kept his eyes forward; this was not his first time traveling in this tunnel.

The exit appeared, and Harvest brought his car to a halt, turning off the engine with a button. He then opened his door and stepped out. Kol reached in the back and pulled his sword from the seat, careful not to cut anything inside. Once he was out and had shut the door, Kol took in his surroundings. They were still in the tunnel, though this one was much larger than the one they had just came through. Kol looked back just in time to see it close and become simply forest again. A bead of sweat slid down his cheek. This place was warmer than the world outside. Yet despite the heat, Kol felt comfortable.

"We have to go the rest of the way on foot," Harvest told him and started forward. Kol gave the gate one last look before continuing. The trees were beginning to thin here, allowing Kol to see more of the surrounding area. Besides the mass expansions of woods Kol could see a lake they were walking toward. The tunnel began to curve to the left, which they continued to follow. After a few more minutes, they arrived at their destination. Kol came to a complete stop as Harvest continued. "Stay here," he said, brushing his hands backwards to emphasize. The sight was breathtaking, and Kol barely heard what he said.

They had made it to a meadow, though not a large one by any means, for that would ruin the magic. The meadow was a pallet of wild flowers, so many that Kol could not name the different kinds, and their color shone bright. The woods around the area bent inward on the center point making a canopy to protect from any form of harsh weather. The wind blew softly, caressing his jacket with a winter chill he found inviting. Birds chirped on branches in the distance and he could hear the soft pat of animals hopping among the fallen trees. Sitting in the middle of the meadow was another sight.

Three huge wagons stood stoically, which were clearly pulled by the two Shire horse that were grazing near the edge of the woods on the right. The wagons stood at least three meters tall, each displaying a variety of color, and circling a designated spot for a campfire, complete with a hanging cast iron cooking pot. Whoever had built these wagons had to be a master craftsman, with the wood seeming to be one piece that murals were painted on. Each one had a window effect that completely wrapped them, appearing to look onto a scene through glass. The first wagon was painted a sky blue, complete with white clouds drifting across the canvas. The second was like fire, and the design of the red, yellows, and oranges were so realistic Kol could not help but think that the wooden wagon should erupt at any moment. The final wagon depicted the same patterns of the ocean, the golden beach seaming to erode with the ebbing tide. Besides the different skins that each wore, the wagons were all similar in design. Four spoked wheels, curving roofs that peaked at either end, and a door framed in the middle of each one, though the paintings made the doors all but invisible.

Pulling his sheath from his bag and sliding his sword into it, Kol threw the strap over his shoulder. He could not help but shake the feeling that this place was not for weapons, so he respected that. Kol walked over to the small campfire, logs stacked just right to allow for moderate heat. Something was cooking in the pot. Kol thought of oatmeal as he moved closer and was assured once the delicious smell of maple and apples hit his nose. He saw blankets laid out around the fire for sitting, one green and the other two blue and purple. Harvest had vanished behind the wagons a few moments before, but Kol paid him no mind as he examined the iron pot and its holder. The triangle rods holding it above the fire on a hook were also made with excellent care. In fact, Kol believed if he checked under the wagons, he would find the brackets that held the axels to the wagons in the same form. The combined hands of the blacksmith and carpenter used on these wagons would be enough to impress both his father and uncle.

"Are you hungry?" Kol stood up hurriedly. The voice was not Harvest's; it was softer and kind, as if talking to a scared animal.

Kol looked around. Harvest had returned, his jacket gone, and he was wearing a black shirt. The person standing next to him drew his eyes immediately. She was shorter than Kol, but the way she held herself made him feel as though they were the same height. Her build was deceptively slender, but she stood in a way that would give anyone pause before attempting to cross her. She wore a dress that went slightly past her knees and was a mix of greens and blues along with several bracelets on each wrist that jingled as she moved closer to him. Around her neck hung a sea shell on a silver chain, which vanished into her long dirty blonde hair that flowed past her shoulders. Kol was trapped in her eyes that looked back into his, with a look that said she was trying to figure him out. They were blue and warm, like a summer sky Kol had never known. She smiled up at him, and Kol felt the warmth of the sun through it. "I said, are you hungry?"

Kol simply stood there, not knowing how to respond. His stomach reminded him that it had been before sundown since he had eaten. "No, thank you." Kol told her, "I don't want to be a burden."

Her eyes narrowed, clearly seeing past what he had just said. "Harvest tells me you're Kol. It's nice to meet you." She placed a hand on her chest and gave a slight bow. "My name is Iris." She turned and walked towards the last wagon. "Find him a seat, Harvest; I'll be right back."

Kol looked at Harvest who was grinning at him and had an eyebrow raised. He walked over the green blanket and sat down. He looked up at Kol and motioned him to sit on the blue blanket next to him. Kol shrugged and sat down, crossing his legs in front of him, laying his sword to the side. His body thanked him as he did; its call was wanting him to rest. He refused, though. He would be on his way the moment he could figure out what all this was. He might, in fact, be close to one of his marks, which was almost enough for him to leave right then. Kol started to rise until Iris came out of the wagon carrying three decorative bowls with spoons. She ignored Kol's attempt to stand and poured a bowl full of oatmeal and handed it to him. He tried to refuse, but she placed it in his hands regardless. She handed Harvest a bowl who started eating immediately. She then turned to Kol with a hand on her hip daring him to protest again. Glaring at her, he took the spoon and skimmed some off the top that had cooled and put it in his mouth. The very first taste left his mouth watering and seemed to bring back some of his stamina. That would be needed for his trip back to the city. He continued his bowl.

Iris did not fix her own bowl. Instead, she went back to the last cabin and came out with a small white box. She sat down next to Kol on the side of his wounded arm. She took his arm to examine the cut, and he tried to pull free. Her grip held strong; he did not think he had lost that much strength or for her to be so strong. "Take off your jacket," she commanded him. Kol stared at her, setting his empty bowl down next to him. She stared right back at him a moment longer before adding sincerely, "Please?"

Kol eased off his jacket, careful with the torn part so he would not damage it further. Iris took it from him and laid it gently to the side. She then carefully took his bicep and peered at it closely.

"Well, it's not as bad as it looks. Will need stitches though." She turned back to her box and started to rummage in it.

"You know what you're doing?" Kol asked. He was not up for a trial and error right now.

"Trust me," she said. "Hold still while I clean it." Kol realized he already trusted her. He watched as she cleaned his wound, taking care not to cause any extra discomfort. Iris did, in fact, know what she was doing. Her hands moved expertly with the swab. "Okay, I have no way to numb the pain. Tell me when it becomes too much?" she said to him before turning back to his wound.

"Go ahead," Kol told her. "This isn't my first time being put back together." She smiled as she made the first incision. The pain was there but it was nothing he could not handle.

"So, Harvest tells me you were hunting vampires?" she asked not looking up from her work.

"Well, if I had not stepped in, he would have killed someone." Kol told her. Harvest got up to refill his bowl, then carried it away from the fire, walking over to the horses. "What are their names?"

"Temperance is the one on the right and Diligence is her mate on the left. They help me when I need to travel, and are two of my close friends." She never faltered as she went on, "There were no humans in that part of the city. Why did you chase after it when you realized what is was?"

"Because it may have been after someone else." Kol shrugged his other shoulder. "Couldn't go on knowing someone could be in danger."

"Well, that is very brave of you, but dangerous, even if you were armed."

"I can handle myself."

"So it seems," she said, tugging lightly on a stitch. She laughed slightly and Kol knew she was only lightening the mood. "So, you've known of vampires?"

"I do, though that was the first time I've ever seen one." Kol said. "Who are you?" He meant both her and Harvest, but it came out differently.

"Well, for Harvest, I cannot fully say but I know his intentions are like my own. I am here for the very reason you went chasing after the vampire last night." She gave one final tug before returning her items to her box. "There, all better." She looked down at Kol's sword, examining it. Her eyes lingered on the guard, then to Kol's white jacket. "Your leg will heal on its own; I'll just clean and dress it. The next question for me would be who you are?" She stood, grabbing Kol's bowl and refilled it with her own. "Chasing after vampires, carrying a sword, and from the sound of your voice, you're not from the city." She sat in front of him, crossing her legs. Kol took the bowl handed to him without any objection. "I put something in that to help with the healing. I hope that's okay?"

Kol nodded. "That's fine." He took a spoon full of the oatmeal. "I'm looking for someone," he said after swallowing.

"Do you have any idea who this someone is?"

Kol shrugged. "I have no idea. The only thing I have to go on is the name Wenn." Kol looked for any realization to cross Iris's face but none came. "Doesn't ring a bell, does it?"

She shook her head, "No, I'm sorry. Why are you looking for this person?" Kol remained silent. this was what he had been afraid of. She took the hint and said, "I understand that you probably can't tell me everything. Maybe just the basic story of who you are and why you have come here."

Kol put another spoonful in his mouth, letting the warmth sink in while giving him time to think. By no means could he tell her everything: the secret must remain for the safety of so many. There was a reason the Scribes had wards placed on them before leaving. If the real world ever found that the North Pole truly existed, there would be no telling what would come of it. Fear of the world is what brought so many refugees there, to both escape it and help it. The children would be joyous, of course, but what of the ones who did not truly believe? The ones who only saw numbers and profit? The monsters Kol has read about were not the only ones out there. Some held their true forms on the inside, and that was what made the city worth protecting.

Taking a moment more, Kol gathered his thoughts before starting. "You're right, I'm not from around here. I'm actually from the north, a small town within the endless forest of Canada. I know of vampires and the other creatures because they frequently believe that a small village in the middle of nowhere cannot defend themselves and are easy prey." That was not truly a lie. It is disputed where the North Pole of stories lay. "Over the years we have learned to defend ourselves. We were attacked recently, which we quickly overcame. My father was not so lucky." Kol pushed away the memories that came while he spoke. "He was stabbed, by a goblin-made weapon. One that puts the wounded into a coma, leaving them at the mercy of whomever sent the attack. There is only one way to wake him and that is to find the blade's brother which will wake him. My uncle said they were called *Clauditis* blades, sound familiar?" Iris shook her head. "The trace came back to here, along with the name Wenn. I arrived yesterday afternoon." Kol was still unhappy with leaving out the whole truth, but it was unavoidable.

Iris nodded as he went on, as if gaining the full understanding. "So that explains your enchanted clothes? Your village knows of magic." Kol was surprised that she knew about his jacket and possibly his boots and pants as well. He nodded at her. "I take it you come from a world of similar characteristics?"

"Something like that." She stood, taking Kol's finished bowl from his hand. "I'll explain more later. Right now you need your rest."

"No. I thank you for your generosity, but I need to head back to the city." He started to get up, but found his strength gone. He looked up to Iris in confusion while she smiled down at him.

"I knew you would be stubborn, even if I told you to give your wounds time to heal." She stood from her spot. "I told you

I gave you something to help you heal. I will not have your stubbornness get you killed. We will talk more when you wake."

Kol looked at her in disbelief. She had drugged him! She must have put whatever it was in the oatmeal when he was watching the horses...wait, he had agreed to it. He reached up and grabbed her wrist. His vision was beginning to fog, and he could not focus his thoughts on one subject. Kol pulled Iris down on him, and she gave a yelp as she fell, dropping the bowl as she did. He was lying back on the blanket, the soft grass and flowers underneath creating a nice bed. He could see Iris's face hovering over his; he had an instinct to hit her. His father had told him to never hit a woman, but his mother had taught him it was perfectly fine to hit anyone trying to put his life in danger. Kol reached up and barely caught some of her hair in his hands, flowing through his fingers like silk. Darkness took him, and the last thing he saw was her smiling down at him.

******

It was the best time of the year; no one could argue that. The night held the compressed excitement and anticipation that was soon to come. Everyone had gathered, both elves and humans, to the center of the city. The tree lit the entire plaza, but the aid from the surrounding buildings were welcomed in full. Kol darted between the jungle of legs as he made his way through the crowd. He was caught up in the excitement as much as anyone else. He sprinted up the stairs, opening and shutting the front door quickly before anyone outside noticed. He would not want to start the excitement early. "Father!" he yelled, running through the entrance hall and entering the workshop. The place was deserted, the work for the year done and the deliveries now needing to be made. Kol went straight for his father's office, taking the stairs two at a time. He was almost to the top when he stepped on one of his untied shoelaces and slammed into the hardwood floor.Kol lay there for a moment, the breath knocked from him. His vision blurred, but he ignored it; he was used to skinning up his knees. Still, small tears came to his eyes. He felt hands take him under the shoulders and lift him up in the air. "Nicholas, now, what have I told you," his father smiled up at him. "Double knot your shoes. Makes for a better bow anyway."

Kol laughed once he caught his breath. "Everyone's waiting for you outside."

"I sure hope they are! Wouldn't be much of a celebration now, would it?" He sat down on the top of the staircase, arranging Kol so that he was sitting on his knee. "They will have to wait a few more moments, though. I have to go retrieve the bells from downstairs."

"Can I come?"

"I'm afraid not, son," He chuckled. "Far too dangerous for you at the moment."

Kol lowered his head. "If you say so."

"One day you will be ready, and on that day, I will be so proud." He pushed Kol's hair out of his eyes. "So, since we are here and it's Christmas Eve, tell me. What would you like from Santa this year?"

"Have I been a good boy this year?"

"Well, according to your mother you are quite the little adventurer. Who holds some form of disrespect towards his parents from time to time." Kol's smile slipped. "But in my eyes, the imagination should never be caged. I personally think you've been one of the greatest children, though I am not supposed to show favoritism."

Kol laughed at his father's sense of humor. Some did not understand it, but Kol did. He thought about what he wanted. Looking over the workshop he could see the empty rolls of wrapping paper and baskets with few bows left inside. Everything had been put to effective use in the months preparing. Everyone was still outside, waiting for the man in the red coat: waiting for the spirit of Christmas to soar into the night. It did not take much more than that to decided what he truly wanted. "I want to be like you."

His father sat quietly for a moment, looking into his son's eyes. At that time Kol had no idea what he had just asked for and what would come later. The smile on his face broadened as his father told him, "Well, that cannot be done in just one Christmas. If you truly want to have this gift, then you must work very hard for it."

"I will!" Kol's excitement was far too apparent.

His father gave his trademark chuckle in return. "Well, first thing tomorrow we can get started."

"Okay!" Kol told his father. He could not contain how happy for what he believed was in store. "I'll do my best."

✶✶✶✶✶✶

The scene changed. Kol the small child who had just been sitting on his father's lap now stood alone in the abandoned work shop. Something was wrong here. The shop no longer held the atmosphere like before. The tables, once shining from the morning polish and ready for the day's work, were covered in dust. The floor was covered with crunched bits of wrapping paper, broken scissors and hammers, and toys laying forgotten with no home to go too. Kol had never seen the shop like this before and did not know what was going on. Terrified, he ran from the balcony and across the workshop. His feet became tangled in a long ribbon, but he quickly recovered and continued running. "Father!" he yelled, wondering where he had gone. "Mother!" he pleaded, but no answer came.

The large doors stood ajar, and Kol had to struggle to push them open. He entered the large entrance hall, finding it also deserted and covered in filth. Rags of torn clothes lay on the floor, the smell of mold wafting from them. What was going on? Leosh would have the entire house strapped for letting it get this bad. She led her troops with an iron fist, where the tiniest speck of dirt was decimated by the whole battalion. The house had been abandoned for months, it seemed. Kol peered closer, looking the rags over. The smell that came from them was wretched, rusted metal mixed along with rot. Kol realized what the bandages had been covered with. He revolted from it and ran for the front door, hoping that someone would be out there. Flickering light could be seen through the stained-glass windows. These lights were not that of Christmas. These were far darker and danced savagely. Kol's hands trembled as he gripped the handle, but he must know what the light was. The latch clicked and he slowly pulled the door open.

Kol stepped outside in a daze, refusing to believe his eyes as he took in the scene. The tree, the great tree his father had planted so long ago to stand for safety and peace was ablaze. The heat from the inferno baked his face, but he could not turn away. The plaza was in rubble, craters that had destroyed the mosaic pattern. The buildings were dark, windows shattered, and booming sounds echoed off them. Somewhere in the city there was fighting. Kol wanted to scream but could not find his voice. He wanted to cry but the tears would not come. Who had done this, who had come into the city and brought war with them? From inside the house a laugh came, the sound so haunting that Kol's knees had could no longer hold him upright. Kol turned to look and saw a dark mass, barely more solid than a shadow walking towards him. It was upon him and he tried to crawl away, but the mass opened its wings wide and converged on him.

******

Kol sat up fast, gasping, then regretted it as his vision swayed. He was back in the camp surrounded by the welcoming wagons. The sun was no longer above them and the stars shone in the winter night. A small fire was blazing before him, one built for warmth and not for cooking. It was a dream. Well, that did not truly describe it. The first part of his dream had been a memory. The second part had no better name than a night-mare, constructed from his own fears of the North Pole's safety.

Kol felt guilty for having the fear. His father preached so hard to accept things not easily understood; that everyone deserved a chance. They horded the secret, protecting it from the outside world. It was for the best, though. It was not the secret of the city that needed protecting: it was those who had come to stay. He could not drop the thought that the fighting that was occurring did not come from the outside. "Sleep well?"

Kol turned to the voice. It was Harvest, lounging on his own blanket. He had changed his clothing and was wearing a pair of kakis and a blue button-up shirt. He was holding a piece of machinery in his hands that Kol could not recognize. He was looking at Kol with a smirk, the type of smirk that came with an inside joke. Kol wondered what it was and then understood. The memory came back to him carried with anger. "She drugged me."

"She did," Harvest told him.

"Why?"

"Because you needed to rest and let your wounds heal," Harvest said simply.

Kol glared at him. "My wounds would heal just fine on their own with or without rest."

"No, the medicine is very specific on rest." Harvest said still smiling, "Just look at your leg."

Kol pulled up his pants leg to look at the damage, noting the fine repair work that closed the hole in the fabric. The light cuts on his leg that had been there before were now a soft pink. They looked as if they had had weeks of healing. He could not feel the searing burn that had been there before, and tensing the muscle he found there was no lack in power of movement. He looked to his arm and it too had the same look, though not as complete as the one on his thigh. The stitches had been removed, and the cut was now a dark scar. A little pain remained, and there was a small amount of stiffness as he rotated his arm, but it dissolved all the worry he had for it slowing him down.

"I would not push that one too much if I were you," Harvest said. He had a screwdriver in hand and was tinkering with the small part. It was probably for his car.

Kol moved his fingers and toes then felt his neck. "So, I've been asleep all day?"

Harvest nodded, and Kol stared at him in disbelief. He had wasted an entire day sleeping when he should have been out looking for Wenn. He could be done with the List and closer to finding the blade if not for them. Kol scanned the camp. "Where is she?" Kol had something very important to tell her.

"Getting you something to eat," Iris said behind him. Kol turned and saw her opening her wagon door and exiting. She walked over to where Kol sat holding something in her arms. She leaned down and placed his jacket in front of him with a plate of food: roast with a side of baked potato and other mixed vegetables.

The smell made his mouth water but he turned up his nose to it regardless. "What makes you think I will eat that after what happened this morning?"

"Yesterday morning," said Harvest nonchalantly.

Kol ignored him, knowing what acknowledgment would do. He had no time for this. Iris's eyes narrowed slightly before she said softly, "The ointment I put on your arm is made from a variety of herbs that accelerate the healing process, as you've already figured out. The patient must sleep or be given a sedative due to both the intense drain of the body and the need to lay absolutely still. After your wounds scabbed naturally, they would slow you in your search."

Kol only stared, though he already knew she was right. He had begun to limp slightly once they had made it to the camp, but he had chosen to ignore it. He would, of course, not let that slow him down, but the facts were hard to dismiss. "That was still no excuse for drugging me. I won't be used, and I'll decide whether or not I can take the pain."

"Will you help us or not?" she said simply.

Kol looked at her confused. "Help you?"

Iris sighed to herself before standing and walking over to the purple blanket. "Yes, we would like you to help us."

Kol still didn't understand. "What do you mean?"

Iris looked to Harvest, who placed his device on the grass along with the screwdriver. He sat upright before speaking. "You remember the considerable number of vampires that chased us from the warehouse?" Kol nodded at him. "Well, that would be the problem. There are not supposed to be so many in one place."

"Maybe it's best we start from the beginning," Iris said, cutting Harvest off.

"Yeah, I think that would be best," Kol said. A full day was long enough to wait for answers, and though he had always been very patient, he could not find it at this moment.

"Well, like I told you, Kol, I am here for the very reason you chased down the vampire." She gestured to the wagons, "Have you ever heard of the circus?"

"Never been, but sure," Kol said.

"Well, I am a part of a festive group of people. But this one is far different from the rest. The people I come from mix themselves with events placed all over the world. The circus, concerts, festivals of all sorts. We do this so that we can protect these large amalgamations of people and find those who are lost and seeking guidance. Both natural and supernatural. " She studied Kol's face before continuing. "During the day we are as we appear at any festival. During the night, however; that's a different story."

"You protect people?" Kol asked.

Iris nodded. "Yes, we protect people, and, as some would say, monsters. From, for lack of a better word, evil. We find those who wish to live a better life and bring them into our circle for rehabilitation."

"So, you kill them if not?" Kol felt unease at the thought.

"Did you not kill the vampires attacking you?" Iris said icily. The new glare she gave Kol was almost enough to bring on guilt, but he discarded it. "We do not kill unless we have to," she continued. "We are people of peace, and always strive to overcome the situations with diplomacy. We know that all life has two sides. We try to help the better part."

"And what about you?" Kol spoke to Harvest, who became intent on his work again. "Are you a part of this circus with her?" Harvest looked up for a brief second before snorting to himself.

"No, Harvest is not from where I am," Iris said. "I met him a few weeks ago in much the same way as he met you. He won't say where he is from, only why he is here."

He looked back to Iris. "So, what is the specific reason? Hunting vampires, you said."

"Yes, to hunt vampires," Harvest said, bored. "The number here is unnatural."

"Unnatural?" Harvest looked up at him, bemused. Kol clarified, "I know of vampires, but have only seen the few who have come to my village and those from last night. So, excuse me for seeming ignorant." The part on his village had been a lie. The only truth was the Cadence occasionally found them among the floating ice in the north.

Harvest nodded, not to make fun but in understanding. "Well, for one, the vampires you saw the other night are not full-fledged vampires." He set his machine part down again and crossed his fingers, leaning on one elbow. "They are still dependent on their host. In fact, only one true vampire was there last night."

"Their master," Kol said.

"Exactly," Harvest continued. "You see, when vampires change a human, the ritual can be done instantly or drawn out. The ritual consists of the human's blood being replaced by a large amount of vampiric blood."

"It's not just a bite?" This was news to Kol.

"No, the bite is necessary to both infect the human with the virus and drain them. This is so the human body will rely on the vampiric blood faster when it is placed inside of them. All this is important so long as the vampire has an instant creation in mind." Harvest took a second before going on. "But, if the vampire wanted to take it slow, he could spoon feed his blood to his disciple after the initial bite. The human begins to become dependent on it for the transformation to finish or they will die. It is an addiction."

"If they are not complete, then how are they so strong? Why the loyalty when they are being pulled along instead of being completed?" Kol asked.

"Well, there are two reasons for that." Harvest held up two fingers and counted them off. "A vampire usually takes the slow route because they want to test the potential of their offspring, mostly out of fear. If the new vampire becomes too strong they could simply kill their master, which has been known to happen. The more blood they have the more vampiric they become. The second is the loyalty. If you hold someone's life in your hand, it makes it really easy to control them."

"So why is what we found different from the usual procedure?" Kol was concentrated on every word, wanting to learn these things.

"Well, usually a vampire will change one human at a time, and it is very straining. They are also very territorial, wanting to have full control of their food supply. In a city that size I would expect no more than two. After the talk last night, this vampire seems to be making more than the customary number."

"Or there could be more than one vampire doing it," Kol said after analyzing what Harvest had told him.

Harvest's eyes brightened. He had not thought of this. "That is a possibility. But the question is why? There is no way a few vampires could maintain that many half-turns, let alone one."

"With so many, would there not be mounds of bodies piling up?"

"We thought of that too, but there seems to be only a person missing every few days and those reports are reposted from all over the state. The group is feeding on one victim at a time." Iris had been listening quietly until now. "Vampires do not need to feed every day; one person every two weeks usually suffices. We must stop them soon. Even though group feeding is keeping the numbers down, it can only exponentially increase from here."

"Iris told me about the blade you're looking for," Harvest noted, "I have a source who knows everything there is to know about the black market of both the modern world and ours. He can find where the blade came from."

"Where is he, then?" Kol demanded.

Harvest went to sounding bored again. "He is currently out of the country. He says that he will be here within a week. Until then we can check on that name with you and you can help us hunt down the half turns."

Iris added quickly, "There are too many for just the two of us to track. If we can find the supplier we can stop the others, but if we continue to take out the young ones their master will just make more."

"So, you want my help in locating the main vampire and stopping him?" Kol crossed his arms in front of him.

"Yes, and we will help you find your person. More eyes and ears is better than just one." She looked back to him. "I gained word that the disturbance here had grown out of hand, so I took the mission and came. Whatever Harvest is here for, it's the same goal. I know that this does not concern you, but if Harvest thinks you capable to help from your actions and I from your words, then you would be a great asset." A small smile crept across her face.

Kol pulled the roast from his fork and tasted it. The salty taste was welcoming and spurred on his hunger even more; he was starving. He stopped mid chew however, realizing that she had smiled because he was eating her food even after she had drugged him. He would not give her more satisfaction in him forgetting what she did, even for a moment, so he continued eating. He once again used his meal to think about what they had offered. Harvest's source would be helpful, there was no way to deny that. He would have the other locations searched before a week was over, but if they all came up empty then he would have nothing left to fall on. With these two looking he as well could get done faster. But that was not the reason he would say yes.

He did not know of this "circus of protectors," but he did not see why she would lie to him. Well, at least tell him as much as she could. As for Harvest, he was still not so sure where his allegiance lay, but his good feeling was still there. People were in trouble, and was that not what he had been preparing for all his life? How could he live with himself looking for his father's attacker knowing that people were mere moments from being harmed? Both of them were here to save these people, and his father would support his decision if he knew. He finished the last bit of potato before setting the plate down. He would find this vampire and put an end to his game.

Kol looked behind him and found his sword laying in the grass. He reached for the sword and brought it in front of him. Looking from Harvest to Iris, Kol said, "You have me."

CHAPTER ELEVEN

Within the Wrapper

The Christmas Tree Kol stood before shone brightly, the only source of light that illuminated the room. It was a small living room: light brown walls with only a few pieces of furniture, deep brown couch with two matching comfy chairs, and a television set on a large dresser full of books. Turning back to the tree, Kol couldn't help but enjoy the simple hanging of baubles and white lights. Sure, the tree was fake, but that really didn't matter. The spirit was just as strong here as any other. It reminded him why he was doing what he was.

Kneeling, Kol looked through the tags of the neatly wrapped gifts: winter blues and shimmering gold with store bought bows of red and white taped on. Bows were attached to the many Christmas themed bags that had been stapled shut. Kol had no doubt the grandchildren who would be receiving them would be struck in awe when they opened them to see what was inside. Kol turned his head slightly and found the soft noise he was listening for coming from deeper within the house. Mr. Wenn and his wife lay peacefully, perhaps dreaming of their coming family who scattered the portraits in the entrance hall. Nodding to himself, he rose from the tree and pulled his List from his bag.

Kol found the correct marker on the displayed map and added his conclusive notes to it. Another house full of simple families readying themselves for the holidays. All but one of the locations of interest within the city had now been investigated. Kol was thankful that Harvest's transportation made this job easier. Iris was helping too by checking on the locations outside of the city limits. Of course, Kol wanted to check each site personally, but seeing how time was not on their side, the logic of providing Iris with the four locations outweighed his stubbornness. If nothing was found, Kol could only hope that Harvest's mentioned source was as good as he said. Tucking the List back into his bag, Kol left the room and made his way down the hall with the photos and out the door. He made sure to lock it behind him.

The Impreza was parked across the street. Kol knew Harvest was waiting within even though he could not see through the tint. Kol removed his sword from his belt as he crossed the yard, stepping carefully over the bicycle and into the street. He heard the car unlock as he touched the passenger door handle and opened it. Placing his sword in first, Kol climbed in and shut the door.

"Well?" Harvest asked. He had his arms crossed in front of him and his eyes closed.

"Nothing," Kol replied, shaking his head. The car came to life and in moments they were speeding down the suburban street.

"How many more in the city?" Harvest downshifted as they took a left at a crossroad. Another street and they would be back on the highway.

"Just one." Harvest nodded and handed Kol a GPS for him to put in the address. Kol entered it, then handed it back to Harvest who gave it a glance and placed it in his pocket.

That's how it had been since Kol made the decision to join them just a few days ago. The first night they had left the camp and returned to the warehouse, looking for any form of clues as to where the vampires had gone. There weren't any—only dust and rubble. The place was not going to be used for any form of meeting again, that was for sure. Why would they risk it? The rest of the night was spent driving through the city looking for anything suspicious. They would park in areas where Harvest had spotted them before and Kol would hit the rooftops in search as Harvest hunted below. Several times they did this and still found nothing. Once Kol believed he saw someone watching him from across a street but whatever it was had gone before he could investigate. When he told Harvest, who was in his other form, he said that there was a scent like wet earth, but no vampire or human. Even listening to the police scanner that Harvest had in his glove box did not help. They were either using more caution in their movements or they simply were not in the city. Harvest believed that it was the latter, and with hardly any experience on the creatures Kol went with that too. A new question was added: where had they gone?

"How did you find them the first time?" Kol had asked, dropping from an emergency ladder.

Harvest shrugged, his crimson eyes scanning the small outlet they stood in next to a parking garage. "Same as you; just so happened to find one and followed. They are quite elusive."

When the sun came up, Harvest turned from looking for their hunting parties to finding their den. This also turned up nothing. There were plenty of abandoned buildings in the city for them to hide and Harvest wanted to check every single one. Kol did not object. The sooner the better, though it would not be so easy because Harvest could not track them in the sun.

"When I'm like that, I'm susceptible to everything they are. Sunlight is the number one weakness," he said when Kol questioned him. "Usually I can catch their scent. The other times I've had to deal with them. Here, though, it's strange; they have no scent."

"A ward could do that," Kol said.

Harvest nodded. "Yeah, I thought of that too, which would mean there may be more involved than we hope to find."

Kol had been surprised when he answered him about his own weakness. He too was at a lack of ability after changing out of his white gear into more casual clothing. White was not the best color when trying to sneak around in a place that was not covered in ice. As they combed a part of the city looking for dens, Kol could not stop himself from asking more questions.

"What else are they susceptible to?" Kol asked as they climbed into a boarded office building. Someone had been here recently, contractors though, attempting to fix up the place in hopes of sell-ing it. "So that I know more about what I'm fighting." He walked after Harvest, stepping over piles of broken sheetrock. From his readings he had a general idea of their weaknesses already, but he wanted to make sure they were accurate.

"Well, other than sunlight, there's not much more that can stop them. Most of the stories heard about them are wrong." Kol nodded: he knew how "off" a tale could become. Harvest went on, considering a small mailing room, "Garlic does nothing except make them angry when they're trying to eat you. A stake through the heart works, but only if you have enough strength to piece their skin, which is as hard as rock. Their entire body is like a suit of armor, really."

Kol grinned. "Glad I was right on that one."

"Best time to catch them is while they are sleeping," Harvest said. "Fire is another, though there needs to be a lot of it. Waving a torch at it won't slow it down."

"I'll stick to my sword," Kol said, gripping his hand tighter on the sheath he was holding. He made sure to keep it in his bag until he was off the street. "What advantages do they have?"

"Strength, for starters," Harvest replied. They had now combed the first floor and made it to the second. Usually they would not talk while searching, wanting the element of surprise, but this building already showed no promise. "They are fast, but there are several other creatures that can easily outpace them. You being able to keep up with one is proof of that." Kol ignored the comment. "The younger ones won't be as strong. They would only be able to lift about three times what they could as a human. A full vampire, however, may start flipping cars to slow you if you're chasing it."

"So, don't let them grab you."

"If they do, they can tear you to pieces." They were standing in a large conference room. "So yeah, stay away from their hands, and, of course, their mouths." Kol nodded, knowing this already but accepting the advice all the same. "I think this one is another failure."

They did not return to the camp after a day's search. When night came again they returned to the same routine as before. Kol would take to the roofs while Harvest was on the ground. There were no disturbances like the first night Kol arrived with the local law enforcement: he had learned from that experience. By the end of the night, they had covered at least a fourth of the buildings closest to the river and still nothing. Kol felt the fatigue dragging his limbs but did not care. Even with no activity, he felt progress was being made. Harvest suggested neither sleep nor returning. Kol was not sure, but he believed Harvest too felt a sort of progress coming. When they grew hungry, they would stop for food at a local grocery store, then hurry back on the trail. Harvest mostly kept to himself, despite Kol's attempts to learn more about him.

"How long have you been doing this?" he had asked.

Harvest glanced at him, scanning Kol's expression, which was vacant, for a moment before replying. "All my life," he said. "And you haven't?"

"In a way, yes, but then again no." Kol knew that this information thing was a barter system. "I grew up knowing about them, reading about them or seeing pictures, but I've seen so few creatures in real life. Where I'm from I help protect the people who live there from outsiders but also from themselves. Very rarely does something come around, but when it does, it typically wants to stay a while. I was never around when they did." Which was true, as his nightly routine back home had only started four months ago. It was then he had decided that he was truly ready, after years of training, for what he planned to do. Harvest only nodded, meaning he was not going to say any more about himself.

The second day was another failure when they started on a more popular part of the city. It was after this that Harvest suggested they start on Kol's problem. Glad to finally be on his own work again, Kol handed Harvest the four addresses within the city. When night came, they continued with their vampire hunt for the first part of the night as Kol suggested, figuring that the residences of the addresses were guaranteed to be asleep. Kol climbed down from the outside of a safety ladder around midnight with no luck again. When he climbed into the car, Harvest showed him a planned route before driving to the first location.

The first house they came to was a one-story home, painted white, and held within a low brick wall. A little stone porch stepped up to the door between two windows. Scotch tape held two white strands of Christmas lights around their frame. Seeing no activity within it or the houses around them, Kol hopped over the wall and walked up to the door. After a quick once over he found a spare key to the house under a small stone elephant next to the door.

He stood in the living room of the home, a small widow in the wall showing the kitchen beside it. Beside the kitchen door was the hallway to the rest of the house. Kol already knew that no threat was here. The living room had a couch and love seat set centered on a television. The Christmas tree sat beside the small fireplace with stockings hanging from it. From the pictures Kol could see a middle-aged couple and a small child who was their daughter. They were all smiling from a boat, possibly out for a day on the lake. Kol had to make absolutely sure, though.

In the kitchen he found a small mess of dishes in the sink, the dozing denizens probably too tired from the day's work to get to them. A newspaper from yesterday sat on the small kitchen table. Next to it was some opened mail, which Kol looked at closely. Wenn was the first name of the husband, as he found on a credit card offer. With this confirmation Kol left the house, but not before checking his List for the little girl's name. He added positive marks on Lucy's name. The Santa Claus picture she had on the fridge had won him over.

The second destination was much in the same mold, though the person living there had slightly less income. It was close to the edge of the city, in a mobile home. The owner was not home when he arrived. The living room had no Christmas decorations, nor did the outside. Though it sounded corny, Kol felt he may have found the right place, but was wrong when he found the shipment papers. This Wenn was a truck driver and was currently on his way South. The man must have constantly worked, and after considering the man's room he found the reason in a photo beside the man's bed. Two boys, one around twelve, the other seven, stood next to a large man wearing a baseball cap. Kol could not resist: he looked up these children, too. One was on the naughty list, and the other was right on the border. He added a few positive marks to them both, making sure they got at least what they needed.

"We're almost to the final stop," Harvest said plainly.

"This one should not take long," Kol told him.

They had ridden north, riding along the interstate mostly until Harvest exited on a ramp, then continued down a winding road. Every few acres a house would be sitting, some decorated in the season, some not. Harvest slowed and turned onto a dirt road, creeping along carefully on the accelerator so as not to make noise. The trees were thicker here, and Kol could no longer see the main road after a minute into it. "We won't be able to go the whole way," Harvest said, slowing to a stop. "Can't risk someone seeing us."

Kol gripped his sword and opened the door. "I don't mind walking." He eased the door closed behind him and continued on foot.

Taking his sword, he placed it where it belonged on his hip, then flexed his arms, enjoying the night. The heat was still intense, but he was starting to adjust. The night made him feel more at home, from both the lack of light and crisp wind. This would usually spur him to run, but he needed to retain any energy he had left. He could easily see; the small bit of moonlight outlined the trees around him, and he wondered how far ahead the destination was. He pulled out his List to check and found the spot a little less than a mile away.

He had no idea what he was going to find at the end of this road, but the sinking feeling was still there: that it would be just like the last. Why would someone who was after his father stay in a place like this? True, whoever it was did not count on someone gaining the blade and using it to track his location, but if he had it could be a trap set for whomever came to investigate. He turned and saw the car disappear behind a set of trees as the road curved around. He was glad to have Harvest and Iris as well. He knew what Harvest could do though he was still something of a mystery. And Iris: he had no idea how she would investigate the other locations, nor how she would react if something turned up. The thought of putting her in harm's way was unsettling, but he chose not to underestimate her. Kol knew not to underestimate anyone.

He hoped the city was holding strong still preparing for Christmas Eve. His mother would be furious with him when he returned, but maybe not after he brought his father back. The North Pole would continue its mission, hoping for a miracle. The factories would be pushing strong, the wrapping process beginning soon, and the List being checked. His new additions should go unnoticed. Slee must have programmed the device to not give him away. He would thank his friend for that later, whenever later came.

Kol had been walking from some time, placing one foot in front of the other, his mind still full of thoughts of home and of the vampires. He almost passed the gravel road on his right but stopped when he saw the small white mailbox. Kol searched up the path that lead to a gated fence constructed between high brick walls. He moved closer and found letters welded across the iron bars, holding him from the mansion sized house he could see in the shadows. Kol could not see any details of the house but the yard was vacant. Kol stepped back to read the gate: "Cindervale."

A feeling of unease crept over him as he looked over the wall. It was easily twice his height and capped with iron points imbedded in the top. A large lock held the gate in front of him closed, the thick linked chain gripping the first two bars to either side. His thoughts from earlier about not finding the culprit behind the attack vanished. The place had the look of something menacing living there. He thought of going back to alert Harvest and bring him along, but he decided it was better for him to go alone. He wanted to find some form of evidence first. Stepping to the side of the gate he judged the distance well, bent his knees, and jumped. His feet landed smoothly between two spikes and he crouched to keep his balance.

Scanning the area quickly he found nothing threatening. The wall continued in a circular style around the house. There may have been one towards the back but from what he could see there was only the one gate. Taking one last look to be sure Kol dropped from the wall and landed, hand on his sword hilt. Still the area was calm, so he slowly moved towards the building. He could see that it was three stories tall, the walls a dark red brick. The graveled driveway circled the front door and wrapped into itself to lead back to the exit. It had double doors painted white, and on either side were five window panes with a short-cropped hedge beneath them. No light came from the windows, but he could see the bars decorating them. There was nothing around the area that needed this kind of work.

Kol pressed his ear to the glass; he could hear nothing moving inside. Ready to move at the slightest sound of danger, he neared the door, pulling his lock picks from his pocket. He knelt to insert the first pick when he stopped. So far, he had not run into any form of alarm with the other places he searched. If this place was so strongly fortified, who would say it was not on the inside? Just for kicks, he tried the handle, which held disappointingly firm. Kol decided to walk the house, careful of the windows. The side of the house was only another row of large windows with the hedge following along. Kol crouched by the hedge until he came to the back of the house. He found another door here, a smaller one that opened into a stone patio with cut firewood piled on it. It too was locked. How dare people secure their homes while they sleep at night.

Kol walked past the firewood then stopped, a small smile creeping across his face. He turned and looked the side of the building over paying more attention to the bars. There was a great deal of space between them. Two support bars held them in their row and bolted them to the window. Walking up to the nearest one, Kol looked into the window to make sure no one would see, through it was too dark for him to tell. Shrugging to himself, he grabbed two of the bars, readied himself, then jumped. He made it to the second floor and pulled himself up. Firming his grip, he repeated the same motion and caught the edge of the shingled roof. One more hoist and he was standing on top.

Kol made his way to the top of the crest and gazed around. He could see the entire yard from where he stood and much of the woods on the outside of the wall. He looked toward the road for the car, but of course the trees blocked his view. Nodding, he turned to find what he had come up here for. The chimney was a square shadow on the edge of the rook closest to the side of the building he had come around. He walked over to it and was glad to find that it was a large size, large enough for a person to fit in. There was only a netted guard on top to keep animals out, which he easily pushed backward. He could not help his smile as he thought of what his father's reaction to this would be.

Reaching into his bag he pulled out a tightly woven rope. He figured that rope tended to come in handy, so he always had some, just in case. He made a loop and secured it around the chimney, careful to double knot it. His father would simply use magic to descend into the many houses he visited, but Kol lacked that specific quality. He could slide, but the way out was also needed. Plus, stealth was still necessary despite the noise he had already made. Stepping up onto the chimney he placed both feet to either side. Gripping the rope in his gloved hands he let the rest fall from his bag down into the dark. Taking a deep, breath Kol took another look into the sky and then dropped in.

The space was cramped, but if his father could manage with his size then so could he. Shaking away the thought he steeled his mind. This was no time for games, though the jokes were too hard to miss. He made his descent slowly, tightening his grip every few meters. Looking down, he could see a faint glow growing. Only a few more seconds and his boots touched the bottom. The hearth opening came to his waist, so he needed to crouch to step out, and he was not expecting the scene he saw. He was glad that no one had started a fire in some time, which was apparent from the old ashes.

It was a living room and a dining hall. He stood in the latter part, three couches circling him. Behind that were a few tables with board games stacked on top of them. To his right was the long dining table, and he counted twenty chairs around it. At the other end was a swinging door, most likely going to the kitchen. A set of double doors was to the left of the ones to the kitchen. The windows were covered by thick curtains, explaining the darkened view from outside. The only light was a faint glow from behind the couch. Thankfully, no one was in here waiting on him, giving him time to take a closer look around, which started to reveal more to him.

The sofas were a dull gray with splotches of color. The splotches were patches of cloth used to cover many holes. The board games sitting on the tables were worn from multiple use and looking over his shoulder he found an ancient looking television. The dining table was also old, chips of wood missing from the edges. The chairs matched—at least, twelve of them did. The others were of a different build entirely. He wondered where the light was coming from, so he stepped closer to a sofa to look over it. Sitting in the corner was a small Christmas tree.

The tree was real, but fragile. Pine needles scattered the floor around it, and open spaces could be seen where branches were missing. The ones that were still attached held homemade ornaments of snowmen, reindeer, painted balls, and snowmen. A star sat on top, making the tip bend slightly to the left. The Christmas lights around it was only a simple strand of white. No presents sat beneath it. Though the spirit was still there, Kol felt bits of sadness come over him. Turning from the tree, he made his way to the kitchen. Not wanting to leave rope trailing behind him he detached his bag and left it on the table. He didn't think anyone would come and mess with it.

The cabinets were old too, some of their doors missing, showing the different stacks of dishes within. It was a simple kitchen complete with all the tools. The odd thing here was the two fridges and deep freeze present. He walked over to one of the fridges and opened it. Inside there was plenty of food, stacks on stacks of plastic containers. He opened the other and found several gallons of milk and orange juice. Shutting it, he exited through the second door into the main hall. He followed it towards what he believed was the entrance hall, passing several closed doors that were locked. His eyes adjusted with the dark again, the small light coming from under the curtains enough to still see. He was correct: he found it barren with only a staircase leading up and another hallway across from him. There was no alarm system next to the door, but he was not going to give up the chance to climb a chimney.

The staircase was large, taking up the entire wall. Kol placed his hand on the polished banister as he made his way to the second floor. The ceiling here stretched to the second floor, the stairs splitting into two hallways. Going with his favorite side he went to the left. It was a simple one, with four doors lining either side. They were painted a light blue that was paled from age. He figured he had to start somewhere so he went with the second door on his left.

The place was illuminated by a little night light sticking from a plug at the door. A single window with the same dark curtains hung here. On either side of the window sat two full sized beds, with small lumps under two blankets of green and blue. Desks were on either side of these with lamps placed on them with dressers beside them. The walls were painted with stars and circles on a field of blue like the doors. Kol slowly closed the door behind him with a soft click. He then turned and went for the stairs. Moments later he was back in the living room and attaching his bag to his belt. Picking up the rope he coiled it as he made his way to the chimney.

"Santa?" a soft voice said behind him.

Kol froze, not expecting someone to have had heard him or followed him. He turned slowly and found the source of the small voice. It was a child, a small boy no more than four standing in onesie pajamas. He had scraggily dirty blond hair and brown sleepy eyes. He had come in through the main hall entrance. He looked at Kol with confusion, and Kol knew why. Calmly he said, "No, I'm not, but you're close."

"Then who are you?" The child would not come away from the door.

Kol saw his slight fear and knelt to one knee. "I am a friend of Santa, one of his helpers."

"What are you doing here?" he asked. "And why do you have a sword?"

"Only checking on everyone, making sure that the List is being written right," Kol told him. He hated to lie but scaring him seemed worse. "My sword is to take care of any monsters in the dark."

"Are there any monster here?" he asked, cringing.

Kol shook his head and laughed softly. "No, you are perfectly safe."

"Am I on the List?" he asked, stepping further into the room.

"What is your name?" Kol asked him, smiling.

The kid thought for a moment before answering, "David, but my friends call me Davie."

"Well, Davie, I'm sure you're on the List. I'll check on my way out, is that okay?" Kol said to him. Davie stood quietly and Kol thought about what he would like. Standing, Kol walked over to a couch and sat down. He gestured for Davie to come over and sit on his knee. He did after a moment's hesitation, and Kol helped him up. "Though I'm not the big man himself, I can stand in for him. Tell me, Davie, what is it you would like for Christmas?"

"Well..." he said, and then Kol saw it, a hint of hope in his eye. "Could I have a family?"

Kol felt it, the sadness hitting him hard. "A family, huh?"

"Yeah, I don't have one anymore." Davie looked at him confused. "Didn't you know that?"

Kol shook his head. "No, I was not told. But Santa knows."

"So can he bring me one?" he asked excitedly.

Kol took a minute to compose his thoughts. "Well, you see, Davie, a family is difficult to move here. Lots of people, you see."

"But he's Santa."

"I know he is, but sometimes..." Then Kol stopped. He could not say it. Who was he to take this away from a child who truly believed? Though he was Santa's son, he had no right to say one way or another. So, he went with this instead, "Have you been a good boy this year?"

"Yes, I have!" he told Kol.

"Well then, we will see what we can do, okay?" Davie nodded rapidly. "Now, it's best you head on up for bed. 'Less you want to be counted naughty."

"Okay, be sure to tell Santa," Davie said, dropping from Kol's knee and starting for the door.

"Oh, one thing, Davie," Kol said.

"Yeah?" He stopped at the door.

"Anyone here named Wenn?"

The boy nodded again. "That's my friend upstairs."

Kol nodded and smiled, "Thank you. Be sure he sends a letter, will you?"

The boy nodded again, "I will. Goodnight, Santa's helper." And he shut the door behind him.

As soon as the door closed, Kol moved quickly to the chimney, gathered his rope, and started to climb. In a matter of minutes, he was back on the roof. Taking his rope and placing it back in his bag, he walked over to the side and lowered himself down to the first window, then down to the next before dropping the rest of the way. He saw a light come on from one of the windows beside him. Feeling motivated he dropped from the second window, landed lightly, then sped across the yard to the fence, clearing it in one leap.

Drums in the Distance

Holly stood with her squad in front of one of the several coffee shops in the Reciprocity District, reading the owner's menu. It was a lovely menu, written beautifully in several assorted colors of chalk on a charcoal board. A regular coffee was only a glint, one of their four-coin currency system, and any additional fluff was only a few additional branches. It was twenty branches to a glint, five glints to a jingle, and three jingles to a wreath. Holly absently fidgeted with the coins in her pocket while finishing the menu and turned her gaze to the coffee shop owner's letter of best services to her customers. The smell from inside the chocolate brown door was intoxicating, and the warmth from the hearth radiated slightly from the large window next to it that held the material for Holly's attention.

The rest of Holly's squad stood nonchalantly around her talking amongst themselves, drums slung on their backs. They waited on their leader who had stepped into the bookstore next door to pick up a personal package there.

"What are you distracted by now, Holly?" That husky voice belonged to Mia, the only other squad mate that was still in training to be a Cadence member. She was the only person Holly knew, the two of them having been assigned to this squad the day before for field experience. They had been training together since they had first arrived at the Island and had quickly become friends. Mia was taller than Holly and had more of an athletic build. Her eyes were a warm brown and the caramel complexion of her face was adorned with a grace of freckles. Her black hair was twisted into a thick braid and pinned behind her head. She smiled down at Holly, waiting for a reply.

"Oh, you know. Anything that I can find to pass the time." Holly then dropped her voice to a whisper, "Is this really what the Cadence do all day?" The rest of the squad was standing as casually as they could, carrying their instruments.

"Sí, I know, training made it seem like constant vigilance was the only option," Mia squinted her eyes at the others, "And here we are, running personal errands. Even after that attack, you would think they would start acting more professional."

Holly's eyes followed a green carriage rolling by, pulled by a brown horse. Sadly, there was nothing on the side of the carriage to examine as it continued down the street. "Maybe to them it's better to enjoy the good times while they have it in case things continue to get worse."

"I don't know how much worse it can get with our king being attacked," Mia said, looking around them to make sure that they were still being ignored. "The paranoia of the people is getting worse every day."

"Don't worry. I'm sure that the Crafted Council is getting closer to solving the issue. They will have Santa back in his workshop in no time." Holly smiled encouragingly up at Mia.

Mia gripped Holly's forearm in thanks. "No lo haré. Gotta believe, don't we?"

Mia turned away and Holly's smile toward her only lingered for a second before dropping. Her eyes scanned the area frantically for a distraction but could not find any, so she had to be irritated now. Holly was not irritated at the street or its shops, the owners or their guests. She was irritated at Kol. Kol, who had taken that nasty blade and vanished off to the Flakes. Kol, who she had brought the item to because giving it to her superiors would only fan the flame of anger towards the Snow People. Kol, who she hoped had given the blade to the Crafted Council, as she had originally intended. Kol, who she was going to punch the moment he decided to show back up again.

Holly had no way to know if Kol had delivered the blade or not. If she asked the Council, she would have to answer. Answer all their questions on why Holly had not just simply brought the blade straight to the Council herself. Why did Prince Nicholas need to see the evidence? He would not be that white clothed vigilante that has been reportedly seen in the city, now, would he? Well, I guess your career is over Holly, thank you for your time. The Major was not fond of secrets among her Cadence.

Holly had tried to write an instant letter to Kol, but the paper had poofed right back into her hand after she had sent it, which meant that Kol was no longer in the city. Holly was sure that if Prince Nicholas had vanished against his will, the city would know about it. Holly was also sure that Kol would at least tell his mother where he had gone, so Mrs. Claus would not worry as much. This gave Holly a sense of peace. If Kol had told his mother, then she would have told the Crafted Council and that was as far as it needed to go. The Prince being away from the city was not unheard of since he used to do so when he was younger.

"Kol," Holly whispered to herself, "wherever you have magicked yourself off to I hope you hurry back with a solution."

"Holly, come on." Mia yelled, marching down the street. "We are continuing our route. Vamonos."

Holly yelped and quickly caught up to her squad. Their squad leader had rejoined them and got the bustle moving again. They had to make it down to the Hearth District before lunch, and thanks to their leader's personal detour, they marched at double time. Holly didn't mind: it was a way to distract herself. The decoration among the street were enough to do that. Holly made sure to reach out and touch every lamp post they passed. She knew Mia was trying to give her a look of exasperation, but Holly ignored it. Pestering Mia was far more enjoyable than pestering Kol. Mia made it too easy. After one last lamp post touch they entered the Hearth District.

Holly switched to drumming her fingers lightly on her drum now. She was not playing any trained beat, just tapping in the rhythm of their steps. It was easy enough to follow. Ta, Tap, Ta, Tap. Holly loved her drum. It was the best part of being in the Cadence. Out of her entire class the music was easiest for her to learn. It was like breathing, natural from the beginning. She could feel a constant flux of rhythm around her. When her hands were idle, her drum was their default station now. As she tapped, the drum would begin to warm to her rhythm. The magic would activate and wait to see if its power was needed. Those of the Cadence would use the drums' standby mode to keep warm during the chilly nights. Ta Tap, Ta Tap, Ta, Ta…p, Ta, Tap, Tap, Tap, Ta, Tap, Tap, Tap, Ta, Tap, Tap, Tap. Holly looked down at her hand, confused. The beat had changed. The generic march her fingers mimicked switched to a more concerning beat. A beat of danger. "Mia," Holly's voice shook slightly and her ears had picked up drum beats in the distance. "Can you hear that too?"

Mia's expression became focused as she listened. "Danger ahead!" she shouted to the squad leader marching beside them.

The squad leader, who was a short trimmed-haired elf with shocking blue eyes snapped his gaze to look over the top of his unit and listen. He picked it up as well and shouted for the squad to form more tightly and make a pace for the drum beats. They had to pass five streets over before they found three other squads and a wreckage that made Holly's blood run cold.

The wreckage was the remains of a recreational building that had been built in a small circular plaza for the children in the surrounding area. They would enjoy their after-school activities here.

The roof had been completely caved in from the center, as if struck from above. Then the remaining walls had been scattered out into the street circling the building. Whatever had done this, and Holly already feared she knew the answer, was gone now. One of the squads there was drumming the beats of warning while the other was shifting through the wreckage. Holly's Squad was ordered to help move the debris for anyone that may have been trapped inside. Mia and Holly sprinted to the closest bit of roof and began to lift it away. They labored hard for fifteen minutes before one of the other squad members gave a yell. They had heard a soft groan somewhere just on the other side of some collapsed wall.

The two debris squads gathered there and formed a plan to move the wall without crushing whoever was underneath. The plan was to have the younger squad lift the wall up and the leaders would use their drums to blast it away. Adrenaline fueling their action, the squads formed ranks and lifted. The strain was almost too much. The leaders had started their rhythms and their drums began to glow a soft green. As soon as the wall was up they finished the beat in unison and a shock wave of sound blasted from their drums. The wall moved exactly as planned, thankfully.

The person who had been trapped was a middle-aged woman with black grey hair, wearing a simple uniform. Fortunately, there was a medical Cadence member among one of the other squads who quickly assessed her condition. The medic, with the help of Holly and Mia, moved the wounded individual safely away from the wreckage. They sat her in a chair that had been brought from one of the nearby houses by another Cadence member. After a few minutes the medic stated the woman was injured but would recover. She was still in shock and would need to be taken to the hospital.

A black all-terrain vehicle came screeching to a halt outside the plaza. The door swung open as Drum Major Eileen Smithson jumped out to assess the scene. The Drum Major waved for the drumming squad to stop playing. She was a woman in her early thirties with deep red hair cut short and in a military style. Her green eyes scanned the scene in an instant and determined all possible scenarios. The Major might have been young, but anyone who would underestimate her for her youth would quickly learn how wrong they were. Her red uniform and boots were no different from the rest of the people she led. Only the emblem on the back of her jacket had the words "Major" stitched over it. The Drum Major was a brilliant tactician, organizer, and motivator.

"Report," she demanded to the squad leaders.

"We've found only one individual in the debris," Holly's squad leader said. "We think…"

The Drum Major held up her hand to stop him. "You've done well, Gray. I'll speak to the woman if she is able. Let's not jump to any conclusions. We are better than that. Facts only." Gray, Holly was glad his name was said again, so she could try to remember it this time. She could not count on Mia every time to remind her who people were. The Drum Major turned to the other two leaders. "The rest of you keep the civilians back. We don't want anyone else to get hurt." Holly looked around quickly and saw that a small crowd had started to emerge to investigate what had happened to their recreational building. The squad leaders nodded in agreement. The two barked orders at their squads, and Gray led the Drum Major to the injured woman. Holly, who was still standing close to the wounded individual, grabbed Mia next to her and stepped aside. The Drum Major gave them a brief nod before kneeling down to speak to the woman. "Everything is going to be okay. Can you understand me?"

"Major! Thank you for getting here so quickly. It all happened so fast." The woman sounded frantic.

The Drum Major gestured for the woman to lower her voice. "Easy. Was there anyone else inside with you?"

"No! It was only me. I came in early to start getting out the equipment." The woman had listened to the Major's gesture at the beginning of her sentence, but her voice started to increase again. Before anyone could stop her she blurted out, "It was a Snowman, Major. It came right through the ceiling and then tried to attack me! It brought the rest of the building down with it before changing back into snow and slithering away on the ground! I was so frightened!"

The woman started to sob into her hands. The Major rubbed the woman's back trying to calm her until the ambulance arrived.

Her eyes watched the crowd and the Cadence around her. Holly looked as well, and her heart sank when she began to read the crowd's expression. They had heard, and it was too late to stop the ripples of fear that reverberated from the whispering crowds.

CHAPTER TWELVE

Festive Exchange

The door opened easily when Kol made it to the car. Tucking his sword in the back seat, he climbed in and shut the door behind him. Harvest watched him, waiting. Kol sighed. "Nothing: another dead end." Harvest eyed Kol for a moment longer before nodding and starting the engine. He shifted into first gear, sliding the rear end of the car around. Kol wondered how he managed to avoid hitting a tree as a cloud of dust filled the road behind them.

The car hit the interstate, the front suspension dipping as they exited the ramp. Kol barely noticed the speed as he had become used to it. He placed his head against his passenger window, cool against his scalp. The sky had become a light purple, meaning the sun was soon to rise. He closed his eyes, feeling the exhaustion from the day of searching. He wanted to keep going, and check the others, but he knew his energy was almost depleted. Hopefully Iris found something to save him some time. Harvest nudged Kol, causing him to open his eyes.

He must have dozed off because the sky was now a light pink. He could see the sun's rays above the trees. The groaning noise pulled his attention to the front: they were at the mouth of the tunnel. The wood stretched to make way for them, as if waking to the morning. Harvest eased the car over the wooden path, turning down the thumping music as they went. A soft wind was swaying the trees back and forth. The soothing motion of the trees and the susurration of the roots as they shifted into the tunnel was strangely calming and mesmerizing.

Harvest parked his car in the usual spot and they exited, Kol almost forgetting his sword. Putting the sheath on his shoulder, he walked with hilt in hand. Harvest was walking ahead of him, and though he did not show any signs of fatigue, Kol figured he too was suffering. A quick rest, then they would head back out. If Harvest would not go, he would walk. Thoughts of his plan stopped abruptly as the aroma of breakfast hit his nose. He noticed his feet had picked up the pace and his stomach began to rumble.

Iris had just finished cooking scrambled eggs, the last item of the prepared feast, as they entered the meadow. She knelt over a large cooking pan. Kol figured she had been back for a while, since they had been gone for almost two days. Behind her was a large wooden table close to the ground, and on it sat a dish of bacon, eggs, and fruit. Iris had also brought out silverware and plates for them, along with glasses and a jug of orange juice. Kol's mouth was watering as he sat down in front of the small fire. Harvest did the same, but laid back in the grass. Iris looked up at them and smiled. "It's about time you two made it back." She placed the pan of eggs on the table. "Come and eat. You look hungry enough."

"More than you think," Kol said. He hardly thought of the first meal she had given him. He moved to the table and sat down with his legs crossed at one end of it. Harvest took a place in the middle, finding a glass of juice. Setting his sword down, Kol had to ask regardless of his hunger, "Did you check all of the locations?"

Iris took a seat at the other end and had begun to butter a biscuit. She glanced up at him and said, "Yeah, I finished early last night." She looked at his plate. "Fix yourself something to eat."

"Any luck?" Kol could not keep the hope from his voice.

Kol knew the answer before she said anything else. Her eyes gave it away as she considered his. "No, I'm sorry to say there was nothing abnormal about the addresses you gave me."

"Nothing with ours either," Harvest said, before starting on his food.

Kol felt a sinking feeling come over him, and he forgot his hunger. The locations were the only thing he had to go on; a simple name an elderly wizard had just so happened to overhear. The blade had been traced here, but now who knew if he had a larger search diameter than just the city? He reached into his bag and pulled out his List, typing in the name. In just the United States, the count was over a thousand, and only for the direct name and without any chances of expanded names. "Kol, we still have Harvest's friend to ask." Kol looked up at her, too lost for words. "Will you please eat something?"

"Sorry, I can't." Kol stood and walked away from the table. "Thank you for your kindness, though."

He was walking towards the lake, removing his jacket as he descended down the slope. The trees were thick, and he had to walk around underbrush before he made it to the edge. He followed it for a while before finding a secluded alcove surrounded by large granite rocks. Laying his jacket down, Kol undressed and pulled shampoo and soap from his bag along with a clean towel. With everything in order, he turned to the water and dove in.

The water was cold, and to anyone else he would appear mad to be bathing outside in December. To him it was refreshing. His head breached the surface, the water streaming down his face, pulling his fatigue away. He knew it was only the shock; fatigue never left that easily. Swimming over to the edge, Kol found a granite bottom to stand on and started to lather his hair in shampoo. His thoughts drifted home despite his avoidance.

His father still lay in that bed, his features suggesting he was moments from awaking, like when Kol used to nudge his shoulder. His mother must have been worried sick. The city had to continue working. It was the only hope they had, praying for a miracle to come just like in the old stories. This was far more severe than any of them, though. The difference before was that his father had always been there to make right what had gone wrong. Kol had to keep searching, but where? The entire idea had become so frustrating. Kol slammed his fist in the water to try to relieve some of his anger.

No trace of anything, and so many people counting on him. They did not know he was here, but they hoped, a hope so strong, and he was that hope. They relied on him and he had nothing for them. Not one single trace of evidence. The only thing he had left to put his own hope on was this person that Harvest knew. That was still only a few days away, more waiting he did not want. The city was more than halfway searched. He would have to suggest searching the center of the city, where it was busier. They had gone through there, but not with a fined toothed comb as they had searched the abandoned warehouses and cargo yards. A change of tact: it would be a good place to hide the other dagger, and he would suggest as much to Harvest.

Then there was the fact of those vampires. Even if he found the other blade, how could he just leave Harvest and Iris? They needed his help; the number that had chased them proved that much. The portal would not reopen until close to Christmas, and he knew his father would come from that bed with all his strength, his spirit afire, and ready to travel. So, he would dedicate that time to helping them. Maybe once he returned he could come back and continue to search for the leader of the vampires. He feared that with no evidence they would have to move, and he could not join them if they did.

Thankfully the day was far cooler than the usual in this climate than previous days. Kol dried off, put on a clean pair of jeans, and lay on a rock to warm in the sun. All his anger had been drained in the water, and he wasn't as tired; only sadness remained. He remained there, eyes closed, listening to the quiet of the woods. Sleep crept up on him quicker than a wolf in the night and just as silently took him under.

He woke to the sound of leaves rustling to his left. His grogginess left instantly as his heart sped, and he raised his hands, preparing his guard. Iris stepped from behind the rock, a look of searching replaced by curiosity as she saw him. Kol recognized it was because of his stance, so he quickly dropped his arms and gave an apologetic smile. She turned her head slightly, regarding him, and gave a small smile. "What are you doing?"

"I felt dirty, so I took a bath." He shrugged.

She glanced at the lake and then scanned him. "In that water? Isn't it cold?"

"Do it all the time back home," he told her. "Clears the senses, washes away fatigue, wakes me up."

"It wakes you up because you're kickstarting hyperthermia." Her voice became stern. "I have a perfectly good camping shower you could use."

"I'll be sure to check it out." He looked down to find he still didn't have a shirt on. Feeling a sensation of foreign embarrassment, he pulled a white t-shirt from his bag and pulled it on. Not wanting to hear any more concern he pulled out a jacket. The fabric was light, so if anything, it would help shield the sun while breathing in the wind.

"You know you shouldn't leave the meadow or the tunnels." So much for the concern, he thought.

"I just wanted to get away for a few minutes," Kol said, pulling on his white boots, always thankful they were practical to wear.

"More like a few hours. You've been gone for four." She walked closer to him and looked up at him. "You also can't enter the Encampment and return as easily. You have to have a whistle from me and know the tune, or else you would not have been able to return for your sword." Kol had not realized that she had brought it, laying it behind the rock as she came around. Iris tossed it towards him.

Kol caught it. "Thank you." He placed it into his bag.

"You're welcome. Now come on back with me." Iris started back before looking over her shoulder and finished, "Please?"

Kol nodded and walked after her, both of them climbing the four or five hills. Iris stopped and pulled the little wooden whistle from a small pouch on her leather belt and blew the sweet tune. Kol was amazed that all he saw in front of him was the continuous wood, but two trees that had grown lushly into one another before pulled away and formed an arch. Beyond it the meadow appeared, the bright wagons pulled cozily around the campfire. Iris stepped inside and Kol followed, feeling that familiar wave of contentment wash over him. The arch broke into the two separate trees and stood as they had before.

Kol stopped and stroked Diligence on the nose as the enormous horse looked up from his grazing, regarding him stoically through a fringed mane. Temperance neighed at him softly. He noticed they had no restraints on them. He smiled and asked, "You're not afraid of them running off while they are gone?"

Iris had walked over to the campfire to warm her hands. "No." There was amusement in her voice. "I've had them both since they were a filly and colt. I've raised them, trained them, and told them everything. They understand me, and I them."

"And they are mates?" Kol left the massive horse to his grazing and stood next to Iris, who was stoking the fire with an iron poker that had detached from the cooking frame. The breakfast had been cleared away already and Kol kicked himself for not being here to help. Hopefully his mother never found out.

"Yes, they had their first colt a year ago. He is with my sister." She replaced the poker and looked up at him, "Would you mind going to town with me? I need to get some groceries."

Kol wanted to ask about her sister but decided not to. "Well, I was hoping to head back to the city."

"Always so stubborn. You don't have a vehicle, and finding a ride this far out will be difficult. You won't make it until sometime late tomorrow." She placed a hand on his arm. "Please come with me."

Kol looked down at her hand, which spread a slow warmth, then into her eyes. She was right, whether he wanted to admit it or not. "So how will we get there? Harvest's car?" He looked around. "Where is he anyways?" Kol had not noticed his absence.

She gestured behind the far-left wagon and Kol saw Harvest laid out on a mattress sitting on a raised wooden frame inside the open flaps of his tent. He was under a thick brown comforter and fast asleep. "I think he might mind if we use it without him." Kol gave a laughed lightly.

Iris looked at him crossly. "How do you think I've been getting around? Taking my horses into traffic?"

"Well, I wondered." She turned and started walking toward the path to the tunnels. Kol followed and they wrapped around the meadow, descending towards Harvest's car. Iris walked past it and into a new tunnel Kol had not seen before. Nestled behind a large oak tree was some form of a vehicle with a brown tarp over it. Iris grabbed the corner and pulled the cover free. Underneath was a gold pickup truck with chrome accessories shining in the afternoon sun.

She opened the driver's door and looked back at him. "Well, get in."

They exited the tunnel a few moments later, the engine a deep roar. She did not drive like Harvest: she took her time, being in no rush. Kol looked over the interior of polished vinyl. The seat was one piece, and the leather was a light brown. "So, this is yours? Do the horses pull it?"

She laughed. "No, it's borrowed from the city. My organization has connections. No one that can help with what we are doing, or know of it, but helpful altogether. I can use it as long as I'm here," she half turned to him, "and as long as it doesn't get destroyed."

Kol nodded. He looked out the window and saw a few houses pass by as they turned on the pavement. Iris reached to her radio and turned it on. Soft rock began to play from the speakers. Kol did not recognize the song, but he liked it. Another noise came and he looked over at Iris who was singing softly. Kol didn't know why but her light singing was compelling. The singer was male, but Kol thought it sounded better coming from Iris. She noticed him watching her halfway through the second song and looked away, a small blush on her cheeks. He also turned away, not wanting to embarrass her anymore. They rode the rest of the way listening to the music in silence.

They entered the town Kol and Harvest always sped through, and Kol took the time to look at it. The main road they were on ran along the edge of the town, and Kol had a perfect view of the area from there. A small cluster of buildings sat against the river that ran through the city. The town was built in a small valley and Kol could see a cement bridge arching over the water. The side they were on had buildings of importance and small businesses. Across the bridge a neighborhood was scattered out along with a large church. The buildings were old and some of them were boarded up, but the small shops seemed to have some business. Each window held an edge of Christmas in it, and his dad appeared frequently, which only reminded him that he was not searching. All the lampposts had light fixtures in the shape of Christmas items attached to them. Iris slowed the truck and pulled into an empty space.

Kol looked the street over. "I don't see a grocery store." He looked at Iris questioningly.

Her face gave it away. "Well, I thought we could take a detour beforehand," she said shyly, stepping out of the truck. Kol glared at her through the glass, and Iris gave him a sideways look. "Would you come on?"

Kol walked beside her in silence as they descended into the town. He thought about remaining that way, but after passing several buildings his curiosity had gotten to him. "So where are we going?"

"The river," she said simply.

Kol saw the sidewalk curved to the right, limiting his view of what was ahead. He looked back behind them and noticed they were the only ones on the path. "What's at the river?"

"Something."

"What's something?" The small stores they passed were all closed as well.

"You don't have to know the details of everything." Kol glared down at her, but she only smiled back. They started to twist back towards the left, and the steepness of the ground began to level out. Kol's ears picked up a faint sound, music intertwined with voices, a lot of voices. Kol began to slow as the street straightened out and the waterfront came into view.

If Kol had to guess, the entire town was down on the river's edge. They were walking down to a park alive with a Christmas festival. The music, "Jingle Bells," was being played by an assortment of elderly men with acoustic instruments. A crowd watched upon them as they played, people singing along and children dancing beneath them. Venues lined the sidewalk that cut the park into two sections, the path leading all the way to the bridge and parallel to the river. Some sold food and candy, toys, and books. Others were stations set up for face painting, arts and crafts, and games for the children to win prizes. Red and green shone everywhere, with tinsel around the stands and draped from the scattered trees. The place was full of joy, and Kol could not help but smile.

Iris had been watching his reaction, and appeared satisfied with it. "Are you still mad at me?"

Kol glanced down at her, his smile still on his face. "I'm not. Come on."

They made their way through the loosely packed crowd. It was easy enough. Everyone was in such a great mood that they politely moved to let them pass, and they returned the favor to others. They had to be careful not to run into the children who sprinted in between the adults' legs playing tag. The sun must have been warm enough for them, since the crowd was lightly dressed. No wind came off of the riverbank, and the trees were scattered enough to let in the warmth. He still glared up at it. Iris noted his grimace and smirked. "Really not a fan of the sun, huh?"

"Honestly, no." Though he was growing used to it, it was nowhere near pleasant. "I love the cold, and the night. Things are quieter then. The world can be seen on your own accord and without the commotion that comes with the workday." It was close to true, though the North didn't run by the sun, or they would hibernate half the year. "People are more at ease when they are safe in their beds. They are at peace."

Iris laughed a little, dodging another child. "Does it get so busy in your village?"

Kol smiled at that. Iris paid attention. "You'd be surprised. We live so far away from any other society, we must be self-sustained. So, farming, carpentry, smithing, things like that." Not another lie. They *were* self-sustaining in the North. To maintain the secret, they couldn't import goods: too much of a chance of discovery. The city was no place to grow crops and maintain livestock by any means due to the cold. Thanks to the combined help of farmers and engineers, and of course a little magic, they had found a system that worked. Kol had only been to one twice, but at least twenty of the mountainous buildings housed enclosed ecosystems.

Walking into one of those giant rooms was like walking onto a large plot of farm land, soil and all. The rooms were so large combines seemed to fit naturally as they harvested the yearly crops. Other floors would hold hundreds of trees lined for an orchard, and in others farm animals roamed for milk, eggs, and eventually meat. The fisheries were also a sight to see as the schools would swim in massive tanks. The system created many jobs, and the people were desperate to have them.

"Sounds like you're living in the Medieval Ages." They had made it to the stage where the elderly men were playing. They were a charming sight and brought joy to anyone's heart. All of them were in their late seventies, wearing fuzzy old Christmas sweaters tucked into khaki pants held by suspenders: one red and one green. The singer was a slender, tall man rasping into his old mic stand, a long white beard reaching to his belt loops. The bassist, guitarist, pianist, and drummer all had more weight from age on them. "They sound really good," she said, as they stood in the crowd watching.

"Well, yes and no. We have modern technology, but you could say we've kept to the old ways." His father wanted it this way, and the citizens their cozy, old fashioned homes surrounding the city. The houses were built strong and hearths warmed their walls, but modern household appliances were there as well: electricity, kitchen tools such as fridges and microwaves. Television for the North Poles news, cooking shows, and movies. Of course, sports were available: hockey was a hit, naturally. Bards filled inns, and artists painted great works, sculptors created masterpieces, pottery, and textiles. There was a large market for their items. "Everyone has their job and they do it well."

"What is your occupation, or do you just run around with swords and fight the occasional monster that comes by?" The sarcasm didn't bother Kol; he enjoyed it. They had left the "Fruit Cakes," the cheerful band, and continued down the venues. "You said your father was a carpenter. Did you take that on as well?" Kol slowed at the mention of his father. On the table in front of them sat carved wooden animals small enough to sit in his hand. Iris picked up a small wooden deer made from pine.

"Your work is well made," Kol told the craftsmen, who was a rough looking gentleman, his thick red beard shaking as he laughed. His father would have admired his skill, and he would have said as much. Iris replaced the deer and smiled at the man.

"Thank you, all made by myself and two sons." His accent was thick. Kol had heard it before in some of the inns. "Care to take that off my hands, miss?"

Iris replied before Kol, "Sorry, I can't right now." She started back on the path, Kol nodded to the man, moved swiftly, then caught back up with her. "I would have got it for you."

"Not needed, Kol, but I thank you. You didn't answer me," Iris persisted.

Right, his occupation. Memories came, then. Ones when he was very young. He was at his father's workbench one spring, just the two of them on a weekend. They had been working on a project for a month now. One large mansion dollhouse, completely furnished, each small item sculpted to perfection. Now, his father could complete something like this in no more than an hour, using magic to control multiple tools at once, and by multiple he meant all of them. When Kol asked why he did not, his father told him he wanted to teach him about carpentry and wood. He also said that he should be able to build a house, and the miniature scale would show as much as a real one, since his father was putting in working plumbing and lighting.

They used both stationary and power tools, starting on the frame of the first floor. After his father showed him how, Kol cut the frames and set them in place. He accidently knocked a wall down which caused his father to laugh and said he had to learn patience, take his time, and look over all the details so nothing would be missed. When it was done, the floors and ceiling were of dark hardwood, the furniture in place, the walls logged and smoothed, and the roof shingled and sparkling in the light. His father then asked him what he wanted to do with it, and that Christmas he had given it to a little girl in the village who had lost the one she had in a house fire. "I worked with my father for a long time. Learning all the skills he could give me. Every day after I finished the school work my mother would give me I would go into his workshop. According to my father, I was a fast learner. That's not what I ended up doing, though."

"Well then, what did you do after that? The suspense is killing me." He gave her a smug look, and let her suffer. Bringing Kol here without telling him! A horn sounded before he could speak. A train drew everyone's attention as it traveled on tracks across the river bridge. The horn blasted again as the engineer saw the festival, and the children cheered and clapped, watching as the graffiti-covered freights clattered by.

The steady ring of the wheels on rail brought Iris his answer. "I also learned how to be blacksmith. By my uncle," he told her.

"So, you're a farrier," she stated. They walked past a food stand and Kol's stomach growled. She heard it because she bought three hotdogs and went to hand him two.

"You don't have to..." Kol started.

"Take them and eat, or I'll make you eat them." Her tone was fierce, almost making Kol do it right then. "Won't want a girl to embarrass you in front of all these people, do you?"

"Like to see you try," he replied, and started to turn.

"Please, Kol." It stopped him and he turned back to her. He saw the softness in her eyes and took the hotdogs. He dressed them in ketchup and mayo, since he was never fond of mustard.

"Thank you," he said. Kol spied an empty park bench down by the river walked toward it. "Let's sit while we eat."

"Okay." As they settled, Kol gazed at the water. The current flowed smoothly and constantly.

"It's powered by a hydro-dam. Two of them several miles upstream. This river was originally two separate ones."

"I'd like to see that before I have to go," he said after swallowing a large mouthful. The taste was heaven, and he finished it quickly.

"Careful, don't choke," she worried him. He shrugged and wiped his mouth on his sleeve. He did not much care for the others scolding him on this, but with Iris watching, he realized he wished he had listened.

"I wasn't technically a farrier since I finished my apprenticeship." Kol told her. Seeing how Iris owned horses, he figured she knew the difference between a farrier and a blacksmith.

Iris squinted at him, "Well, that's an interesting skill to have." Kol smiled and continued his food. The memories of his training drifted to the top of his thoughts.

The great forges had all been a fire in the large underground caverns of the Flakes. The Snow People needed their forge like humans needed food or air. Creating was sustenance for their existence. While the Snow People worked their craft they wore aprons, enchanted to protect them from the flame, though the cold was so strong it hardly went further then the pit, and they had plenty to rebuild themselves with if needed. He had been rather young when his uncle came to the city one night, after the mishap of when Kol was a baby. It had been right around the time that he had learned he could not follow his father's footsteps, and Frosty was only a Snowman to Kol. He knew the story and respected him, but that was it. His father knew about the state of his depression and came up with a plan to help distract him from it.

His uncle and his father sat together one night, heavy in discussion, and after they talked with his mother it was agreed. The next morning Kol woke, dressed, and made his way to the plaza outside where his father had summoned him. His father, mother, and Frosty had been waiting for him before the tree. His father had been smiling at him, though his mother looked concerned. Frosty had no features, but Kol took his posture for stern, with even his black top hat adding to it.

They explained to him that since he had learned more than enough in carpentry, he could learn about metal working out in the Flakes. Once his school work was done during the day, Kol and his father would fly out to the Flakes so that he could learn. Once Kol was familiar with the path he would fly himself there and stay on the weekends in a room built specifically for him. Kol admitted that he was slightly scared of the fifteen-foot giant at the time. Frosty must have sensed his trepidation because he told Kol not to worry, he would be safe, and he would send him home if he did not want to stay there, with his father seconding him.

The first day Frosty had come to greet him at the entrance to his kingdom. Together they descended to the forge. It was cold on the surface, the cold of the wasteland and not the cool beneath the city's protective barriers. Kol had to put on several layers of clothes just to reduce the shivering. Down in the forge it was better: the warmth came from the forges was enough for only one jacket. He was not to be mentored by the Frost King as he donned his apron, but to work with one of the younger journeymen. He worked with Snow Children, not knowing that they even existed before. Frosty later told him how the Snow People brought their children into the world. Kol treated them like he would other children, and after the shyness wore off he began to make friends.

The labor was hard. Kol would work first, gathering all the extra metal from the floor and putting it in a bin to be reused. The rest of the day he would run errands, work the bellows to keep the fire hot, run for more coke to fuel it, and once the day was done he would be left to clean tools and return them to their proper place. By the end of the week he was sore and fatigued. On the nights he slept there he had to make sure his own chores were kept up in his room, such as waking in the night to feed the fire, so he did not freeze.

He pushed himself hard. Kol focused the bellows to not miss a stroke to hinder the flame, carried more coal than he usually did, and he even encouraged the other children to do the same, which they did. Frosty noticed and drew him aside from his giant forge to tell him he was doing well and to keep it up. Months passed, and he no longer became tired or sore as his body grew used to the work. He learned that the North Pole relied on their work and they never knew; most of the metal needed in the city was created here. Frosty said it was best that way. They didn't mind doing, it and one day they would be known, but not quite yet.

When Christmas came that year Frosty gave him a gift. Kol almost cried when he opened the small bundle and found his very own set of tools, including his hammer. He learned how to make nails, screws, and chains. Simple things for him to sharpen his skills. His uncle, as he called him now, told him it was not just physical strength: it took more to forge worthy metal. His mind would control his movement, always steady, no matter the fatigue. The most important thing was his heart, and Kol should channel his emotions; joy, fear, anger, and sadness, into his work.

Kol realized he had grown quiet, and by the position of the sun had been for a little while. "Sorry," he turned to Iris, who turned from the river to look at him. "I finished a few years ago. I had been schooled at home and wanted to attend school with others my age, so my training had become a weekend thing after that. My uncle says I would have been finished a lot sooner if not for that silly education nonsense." Frosty and his dad could not have been prouder. "It was my uncle who taught me. He isn't truly my uncle, but my father and he have been friends forever."

"That's wonderful. Your dad sounds amazing, and your uncle too."

"They are. I hope to one day to make them proud."

Iris looked him in the eye. "The way you think of them and have come all this way… I'm sure they are more than you know." She tugged at his small white bag. He saw the softness had caught her off guard. He didn't mind; only he could pull things out. "So, what about the sword?"

Kol, nodded. "It was the final item I made to finish my apprenticeship." He felt a sense of pride swell up. "My uncle and I forged it from an alloy made from two specific metals. The edge will not dull anytime soon, and it cuts deep in many materials. Of course, some are more stubborn than others." He gave a small laugh. He'd tried to show off his blade to his father in one of their sparring matches, and his father had matched it against his own, stopping Kol's blade cold.

"It is also enchanted," she noted, and she was right. It would not break or rust due to its enchantment.

Kol looked at her curiously, remembering her comment on his clothes. "How did you know it was?"

She blushed slightly. "Well, where I'm from magic is used a lot, and it is also necessary for someone of my trade to be able to spot it. In case a magic user has gone renegade." Kol wanted to question her more on her trade and the people she worked for, but she darted another question out. "So, since your sword is enchanted then you have magic users in your village?"

"My village actually has quite a few wizards and witches. Part of the reason I know all about monsters. They are attracted to power, or so I have been told by my father."

"So," Iris seemed to be choosing her next words carefully. "You took up the sword because you cannot do magic like the others?" Kol's face gave away nothing as he smiled at Iris, but he did not respond. Kol was impressed: she had a talent for piecing information together. No, he could not use magic himself, mainly the abilities that his father possessed. The only bit he had been able to do was his skill with his bell. He touched the case holding the bell, knowing he could never use it like his father could. It is exactly why he took up the sword. If he could not use his father's abilities, he could gain the art of the sword.

"I'm sorry, I hope I didn't offend." Iris put a hand on his knee, looking up at him when he had not responded.

Kol looked to her and sighed. "No, you didn't offend. You are right; I cannot use magic. Like my father, at least." Her gaze never changed but Kol could feel empathy flowing strongly from it. It made Kol want to trust Iris. A brief desire flashed through him to tell her everything, but instead he continued, "He is a great man, full of wonder and adventure. He is very good with a sword, a tradition passed down through our family, you see, and when I was not studying or at the forge I asked him to train me while growing up. He taught me well. Though I have yet to beat him in a spar." An image of him sliding across the ice training room, sword gone and his father laughing, came to him.

"Something you can share then. Perhaps you can best him one day." She tugged at his sleeve. "What about your field gear?"

Kol nodded. "That was a gift from my aunt. She made and enchanted them to go along with my sword after I finished my apprenticeship and my education. They allow me to become lighter when I need to. So, when I'm running with my boots, which are enchanted to help me move faster, the clothes take off the strain my usual weight would give. Same concept when I jump and pull myself up buildings. They also keep me at an ideal temperature if I'm ever in an extremely cold situation. Maybe I should ask my aunt to change it to keep me cooled off in a place like this. Also, resistance to damage, but apparently not as well as I thought after fighting the vampires. My aunt and uncle said I would be great in the town guard and so I made that my goal."

"Well that would explain what Harvest told me about your ability. Let's keep moving," Iris said, standing and stretching her arms. "I want to see the rest." Kol nodded and started on the path with her.

A warm gold filtered the park; the sun was preparing for sleep in a few hours. They stopped to look at more shops, Iris eyeing some paintings done of the small town. This spurred a question: "Who painted your wagons?"

She smiled and moved on. "My sister."

"She's very talented. Where is she?"

Iris gave a sidelong glance. "Back home with the rest of the family."

"They don't do the type of work you do?" Kol did not mean to pry, but if she had learned a few things about him, he wanted to know more of her.

"Not exactly. I'm the only one who took on this profession, though they give aid when they can. I am at a very delicate part of my training, so they cannot help me right now."

Moving around an elderly couple, Kol questioned, "What do you mean?"

"Well," she hesitated a moment, considering whether to tell him. She made eye contact with him then nodded. "For the work we do, we have to be able to overcome anything thrown in our face." Kol looked ahead to see that they were close to the bridge. "We base ourselves strongly on the family; it's all we have in this world. That we promise to each other. Rely on each other for comfort and help, but that can become a weakness." She had noticed the stone bridge too and was examining it. "So, during the last year of our training, we have to live away from our family. No contact, just time to reflect, develop independence, travel and see the country, and above all to firm our reasons for what we do."

"How long have you been away?"

"Ten months." The sadness in her voice could not be missed.

"You miss them, then?" He hoped he was not pushing too hard.

"I do, Kol, very much." She reached up and squeezed his arm. "But I'll see them again soon. Just as you will see yours."

Kol wanted to walk across the bridge so he led Iris to the small ramp and up they went. There were people standing on the structure, watching the water or over the festival. They found a spot at the top and leaned on the railing. Standing over the water, Kol saw the warm gold reflecting off the water. Iris looked with him, enjoying it. "So, do you specialize in medicine?"

She answered, "It's one of the specialties I have. Though I have to know how to hurt just as much as heal."

"So, you can do the other just as well then," Kol stated. She didn't respond, only nodded softly. Before asking something else Kol's ears perked, and he turned his head to the other side of the bridge. He could not see it, but he knew it was coming. "Do you hear that?"

Iris looked around. "Hear what?"

He didn't answer. She would know soon enough. Everyone standing around them must have already. A marching band, from a nearby high school by the looks, was heading down the street towards them. They marched around a street corner, clad in black uniforms and Santa hats. As they played "Dashing Through the Snow," floats followed behind pulled by well-cleaned trucks. The band was on them and passed, the sound of the drums reminding him of home. The floats were from different organizations around the town and schools, built to theme with the season of course. A group of tractors rumbled by, followed by fifteen motorcycle riders. Kol laughed at the fierce looking men wearing green and red vests of wreaths, snowmen, and Christmas trees. Another school band followed, then more attractions.

Kol saw the rear coming and his father sat in a sleigh, waving to the crowd. Of course, the man was only someone asked to be Santa this year, but it tugged at him all the same. He wondered if the man was a Secret, which was possible, but there were people who did not live in the North who carried on the tradition too.

Kol looked at Iris. She was laughing at the parade, trying to catch the thrown candy canes and beads. Smiling, he reached out to Iris and she grabbed his hand in return as the parade finished. The streets became instantly filled with people following the line. The parade was moving down the road closest to the park and naturally everyone had left the venues and games to watch it pass. The merchandise owners began to pack their things and lower their tents. The festival had come to an end, the anticipation for Christmas only continuing to grow.

"Christmas is important to you, isn't it?" Iris was studying Kol, but he kept his face forward.

He had to be careful, yet he nodded to her. "It is." It was all she needed. "I thank you for helping me," Kol told her. They began making their way back to the truck, the warmth of her hand still in his.

"I thank you in return as well." They had made it to the truck, and Iris spun to face Kol. "The way I see it, we all have a common goal. Even Harvest, though he won't say."

Kol saw that she truly believed it, and he could put faith in her. He nodded. "Right." She smiled and gave his hand firm squeeze as they let their hands fall. Kol reached around her and opened the door, helping her inside. She fired up the engine and they were away, soft music once again coming from the speakers. Kol saw buildings become woods and turned to Iris. "Thought we were going to the grocery store?"

Her face once again gave her away. "Well, we were until I remembered that I already had what I needed in my wagon."

"And when did you remember this?" Kol asked. He made his voice sound annoyed. He was not going to admit it, though he believed Iris already knew. He had enjoyed himself. If anything, he had needed it. Not only did the festival excite the children for his father's visit, it empowered him more to see that it happened.

"A few seconds before I asked you to come with me." Kol shook his head and smiled.

CHAPTER THIRTEEN

The Green Smile

When they returned, they found Harvest still asleep. Iris wanted Kol to see the inside of her wagons since he had complimented her sister on her painting skills. Kol remembered his thoughts about the craftsmanship in constructing them and asked her about them. She told him it was a combined effort of her family, adding that it was her father who had made the hinges, axels, and reinforcements. He asked who designed them, and apparently she had. Kol was not surprised. Sadly, before the tour had even begun, Iris told Kol he would not be seeing her bedroom, which was at the front of the wagon train. It was in the wagon painted with the colors of the ocean.

The one in the middle was a small mix between a living area and kitchen. The front of the wagon was a sitting area, with no chairs, but the brown carpet was nice and soft, with plenty of room to stretch out. The walls were lined with three bookshelves and resting in them was everything from books on monsters and magic herbs to classic novels from Europe, America, and even some from Asia. Iris said he could come in and borrow one whenever he pleased, so long as she got it back. The other half had a white tiled floor, oak cabinets, a medium sized fridge, microwave, sink, and stove. They were rarely used: Iris liked to cook by a campfire. The kitchen was only for emergencies and baking. The last wagon was used for stored supplies, she assured him, and Kol believed her as she opened the door and a few brown boxes fell out. Kol helped Iris push the boxes back in before the two of them had to force the wagon door shut again. After the small tour she asked him to help with dinner.

When asked what he would like to make, Kol took two whole chickens from the well-stocked fridge. Iris had a recipe for him to follow, but he ignored it. Waiting for her to leave, Kol opened her cabinet and found a variety of spices. Making sure Iris was busy chopping vegetables outside and kneading bread, he replicated one of his mom's creations. Once he was done marinating the chicken, he found the rotisserie spit and set it above the hot fire. He had mixed up a sauce to pour over it as it turned, and after an hour the skin slowly cracked and turned a delicious gold. Iris dressed the mixed vegetables in a tangy sauce and cooked them in a pan next to the chickens. Once they were done, she went to the kitchen to retrieve the bread she had left to bake, almost catching Kol at work.

The smell had been enough to wake the dead, so Harvest joined them. Stumbling, he pulled a knee-high table from a compartment under the middle wagon, setting it up so they could sit on the grass and eat. Iris tossed dishes, cups, and silverware from the door, wanting to catch Harvest off guard. Harvest and Kol caught every item, including a cup that had to be bounced off a foot, then set them appropriately. Taking the chickens from the fire, Kol slid them onto a serving tray and began to cut them into portions as Iris brought a pitcher of cold brew tea. The three of them settled, and Kol started on the vegetables after filling his plate. The mix was life-giving, the spices delicious, but more importantly it woke his muscles that had grown stiff and replaced energy long lost.

Iris smiled at his reaction. "I mixed some special ingredients. Hope you don't mind this time," Iris said before biting into a piece of chicken.

"Only if you don't mind some of mine," Kol told her. Harvest ignored them, groggy from too much sleep or possibly just not caring. He wolfed it down regardless.

"It tastes wonderful." She took another bite then swallowed. "Where did you get this recipe?"

"My mom," he said, taking some bread. He was once again ashamed of the taste rivaling that of his mother's. "She is the main cook in the town inn back home. Everyone comes during holidays. I often have to help her." Still not so much a lie.

"Well, my regards." They continued in silence, enjoying the food and the sounds of the woods around them.

Once the food was gone, Kol helped clean the dishes and pots as Harvest put the table back and Iris tended to the dying fire. After he was done, the moon was well up. "Ready to go, Harvest?"

"No," Iris replied before Harvest could. Looking from Kol to her, Harvest smiled and took a spot on his blanket before the fire.

"Iris," she had not heard Kol this serious before. He had to be stern on this matter. "I can't waste any time."

She placed another log into the fire and walked over to him. "Kol," she said up to him, "Please, just for tonight, rest. I worry about you and Harvest when you leave."

"What about you? I don't like the idea of you going alone." The words left him, and he knew they were true. She would always leave after them and return beforehand. Each time Kol had felt relieved to see her. He never mentioned it, feeling it was not his place.

"I can handle myself."

"So can I."

"I'm not so sure you can."

Kol stepped closer towards her. "Would you like to find out first hand?"

Iris cocked her head to the side, not backing down. "Don't challenge me." She sounded irritated. "I can close the Encampment where it won't let you out."

Kol took it for a bluff, but he wanted to continue the other matter. "What happens if you do find them? Harvest and I search the city together because it's more efficient, yes. But we also watch out for each other. Who is watching you when you're traveling to these towns or in the woods? What if we can't get to you quick enough?"

Iris was silent for a few moments, and her eyes searched his for something Kol did not know. She turned her gaze from him. "Look," she kept her voice soft, not wanting to anger him. "If I find them, I'll contact Harvest immediately, and wait for the two of you to join me." She glanced back at the fire before turning back to him. "But you have to find time to rest and eat. We will need all our strength when the time comes, I know it. You may be able to ignore it, but I can see your body is tired. So, Kol, if you promise to listen to me about this, I won't put myself at risk without you there. Deal?" Kol only looked at her, not knowing what to say. She took his silence for a no, so she added, "Please?"

Kol only looked at her. He hated himself for it, but he gave in and nodded. She smiled thankfully at him and they went to sit with Harvest at the fire.

"I see she changed your mind," Harvest said.

"I didn't see you standing up to her," Kol retorted.

"Don't need to when I agree. We need rest." He reached into his pocket and pulled out a folded piece of paper, which he opened into a map. Kol couldn't say the same to him: Harvest had been asleep all day. "And we can use this time to sharpen up the plan." He pointed to a few locations. "We've already searched these areas, as much as possible. Seeing how they were at the river, I think they're hiding somewhere on the edge of the city. Plenty of woods for them to hunt if they want to stay hidden."

Kol nodded. "Makes sense. Can they eat animals as well? What about the number when we find them? Can we take on so many?"

"Anything that has a heartbeat and is warm. As for the number, I know I can take them, but with you it'll go easier, and I'd rather not spend all night on it." Harvest didn't even look up as he said it. Kol let it roll over him. Kol believed he found good humor in it, so who was he to deny him his joy, even if the jibes were so bland.

He thought back to the spiked haired boy, his face an expression of human fear, as he landed on him with his sword. "Can they be saved?"

Iris looked at him, and was sympathetic when she spoke, "No, Kol: the only way is to catch them extremely early on, and even after that their bodies will be drawn to it like an addiction. It's like a high to them. The ones you spoke of have gone too far, and must either find a place for themselves in the world after finishing the transformation or be stopped as a monster. There is no cure."

Kol nodded; he understood. "So, reasoning?"

Iris nodded. "Yes, that is what I will do. We have a place for them if they want it and work hard for it. If not, and they want to live a life of bloodlust, then there is no other option."

"I will kill them if they try for my life. Looking at me counts," Harvest said, bored, and scratched some words in a small notebook that he kept in his pocket. Kol agreed, though he would want to try to reason if he could. "Iris, I see you're making progress southwest. I'd suggest continuing clockwise, same as us, so we don't leave any stones unturned." Kol glanced over the map and saw that Harvest had placed her just ahead of them outside the city. The idea was to catch anything fleeing as they drew closer, but Kol also found comfort that they had the quickest route to Iris if needed. Harvest was looking out for her as well, though Kol knew he would never admit it.

They finished going over the map, and Iris decided she was going to sleep. Kol denied from her anything he could use for bedding. She seemed distraught at this, but let it go. She had one victory for the day: best she did not try for another. He walked over to the tree line and pulled a hammock and thick blanket from his bag. Securing the knots, he climbed in, hearing Harvest hit the mattress in his tent with a grunt. Kol wondered why, since he had slept all day. The hammock was tied far enough that Kol was almost horizontal, and after finding a comfortable spot he settled his gaze on the stars to distract from his thoughts.

This was the first time he had slept willingly in the Encampment, and he had to admit it was comforting and peaceful. There was nothing wrong with the frequent naps in the passenger seat of Harvest's car. Diligence nuzzled him with his nose. Kol laughed, patting him before the horse went back to Temperance. Seconds later he was asleep. He was awakened by Harvest. Iris had already left, and they were to head to the city. Kol realized that he had slept dreamlessly through the day. Thankful for that, Kol quickly donned his gear and they left.

The view from on top the bank they stood on top of was amazing. Kol could see over the smaller buildings along the river. He believed the water was far larger than upstream. Maybe more rivers emptied into it. He would look on his map when next he had time. Kol looked up at the three spinning spotlights Harvest had noticed coming in. They led down to a well-developed part of the city. Harvest had called it the River Front. These were where the popular clubs and restaurants were found. Tall hotels with glowing roofs, red and green of course. It was the place the young and foolish went to enjoy themselves, and tomorrow they would journey there as well to hopefully gain a lead on the dagger.

Harvest appeared beside him, his skin pale stone and eyes filled with blood. He made no noise coming through the roof hatch, but Kol had sensed him approaching. He could not explain how, and yet he did. The only thing he could figure was that it was their honed teamwork forced on by their combined desperation. Still, this did not seem enough of an explanation, but he was thankful for it. "Find anything inside?" he asked Harvest. While searching the building, Kol had waited on the roof as a lookout and to watch for anyone fleeing.

Harvest shook his head. "Another dead end." He placed an object back into his coat. Kol knew it was a magical device Harvest had showed him that disabled any simple electronic alarms.

Kol scanned the city, his eyes falling on the center building. Standing many stories above the others, the structure was impressive for the city. Stationary spotlights illuminated all four sides of the building. The original color was white, so when the red and green hit it, the building shown powerfully. He could always see it several kilometers off when coming on the interstate. "We haven't checked that building yet," Kol nodded to it. The suspicion with which Kol looked at it made the red side of the building seem like blood.

Harvest followed his gaze. "You're right, we haven't."

"Would be like hiding in plain sight." Several of the office lights were on. "Though it appears normal all night."

"It's definitely worth looking into. For now, though, let's maintain our search pattern so we don't miss anything." He took a step and dropped from the ledge and Kol followed after, his gear slowing his fall. He landed softly, his boots never making a sound, and walked over to the car parked down an alley way. Harvest floored it, and they made their way to another location. This area was completely searched, and they had enough light left for one more location.

Harvest parked on the road, not having any alleys to pull into. Kol helped him with the tarp to keep away unwanted attention. Once secure they continued in their usual scouting fashion, with one of them on the ground and the other along the roofs. They moved several blocks, nothing catching their interest. At least they were moving quickly: the section was almost complete. Kol stopped abruptly on slanted tin, he had heard someone scream. He whistled to Harvest, the sound meaning "follow," and they raced a few blocks over.

The yelling became louder. Kol could easily hear "help" echoing from down an alley. Harvest whistled for his attention and pointed to the source. Kol made it to one of the buildings and dashed for the far exit; Harvest would hold the other side. Looking down into the dark, he could see two individuals. One was holding the other by his jacket. Kol dropped in, sword unsheathed as he fell. "Pleasant night," he said.

The reaction was expected. The man released the other's jacket. "Who are ya? You don't want none of this."

"Just going to do as you please with someone else, huh?" Kol asked. "Now that's not right, especially for this time of year. Tis the season, after all."

"Matter don't concern ya. So leave or I'll get ya next." His speech was slurred, and Kol smelled the alcohol. A large knife was in his hands. He smiled though, and the man looked at him, confused. A hand fell on the robber's shoulder. It was clear the knife wielder was no vampire now. Unfortunately for him, right then Harvest was. He spun the man around and grabbed him by the throat. He did not squeeze, only held and lifted. The man was dumbstruck, unable to believe what was occurring. Harvest opened his mouth, displaying his fangs, and then let out the blood curdling scream vampires made. The man began to scream and cry, frantically thrashing his body to get free and dropping the knife. Harvest tossed him down the alley where he stumbled over himself before catching his feet and running.

"Best you leave as well," Kol said to the other man, who nodded and crawled past Harvest before he too could run. His disbelief was no less than his assailant. "Horrifying," he told Harvest.

"Let's get back on the searching," was all he said.

Dawn was an hour away, the sky turning a dark purple. They had searched the next set of buildings, once again finding nothing. The robber had been their only entertainment. Kol hated they had nothing again, but the following night they were going to talk to Harvest's friend. His stomach growled, and he hoped Iris had breakfast going. Kol could already smell it when he bumped into Harvest. Looking past curiously, Kol saw someone standing next to Harvest's car. The tarp was thrown off, and Kol heard a deep growl come from Harvest. The figure heard, though at that distance he did not know how, and bolted down the street.

Harvest was after him instantly, Kol not too far behind. The figure turned onto another street, they barely saw him do it. This did not deter them. Kol pushed himself as hard as he could. Noise came from above their heads and dust fell on them. The person had just vanished around the small restaurant they were beside, but it was impossible for whoever it was to get up there so fast. Harvest hit the wall regardless, clawing his way up the side of it. More rubble fell as his fingers easily imbedded in the brick. The "leaving no trace" speech that Harvest had given him day one seemed to not apply to him. Kol scanned the grey building but found nothing he could use to climb the two stories. He dashed down the side of the building, listening for Harvest's screeching and cursing to lead him in the right direction. He was angry, and Kol hoped he did not kill the creature when he caught it. They needed answers.

Kol lost count of how many buildings he had turned down and the several streets he had crossed. Sprinting across a new one he was blinded from his right, instinct causing him to leap into the air and roll over the top of the small car. The driver yelled but Kol was already a blur into the night. An emergency ladder appeared in front of him, and he made for the exterior casing. He climbed hastily, hoping to make it on top of the third floor before Harvest was out of sight. He put his hand on the ledge, hoisted, and his face came centimeters from a smiling mask. The person had flipped from the adjacent building and laughed as his momentum pulled his body away. It was pure hysteria as he sped on. Kol finished his climb to pursue.

Harvest landed next to him the moment he was upright, and they chased after the strange figure. Several buildings in front of them were built together, just like so many others in the city, the roofs only differing by a meter or a little more. This was a blessing, and Kol became more motivated because they were gaining on the laughing mask. Watching his footwork, Kol stayed alert for any incoming turns. The person seemed to be skipping. A few more yards though, and he could use his bell. The yards never came. Instead they went as the figure lightly stepped onto the ledge and leaped across a space far greater than Kol or Harvest could, feeling the air with sounds of pure enjoyment.

They both came sliding to a halt. Kol was panting, looking at the masked man standing on the building opposite them. The sun had breached the horizon, but not enough to see what the man was wearing. His mask was a bright green color, though, the smiling features crudely drawn in white. Harvest went to leap down, but Kol grabbed his arm. Smoke was beginning to rise from inside Harvest's clothes along with his hands and face. It was a warning sign of coming day. Harvest glanced down then back at the green smile. Taking a deep breath, Harvest gave one more screech of rage before pulling his right fang from his mouth. The screech became a yell as his skin regained color and the blue came out in his eyes.

The person was done observing them, so he gave a delighted laugh and leaped beneath them and landed on the street. Harvest made to move again but Kol gripped his arm tighter. He stepped to follow himself but the figure dropped to his belly and slid into a storm drain. Kol dropped and landed by the hole, too small for him to fit, and somewhere inside a whistling tune was growing fainter. "Really!" Kol heard Harvest cry, and after looking turned the direction he was looking. The car was only a few meters away. The Green Smile had been playing with them.

Kol waited beside the car as Harvest found a way down from the roof. He waved at a passing car, not caring about his sword on his hip when his partner appeared on the street moments later. Harvest walked passed him and climbed into the driver's seat. Kol barely had time to get in himself along with the car cover before the car shot forward. Other cars were crowding the street, but Harvest weaved around them. It wasn't until they were back on the interstate that Harvest spoke. "Touched my car."

Kol smiled. "How dare he." He had to admit, them ending back where they started had been humorous.

He must not have heard Kol. "When I catch him, I'll drag him behind it, then he can see it all he wants."

Kol only shook his head. Harvest, who rarely showed emotion, did so only in concern with his car. Kol made a mental note of that as well, in case he needed it for later. He decided to try discussing who or what the person was. "Have you ever seen anyone clear such a distance?"

Harvest shook his head, "No, and I couldn't get a scent, either. At least not anything that would give him away. All I got was earth, which only says he needed a bath."

Kol nodded, "Well, no vampire, but I'm not going to ignore it. The two could be connected." Another oddity came to him. "The sewers? Could vampires be there as well?"

Harvest shrugged and shifted gears as they entered the freeway. The car seemed to be feeding off his mood, the engine roaring with as much anger as Harvest held. "It's possible, but usually vampires are prideful and wouldn't stoop to that. New ones, on the other hand…" He left the rest for Kol to figure. "We will check it out regardless." Nodding, Kol turned to look out his window, away from the blinding sun.

CHAPTER FOURTEEN

Colorful Breakthrough

Parking in the Encampment, Harvest's walk seemed less hostile, but anger was still there. "Find anything?" Iris's voice called from inside one of her wagons. She peeked her head out. Harvest ignored her and went straight for his bed. She raised an eyebrow at Kol, who came up moments behind him as Harvest landed on the mattress.

"Nothing all night, but when we returned to the car there was someone there." Kol walked over to his blanket by the fire. "We chased, but he got away." Lowering his voice, he added, "Sun came up."

"One of them?" Iris asked, sitting down next to him. She handed Kol a large bowl of oatmeal he accepted graciously.

He shook his head, placing a spoonful in his mouth. "Don't know. According to Harvest, he didn't even have a scent."

"No, I said he smelled like dirt," yelled Harvest.

Iris smiled and nodded in agreement, stifling laughter. "What did he look like?"

"Couldn't tell, wore a mask. Bright green with a simple smiling face." Kol used his finger to show the size of it. "Didn't stop there, he added his own laughter to the image, before disappearing in a sewer." Kol yawned. "Only got away because he could clear a four-lane street, with sidewalks, mind you."

"A laughing sewer diver?" Iris shook her head in disbelief, still holding back her own laughter. "So insane."

"When he was done playing with us, he left. We ended up back at the car." That did it, Iris lost it, causing Harvest to become angry again and yell at them to be silent.

After breakfast Kol decided to bathe, asking Iris for the location of her camping shower. Once he had cleaned up, he packed away his things, pulled on shorts and a shirt then returned to the camp. Iris was gone, probably asleep in her wagon. Kol headed for his hammock, deciding he needed to do the same. It was not an easy sleep, as he woke up several times to the sun in his face. The last time he woke was to a different sun in the form of Iris walking towards him, wearing orange pajama bottoms and a yellow shirt. As she approached, she put a hand on his chest and placed a plate on his lap while keeping one for herself. On it was a sandwich and sliced apples. "Thanks," he said. He definitely had not had enough rest.

"No problem. I figured if I don't feed you then you will die." She took a seat against one of the trees his hammock was tied to, placing her own plate on her lap. "This thing can't be comfortable."

"I like it," Kol said, taking a bite of sandwich.

She sighed. "Whatever you say." She popped a slice into her mouth. "Ready for tonight?"

"As much as I can be." Kol didn't want to think about what would happen if he did not gain any useful information.

"Don't worry," she said. "We will find something." She smiled up at him. "Besides, we are going to a club, so we can loosen up a little."

He had never been to one, so the familiar curiosity mixed with a little fear welled in his stomach. "Yeah, I would imagine so." He forced the rest of his sandwich and apple, losing his appetite from nervousness.

Kol did not believe Iris had noticed, and he got off his hammock and snatched her empty plate from her. She complained that she could get it but Kol ignored her and went to the kitchen to wash them. She glared at him from the doorway, but made no move to stop him. "Guess I'll go get a shower and get ready."

Kol looked over to her. "It's only the afternoon. We're not leaving until later tonight." The next look she gave made Kol's thoughts hesitate. She did not reply, but only walked away from the door. What had he said? Placing the plates where they belonged, Kol went back to his hammock and tried to rest a little longer. He ended up just laying with his eyes closed, thoughts racing in all directions. He must have dozed or skipped forward in time an hour or so because he opened his eyes and found night had set in, where moments ago the sun was still shining.

"Don't have to dress too fancy tonight," Harvest called to him. He wore faded jeans and was drying his head with a towel.

"Why is that?" Kol really did not care.

Harvest smiled at him. "You'll see: don't want to ruin good clothes." Kol wanted to ask how they'd get ruined, but knew Harvest would not say. He pulled on a pair of jeans and a black shirt, thinking it was fine enough. Lacing up his boots, he walked to the fire to join Harvest, who was now wearing a red shirt with a car brand on it Kol did not know and a leather jacket. "Really don't get cold, do you?"

"No," Kol replied shortly.

"Let's go, Iris," Harvest shouted. Nothing happened. Harvest looked slightly annoyed. "We are already late," he said to Kol. "I did that on purpose."

Kol glared at him. He hated being late. Pushing past Harvest, Kol walked up to the first wagon and knocked on the door. He heard movement, and it opened. Iris stepped out wearing jeans that fit close to her legs and a grey laced shirt. Her hair was straight. Kol was used to it being wavy, but thought this looked good, too. Her wrist carried the usual assortment of bracelets, and around her neck was a necklace of golden rings, more than five, he noticed. She smiled down at him, and he had not realized she had spoken.

"Huh?" he said stupidly,

"We ready?" Iris repeated. Her knowing smile made Kol forget to answer for a moment.

Harvest answered instead, impatiently, "Waiting on you." Reaching into her wagon, she pulled a fine cut black jacket and threw it on. She brushed past him, her flats ringing on the wooden wagon steps.

Harvest turned over the car once they were all in. His rage had appeared to pass and the gentle ease of the car added to his serenity. Harvest turned up his stereo, the hard bass sound pouring from the doors and rear. Kol looked in his rear-view mirror and saw Iris behind him. She caught him staring and he quickly looked away. Harvest sped through the small town, and soon after onto the interstate. Kol wondered why they had not seen a cop try and pull them over the entire time he had road with Harvest. He had a feeling that if a cop did flag them, Harvest would not be pulling over. It was odd, coming to the city and not searching tonight. Odder still, Iris was with them. She preferred to go solo, usually, but he was glad she came tonight.

Hitting the exit ramp, Harvest slowed the car. Kol glanced at the driver, finding his going slow unsettling. "Need to blend in tonight," he said tartly, not looking away from the windshield. Kol looked up through the window and found the spotlights from the night before. They grew larger as they approached, and Harvest turned down a street that was brightly lit. In the rest of the city, it was rare to see vehicles moving about or even more people. Not in this part of the city. This was where the people who could not sleep came. As they moved down the street they passed several expensive-looking cars. The sidewalks were busy, everyone heading to a party judging by the way they were dressed.

He noticed something more. Everyone they passed was looking at them. "Blend in, huh?" he asked Harvest. Harvest simply revved the engine, drawing more eyes to them. Iris laughed behind him and Kol nodded his head—Harvest couldn't resist.

Harvest pulled into a parking garage and drove to the top and parked. They used the elevator to return to the ground level, another oddity. Kol figured why, since they were acting normal: well, at least Harvest and he were. He had no idea what Iris did in the field. Wasn't so bad, though. Kol thought of it as taking a different direction than usual.

"So, where is this place?" Iris asked.

"Not too far; I parked close for a reason." He flashed a wicked smile, rare for him.

Harvest led them down another road, passing bars and restaurants full of people. One had a band playing inside, causing Iris to slow for a few seconds. Kol laughed at her and she glared back at him playfully. Kol inspected his surroundings more closely. Besides the street lamp ornaments, Christmas did not belong here. Harvest continued to lead them on, the people in front of him moving out of his way. He wondered what would happen if they didn't move. Remembering the robber, he grinned. People would definitely talk. Finally, Harvest halted in front of a building. They had made it to the club.

From the outside, "Revs' Hold" did not have much to it. The neon sign shone white above a large metal door surrounded by brick. No windows let anyone see what was inside, and no sound came either. A bouncer stood at the front door, large, bald headed, and sporting a collared shirt with the club's name. A line of people ran to the right of the building, standing between the building and a velvet rope. At a glance Kol figure they had been standing there for a few minutes. "Guess we have to wait," Iris said.

Harvest laughed sarcastically and walked up to the bouncer. After a few quick words the two were laughing. Kol couldn't hear what all was said, but the bouncer appeared to agree with Harvest and stepped to the side to let them in. Shouts started from the line, but Kol ignored them and followed Harvest into a red hallway. The bouncer shut the door behind them, enclosing them in the hallway. He felt Iris up against him, as the hallway was tiny. A window opened to their right and a voice called, "Mr. Harvest, The Rev is currently busy. He asks that you please enjoy yourself inside until he calls for you."

"Thank you, we shall," Harvest replied. The window slammed shut, and they were once again closed off in the quiet hall. The sound of metal sliding filled the room and Kol looked over to see that the door in front of them had a locking system. Multiple pulleys and gears moved in synchronization. The well-oiled machine unlatched from its frame smoothly. A soft click finished the process and the door slowly began to open.

The sound hit them instantly, the bass so strong Kol felt his clothes vibrate with it. It was the same type of music Harvest listened to. Harvest stepped into the room and stepped aside to let Kol and Iris enter. Darkness and color was the simplest way Kol could describe the vast room. They stood on a blue glowing walkway above the dance floor beneath them. At least, Kol believed there was a dance floor, but he could not see it for the amount of people on it. The DJ sat on a large platform above the crowd, the music and lights flowing with his rhythms. He was decked in a multitude of neon ribbons, one even covering his eyes. Three circular platforms ran the center of the floor, and three dancers garbed in neon circled to the beat, the floor beneath them changing colors along with the hanging lights. The catwalk they stood on ran the length of the room, the stairs leading to the pit on the opposite wall. One second the room was pitch black, the next lasers streaked the walls and strobe lights cropped the people's movements. The people dancing were also colored, splattered in a rainbow of neon. Tonight, the club was a paint party. Kol spotted several stations where the dancers could paint themselves near bright sitting tables and couches.

Iris and he had been observing the room, so they did not see Harvest walk away. He stood by the bar, which was located on the same level as the entrance. The catwalk was larger here with a platform in front of the bar made to hold several tables and stools for relaxing. Two bartenders manned the drinks, a dark wood top set onto a solid panel of light. The color of the bar and both the structure and shelves shifted with the beat of the song. They joined Harvest, though he was busy talking to the female bartender with short blonde hair. She smiled at Harvest and a few moments later Harvest was sipping on some clear liquid. He offered it to Kol, who denied it with a wave. Iris took a sip of it before returning it back to Harvest. It didn't bother him if they were drinking, it just wasn't his thing.

The song had changed, the dancers all moving on the same vibe. Iris walked to the handrails and peered over watching them with interest. Harvest took a seat at the bar, motioned for Kol to join him. He yelled something to Kol, but the music was too loud to hear. He smiled and nodded, watching a few more people come into the entrance. Harvest had turned his attention to a brown-headed girl when Kol looked back. Not wanting to interrupt him from his new friend, Kol looked to the railing and found Iris had vanished. He tapped Harvest and pointed. Annoyed, Harvest shrugged and turned back to his new friend. Kol walked over to the handrail. Iris had folded her jacket and laid it here. Kol scanned the catwalk in a glance then examined the dance floor. The crowd was swaying in unison, some people alone others with couples. It did not take him long to find her.

Iris was standing in a cleared spot, dancing along with the music. The way she moved made the professionals on the stages look plain. Kol could not help but look, and when Iris glanced up and saw him, she didn't stop moving. She had found one of the glow stations and had painted pink, blue, and green on herself. Under her eyes she had two streaks, reminding Kol of a sort of war paint, her arms caressed in swirls. She shone, to Kol's eyes, brighter than any other. A few guys tried to come up and dance with her, but she quickly turned away from them, shaking her head. Kol felt a flash of anger seeing guys come up to her. He didn't know why, and before he could figure it out, he felt a tap on his shoulder. Harvest was standing next to him looking down on the dance floor, too. The brown headed girl was trying to grab his attention, but Harvest nudged her away without even looking. He gave Kol a hard look, then pointed down to Iris. Kol understood and removed his own jacket and started for the stairs, not knowing what was pushing him along.

Iris had moved to the center of the floor. Kol had to carefully move a few individuals who were lost in themselves. Iris saw him coming and smiled. She turned gracefully and Kol found her in his arms. The song changed, and they began to dance. Kol had no idea what he was doing. His body seemed to be moving on its own, so he let go and let the music fuel him. Dancing with Iris felt natural. She would turn and smile up at him and he could not help but return it. Kol took a quick glance up and saw Harvest watching. He smiled and nodded, raising his new glass to them. Only a moment though, and Kol was swept back under the tide.

The song ended far too soon and Kol did not know how many they had danced through. Iris stepped away from him but held his hand. She pulled him though the crowd and over to one of the glow paint tables against the wall. She gestured for him to stand still while she poured paint on to her right hand. His arms already had small bits of paint on them from Iris, but he didn't object when she turned back to him. Reaching up slowly, Kol noticed her hand was unsteady. She placed her hand on his left cheek, holding it there. The moment she touched him the world vanished. The dancers gone, the music gone, the lights gone. He only saw Iris, and she only saw him. He reached up and put his hand over hers, energy pulsed from it. He started to lean towards her, and she him. Kol could see that she wanted to as much as he did by looking in her eyes.

A hand reached out and gripped his shoulder, bringing him back to reality. He shrugged it away, wanting to act like it didn't happen, but Iris had pulled away, blushing hard. The moment, whatever it was, had passed. Slowly he turned and found a new bouncer looking at him. Kol wanted to hit him. The bouncer gestured for them to follow him, and Kol looked to Harvest who was glaring at the bouncer, but he nodded down to them. It was finally time.

They ascended the stairs, Harvest joining them by the bar. No words needed to be said between Kol and Harvest as he handed Kol his jacket. Harvest patted him on the shoulder when Iris was looking down towards the dance floor again. Iris picked up her jacket and threw it on as they walked. The bouncer led them over to a wall and looked back to the bartenders. The short blond haired one nodded and reached down below the bar. It must have been to press a button because the wall in front of them folded away and the bouncer walked in. They followed him, the hidden door closing behind them.

An entrance with sliding locks and hidden door, what else did this fun house hold? Kol was excited to find out. They had walked down a hallway, backlights illuminating their way, the music muffled behind them. Kol looked to Iris who glowed from the effects. He smiled at her and she looked away, but couldn't hide her own smile. They walked into a set of stairs and quickly made their way up. The top let out into a circular room with two large wooden doors and couches lining the wall. The bouncer turned to them, and Kol continued to glare at him. "The Reverend will see you now." With that, he left back the way they came. Harvest walked across the room and pulled both doors open, and Kol and Iris followed.

Kol had to squint to shield his eyes. The backlight hall and club had his eyes tuned for dark, but this room was complete opposite. It was a long rectangular structure, and Kol could not help but notice how clean it was. The floor was a dark stained wood, the same color as the entrance doors. Their images reflected back at them almost perfectly. It was the only dark color in the room because the rest was white. The walls held intricate designs in the faintest of grays: mountains wrapped in a shrill wind set during the night, with a clouded moon. Stiff leather sofas lined both walls at the back of the room and a small glass bar was set to their right with a small lounge to the left facing a large television. The back wall was completely glass, the multiple lights indicating it overlooked the club. A large desk sat before it, made of marble. Two lions were carved on either side to hold up the glass top and in between them was a symbol Kol did not recognize. A brown leather chair was turned towards the glass, no doubt Harvest's informant. The bright light and cleanness made Kol think of the paint that was on his face, arms, and clothes. A glance at Iris assured Kol she was feeling the same way.

"Don't worry about it." The voice had to be the Reverend's, though he still faced away from them. "I am glad you enjoyed my establishment." The Reverend was no religious man: he gained his name from the vast knowledge he had obtained from his years in dealings with monsters both supernatural and human. Yet when he turned around, Kol would not be able to say that about him. The Reverend was young, and Kol put him at only a few years older than they themselves were. Kol always looked into the eyes of the people he talked to or met, but with the Reverend he could not. He wore large white sunglasses, matching the white robe he wore as well. He had his brown hair cut short and the bangs spiked slightly. His fingers were crossed on top of his desk, and on his right hand he wore a silver ring made into the likeness of a lion's head. Despite this display of mystery, the Reverend had no aura of intimidation, and his small smile completely welcoming and joyful.

"I wouldn't want to be rude," Kol told him.

The Reverend continued to smile. "They are just things," he assured him, standing from his chair. "Harvest, how good it is to see you, old friend."

They walked closer to the desk as the Reverend came from behind it. "I would not say too old." Harvest grasped the Reverend's arm. "Only a year."

"That short?" The Reverend laughed again, "I thought that deal with the witches took place years ago. Well, work does get clouded over time." He looked past Harvest to the other two. "And who have you brought to see me?"

Harvest stepped aside to allow Iris and Kol to be seen properly. Kol waited for an introduction, but when Harvest remained quiet he took it upon himself. Stepping up he offered his arm in the same fashion Harvest did. "My name is Kol. I'm glad to finally meet you, Reverend."

The Reverend took his arm, giving it a firm grasp. "You can call me Rev. I keep my full name to myself, proper due to my line of work. I hope you understand."

Kol nodded, he did. Iris stepped closer to Kol. "I'm Iris." She too offered her arm.

The Rev released Kol and turned to Iris. "I see." He smiled and grasped her hand in his, different from their gesture. He released it and turned from them, going to sit at his desk. "So," he started once comfortable, "What is it you need from me, Harvest? I am very busy up north and would like to know why it was so important that I come down."

"A few things," Harvest started. Kol felt an unease slowly come over him. What business in the north? "First, have you heard of the increase in vampire activity?"

The Rev took a moment to consider this. Kol glanced toward the window while they waited, the sound from the DJ only faintly heard. "I have not heard anything of it." He gave a soft laugh. "I thought you could handle a few vampires."

"More than just a few. Over twenty I know of." Harvest made a small gesture towards Kol. "We ran into them."

"A family so large?"

"Not a family; just a group of them."

"So what is the problem? No attacks, and with so many, they will die out eventually. Most likely killing one another for the blood before the worst happens."

"We can't leave that to chance; we've only searched a little over half the city."

The Rev nodded. "I see." He pulled a piece of paper from out of his desk. "I'll have the Brothers look into it."

Kol could not truly tell, but he thought Harvest was relieved. "Thank you. It won't take us so long."

"So let me see this blade."

Kol froze a moment. He did not know that Harvest had told Rev about the blade. He felt Iris slightly nudge his elbow. He nodded and reached into his bag. "Be careful not to touch it. The last one dissolved on me."

"I have never seen a bag like that." The Rev was analyzing Kol evenly.

"It was a gift," he said. "I wrapped the blade in the fabric for safekeeping." Kol gently placed the item on the desk in front of the Rev. He knew he should have given it to Holly when he left, but after what his uncle had told him there was no point.

The Rev did not respond, but instead pulled out a pair of thick white gloves, then slowly opened the cloth. A few seconds later and it was free, the sickly green shining faintly in the light. Kol caught himself glaring, as the sight of the blade causing anger to flow through his veins. Internally he was like a raging storm, but the outside was cold and collected. "Goblin made."

Kol nodded. "Yes, my uncle said as much." He was surprised at the calm of his voice. "Dual enchantment."

"I can see that." He pointed at the blood. "This is how you tracked it, correct?" Kol nodded. "As I suspected. A strong controlling hex placed on top of the Lock's original purpose. Very difficult to place two spells on an object without them canceling out."

Iris stepped closer to the desk. Kol realized this was the first time she or Harvest had seen the dagger. "So, a strong user, with years of experience and natural talent."

"Yes, I would assume, but they are as rare today as the alloy this blade is made from." He pointed to the green tint.

Kol decided to be blunt. "So, can you tell us who made it?"

"No."

Kol almost lost his nerve at how careless he was when he said it.

Harvest took a close look at the blade. "Any clues you could give us? Anything that might help?"

"Ah, I have something that is now starting to be answered for me." The Rev opened another drawer on his desk, and Kol heard him shuffling papers. "Here." He pulled out a piece of paper. "I have a location to a goblin forge located on the east coast: the information came at the beginning of November." Harvest took the letter from the Rev's hands and glanced over it.

"Excuse me," Iris stepped forward slightly. "But how did you get this address?"

"Oh, Harvest didn't explain?" Harvest had told Kol while in the city. "I am over a large organization of creating and distributing illegal contraband. Not only in the human world, but in the supernatural as well. Weapons, drugs, immigration: all of it comes under my jurisdiction. A business that I accidentally inherited. I've participated in many deals, both monsters and individuals from your little family as well." This caught Iris off guard. "So whenever a group of the supernatural comes together on the east coast, I like to know why. Which is why the news of this increase of vampires is irritating me." The Rev stood and walked over to look down into the club. "I received news that a goblin associate of mine had a family member who received a rather expensive contract. He gave me the address along with this information."

"So what were they doing?"

The Revs' mood altered. Kol could feel a darkness coming over him. When The Rev spoke his voice was not that of talking to a friend but one that spoke within his organization. "That would be the irony in this situation. Asking me about a goblin-made weapon." Void of emotion he continued, "I had to fly to New York to deal with a large investment. When I heard of the small gathering of goblins I asked one of my employees to investigate and deal with the matter."

Kol believed he understood. "What did he say?"

"He didn't." The Rev turned back to them. "It so happens that I would have been back in town, regardless if Harvest asked me here. My employee went missing when he went to investigate, along with two other persons under him. I had only heard a few days ago. I was planning on sending the Brothers tomorrow."

Kol nodded. Harvest folded the paper and tucked it into his pocket. "We'll investigate it for you. If you can send the Brothers into the city."

The Rev thought on the matter for a second. "I will agree to that on one condition. If you find my subordinates. If you don't, bring me whoever is responsible."

"I will," Harvest said simply, and Kol knew it was all that was needed.

The Rev nodded. "So," his cheerful tone was back, "Where are you from, Kol?"

Kol did not want to say anything. He believed that the Reverend would start digging for an answer and would not stop until he found what he wanted. He opened his mouth to reply, but was interrupted by the floor moving. It was sudden, and it was as if an explosion had occurred nearby. The lights gave a quick flicker and Kol had to place a hand on the desk to steady himself. The vibration came and went so suddenly that Kol did not notice the music stopping as well. Next came the screaming.

CHAPTER FIFTEEN

Night of Misunderstandings

The four of them ran to the office window without hesitation. The music had stopped, and it was difficult to perceive anything. Yes, strobe lights were still going, but they only illuminated the cloud of smoke that was slowly rising to the ceiling. As the smoke dissipated, they found that what had made the noise was the twisted remains of the vault-like front door now lodged into the concrete wall on the opposite side of the entryway. Glancing over the frantic crowd and towards the metal frame that had held the door, Kol saw that it was now just an archway of crumbling wall.

Heavy noises came from the shadows of the front hall, footsteps echoing into the room as everyone froze in horror. An unrealistic being stepped forth through the newly gaping hole. The thing was giant, and Kol was instantly reminded of the Snow People, but quickly felt a small amount of relief as he saw that it was not from home. It was a massive suit of plate armor made for something far larger than the average human. When the behemoth leapt from the catwalk to the center of the dance floor, the crowd had to shove each other in a frenzy to avoid being crushed. When the metal being hit the ground, landing in a crouch, the building shook again. Steam hissed from its joints as it slowly stood back to its full height. "Get Out!" it commanded in an amplified deep metallic voice. The crowd did not hesitate as they pushed and shoved their way up the stairs and out the door, screaming the whole time.

A spot light illuminated the suit of armor, allowing Kol and his team to see more detail. The armor was towering, clearly a little more than two meters. Its width was immense: it was easily the same distance as Harvest and Kol standing side by side. Every piece of it was intimidating, a creation designed perfectly for battle. The armor was dark grey, with accents of silver. The thick plates covered every portion of the body that did not need to hinge. Where there were joints, the protective metal was smaller and overlapping. The gauntlets and the spaulders seemed to be a bit larger than they should be, despite the armor's already massive size. Though it was now stationary, the plates of the armor made small adjustments as if checking for any faults. The helmet was made from only two pieces of metal: the rear encasement and the face guard. The face guard fastened at either ear and was unique because both the eye and ventilation slits glowed a menacing deep purple.

Kol could not help but think that this was something from a time past, only read about in books and dreamed of being saved by or becoming one across the world by many children. Protector of kings and slayer of giants and dragons. A knight, shining as bright as its legend even with the armor dark, stood on the floor below them.

"Well, that is a sight," Iris commented. She reached into her jacket and brought out a small leather parcel.

"A sight!" There was no masking the Rev's outrage. "Do you see what that Knight did to my door?"

Kol only barely paid attention. "He's looking right at us." A slight smile was displayed on his face. This was far too impressive and exciting for him not to. Slowly he reached into his bag and retrieved his sword.

"He can't see us," The Rev said. "That glass is made special. Nothing can break through it, and it's enchanted to look like the walls in the club." He turned to Harvest. "Take care of this for me. I can't fight, not anymore. That thing," he thrust a finger at the Knight, "just cost me money, and you know how we are about that." He glared. "I want the armor for the payment of my door and who it is beneath that armor. I know where it came from, and if Knights are involved I can't be here. I have to get back north."

Harvest was still staring through the glass. He gave a light chuckle. "I wasn't a part of this club and made no profit. Why should I help you here, Rev?" He glanced over his shoulder at the Rev. The humor was too plain to miss.

The Rev missed it. "Are you kidding me?" His voice was raised. "After all we have been through!" Kol slowly stepped away from the glass. Maybe, just maybe, his blade could make it thought the thick metal. He doubted it: it was probably just as enchanted as his sword.

Harvest started to make another remark but was interrupted by the window shattering behind him. Kol expected no less: he figured that's why the Knight was moving. Iris had seen it too, moments before the strike and had made it clear as well. Harvest was pelted with glass, and sticking in the ceiling in front of him was a long silver shaft, which Kol took for a javelin. From its position in the ceiling, it must have passed within centimeters of Harvest's head. His demeanor instantly changed, his face hard and that darkness crept over him again.

"Vampire," the Knight boomed. It was able to amplify its voice. "Your actions have been judged, and I sentence you to your fate. Come now and die with any honor you can find in yourself. Run, and I will chase you. Hide, and I will find you. Fight, and I shall end you quickly." He paused before finishing, to allow Harvest to consider. "It's more than you deserve."

"That was original," Iris said. She had removed her own coat and set it on the desk along with the now empty leather parcel. Around her waist was a dark leather belt that had several small leather cases with bronze clasps attached to it. Her forearms and hands were now encased in leather gauntlets with brass buckles and extra padding on the knuckles. Her fingertips were still exposed as they flexed from an open hand to a fist and back. Iris also had her hair pulled up into a tight ponytail and tied across her forehead was a leather headband. All the gear she wore matched with a thick stitching of red, orange and yellow in the shape of flames. Iris was adorned in fire. "Who does he think he is?" She turned to look at Harvest. "Vampire?" she raised an eyebrow. "What have you been up to, Harvest?" She gave a small grin then slammed her fists together.

"The only thing I know of the Knight can judge me for," he spoke quietly, but that was a warning with Harvest, "is what's about to happen to him." He turned and Kol saw a large cut where the spear had grazed him, and the blood ran freely. He walked to the edge and looked down on the Knight, reaching into his clasped jacket pocket.

Kol spoke to the Knight while Harvest prepared. "Your perspective on this situation is incomplete. We can help fill in the gaps."

"Maybe we can negotiate and find what you're looking for," Iris added, "Maybe we can work together. If I know anything about you, your cause may be the same as ours. It's the only reason to explain why you're here. We too are looking for the vampires who are in the city."

"Lies!" the Knight yelled. "The trail I have been following for the last day has led me to you. I don't know what type of trick you have on you to appear human, but I know what you truly are."

"You do not know what I truly am." Harvest was outraged at her last comment. His body was shaking slightly and his voice was even sharper. He lifted his hand to his mouth and inserted the fang on his right canine. "But you will see what I can become."

Kol pulled his sword free and assumed a two-handed guard stance learned from his father. Iris shifted her body sideways and assumed a fighting stance. Harvest of course simply stood straight and proud as the change took over his human form. Once finished, Harvest crouched and let out the horrendous vampiric shriek. The Knight only stared, no emotion available behind the helmet, and reached behind his back. There was a soft click and the Knight brought around a large shield that swiveled into place. The shield had a silver family crest crafted into it. The

Knight gripped the black leather hilt of a sword attached behind the shield. A double edge sword was freed and gleamed in the bright light.

Music erupted over the speakers. Kol looked and found the DJ behind his table again. Apparently, some form of insanity had compelled the artist to give their fight a soundtrack. Harvest moved, leaping straight towards The Knight. Kol was right behind, his boots helping him fall to the left of their opponent. Iris landed next: she had slid down a black rope she had quickly attached from above. The Knight quickly stepped forward and brought up his shield to collide with Harvest. Before Harvest could leap away, the Knight slammed him to the floor and brought his sword next. Harvest rolled backward and Kol took the opportunity to attack the Knight's flank. His sword met the Knight's as the armor pivoted and swung upward. Kol locked his arms to hold the strike but was knocked off his feet and slid across the floor. Iris had used their attacks as a distraction to move behind their enemy. As Harvest launched into a frontal strike again Iris ran forward. The Knight effortlessly stepped sideways, swinging sword and shield wide. Kol's companions had no choice but to retreat from the Knight's reach.

Seeing them staggered, the Knight advanced on Harvest, the large sword aimed for his raised forearm. Kol had regained his footing and ran to connect his sword with the Knight's. He now knew better than to take all the force, so he parried it over them both. The impact was still strong, and Kol felt it vibrate through his arm. Kol gripped his weapon tighter as the sword swung back, his second parry almost a failure. Harvest darted beneath the arm and delivered several strikes to the Knight's abdomen. His claws did nothing to the metal and Harvest hissed in frustration as he darted back to Kol. The Knight brought his shield around and shoved them both back. Kol's instinct made him bring his sword up and he quickly cursed them as his sword bounced away and hit Kol in his jaw. He spat the metallic taste of blood from his mouth and wiped it on his arm.

Iris had taken another opportunity presented. She vanished for a moment, and then her head appeared above the Knight. Iris had her feet against the Knight's back and one hand on a spaulder, the other beneath the face guard of the helmet. She seemed to be trying to pull it off, but it was no good as the helm was locked down tight. The Knight's sword came swinging up to meet Iris. She released and flipped backward from it. The Knight appeared triumphant from causing Iris to flee so easily but was surprised when the small explosive under the helm detonated, which knocked the Knight slightly off balance. With a grunt of frustration, the enemy took a moment to regain composure.

The Knight ran toward Iris then, swinging the sword wildly at first, then falling into precise swings. Iris began to dance, the same graceful movements she made earlier, but this time she was dodging death, making it look easy. Kol imagined the music helped. A quick glance to the DJ showed him watching and nodding his head to the sound, as if his part were just as important as theirs. Entertaining as the thought was, Kol knew it was foolish. Iris could move like that because she had trained hard to do so. No one was that efficient with controlling their body unless they had dedicated an uncountable amount of time to it.

Harvest darted past Kol after giving him a quick hand signal. Kol knew instantly it was to divide. Despite the Knight's efforts, not all his sides could be protected at once. Kol only waited a second for Harvest to be in position before he moved. He jumped, aiming his sword for the Knight's head. Iris was almost against a wall, dancing away from a paint table the Knight swung through and destroyed. Harvest collided with the lower back right before the paint table shattered, causing enough alarm for Kol's swing to go unnoticed. It rang true, hitting the joint holding the face guard to the rest of the headpiece. Kol then landed, ducked to miss the approaching sword, then darted back to a safe position. Both Iris and Harvest were able to get to safety as well and came to Kol's position. The Knight turned, and Kol felt his adrenalin spike harder than it was already. The joint had become loose, the face guard slightly drooping on the left side.

Good, Kol thought, it can be hurt, and thus, beaten. The Knight noticed and gave a frustrated yell while banging his sword on his shield. The light from the face guard glowed brighter. It started for the three of them, moving faster, the boots thudding hard on the ground. Iris and Harvest moved forward and parted so they could gain the position advantage again. The Knight was not going to allow it. With a quick side step the Knight's shield collided with Harvest. Steam came from the shoulder and elbow and then Harvest was hurtling through the air. He hit the concrete wall and gave a yell of pain and the stone caved slightly. Iris had let her guard down for a second as she watched Harvest fly, she was punished in the form of the Knight's armored foot contacting with her chest. Not as much power was used for the kick but Iris was still sent airborne to land on one of the couches in the room. The Knight then refocused on Kol. There was another soft explosion from the Knight's foot and thick white smoke began to surround the enemy from a small canister.

Kol was grateful, but the lack of vision did nothing to slow the brute. Coming through the smoke, The Knights sword was raised high. Steam once again came from the arm and the Knight swung straight down at Kol with a yell. Kol stepped sideways, barely missing the strike. The great sword had contacted his own for just a second, and from the strength his arm gave away and the blunt of his own blade struck him again. The Knight's strike continued and collided with the floor, sending shrapnel flying. Kol winced away as rock hit him, the Knight gave a grunt and pulled his sword free, standing from its crouched position. "Be careful when you see steam in the joints," Kol yelled over the music, as he raised his guard for the next attack and slid from around it. "It must be a type of overdrive system. Burst strength."

"You think?" Harvest yelled back. Iris had sprinted to Harvest and helped him up.

The Knight continued to assault Kol after witnessing his stagger from the overdrive attack. Kol kept moving, blocking, and dodging. He saw an opening and stuck for it, hitting the shield before he could make it. The Knight then slightly moved the shield, thrusting the great sword from behind it. Kol went up on one leg and tried to pivot his body away from it. He missed the point but not the edge. It parted fabric and grazed the skin before Kol moved from underneath. That sword would take limbs if he stood still. The armor flexed and Kol was to off balance to react fast enough. The Knight's sword would cut up into him. Panicked, he felt a hand grab his jacket and pull.

Iris darted around Kol and towards the enemy. She made rapid palm strikes along the sword arm. It was Harvest who had pulled him from the blade and set him back on his feet. Iris flipped away from her assault and landed in front of them. She then touched the top of her glove and the explosion she had placed along the armor erupted. Slightly stronger than before, the explosions were a chain reaction from hand to shoulder. The great sword clanged on the ground, and the Knight moved a couple of steps back. Harvest dashed for the blade, grabbing it before the Knight could regain footing. Even with the vampire strength he strained to hold its awkward size. The Knight saw and reached for his gauntlet.

Kol yelled to his ally, "Harvest, drop it!" The strobe lights were joined by electricity surging from the sword and into Harvest. He yelled in anguish, unable to let go of the blade. As Iris reached and grabbed the blade, fear for her hit Kol, but the gloves she wore protected her. Kol then tackled Harvest away from the blade. Iris tossed the sword as far away from its owner as possible, but it did no good; the Knight pressed another button and the sword flew back to the gauntlet.

Kol checked Harvest over. He was unconscious and smoke was coming from his face and within his clothes. He was human again, the fang laying behind his head. Kol quickly put it in Harvest's right pocket. The Knight was coming towards them again from across the room, arrogantly taking its time. Iris stood between them fighting, stance ready. "Harvest!" Iris yelled over her shoulder. "Wake up!" Nothing. He lay still.

Kol looked over his shoulder and saw a spaulder opening. Iris had no time: a steel net shot from the Knight's shoulder and ensnared her within. She hit the ground yelling curses and fought to escape, but the net had fully engulfed her. Kol stood bringing his sword to bear both hands. He had to stop the Knight from hurting them further. If Harvest was not already.... he stopped the thought. Iris tossed an object from out of the net she was in and another explosion occurred. Iris suffered from her own device as the compression hit her but in return it had caused the Knight to stagger backwards away from them. Kol sped through all his training to decide what he could do next and felt panic attempt to grip him when he was unable to determine anything that he could do.

Light appeared beside Kol, a beam that quickly reached towards Harvest. He looked for the source and found the Reverend standing by the bar on the catwalk. He was outlined with light, a blinding beacon of white. The light was reaching from him and separated into two beams that touched his friends causing them to also shine. "I'll help them," he yelled down over the music. "Hold that thing off while I do what I can." Kol nodded, and the two of them were lifted from the floor by the glowing power and placed gently next to the Reverend on the catwalk. The beams retracted back into the Reverends hands. The Rev then knelt beside Harvest and closed his eyes. The energy outlining his body pulsed into Harvest's still form. The bartender was trying desperately to free Iris from the net. Kol turned back to the shield slamming into him, hitting his full body.

Kol was on his back, the room spinning. His left eye was covered in something, and it was hard to think. Blood, from his own sword. He had been wiping it all this time. Now the cut above his eye went unchecked. His head slowed, swimming, and the point of the Knight's sword was centimeters from his face. "Yield," The

Knight told him. Kol knew who ever was underneath was giving a triumphant smile. That sound was too noticeable. "Or die on your feet. I am here for the vampire, not you or your tricky female." The blade came closer. "Choose."

Slowly Kol stood, his abdomen on fire from the Knights sword. His shirt was deeply stained. As Kol stood he saw his sword was behind him: no time to reach for it. The Knight's own sword prodded him as he looked, making sure Kol did not try anything. Kol slowly reached for the pouch on his belt grabbing his bell inside. He stood straight, looking directly into the glowing slits of the Knights eyes. "No," he said. "I do not yield."

"You decided your judgment." Kol watched the sword slowly rise then fall. He lifted his bell in front of him. It shown bright and silver. So simple, but to him so dangerous. The more times he used it in a row, the weaker he became, but right now it was not important. The sword was close to him, the steam spewing from the arm. He gave it a light shake and listened for the Sound. Soft as snow it chimed, a noise so pure it silenced the rest of the world. He saw the Sound wave from it and embraced it, drank it into his body and making it a part of him. The sword stopped its swing, the steam from the armor held in place. The strobe lights had stopped moving, and a quiet set in that was far deeper than anything the earth could find. So vast yet so small, and his body instantly ached as it always did, rejecting the Sound. As ever when using the Sound, he ignored the pain. He stepped over to his sword and picked it up. Kol could not breath here very well: the air was far too thin, so he often held his breath beforehand. Only a few seconds, Kol thought, and the Sound left him. Slowly his surroundings caught back up to speed.

The Knight's sword hit the ground with the same force as before, causing more rock and rubble. More stationary spotlights came on and the colored ones switched off. The dust cleared swiftly, and the Knight saw his strike had missed again. When the helmet looked up Kol looked back calmly, his weapon eased in his hand. He knew the Knight was shocked: who wouldn't be? First he was standing there, the next he was in a completely different spot. A distance that could not be traversed so fast. "How?" the Knight asked, the shock Kol had already assumed easily found on the Knights voice.

"It's simple, really," Kol raised his sword and attached his bell to it. It jingled, but he could always choose whether to use the Sound or not, regardless if he heard it. Letting his arms rest again, Kol continued, "All you have to do is believe."

A roar came from the Knight and it moved on him. Steam bellowed from every joint, the Knights speed increasing. Kol rolled beneath it, and came up from behind, wanting to make a strike. The Knight had turned with Kol and was swinging the great sword wildly. Kol dodged back, the blade always close. He checked and almost ran into a table, which also was destroyed after they passed. His back hit the wall and the Knight lashed out. Kol embraced the Sound.

With time stopped, Kol struck several times into the elbow joint of the arm holding the sword. When time started again, the Knight hesitated before looking around for him. It tried to pull up the sword, but the arm would not torque. The Knight noticed that the joint was damaged, and in a fit of rage he spun and flung his shield like a disk. Kol just barely embraced the Sound, which slowed time just enough for him to step to the side before things snapped back to normal speed. To the Knight he only shimmered to the side or blurred; he knew that from watching his father teach him the levels of the bell's power.

The Knight used his shield arm to pull the sword free of his broken grip. Kol noticed that the Knight's left arm was not as well trained with a sword, but it was only a fractionally less trained and still just as dangerous. With the shield gone the Knight switched sporadically from two hands to one. The right arm must have been good enough for support but not for actual striking. Kol moved from an attack and the right gauntlet almost collided with his stomach. Stepping between the Sound again he could give eight strikes before he was back. Kol aimed his attacks to the right leg, but he found no weak points. The legs must have been built with stronger armor. He moved back, but the Knight's sword point caught his right arm. He gave a shout and continued to backpedal. This wasn't good; his body was in agony from his bell and fatigued. It had to be all or nothing. He heard the Sound again, and this time only able to land seven strikes. He listened again the moment he came out, and delivered six more. The more he used it, the less amount of his own time he could spend away from everyone else's. Listened again and five strikes, then four. He was jumping around so quickly the Knight could not keep up. Whenever he struck Kol was gone, already striking and appearing elsewhere. He had just made three more hits when he almost collapsed when time returned.

He coughed, the taste of blood once again in his mouth. Rejection. His body could no longer take it. He looked to his friends. The Rev was trying to untangle Iris alongside the bartender. Iris was shouting for him while she struggled from the inside. Harvest was awake and struggling to his feet, wanting to rejoin the fight. Kol looked back to Iris and realized he could not hear her. The world was quiet to him. A reaction to the bell: it would pass eventually. He coughed again, and this time blood hit the ground. The Knight saw, his spaulder opening and launching another net. He brought his sword and spun it before him as the links wrapped around it instead of Kol. It was heavy, so he would not be able to fight with his normal speed. Kol tried to pull it free but couldn't, and then the Knight was above him. Kol was able to set the point of his sword free and aimed it for the Knight's neck. Kol hoped to break through its armor when he was slain. He had failed his father, but hopefully his friends would continue to look and somehow help his home.

The sound of laughter came and he smiled despite himself. His hearing had returned quicker than he anticipated. However, it was not the Knight or Kol laughing: this one came from the entrance, joyous laughter mixed with what Kol considered insanity. The figure darted in and leapt towards the enemy from the gaping hole. The Knight forgot Kol and focused on the newcomer, who landed on top of the armor. The new ally was quickly away again holding something shiny. Kol knew who it was instantly: it was the person they had chased on the roof. His green mask with the crudely drawn smiley face peered at the Knight. Kol looked at what he held in his hand and saw it was the left spaulder. Red mesh covered the Knight's shoulder where the piece of armor once was. There was so much anger incased within the armor. The Knight snatched at the Green Smile, but he hopped away, dropping his prize and then leaping back at the Knight again. Landing on the right arm, he held himself there in a way Kol could not see.

He had the right forearm guard now, then the left thigh. The Knight's movements were slowing. Kol saw that if the machine was not whole, it could not function. The Smile completely stripped the left arm, and the gauntlet came away clutching the sword. Kol had to lean left to miss it. The right boot came off and the Knight kneeled. The Smile would place a hand on a piece and just pull away with it in his hands. Kol had no idea how he was doing it when Harvest couldn't. Not strength; it was something else. Metal hit the ground around them, and Kol felt someone grab his arm and looked to see Iris. Harvest was next to her and the Rev. They all looked in astonishment as what had just been wrecking them was now in several pieces. Second to last was the top chest piece, after which the Smile stepped behind the person, who faced them now on both his knees. While laughing hysterically, he carefully pulled the helmet up.

Kol admitted he was not expecting what he saw, and neither did the others. Tightly braided hair of purple and black was held back in a tight braid. The Knight looked up at them, eyes burning with hatred, but still a warm deep brown. The Knight was only a girl, with chestnut brown skin. Kol only said girl because she was younger than him, by two or three years at the most. The Knight snatched her shoulders away from the Green Smile as he went to lift her to her feet. Instead she stood on her own, and Kol could not figure out how someone so small could fit in armor so giant. She stood shorter than Kol's shoulders. She had a slender build, athletic and compact, obviously from the crimson skintight suit she wore. The fabric looked like chainmail covered in a rough texture. All of her was encased in the outfit, all the way up her neck and stopping there. A white image was sewn onto the front, the family crest from her shield.

Harvest stepped up to her, kicking her sword aside. "What is your name?" His tone said he had no room for trouble. The girl glared at him, mouth locked shut, crossing her arms. Harvest continued to stare. "If you don't talk, I will tie you up and take you with me. You will remain so, until my business in this area is done. When I leave I will leave you as you are now. Your armor and weapons will come with me and I will sell them to someone in the underground." He gave her a moment to think. "I know who you work for, and I also know what they will do to you once they found you've not only lost your armor, but some unworthy creature out there is probably killing your own people with it, let alone innocent humans." The girl's face softened at this. "My questions are these: what is your name, how are you here, why are you after me, and how many more is with you? And be truthful. My friend the Rev can sense lying."

Kol looked to the Rev, who gave no indication as to whether he could or not. He noticed Kol looking and made a face like he had forgotten something. He walked up to Kol. "I need to heal you; the sword could be poisoned." His hands began to glow. "This will be unpleasant, Kol. This type of healing magic is the purest and rarest, and can save someone from an inch of death. At a price: it will drain you. I have an herb you can eat to restore the stamina this will take but it will only last a few hours. I'm not sure how you were doing what you just did, but I am sure you're the worse off of the three of you." While explaining, the Rev pulled from inside his jacket a wrapping of some foreign leaves. "You will need to rest once your temporary energy diminishes."

"My sword's not poisoned!" As Kol believed, the armor changed the voice of the wearer. Intimidation purposes, he imagined. It also masked the accent. British, or close by. The voice was forceful and angry which seemed to suit the way she was glaring. "I would not stoop so low as to use that form of a coward's method."

Kol glanced at Iris who leveled a glare towards the girl. It was gone in an instant as she turned to examine the Rev's medicine. "She's telling the truth. I recognize that."

Kol grabbed the herb and ingested it. "Do it," he said.

"You may want to sit; the first part is the hardest." Rev rubbed a clear salve in his hands.

Kol just stood there. He did not want to pass out, knowing he would if he sat down. He crossed his arms and the Rev sighed before placing his hands on his shoulder. He went rigid, his entire body locking in place. Fire, it was fire coming from his hands, and then it was ice so cold even he could hardly take it. In waves it came, pulsing into him and back out. He did not shout, but the pain was searing. It seemed to take forever, but eventually the pain decreased to where he could tolerate it. After a few seconds, the pulsing temperatures left him. Kol turn to see the Rev stepping away. Kol's vision started to go black as his energy vanished from him. Thankfully the medicine he swallowed kicked in, waking him back and making him feel like he could run forever.

Kol lifted his shirt and saw his wound was now a faint scar, the same on his head and arm. He scowled at his arm, not for the cut but the fact his jacket had once again been damaged. Kol would ask Iris to patch it up later like she did before. To the Rev, Kol said, "Thank you."

"Don't mention it," he replied curtly.

"So you can speak." Harvest had not looked away from the Knight. "You have only one chance to tell me."

If looks could kill, this girl would never need the armor. "I was sent here by the First Sword and Shield to look into a matter of increased vampiric activity."

Harvest nodded. "Where is the other?"

"It is only me. I came alone." She looked away. "The Firsts thought I could handle it."

"I don't doubt that, seeing what you just did to us," Iris said, and she looked slightly impressed.

"I arrived yesterday and saw you two running over the roofs." She looked to Kol and Harvest. "By the speed I figured that you were vampires. I was too far away when I glanced at you and you were only shadows. I only got residue for the equivalent of one vampire. I made a note to find out what human could keep up with running with something supernatural." Her focus stayed on Kol. Despite her now being at their mercy, she was demanding. "What are you? What did you just do before the hoppy thing came in?"

Kol only stared back and did not answer. Harvest ignored it as well. "I'll be asking the questions here, and maybe after we answer yours. What is your name?"

"Lady Shield Wilhelmina Dulon," she said proudly.

Harvest pressed on, "It is difficult for me to believe there is not another one of you here. How old are you and when were you Knighted?"

"Sixteen, and I was Knighted mid-way through this year."

"If the Reverend has not said that you are lying then I have no choice to believe you." He pointed to the Green Smile. "You." The snickering person had been rummaging up on the DJ booth. Kol had not seen the DJ leave. He looked up towards Harvest, making a soft chirping noise. "Go up to that office. The doors are hidden behind the wall. Bring me that rope." The Green Smile laughed then darted off, making it to the top of the stairs and pushing past a couple of bouncers Kol had not noticed there before.

"I'll use your nets to carry your weapon. A great sum of loot."

"NO!" Wilhelmina shouted. A tear fell from her eye. She was trying to hold it together, but the events had flipped on her so fast that the stress was too much. Iris walked up to her and placed an arm around her. Wilhelmina slid away. She was indeed full of pride.

Harvest let the silence come, which broke at the Green Smile's return. He gave the rope to Harvest. "You will be coming with us now."

"I WILL NOT!" Kol wondered if there was no limit to the anger.

"Yes, you will. We can use you." He gestured to the rest of them. "We are here for the exact same reason you are, and it would be best if we joined forces. You will be coming back to our camp and we will talk more on negotiations."

"What negotiations?" she demanded. "I'm not leaving with a vampire."

Harvest reached out and grabbed her hand before she knew what happened. He took her palm and placed it on his chest. "Can you feel that? My heart is beating, and I'd expect you to know that no matter what type of magic is used the heart of a vampire will never beat. You feel the warmth? Vampires cannot hold that either. Yes, when I take that form I am the actual thing, but I have control. Completely."

"Lies." She snatched her hand away and started to move. Harvest was too quick. He had her on her belly, hands and feet tied together. Finding a piece of fabric, he wadded it up and stuck it in her mouth, which barely quieted the noise.

"You should not treat her so," Iris said. She moved to untie Wilhelmina.

"She's far too angry right now to listen to reason. You saw what she can do, and we can't take any chances." He walked towards the closet piece of armor. "We need to be cautious. If someone is watching her they will be after us. Once she calms down we will untie her. Unless you want to fight her again on the car ride home?"

Kol nodded to agree with Harvest. This person had almost killed them. Tying her up for an hour or so would not be the worst. Breath touched his face to Kol's left as he turned his head.

The green mask was completely in his field of vision. "I thank you for saving me, us. Who are you?"

The person bounced away, giving Kol back his space. He lifted the mask from his face and tossed it to the floor, grinning. Kol's breath caught. He knew him. This person was the first person he saw after coming here. The same deranged look he saw then was there now. His stare could be unsettling, since it was both focused and distant at the same time. He had to be seeing an illusion of some sort. He bowed comically, flinging his hand high behind him and almost touching the ground. "My name is Lloydric," he stood back up, "but I won't answer to it. Lloyd will hold more chance than Lloydric to catch my attention."

Lloyd was mad. That was Kol's only thought before asking, "Why are you here?"

"Heard a shout." He cocked his head to the side as if to hear another.

Iris was smiling at him, and Kol found he was too. Harvest did not. "You're the one who touched my car. I should drain you dry for that." Lloyd snickered, bounding away. Harvest returned his attention to the armor and the irate, struggling Knight. "Here," Harvest handed Kol one of the steel nets. "Collect all the pieces and weapons too." Kol stared at him. "Don't you want to know how it works? I've never had a chance to examine a Knight's armor."

"Wait, I said that was mine," The Rev stepped up, "to pay for the damages."

"Send me the bill." Harvest gestured to the Knight on the floor who had started yelling again when she heard intentions for her armor. "It belongs to her. I have a feeling that the situation is far greater than we believe and we will need everyone we can."

CHAPTER SIXTEEN

A Sound Stipulation

"**W**hy haven't the police shown up yet?" Kol stood with Iris and Lloyd in the entryway facing the Reverend. Wilhelmina was there as well, still tied up and laying on her side behind them on top of the two steel nets she had launched from her spaulders that now held the pieces of her armor. Lloyd had used the javelin she had thrown to drag the armor in the nets attached to either side. Kol made a note—this person was also stronger than he appeared. Iris kept close: Kol knew it was to keep an eye on him in case he passed out. Every couple of minutes Lloyd would kneel down and poke Wilhelmina, causing her to scream, yell, or growl in anger through her gag. Lloyd only made cooing sounds at her. Inside they had spent an hour packing her weapons and armor. They would have finished the job sooner, but it took Harvest, Iris, and Lloyd to pull the shield from the wall. After they had placed everything at the entrance, Harvest departed to get the car and check that they would not be attracting unwanted attention.

The Rev smiled at him. "Well, I don't really like the authorities to come searching around my places." He walked to the wall and placed a hand on it. "No sound can escape the walls; built them insulated that way. When this place was built I also had a few wizards place cloaking spells into the walls and foundation. So if anyone I didn't like came snooping around I could simply make it disappear."

"Wouldn't that be bad for business?" Iris asked. She reached down to slap Lloyd's hand as he tried to poke Wilhelmina again.

"Shouldn't they still come because of all the people who left pan-icking?"

The grin the Rev gave this time was definitely sinister. "Cloaking wasn't the only thing I had installed. When I activate the cloak I also activate a memory spell. Quiet, but powerful, predesigned to switch the end of the night's actual events with the club closing early due to electrical difficulties." He pulled a piece of debris from the front door frame. "Have to make sure they come back and spend their money."

"That's wrong," Iris told him. "It's wrong to tamper with someone's memories."

The Rev smirked, "They probably had enough to drink to take care of that anyways. Now don't get all up-tight with me; I don't pretend to be a nice guy. This place is a haven for any-one wanting to lose themselves for a few hours. I won't let some self-righteous zealot like this Knight come in here and ruin that for them." Wilhelmina really started to buck at that comment "If I don't want it getting out people can come to harm here, I won't."

"So you're a wizard too?" Kol asked him. "With the healing and all."

"No, I can't say that I am." He raised his hand and emitted a soft glow. "I'm only a healer, and no wizard can honestly do what I can, though they wish they could. On that topic I'd like to have your word that news of my abilities are not spread. I'll do the same for you." He gestured to Wilhelmina. "I should have her modified by one of my men. Last thing I want is her other coming after me."

"She won't say anything." They turned as Harvest came through the door.

Kol and Iris stepped aside as Harvest stepped over the Knight. "We are going to be leaving now, Rev. Don't worry about the Knight—I'll take responsibility for her." He had replaced his fang and was once again a vampire.

"That I hope, and I also hope I receive payment for the repairs of my club."

Harvest smiled. "Get me an estimate."

"Oh I will." The Rev let out a soft sigh, and, to Kol he appeared tired for the first time tonight. Despite seeing his own face in the white sunglasses, the Rev's cheeks looked to have sunken and his shoulders drooped as if letting go of a large load. "It was great seeing you again, my old friend, but I must admit this was too close. I can no longer come to the front lines anymore. I have the Brothers coming in two days from now and they will search the city and let you know. Be sure I get a call about what you find at that address. "

"I will," Harvest nodded, and without even a goodbye walked up to Wilhelmina and pulled her up, struggling and suppressed shouting onto his shoulder. Lloyd, Iris, and Kol lifted the armor with difficulty and followed Harvest out of the club. Lloyd had to stop for a moment outside to retrieve a large hiking bag from the sidewalk. The car was parked on the curb directly in front of them. Looking over his shoulder, Kol saw the Rev was not lying about the cloak. The white neon sign no longer hung bright on the wall, and it was now just a boarded up antique store. Magic always spurred a smidgen of joy in Kol. He did not know if others shared his amazement, but even though he had grown up in a world full of magic, magic to him was, well, magical.

Harvest walked directly to the car, opened the back seat, and tossed Wilhelmina inside. He shut the door after so as to not draw any attention. Kol scanned the empty street while Harvest opened the trunk. Either everyone was in bars or clubs or, for them, the night was over. He placed his items in first, then helped Lloyd and Iris with theirs. Harvest had to put his back against the door to close it completely. Kol noticed the car was moving as Wilhelmina was in the back struggling to move. "She's going to break your back window."

The soft thud came like he knew it would as Wilhelmina's feet hit the back window. Cursing, Harvest opened the door, grabbed the Knight's back legs and tied them to her hands behind her back. "There."

"It's going to be a tight ride," Iris said, looking into the car.

Harvest nodded. "Yeah, but I believe you two can handle her."

"What if she bites me?" Kol asked.

"Bite her back," Harvest said simply.

"Where's Lloyd?" Iris asked.

Alert, Kol spun: he was gone. He did however, hear a noise and followed it. The source was easy enough to find. Lloyd was making the engine noises on the motorcycle he sat on. "I just take off on it, crash it into your car."

"Get off the bike," Harvest snapped. Laughing, Lloyd did so.

Kol walked over to the machine, and he could not help but be impressed. The motorcycle was a beast, simple as that. A cruiser design, it looked heavy. From the moonlight Kol could make the chrome pieces out clearly. He had to look closer for the crimson color. Attached behind the bike was a trailer that kept the bike standing upright. A very large trunk was built on it, almost as big as the bike, polished crimson to match. "I think we know how our Knight was getting around."

"Yea," Harvest said. He quickly went to his car with Lloyd to take the armor back out of his car and placed it in the bike's pull-along.

Kol threw a leg over the bike and sat down on it. The key was still in the ignition, so to pacify himself he turned it over. It came to life with a deep purr. "I'll follow you, then."

Harvest nodded. "Where are your things?" he asked Lloyd, who laughed as they walked back to the car.

"You can't possibly think to ride that thing back to camp," Iris said. Kol had never heard that tone from her before. There was a heat to it that almost made him shy away from it. Stubbornly, Kol reached down and picked up the helmet hanging on a small peg. It barely fit, meaning it was too small for him anyway. "Kol, you don't have the strength. You could fall asleep at any minute if that medicine burns out too fast."

"I'll be fine, Iris. Don't worry. I promise..." But Kol did not get the chance to promise anything as Iris grabbed his coat with her left hand. Kol tried to knock her arm away with his left hand instinctively, but Iris easily countered him as she grabbed it with her free hand and twisted it so fast Kol's face found a resting place on the bike's gas tank.

"I'm well aware that you are capable of a lot of things, Kol," the fire of Iris' tone receded but still held the capability to burn. "You pushed yourself too far. You didn't come all this way to dishonor your father by being unnecessarily reckless, did you?"

Kol tried to sit back up, but Iris' grip was iron. His pride wanted him to get angry, but his sense of reason was stronger. Kol's stubbornness faded before he said, "You're right, Iris."

Iris released him. "Thank you. I'll drive us home, just sit back and rest."

Straightening out his coat, Kol hesitated to move as long as he dared. "You just caught me by surprise. Just so you know." Iris tilted her gaze in such a way that Kol quickly held up his hands and slide backwards on the seat. To be honest, after he had seen her in action against the Wilhelmina, he wasn't sure if he was a match for Iris.

Taking the helmet and sliding it on her head, Iris gripped the handlebars and turned back to Kol. "Hold onto me if you feel yourself getting weaker." He did not get to answer her before she kicked the motorcycle into gear and pulled them out onto the road, Kol just barely managing to wrap an arm around her waist to stable himself. They returned the way they came, following behind Harvest. There were just a few lights before they could increase their speed along the highway. Halfway back to the encampment Kol was glad more than ever that Iris had stopped him from driving. The artificial stamina had faded to just a sliver of what it had been before. His head felt heavy, so he rested it against Iris' back. She was warm and that was appreciated in the chilly night. Her helmet turned to check on him before focusing back on the road. Kol closed his eyes and just held on.

The sky was a dark grey when they made it to the end of the dirt road. The morning sun was on its way and Kol wished for his hammock. The thought of moving was so uninviting that he considered sleeping on the bike seat. The tunnel began to open in front of them as Harvest rolled his window back up from using the whistle. "Are you awake, Kol?" Iris asked.

Reluctantly, Kol sat up, "Yeah, I'm up. Not sure for how much longer."

"Just a minute more," she said comfortingly.

They crept through the finished tunnel and parked their vehicles in the clearing. Iris shut off the motorcycle and they both dismounted—well, Iris dismounted, and Kol tried to fall off gracefully. He watched Harvest and Lloyd exit the car, the driver almost doubled over in laughter. Lloyd was smiling too, though Kol suspected it was about something entirely different. He knew what was making Harvest laugh because of the other muffled sound coming from the back seat. When the latch was unhitched, an uproar came pouring out.

"I SWEAR I WILL NOT LET YOUR DEATH BE QUICK!" She was red-faced. "I WILL MAKE YOU WATCH AS I BURN EACH OF YOUR LIMBS." Her gag had been removed.

"So scary," Harvest told her as he lifted her onto his shoulder. "Leave the armor on the bike, everyone. We will get it later." And he started up the path, easily followed from the sound of his luggage. Lloyd pulled a large duffle bag from the back seat and slung it on his back. It was an old thing, but it matched the dirty rags the boy was wearing, looking as if it was made of patched scraps of clothing. Kol stepped from the bike and joined Lloyd after he closed the car. Iris continued up the path with Harvest. "So have you been following me since you saw me in the park?"

"What?" Lloyd looked at him with a confused expression.

"The park," he repeated. "I saw you sitting on the ground. You had a bird sitting on you and a squirrel tugging on your pants."

"I don't know about all that." Kol saw he was smiling. Was he always joking around?

"Where are you from?"

"The center," he said simply.

Kol did not think this guy was ever serious. "What do you mean, the 'center?'"

"What do you mean the top?" His expression had returned to that unnatural look of being distant and focused at the same time. Kol did not answer. But, simply, he *was* from the top, so Lloyd must be from somewhere along the equator. A very vague answer because of the circumference of the globe. He did not want to talk anymore anyway now that they were back at the Encampment.

Back in the Encampment, Kol saw that Iris was heading into her main wagon and Harvest was dealing with the Knight. Kol's focus was on that blessed woven fabric swinging between two trees. Taking his jacket off, he groaned. His abdomen had grown stiff from his wound along with his arm. He laid his jacket carefully on his hammock. He would have to ask Iris to help him patch it later on. Tailoring was going to be the next skill on his list to learn once this was all over. Best to wait regardless. His shirt was beyond saving so he simply balled it up and stuck it into his bag, pulling a fresh pair of gray sweat pants back out. Having to continue to move slowly, he changed from his remaining clothes to his new ones. He did not even care about the paint still on his body.

Wilhelmina was not yelling anymore, but it only took one look to see that this particular animal should not be pestered. Harvest had placed her on his king-size bed as he too undressed. Lloyd was, of course, doing something very strange. Kol believed even more that this was his custom. He had made his way to the horses the moment he saw them. He was now talking to them, but not as he had to Iris, Kol, or Harvest. Talking was not even the proper word to use, Lloyd was simply making noises. Kol listened, but his voice was too soft to understand.

"Strange one, isn't he?" Harvest spoke, walking up behind Kol. He was dressed only in his under clothes and had a blanket loosely wrapped around him.

Kol nodded at Harvest's comment. "He is indeed." The horses were both nuzzling Lloyd's face now. "You think it was wise to bring him with us?"

"Well, if not for him, you would not be here right now." He laughed towards Wilhelmina, who could not see them. "Nor her. In fact, you sound as if you're more worried about him than her."

"She's tied up."

"So we should tie him up?"

Kol shook his head and smiled. "No, I believe we can kinda trust him." He was telling the truth. "Even her, though I don't think she will return the feeling. Which in itself is dangerous."

"You're right," Harvest said. Lloyd had parted from the horses, making his way to an open spot near the path that lead back to the cars. Taking his bag from his back he dropped it on the ground, then collapsed into the wild grass and flowers. His stomach rose slowly and fell again, his eyes shut tight. "Think he wants a blanket?"

"Actually, I don't think so," Kol told him.

"We should keep a cautious mindset with the both of them, yes. He seems to be aware of our world and stripped the armor from a Knight single-handedly. We'll question him more later." Harvest patted him on the back, "Get some rest, man; you look as if you're about to drop yourself. Don't worry: I'll stay up and keep an eye on both the newcomers."

Kol was about to reply when Iris emerged from her room. She did not look in their direction. She marched to Harvest's bed, holding a glass bottle in her hand. "I'm going to untie you, but only after you drink this." She displayed the bottle.

Wilhelmina started to build up a storm again. "Willing to drink some liquid from my enemy? How stupid do you think I am?" She thrashed into a position so that she could sit on her knees.

Iris's tone was caring, "I don't think you're stupid at all. I just believe that little ordeal we all had earlier has made you just as tired as we are. This is to help you sleep. How about I untie you first?"

Harvest took a step towards them, "I wouldn't..." He stopped there because both Iris and Wilhelmina's heads snapped towards him. Both of their glares stated not to interfere. Kol placed a hand on Harvest's shoulder and pulled him back. The last thing that was needed was those two teaming up.

Iris's glare slid to Kol, then back to Wilhelmina, softening. "That sound good?"

Wilhelmina held her glare, however. "Whatever," she said. Iris took this as confirmation and pulled a small knife from her belt. In one smooth motion the rope was cut, and Wilhelmina was free. Wilhelmina rubbed her wrist and flexed them to make sure nothing was wrong. Kol feared she was going to attack Iris next. True to her word, however, she took the bottle and downed it.

"Would you like me to get you something to sleep on? I believe I have a cot in my caravan."

Wilhelmina glanced towards Kol and Harvest then back at the bed. "No, I believe I will stay here." She turned from Iris and bedded herself down.

Iris nodded and started back for her room. She reached into her door and pulled out a small bag before walking off towards the location of the shower. "I think it best for you to be a little more careful around Iris. I saw what happened back at the club," Harvest told him.

"And *I* think it best you be careful." Kol nodded toward Wilhelmina, "A person is most in danger when they are asleep and that one has situated herself in your bed, where she can easily stab you."

Harvest nodded, then glanced at the sky. "I'm crashing since they both are out; sun's coming. Judging by what I've seen before, a draft from Iris will keep you asleep for a good bit." He then made his way toward his disadvantage.

Kol glanced at the sky and frowned at the possibility of sun. Grabbing his pillow and his belt with bag and case, he walked into the woods. His hammock was one comfort, but Kol was a light sleeper and the sun's light would make his sleep even lighter. After a few minutes of wandering he found a large boulder sticking out from the earth. The grey polished rock was large enough for him to stretch out on. The trees had grown thick above him, so he did not need to worry about the sun cooking him. He pulled a sleeping bag out and laid back onto his pillow and was instantly asleep.

His sleep had been dreamless. Without the foundations of his dreams to stand upon, Kol almost lost himself back into the depths of slumber after waking the first time. The struggle was difficult, but he managed to open his eyes, their weight as heavy as the rock he lay upon. It was sunset, and the sky was clouded and softly shimmering from the vanishing beams. Right now his eyes were all he was going to move. His body felt wrecked, with every muscle holding a deep sore. He could barely tense any of them; the strain had not set in until after he slept. That brought comfort, at least; he was healing. This would count as the second time he had pushed so far using the bell.

The first time had come sometime after he had received the bell from his father. It was a Christmas present, one that his father had given him after he had fallen. It was an understandable mistake. Who would have thought his own blood would not be able to follow his set path? Training, that's what his father had told him was needed. If he worked hard enough he would one day be able to hold the Sound just like his father. So Kol did. It had taken him so long just to the *hear* the Sound. Sure, he could hear the jingle of the bell, just like anyone else who listened for his father's sleigh. When the day came where he could actually hear, his body finally sensing the ripple of Sound, he had found new hope. His father saw it as well, and told him that he should hurry with his training so that he could lighten the load come Christmas Eve.

Hearing was one thing, but embracing the Sound was another challenge altogether. During the time he was home from the Flakes they would come meet in the training room. If Kol had stayed with his uncle, they would simply train outside his quarters. Half the time would be dedicated to learning the sword and fighting in general. On top of the pride he held for Kol wanting to learn the old, often considered obsolete, fighting styles, Saint Nicholas felt that learning the sword and hand-to-hand combat would help Kol to embracing the Sound. The martial arts would strengthen his body. Whether or not it helped, Kol could not say, he just knew that his hope grew until the day he finally held it.

He had not known it happened and it had only lasted for a few seconds. It had been just them two in the room, so he had nothing to determine from. His father had to embrace it with him, so he did not stop when time had. When it had ended nausea had come over him, which he had ignored because his father had been completely overjoyed. They tried again the next day, and after only a few tries he was able to do it again. They had built on that, his father wanted him to master holding one sound wave, before sliding from one to the other. His father explained that's how he could continuously step apart from time. All the while Kol had ignored what was happening to his body. He thought what it would continue to vanish soon after training. Like muscles growing stronger, so wasn't that what was supposed to happen?

They had not realized until the day to push his limits came. Kol had been able to hold onto the Sound for longer than a few seconds by then. With each wave he accepted the shorter time he could hold it. He had kept going, hoping he could break through the wall he believed was there. It had not been until Kol collapsed, coughing up blood, that his father figured it out. Kol's body was rejecting the Sound. If he continuously used it rapidly, he could die. After this was explained to him Kol made up his mind and stopped any other form of hope that the path of his father's was one he could follow. They had stopped training with the bell after that day. It had not been brought up again until this past November.

Standing was even more difficult, but he managed. The limit he had reached last night was the same he had hit with his father. Kol stretched: this actually felt great. "How do you feel?" Iris' bracelets made their familiar sound.

"Thought I was well hidden." Iris stood at the bottom of the rock looking up at him.

She smiled. "No, I found you after my shower. Been here a few times throughout the day since you like to go outside the encampment with no way to return."

"Ah." Kol grabbed his scattered items. He tossed the pillow and sleeping bag into his bag and throw the belt over his shoulder. "Iris, I'm sorry again for earlier. I'll try to spend a little more time being more considerate."

He made his way down to her as he spoke, and she turned her gaze towards the ground as he approached. "I know, Kol," she said. "You have a good heart, but that impulsiveness could use a little bit of adjustment."

"You're not the first person to tell me that."

"How do your wounds look?" She reached out and touched his stomach. A chill swept over him. "He really did a good job. Looks months old. The scar will not fade completely, however."

"Guess it's the price I'll pay."

"Well, no, you shouldn't have." She pressed more firmly. "But I think it looks good on you."

He involuntarily stepped back at this and laughed nervously. "Let's go back and put together a plan."

"Dinner's waiting." Her words were that of an angel. Food was all he wanted in the world right now.

The small gateway opened before them after Iris played the soft notes. Kol was greeted by the delicious smells she had put together. Harvest had set up two tables this time, to make room for the new guests. He and Lloyd were both sitting around the tables halfway through their plates. Iris had created a salad dish, a large loaf of garlic bread, and a pan of spaghetti for the main course. Kol felt a twinge of guilt over not being awake to help make it or set up the tables. She talked as if the whole meal was still present but in actuality a little less than half was being devoured. The two of them looked to have just woken as well. He looked for Wilhelmina and found her unconscious in Harvest's bed. "She not joining us?" he asked, taking his usual seat.

"I gave her a large enough of a dose to keep her out until late tonight or early tomorrow morning," Iris told him as she also sat and began to make her plate.

"You know that can cause her to mistrust us?" Kol asked while spooning spaghetti onto his plate. Iris just stuck her tongue out at him.

"I'd rather have her that way while we look at her armor," Harvest said. "I don't think 'quiet' is in her nature."

"I like her nature," Iris pointed out. "She has a lot of fire in there."

"Oh you would, wouldn't you?" This time it was Lloyd, who came up for air just for a few seconds to make his comment then went back to destroying his bread.

They all watched him for a moment. He seemed completely oblivious to what was going on around him. "So who is she?" Kol asked. From the way they talked last night whoever she was, it was not a secret.

"Well, simply, she is what she appears to be." Harvest placed his fork on his plate and pushed it away before refilling his cup with tea and continuing, "A Knight."

"We had no idea." Sarcasm from Lloyd again as he went for seconds.

Harvest ignored him. "I'm sure you've heard of them before. Chivalrous, valiant, the ideal warrior. Champion of the Medieval Ages and on through the Renaissance. Slayers of dragons and giants and taking vows to protect the virtues of women." Iris squinted her eyes at Harvest.

Kol let Harvest's arrogance slide around him. "Yeah, I've heard of them. Ran into a bad spot against the long bow."

"Correct," Harvest nodded. "I'm sure you know about this next part as well but I'm just going to continue from start to finish." Harvest slowly started to become distant as he talked. "Between the times of the Medieval Ages and the Renaissance, there was a period where culture as they knew it dwindled down to almost nothing. Barely anything worth historical significance came from the Dark Ages, mostly due to the fact the majority was more focused on surviving in the present than worrying about the future." He took a sip from his cup. "Kol, you know that the stories hold more truth than believed by civilization. Vampires and werewolves, along with many other types of monsters, like the undead, plagued Europe. Their numbers had grown rapidly, an infection spreading with no hope of a cure. Someone had to answer the call, and who else was better than the glorious knights of old."

Kol had given Harvest a questioning look at the mention of truth in stories. "So from what I've witnessed, the Knights are still around, just like the monsters."

"That's exactly right."

Lloyd tossed down his fork. "Yeah, isn't it obvious?" He gave Kol a look as if asking if he were stupid. Then he smiled and stood to walk towards the tree line.

Kol smirked at him, then addressed Harvest. "But how?" Harvest turned back to him. "Wouldn't they be on the news or in the papers? It's not like they can go unnoticed."

"I believe once the monsters started to become nothing more than legend, so did they." Harvest stopped to glance at Iris, who stood and collected their plates. She reached for Kol's, who kept a firm grip on it. After several seconds of a struggle she released it and walked stiff-backed to the middle wagon. "If I am correct, they still exist to continue their fight against the things they deem evil." Harvest refilled his cup again. "You're right about people would usually say something about them. 'Caelestibus,' which is their organization's name, is usually more discreet. They usually don't walk around fully armored in public unless absolutely necessary. That one," Harvest pointed towards Wilhelmina, "Was probably too hot headed and needed to prove herself, so she just charged right in."

"Wouldn't someone be able to get a picture?"

"I believe their suits do more than just protect and assist them. Maybe something in them disrupts imagery equipment. And who is going to believe a person who is saying a seven-foot suit of armor is fighting a werewolf in the middle of a small town?"

Kol nodded. It made sense. The air around him was disturbed for only a moment before Iris acquired his plate. Kol glared at her, and she only smiled back at him. "So, they fight monsters, is that it?"

Harvest took a few seconds before responding, "Yes, but fight is too weak of a word."

"They eradicate them," Iris said, coming back, "regardless of if you are trying to retain your humanity. Anything not human is death when Caelestibus is involved." Iris picked up the empty tray of spaghetti. "No mercy. Where we would give them a second chance, they will not."

"Thought you liked her fire?" Kol prodded.

Iris picked up the stack of dishes. "I do, that's her personality. That doesn't mean I like her organization's purpose."

"So, you two have dealt with them before?" Kol asked. He was not even going to attempt that complex understanding of the given situation.

Iris shook her head. "No, but we know of them and try to keep our distance." She started towards the cabin. "If any of them found my family's organization they would destroy it. Any human believed to be helping monsters is given the same judgment."

"I have." Harvest pulled Kol's attention from Iris's dark expression. "Our shining hero is not the only one who has thought me to be permanently my other self."

"What did you do?"

"Ran," he said simply. "There are always two of them. That's why I find this one strange and glad nothing can be detected from outside the Encampment. You saw how powerful they can be, and that is only half of a single entity. They work as one being separated into two bodies, overpowering and efficiently deadly."

"What about their armor?" Lloyd asked. He gave a small heave and both nets fell to the ground, the metal inside bouncing off of one another and the sound echoing around them. He must have ventured to the car while they were talking. Iris stuck her head from the cabin doorway to see what had made the sound.

"That I don't know much about. Every time they have come after me I never stayed long enough to find out what all they were capable of."

"Shocking," Kol said. Lloyd snickered at the pun.

"That was hilarious," Harvest stated calmly and reached for the first net. "I wonder what it is made from and how it works."

"Kol will know," Iris yelled to them over the sink water. "He knows metallurgy." Kol just shrugged when Harvest looked towards them.

It took several minutes of them finding a way to open the nets and separate the pieces. They placed the pieces of armor on the grass atomically correctly. The shield and sword they placed next to their correct gauntlets. The suit was still as massive as they saw the other night. Though the wearer was asleep, Kol's instincts told him to remain cautious. The armor gave off a dangerous vibe and though shining in the evening sun it held a feeling that it would rise at any moment and attack them. The tone of the armor was not black but indigo. Of course, with a lack of light it appeared much darker. "What do you think?"

Kol picked up a piece made to protect the right bicep. Heavy, the weight seemed unnecessary, and Kol had no idea how Wilhelmina could lift not only this piece but the whole suit. The metal was a few centimeters thick, and inside was a black padding that compressed to fit. Three metal tubes were fed through the padding from the top of the piece to the bottom with other smaller tubes branching off from the sides. The larger tubes must have a purpose for some form of hydraulics, while the smaller ones encased running wires. He saw that he had been right last night: the metal was etched with silver symbols. Though runes were an important part of forging certain metals, these ones appeared to have been engraved after the armor's creation, but in a method Kol did not recognize. This meant that whatever spells existed here were not folded within the metal but applied after. As for the type of metal, he knew at first glance that it was as a simple alloy.

Titanium, he had no doubt there, was the main ingredient for whomever crafted the armor. Titanium was considered a light metal, with far less weight than steel. The weight of the arm plate told him just how much titanium was used. If the metal was considered light, then the heaviness came from a lot of used material. Silver was also present, he believed, leading Kol to think that a werewolf had no chance against a knight of Caelestibus. A defense that fought back was a very effective ally. Spell-forged, he could tell that just by looking. The protected gears that attached to one another were now visible, and Kol saw they too were made of the same. His experience stopped there. Spell-forged gear would need to be examined by someone who has mastered that part of the trade, like his uncle.

"Titanium, a lot of it, forged with silver and others I'm not completely sure about," Kol told Harvest and Lloyd, who seemed to be paying attention. Kol moved to the shield and sword and examined them. After a few seconds he became frustrated. "These two, however, are made from something that I have never witnessed or read about." He went to lift the shield using both hands, straining. On the inside bars ran across to support the face. He saw two hooking devices that attached to the left-hand gauntlet. Another device was attached under that and Kol knew it was where the sword went. Too small for the great sword, though; maybe it collapsed. He inspected the blade. It was flawless to the touch, but he leaned closer and found what he was looking for. "The sword collapses behind the shield, like we saw. As for the type of metal, it glows. Very faintly, but if you put it in a pitch-black room, you will see."

"Interesting," Harvest nodded. "Silver in the armor, an innovative idea." He was looking at the knee guard and front thigh piece.

"How does it hold together?" Lloyd asked. "What is with the mechanics and the runes?" That was the most normal thing Lloyd has said so far, and good questions too. "I've never seen anything like them."

Harvest was giving him an amused look, probably because he thought the same thing that Kol did. He picked up the helmet and gave it a once over before responding. "The wiring system is for sensory input, from what I can tell. The eye slits on the front are for show, I believe, because the entire inside front of the helmet is a LED screen. If I had to guess, I would say it displays the armor's status and the tracking devices that she said are installed." He gestured to the spaulder and a gauntlet with both his hands. "Also, inventory. The armor has compartments all over it for holding items such as the nets."

"These have silver too," Kol interrupted.

"Right." Harvest nodded. He lightly shook the spaulder.

"A hand puppet." Lloyd laughed as he started to put a gauntlet on. He struggled but his hand would not enter.

"Let me see that." Harvest took it from Lloyd and peered inside. "Well, that shows how the suit fits her."

"How?" Lloyd asked.

"The dark material on the inside is fitted to her hand." He turned it for them to see. "Her hand won't go all the way to the armor's fingers. The amazing thing is, she can move her hand like normal and the glove responds in the same way." He set the gauntlet back then went to the boot. "Same here, though it looks like she has to stand on her toes to wear them. All must be compatible with the clothing she wears underneath."

"So, she wears heels into battle," Iris said. She had walked up from her wagon a few seconds ago.

Harvest nodded. "I'm still bothered by not knowing what the runes are for. It's not my specialty."

"I might know." Iris took a seat on the grass next to Kol. She was holding a rather large brown book. The border was a black leather and on the front Kol could not read the old language the title was written in. "It's a book on known runes in the world," she told their curious looks. "Ones used by wizards and witches mostly, but some others as well." She opened the book and began to flip through it.

Kol sat back and watched her read. She was amazing; no magical ability at all, but always prepared for anything that comes in the field. He guessed that you would need to be in this kind of world. Harvest and he both had their advantages: he had his bell and Harvest's had the ability to level the playing field. Iris had to use her intelligence to stay alive. He did not know about Lloyd besides the supernatural abilities, but he did take out Wilhelmina, who also had her armor if she decided to join. Plus, there was something about Lloyd that told Kol more was to come. Hopefully it would be a positive influence to them.

Kol walked to the fire to add more logs from the stack next to it. This place was unusually warm after a few days. Though the cold was his true home, he never minded a good hearth fire to lay beside. The Encampment looked to be a part of the woods, but it was not. Whenever the wind would bend the trees and carry with it a deep chill it would never reach them. Kol believed it hit the protective barrier on the edge of the meadow and caressed around it without slowing in pace. It had not rained since he had arrived here but Kol believed it would halt just a few meters above the trees that bent in around them. He could probably take a shower in the water that would slide off. He decided he wanted to see that, the rain at least. They had artificial grass and rain from the ceiling pipes in the agricultural buildings back home, but the grass was nothing like the stuff back home, and the rain would not be, either. His home was the ice, the cold, and the dark, but for now the wilderness was his home and he loved it.

"That's strange," Harvest said from behind him.

Kol finished placing the last log and walked over to kneel beside Harvest. "What?"

"I cannot find any source of power."

"Is it really needed?" Lloyd asked distantly.

Harvest shook his head. "It has to be. Something must be running the Heads Up Display and the compartments and weapons. These large tubs are the only thing close to what could support this masterpiece. But from the battle, they have to be a part of the overdrive."

"Magic?" Iris asked, raising an eyebrow.

"I don't think so; the pieces in here are far too modern." Harvest carefully turned the chest piece over to examine the back. "This is one of the most impressive pieces of machinery I have ever seen. A balance of modern technology and protective magic, but I don't see how it functions. She obviously can't move this on her own."

"Hmmmm," Lloyd sounded, "Maybe..." The runes began to glow.

When it had started to glow, Kol thought it was only a trick to the fire at first. The intricate silver symbols now shone with, a piercing white light. The eyes of the helmet shined the brightest, and he had to squint to avoid blindness. He could barely see the pieces, moving slowly over the grass, the exposed gears and attachments beginning to interlock and hide themselves as the armor became whole, healing any damage the group had caused in the club. In moments the behemoth was back together, appearing at any moment to stand and attack. They stood, Kol reaching for his bag to grab his sword. Wilhelmina walked up them and she too shone. Her suit, no maybe it was her skin, displayed identical runes to the armor. Every one of them was in the same place they would be on the armor. Even parts on her face were alight. She had her eyes closed when she stepped forward, but now she slowly opened them. They were the brightest of all the essence they now stood in, the fire of anger so hot you could not look upon it. Her eyes held so much fury that Kol was reminded to reach for his sword. She slowly scanned all of them before saying in a voice barely above a whisper, "Do not touch him again."

CHAPTER SEVENTEEN

Another Peculiar Addition

"**H**ow?" Harvest asked incredulously.

Wilhelmina's head snapped towards his. "It is no business of yours." She stepped closer to Harvest. The light slowly started to fade as she spoke. "You have no right to touch my armor."

"I had every right. You attacked us, tried to kill us, and we needed to know what we might be up against."

"So you ask me to join you then continue to treat me like the prisoner?" Her voice started to gradually climb to a yell. "What makes you think I would even agree to helping you WHEN YOU CHOOSE TO DISGRACE MY ARMOR! LOOKING OVER IT LIKE SOME NEW PLAYTHING!"

Harvest never raised his own voice, keeping his demeanor as if he did nothing wrong at all. "I couldn't resist. The whole thing is impressive."

This helped to bring her rage down. "My armor is me. To touch it without my permission is highly disrespectful. If ANY of you do it again I will carve you hollow and hang you from the trees."

Lloyd started to crouch, slowly reaching his hand towards the helmet. "Are you hungry?" Iris stepped in front of Lloyd, causing him to fall backwards laughing.

Wilhelmina glanced at her. "Yes, I'm starving."

"Come with me. There is plenty in the wagon." Iris nudged Wilhelmina's arm and together they headed toward the wagon.

"The moment you touch him again I will know, just as I did when I woke," was her final warning over her shoulder before she stepped into the cabin.

"Lot of rage in that one," Lloyd told them, smiling.

Kol nodded. "You think she will join?"

"She will," Harvest said. "Her honor demands it of her, and her quest to eventually kill me."

Lloyd reached down and grabbed the helmet. The armor had unfastened itself and became inanimate after the light had vanished. He held it above his head while dancing awkwardly and making high pitched sounds with his mouth. Kol laughed and moved toward the fire, not wanting to be caught in the middle if Wilhelmina came back out. Harvest joined him, followed by Lloyd tossing the helmet back down just as Wilhelmina's head peered from the door at them. Kol added another log before relaxing on his blanket. Harvest followed suit and so did Lloyd, except he seemed to like the grass more than fabric. "So who are you?" Kol asked the strange person.

Lloyd looked at him, confused. "What?"

"Who are you?" Kol repeated.

"I'm Lloyd." He gave Kol a look as if he had lost his mind.

"Where are you from?" Harvest tried.

"Nature," he said, smirking.

Harvest squinted at Lloyd, "So you've lived in the woods your whole life, or a town?"

"Are you serious right now?" Lloyd asked, sounding offended. Kol smiled. Lloyd seemed to only speak sarcasm. Kol would just have to think that Lloyd was some person who grew up in the wild, and he was going to respect his privacy. Kol himself did not want anyone asking more questions than needed about his own home. Wilhelmina did not have the luxury, because who she is was apparently well known. The others were just as mysterious as he was. Iris was a part of some circus or festival goers, but she gave nothing else away about them, and Harvest was locked tighter than Kol was. Kol at least gave a very small form of the truth. That was not important, really; they all had a common goal. Well, Harvest, Iris, and possibly Wilhelmina did.

Kol shook his head before continuing, "So, Lloyd." They did need to know this. "Will you be staying to help us?"

Lloyd started to laugh. One thing Kol did notice about Lloyd that was when he laughed, it was not to make fun of anyone. He simply laughed out of joy or insanity and Kol didn't think he would ever know exactly which. It was like he had just remembered a good joke or was contemplating how he was going to kill all of them. Kol believed Lloyd would concoct something original and flashy to do the deed, yet he still felt he could trust him, at least as much as Kol figured he could trust a lightning storm. Fun to watch, but randomly dangerous. The girls joined them at the fire a few minutes later. Iris sat on a blanket next to Kol with Wilhelmina between Harvest and Lloyd. Wilhelmina had a large plate of leftovers from the dinner earlier. She appeared calm while slowly making her way through her meal. Maybe she had more to her than just anger.

"So I am going to pretend that none of you touched my armor." She took a piece of bread, chewed and swallowed. "And maybe the part where my armor was removed and tied up. I will admit that I am curious as to what this is all about. Why people like you were in the club and such."

"Did you forget the part where you logged a steel plate door halfway into a wall and attacked us? Or better yet, tried to kill us unprovoked?" Harvest replied.

"No, so my suspicions will stay." She took another bite. Without her angry voice she sounded very matter of fact. "I don't know any of you, and as such do not trust you. I'll listen to what you have to say and decide from that if I will kill you," she pointed at Harvest, "and capture the others."

This stabbed at Kol lightly, but he remained quiet. He would like to see her try and catch them, or harm Harvest again. She no longer had surprise on her side. "She does have a right to that,

Harvest," Iris said. "It is her purpose to slay monsters and protect the innocent."

"And act irrational," Lloyd put in, smiling.

"So, you would like to know what we are doing." Harvest ignored all of them. "We won't tell you of our origins but the three of us," he gestured to Iris and Kol, "have a common goal, which is to stop the infestation of vampires that had occurred here. We are also helping Kol find the person responsible for sending someone to kill his father."

"How is it that I can't know where you are from but you can know that about me?" Wilhelmina interrupted. There was the anger again, slight but appearing so easily.

Harvest said, "It isn't our fault that Caelestibus is well known. Maybe if they didn't dress in shining armor they would go more unnoticed."

"And what about the things you are capable of?" she demanded, searching for another argument. "You examined my armor and know how it works. Why don't you tell me how you can transform into a human, and how he can apparently teleport?" Close, Kol thought, but not quite right.

"That as well is to remain secret," Harvest stated. His voice was starting to sound bored. "Some of us are protecting others, and our abilities are not our secret to tell. If you have to know that information you can leave now."

Wilhelmina remained seated, jabbing her fork with more force now and eating more aggressively. "Fine. Just tell me the story so far."

"I came here a month ago and walked in on a few fledgling vampires feasting on a cow." Judging by his tone, Harvest definitely did not want to tell the story again. "I spoke to them, in my vampiric form so I could gain their trust, but they decided to attack and defend their meal. I killed them and when the last one was falling, Iris stepped out of the shadows to talk with me. She took me for one of them, but after I showed her I wasn't, we both agreed to work together in our common goal. When I located what I believed was their den, Kol got in the way."

"Sorry for staying alive," Kol quipped.

"Sometimes I question that." Harvest glared briefly at Kol, then continued his story. "Kol is here because he is looking for a magical item that will wake his father from a cursed sleep. The wizard in his village sent him to this location to look it. He somehow scared a vampire during a hunt who then led him back to their temporary den. Before Kol was found, I witnessed the master at work giving out his blood. He told them Kol was spying on them and they attacked, so I stepped in. The vampires remaining after the initial skirmish retreated and brought more with them. We counted a little over twenty. We had to flee, and came back here. Kol told us of his problem, and we decided to help each other out."

"And this one?" Wilhelmina asked aggressively. She was talking about Lloyd, who had been secretly grabbing food from her plate for the last minute or so.

"He came along when you did. I guess he would like to stay and help too." Harvest laid back on his right elbow. "After the last meeting, we have not picked up any trace of the vampires in the city or surrounding area since, so we have been looking into Kol's matter as well, which is why we were at the club."

"That seems logical," Wilhelmina said, back to the matter of fact voice. "My tracking system found no residue of more than you. I rode almost all of the city, and the whole time it was your trail I was after. Which makes it hard to believe you're telling the truth. Despite what my armor has told me, I would not be here if there was not more activity. So if it is true, one vampire could not sustain so many, nor could he have hopes of finishing any of their transformations. They will perish eventually."

"Meaning they are disposable," Harvest said, "and yes, they are disposable, which means we need to find their master and kill him."

"So what is your next plan of action?" Wilhelmina asked.

"Next, we look into a matter concerning the person who attacked my father. We just acquired fresh evidence from the club. I hope to be traveling as soon as possible." Kol glanced at Harvest.

"In the morning, Kol; another night of rest will not hurt," Iris leaned in and suggested. Kol reluctantly realized that she was right again; his body was still fatigued from his bell. The morning, then, and not a moment later.

"So that's it," Harvest said. "If you choose to join us, you will be given back your armor and weapons along with your vehicle and other things. If not, I will send you on your way and leave it somewhere for you to find after we are long gone. We have to establish some trust here. What is your decision?" He turned to Lloyd. "Same for you. You are more than welcome to join us, though I have no idea if you're qualified to handle this. Seeing how you took on the Knight, I would say you are. But if you're crazy enough to help and can't take what's to come, I won't lose any sleep over you if anything happens. I usually have good instincts with this; the danger will only increase. If you agree, you will help us and listen to either Iris, Kol, or myself, depending on whichever of the two situations we are dealing with."

"I'll do what I jolly well please," Wilhelmina snapped peevishly, determined to not be bossed around.

"You will want to follow us if you decide to stay." Harvest laid back on the grass. "I'm tired of talking. Take a few moments to decide."

A silence set in. As they waited for their answers, Lloyd stood, and a second later so did Wilhelmina. Lloyd strode off towards the horses and started to rub their heads. He was not laughing this time; in fact, his face looked serious for once. Then Wilhelmina walked to her armor and peered down at it. She walked around it, Kol guessed to inspect it and make sure nothing had been harmed by their prodding. Lloyd had started back towards them and Kol and Iris stood. Wilhelmina reached down and grasped her sword. Kol thought for a second to reach for his own, but Iris grabbed his arm lightly.

A soft click echoed in the air as the hilt came away from the monster blade. Within it was a smaller version of Wilhelmina's sword, one she could wield easily. Giving it a simple swing, she nodded to herself and knelt beside her shield. Wilhelmina made several presses along the metal, in a spot Kol was not able to see, and the shield opened and the center raised for her to grab. It was also a smaller version of the original it was inside. The family crest was only a center cutout of the original, but that did not matter when it was bashed over someone's head. She swiftly fastened it to her left arm before standing upright.

Harvest stood with them now, the three of them looking on what could be the new members of their team. Wilhelmina stepped toward them, and Lloyd fell in behind her. They both stopped in front of the motley group. Wilhelmina was determined and Lloyd still seemed serious. "I have no idea who you people are, and there is a strong possibility that you are lying to me. I can take care of myself, so in truth I really have nothing to fear from you or what we are after. My instinct says I should slay you now." Kol saw her grip tighten on her sword handle. Kol eased himself slightly in front of Harvest and Iris. He would probably take a hit before he could pull his sword, but at least it would not hit the other two.

Wilhelmina ignored him. "But my honor says I must investigate this matter further and make absolutely sure the innocents are safe." She pointed her sword at Harvest's face. Kol kept his muscles ready. "If you are lying to me, setting me up for a trap, or make any move of harm towards me, I will not stop until I have hunted you down and staked you in the sunlight." She pulled her blade away, then lifted her left arm and stuck it behind the shield where it became sheathed just as their larger counterparts did. "You are right of the dangers, and I am aware that you can't trust me just like I can't trust you. We will need to work together if the future path is as grave as you believe. So, on my honor, this is the most I can do." She stepped closer and held her shield before her. Iris gripped Kol's arm tighter and pulled him aside. Harvest must have known what was needed, because he stepped up and placed his right hand on her shield. "From this moment on and until the deed is considered done, I will be your Shield. As so long as you are true to me, so I will be to you."

Kol knew she had to swallow her pride, a very large amount, to even say that. It was probably worse because she thought Harvest a monster, and Harvest must have known that too, so he replied with the words that must have been proper: "Your shield will protect us. Your service is welcome and in need." He removed his hand and she lowered her shield. Nodding more to herself than anyone else, she stepped to stand beside Harvest and faced Lloyd. "And you?"

"I'm not about any of that craziness, but last night was too much fun. So, I'm going to stay and see what other forms of mischief I can get myself into." He laughed then and stepped beside Wilhelmina and faced the same way as them. "What are we looking at?" he asked.

Hours later, Kol and Harvest stood by themselves near the tree line. After the new members joined, they all decided to get ready for bed again. Wilhelmina had gone to her bike to grab clothes for a shower and camping supplies. She now slept in her own three-room tent. Lloyd was also asleep in his patch of chosen grass after his own shower, though Kol didn't see why he had taken the shower if he was just going to lay in the dirt again. Iris was in her room getting ready for bed and creating a supply list for them tomorrow. "So, you think we are going to find anything useful tomorrow at this address?" Kol asked.

"We may," Harvest said. "It has been over a few weeks since your father was attacked, and it could be abandoned. The location is a long distance north of us so we will be traveling a while."

"It's all we have," Kol stated.

"It is. One step always leads to another," Harvest assured him. "I'm going to bed."

Kol stretched out in his hammock. The fire had died down low so the stars shown brighter than usual above him. So much had just happened that it did not seem real. A Knight straight from history attacking them, then swearing a temporary oath of service. A ragamuffin of an individual saving them who was also possibly insane. Quite the assortment of individuals once you included Harvest, Iris, and himself. They now had another lead but the disheartening part about it was there was not much to go on. If this did not fall in their favor, then the trail would grow cold again. This thought alone kept Kol from any form of peace in his sleep.

CHAPTER EIGHTEEN

A Way Within a Way

The morning light proved him wrong as he observed the golden color brightening the branches above him. That and the smell. That delicious smell would ruin his day if he did not wake to it. Maybe that was his stomach talking, but it did not stop the urge to leap from his hammock and assault the breakfast table. Kol accepted this impulse as a necessary action but had second thoughts at the slightest move. Lifting to stretch his arms he felt drained. His body was stiff and wanted him to move with caution. He waited for the grogginess of his sleep to pass, then ignored his body's pleas and shrugged out of his hammock.

They had planned to leave in the morning. Kol did not think sunrise was the correct form of morning. Night had just ended, and from what he saw from the others told Kol they would like to enjoy a few more hours of rest. Iris was moving about in her middle wagon, but Harvest and Wilhelmina were both dead to the world inside their tents. Lloyd had changed places during the night, as his first patch of grass no longer sustained his needs, so he must have decided closer to the fire was better. Kol was glad to see him in a different pair of clothes, extremely large sweat pants and shirt, instead of the rags that Kol had seen him in for entire time he was here. He stepped lightly over the smug sleeper as he let his nose guide him to the wagon.

"Oh," Iris said, followed by a large book hitting the floor. She was still in her sleep clothes, a grey t-shirt and blue pajamas. She had been sitting at a stool reading a book over the counter when Kol walked into the doorway.

"Sorry I startled you," Kol said, stepping into the wagon and retrieving the book from the floor. "*The Nutcracker?*" he asked after seeing the title.

"Yeah," she said, looking away. "We've been so busy I'd forgotten Christmas had come so close. It's one of my favorite Christmas stories." Kol handed her back the book which she placed on the counter behind her. "Do you have a favorite Christmas Story?"

Kol smiled at her as she turned back to face him. "*The Night Before Christmas.*"

"I like that one, too. I like all of them, really." She moved to the stove to flip a couple of pancakes. Kol's stomach growled as he looked at her creation in progress. Eggs had been beaten and prepared with cheese, sausage links sputtered in a pan next to large strips of bacon, and of course, the fluffy stack of pancakes. He wanted to pull a strip of bacon from the grease and run with it before Iris saw. "Coffee?" she asked him, lifting a large green mug and retaking her seat on the stool.

"No, thank you, not really fond of the stuff," he said, taking Iris's cooking fork and turning the sausages.

"I love it. My life source." She eyed him coolly as he moved the bacon around the pan. "Is there anything I can get you?"

He smiled and shook his head. "No. Iris, you are doing enough already." He placed the fork back where she had it. "Why are you up so early?"

"Wanted to get a head start on the day," she said, looking into her cup. "From what I've experienced, Harvest prefers to be late and I do not, so I try to hinder that as much as possible."

"Couldn't sleep," Kol corrected her.

She gave him a guilty look. "That too."

Kol grabbed the spatula and lifted the two pancakes from the pan and placed them on top of the five others she had already made. He grabbed the purple bowl full of batter and poured two more into the pan. "Why?"

"Just a lot has happened so quickly," she said. "I came here expecting to solve the problem by myself. I had no idea how bad the situation is. Then the four of you coming along." She jumped a little after the last comment. "Not that I don't mind; I'm glad you're here…" a moment's pause, "and the others." She stopped there.

"You shouldn't worry so much about us," he told her. He flipped the pancakes over so the other side could cook. "We are getting involved because we choose to. It's not a burden you need to carry alone."

"If something happens…"

"We will take care of it, Iris," Kol said, then placed the spatula down and faced her, crossing his arms.

"You have your own problems too, Kol."

"We are taking care of that as well." He gave her a smile. "Trust me. This will be done before Christmas."

Her look was hopeful and it rocked Kol. "You believe so?"

Believe. A word Kol held close to his heart, the one that encased his hope and pushed him on. He nodded. "I believe." She smiled up at him, and Kol felt that uncontrollable urge start again. He leaned into her and she did the same toward him. They were only a centimeter from one another but pulled hastily away as Lloyd stepped into the doorway. "Hey," his speech was a faked slur, "Who's got the bacon?"

Iris pulled back instantly. "It will be done shortly," Iris assured him, smiling and hiding her blush behind her hair. "Go wake the others," she instructed Lloyd.

"I love black pancakes," Lloyd laughed.

Iris looked at him questioningly then realized what he meant. She moved frantically to save the burning pancake.

"I'm going to take a shower," Kol said.

"Don't take too long," Iris said, not looking away from the stove, clearly embarrassed. Kol wanted to tell her not to be, but something told him that was the wrong thing to do. He walked past Lloyd, who was still smiling and starting toward Wilhelmina's bed. Looking over his shoulder, he felt an odd sense of fore-boding once Lloyd reached the bed. He quickened his step so he was not caught in what was destined to come. He reached the shower quickly and finished his ablutions rapidly. Now completely paint and blood free, Kol made his way back to camp and could hear talking.

"He was just staring at me making 'pssst' sounds." Wilhelmina was up, and Kol's feeling from earlier had been correct.

"It's better than him yelling at you," Iris teased.

"I can wake up on my own just fine!" Always the hostility.

Kol walked around the cabin and found them sitting around the table, except for Harvest who was still asleep. "Pssst," Lloyd said, reaching out to Wilhelmina with his finger.

"DON'T TOUCH ME!" she yelled, swinging a fist and missing. Lloyd laughed and started on his stack of pancakes. Kol walked up and took his seat next to Iris.

"So is that better than the lake?" Iris asked him.

"Not cold enough," Kol said, helping himself to eggs. They continued their meals in silence, except for the occasional words from Lloyd. Harvest woke when exactly a single plate of food was left, which he devoured half awake. Kol started to put the dishes away after almost coming to blows with Iris. It ended in Lloyd and himself washing the dishes with Wilhelmina drying them off and placing them appropriately. He had sent Iris off to get a shower, threatening to put her there himself. Harvest went to the vehicles to get them ready for the journey. When Iris returned, she was wearing casual blue jeans and a black jacket over a light blue shirt. Her bracelets jingled on her wrists and she had donned her usual pair of boots.

Wilhelmina went down the hill to the shower next, then Harvest after he returned from the vehicles. Wilhelmina looked normal, which Kol never thought of her outside her chain mail fabric. She still had it on beneath her black hoodie, blue jeans, and sneakers. With Harvest in jeans and pocketed jacket and Lloyd in kakis and a lime green muscle shirt and brown jacket, they looked rather normal. Wilhelmina's purple hair may draw some attention, but besides that, they gave no appearance of a group of monster hunters. Kol thought it was good because they wanted to blend in where they were going. When he thought about it, he did not know exactly where the address the Rev had given them was.

"So, where are we headed?" Kol asked Harvest as they packed the back of his car with supplies. They did not know how long it would take to find the location the Rev had told them about, so Iris had prepared them with camping equipment and enough food to last them a couple of days.

"It's a small town on the east coast in Virginia." Harvest reached up and pulled the hatch down securely.

Kol did not know the exact distance, but he was aware of the state's location from here. "So we have a long drive ahead of us?"

Harvest nodded, but Iris disagreed. "Not as long as you think." She and Wilhelmina were loading the armor into the bed of the truck. Wilhelmina had allowed them to help her at least this much to be ready faster. They would be taking two vehicles on this trip, one to help scout and one to carry the armor and supplies.

"Ten hours is a long way," Harvest said back to her.

Iris smiled as she and Wilhelmina finished securing the tarp over the armor and camping supplies. "I'll show you." She snapped the last bungee cord into place and walked around them. The vehicles had been pulled further into the tunnel next to the path leading towards the encampment since Iris had originally wanted them this far up so it would be easier to load the vehicles. With her mysterious comment, it would seem the reasoning for the vehicles' position was a little more important that loading equipment. Wilhelmina, Harvest, and Kol each repositioned themselves to have a better view of whatever Iris was up to.

"Are we all staring into a random direction again?" Lloyd asked, stepping from the trail with his bag slung over his back. It was still different to see him wearing clean clothes. It almost made him seem less crazy. He cocked his head at Iris, erasing Kol's thought of him being normal.

Iris shook her head, either to concentrate or stop herself from laughing. She reached in her pocket and pulled out a new whistle. This one looked like it had several small holes lining the light wood. She brought the instrument to her lips and started to play. There were far too many notes to ever try to mimic, and maybe that was the point, but Kol would want to try after hearing this tune only once. The notes soared high and then came crashing back down, a personification of joy and life. Kol felt it tug at his heart and pull his body to move to it. It had the same effects on the others as well. Harvest was bobbing his head, Wilhelmina held a light smile, and Lloyd embraced it fully and began to move along with it in rapid motions like the ones you would see around the campfire of a tribe. The tune reached further out, to the animals, the sky, to the earth, and the trees. Once it reached the trees, they began to dance as well.

The forest before them came alive, just as it did at the entrance. These trees were far larger and older, so their movement was more strained. Yet the old cedars would not let that stop them from enjoying the sound of the tune. Their branches clasped one another in a tangled embrace and raised their roots to level the way. Iris repeated the main chorus of the song again and drifted into the conclusion. The trees heard the end was near and began to slow. Breathless, she pulled the flute from her lips and spun towards them, the last note echoing down the newly formed tunnel.

Kol walked up to her. "What is this?" The song still had his heart alive and working hard. The others stepped up around her to look into the large entrance.

"A shorter way," Iris told him simply, light laughter in her voice.

Wilhelmina examined the tangled branches above them. "I've heard of this before when you brought me here. I thought they only existed overseas, before the colonial period here in the

States. The way to create them had been lost." She looked at Iris. "Who is it that showed you this?"

"That is to remain with me," Iris told Wilhelmina. "The way was not forgotten, just well hidden."

"These could be used for a better purpose."

"They could," Iris said, "But this was created as a haven for those in need of it. I would have never shown it to any of you if not for the severity of the situation. I don't fear you leaving here knowing this; none of you know the song, and I'm not willing to teach it." Iris turned to Kol. "My Encampment is not the only one that exist on this continent. There are thousands of others scattered from here to the Pacific. Each one has a connection to others through the tunnel you see here. Inside these tunnels another form of magic is at work, one that makes traveling over a large distance shorter. Not by too much, but we will make this trip in fewer hours than it would take otherwise."

"This is amazing," Kol told Iris, and she beamed.

"We should get going," Harvest asserted practically.

Lloyd started to scream and run into the tunnel as fast as his legs would take him. They watched him go. "If anyone should be the one to be worried about it would be him, not me," said Wilhelmina crossly and started for the passenger side of the truck.

"Be sure to pick him up," Iris said and joined Wilhelmina on the driver's side.

The truck roared to life as Kol stepped into Harvest's car. "Are we going to get him?"

Harvest didn't answer, turning over the ignition of the car. He started into the trees at a fast pace, doing so carefully so no harm would come to his machine or the trees. They came upon Lloyd a little over half a kilometer away. Kol still wanted to know how he could move as fast as he did. Kol believed he would find out the moment he found out about Harvest. Harvest slowed the car enough for Lloyd to open the door and hop in. He almost slipped and fell under the tire, and Kol did not think Harvest would have stopped. Lloyd laughed, apparently ignorant of the near bodily harm, and Harvest started his stereo. They journey had begun, and Kol felt he was moving closer north, not only in location but in finishing what he had come here to do.

The path was not a straight shot. It would curve left and right frequently, dip low into bottoms and up high into hills. Bridges constructed over lakes and rivers from stone would raise as they came closer. The stone would even move for them so that they could safely pass through mountain tunnels. It was an amazing sight. They could rarely see past the wood line, but occasionally they would catch an image of the countryside. Not once did he see any form of urbanization, as if the path were truly alive and wanted to avoid the areas. Kol found it hard to believe that there was a straight shot from where they were to their destination consisting completely of nature. He asked Iris at the first Encampment other than their own that they came to.

"We do pass under roads and near farms and small towns. The trees just hide us well from them. Thanks to the ward that is placed, no one can see us going along, either," she told him after finishing a new song to open the tunnel before them again. "Don't ask me how; it's just something we accept."

He had to take that for now, though his curiosity was still active. Kol checked his list to try and get a grasp of where they were, but the screen was blank. "Interference," Harvest said, looking over at him.

"So nothing can get out."

"Nope, we're all alone," Lloyd said from the back in between chips. Kol found the flaw in Iris's organizing the moment his own stomach began to rumble. Why place the food in the same car with three guys that had nothing to do but listen to music? The bag Lloyd had was the third to go, along with some sandwich meat, vegetables, bread, and drinks. They mostly drove in silence listening to Harvest's playlist. Lloyd liked to play a game called "What If," in which he spouted out random events that could happen and what they would do to overcome them.

"What if the path collapsed with us still inside?" Lloyd asked.

"I would be enraged from my car being destroyed by trees," Harvest said.

Kol shook his head. "I think I would try to exit the vehicle."

A few minutes later.

"What if an alien popped out of my head and I, like, died." He pushed his shirt out with his fist to show where it would emerge. "Blood spurts everywhere and guts, the thing screaming."

"Stab you with my sword," Kol said.

"Open your door and push you out and hope your death is slow after Iris hits you so you are well punished for covering the inside of my car with blood and ichor." And they drove on as if the matter were serious. They stopped to use the restroom at the next encampment and were away again. Lloyd had passed out in the back and Harvest was nodding along with his music. They had stopped at six Encampments so far and had been on the road for a little over three hours. The last Encampment they had to leave to find a place to fill up the gas tanks. They took ten minutes to walk around and stretch before they were off again. Kol had wondered how Iris and Wilhelmina would take riding together starting off slightly hostile. At the first stop they had kept quiet, but from every stop on they seemed more and more comfortable with each other. Harvest enjoyed the warmth, and by warmth he meant furnace, so Kol placed his head against the window. It wasn't the arctic cold he wanted, but for now it would work.

He could see the truck following behind them, far enough for both vehicle's safety. Kol could not see her, but he figured Iris was relaxing in her seat with a hand on the wheel listening to her music and talking with Wilhelmina. Iris had a way to open people up and bring out their good sides, Wilhelmina actually stepping from the truck laughing once was the proof of that. There was no lying to himself; Kol liked her and wanted to know her better. She was beautiful, and he often caught himself watching her across the campfire until she noticed. After they had danced at the club something had awakened in him, as if he had just realized that he wanted her. It was not just her smile, the way she walked, or her eyes that dragged him under, but who she was as well. She always worried about others making sure that they had everything they needed. She could take care of herself, which Kol thought was amazing, though he still felt the need to keep her safe. Her stubbornness was even something he was attracted to. He needed someone who would make him rethink his steps. She had the soul of a healer, to take care of the sick and tend to the wounded. The heart of a warrior, fearing no enemy and willing to step into the fire to protect the ones she cared for. Kol looked at her and could only find that she was absolutely phenomenal.

That was as far as Kol could go with it for now. He wanted her and he hoped she felt the same, though he had no way of telling. What had happened in the club seemed to be ample evidence, but was Kol just seeing it all wrong? She had touched Harvest on the arm before and laughed at Lloyd the same as she did at him, so was there anything for him? Kol kept reminding himself whenever she came up that he had people relying on him. His father's people needed their beacon in the storm to lead them and bring back hope. Without his father the North Pole would tear itself apart, and Kol would fall prey to the same desolation. After, he decided. After all of this was done and his father was saved he would meet with Iris and see where their paths went from there.

A deep horn reverberated around them that belonged to Iris's truck, waking Kol from the light sleep he had fallen into. Harvest began to slow as they emerged into a seventh Encampment, pulling to the right of the larger tree line. Iris pulled up beside him and shut her engine off, as did Harvest. Kol opened his door and stepped out, stretching his legs again. "How much further do we need to go?" he asked. He glanced at the inside clock and saw they were four and a half hours into the trip.

"None. We're here," Iris told him. "We were lucky that the area we wanted was a straight shot. There is no way we could make this much time if we wanted to go cross country; the path can only go where the trees are."

"Where is here?" Wilhelmina asked, sternly turning to Harvest.

Harvest reached behind his seat and smacked Lloyd, who woke with a start. "Selma Pine."

CHAPTER NINETEEN

An Abundance of Expression

They unloaded the vehicles before deciding on anything else. Wilhelmina wanted to start toward Selma Pine, but Iris told her they did not know how long they would be here, so the best thing to do was to set up camp first. Kol's time spent in his uncle's lands agreed with that, so he gave the others a hand. They left the armor in the truck, but the camping gear and what little was left of their food supply came with them up into the Encampment. There was a bit of difference between this Encampment and the one they had left that morning: This meadow was smaller, much smaller, and was simply wild grass instead of the many flowers of their first one. The trees were older here as well, thicker and leafless, displaying a grey sky above them beneath the afternoon light. No lake lay between the thickly sprawled limbs, but a beautiful mountain range could be seen stretching across the view from the entrance path. Kol felt great, as his body was not sweating from the humidity here. Inside the Encampment it held a warmth just like the other one, but this one was fainter. The Encampments must be able to hold a comfortable climate, but were limited to its surrounding area. The others might have felt a bit chilly, but Kol definitely did not mind.

Together they turned the small meadow into a temporary home. Harvest and Wilhelmina were busy constructing the five tents they had brought along while Iris and Lloyd were organizing the rest of the supplies from the truck. Thankfully, those in the first car had not devoured all of their food supply as Iris had cleverly given them decoy food while the primary supplies were safe in the back of her truck next to the armor. Kol did his job by choosing a safe place to build a fire and setting up the cooking kit above it. Because his job took far less time than the others, Iris handed Kol an axe and suggested that he start to collect firewood. Kol made sure that the tune to reenter the Encampment was the same, to which Iris replied, "So long as I am here it is." Reassured, Kol started his trek through the underbrush.

Kol walked in the direction of the distant mountain range and stepped from the protection of the Encampment. It did not take Kol long to gather what they would need for tonight and the morning. With rope from his bag, Kol bundled his collection into two easy to carry masses. Using a fallen branch, Kol lifted the work onto his shoulders and made his way back to camp.

Five tents were set around the center of the meadow, spaced evenly and enough distance away to be warmed by the fire. Each one was a different color: white, green, blue, red, and yellow. The blankets Iris had around their previous fire were rolled out here as well. Lloyd had stacked the supplies of water and food into a random circle off on the right, and the four of them were relaxing and talking amongst themselves on the blankets as he moved to drop the logs. "You could have come and retrieved one of us to help you carry those," Iris said, standing and striding towards him to help carry the logs.

Kol waved her away. "Was not a problem; we have to stay warm, right? I'm sure the night will be a lot colder here."

"You're right," Iris replied. "I'll place some in the pit to get started, later."

Untying the wood, Kol asked, "So what's the plan?"

"That's what we were discussing when you came back," Harvest spoke up. "The most important part is to remain undetected. If anything is still in the region we will need to not disturb it and give it a chance to run away."

"My armor can track goblins if there are any in the area," Wilhelmina commented.

"What creature would stay in town if rumor started that a Knight was in the area?" Lloyd asked her.

Wilhelmina turned on him, her anger starting to boil, "Wouldn't matter if they ran. I can track them."

Kol finished with the wood and joined the others at the center. "I don't want to spend more time on this than needed. Chasing them would take too long."

"I agree; the quicker this is done the quicker we can return south and finish the other job," Harvest decided.

"A waste of time." Wilhelmina crossed her arms defensively.

"Willa," Iris said. Willa? The two of them must have become closer than Kol believed on the trip here. "We will be taking the vehicles, so you won't be too far from your armor. If we find them and they run, then you will be able to go after them."

Wilhelmina remained obdurate. "I would just feel more secure with my armor on in the field."

"Against a few goblins?" Lloyd laughed at her.

Wilhelmina turned on him, throwing a piece of firewood. "WE DON'T KNOW WHAT ELSE IS OUT THERE!"

Kol caught the piece of wood before it hit Lloyd. "So when do we leave?"

"Dusk," Harvest replied.

Kol looked to the sky. "A few hours then. Iris, let's fix dinner. It's going to be a long night, and though we have been riding all day, we will still need the energy."

She agreed and they all started to pitch in, even Harvest. He started the fire while Lloyd filled a pot of water for soup from five-gallon jugs. Wilhelmina wanted to use the knives, so she and Iris chopped vegetables while Kol cooked the chicken breast in a pan. He then cut them into chunks and they added all the ingredients into the pot to boil. Iris manned the wooden spoon while everyone else relaxed on their blankets.

"So, how will we proceed with tonight?" Kol asked.

"Splitting into two teams. Lloyd, Wilhelmina, and I will check the shipyard while you and Iris will check the town then come help us finish the yard. I don't think we will find anything at either of these locations, but it would be best to get them out of the way regardless," Harvest stated calmly.

"That's stupid. We should go to where they will most likely be. A cave would be a good place to start." Wilhelmina added.

Harvest nodded. "I won't argue. That's why Iris and Kol are going into the town, to ask people if they know of any in the area or something along those lines."

"You talk of not wasting time but your plan is full of useless actions." Wilhelmina gave them the verbal equivalent of rolling her eyes.

"I agree with the plan," Kol said. Wilhelmina's comments were slightly annoying.

"I should go with Kol and Iris should go to the shipyard with the rest," Lloyd spoke out, smiling.

"Why do you say that, Lloyd?" Iris asked from the pot.

He shrugged. "I'm a people person."

Harvest looked at Iris to make sure she was okay with it. She watched Lloyd, seriously examining him, then smiled and shrugged. "That's fine with me, but I'm going off on my own in the harbor. Save more time like Wilhelmina said."

When Kol first met Iris, he had made the mistake of thinking that he needed to be worried about her when she went off on her own. After their fight with Wilhelmina in the club, his previous worries were unfounded.

They ate their soup quietly. When the cleanup was done, the group began their usual gear checks before going out into the field. For the first time since the night of the vampire den, Kol wore all of his gear. His sword stayed in his bag, and a second pair of easily removed jeans had been pulled on over his field pants to better blend in with crowds. They could be removed with a knife in the event of an emergency. Harvest had put on his worn out blue jeans and running shoes. His six-pocketed jacket was snug on his shoulders overlapping a black shirt.

Wilhelmina had dressed in her chainmail-like fabric before putting on common shoes, jeans, and jacket. She wore a large hiking pack on her shoulders that seemed lightly stuffed. Kol had seen Wilhelmina place her sword and shield inside when he was putting on his jacket. Lloyd had changed his clothes as well, but all Kol could see was a long dark brown coat wrapped around his front and falling to right above his knees. Lloyd was also wearing a small pair of square-paned glasses. His features were, well, normal, with not a strand of insanity left.

Iris also dressed in her full field gear, for the first time Kol had ever seen. Her hair was woven into a tight braid, to stop it from getting in the way. She wore a black high-necked shirt that had gloves of the same material built into it. Her leather belt that held several leather pouches and other tools of her trade was looped through a rust colored pair of pants with leather capped knees tucked into boots. Fastened across her back and chest was a spaulderless leather cuirass. It was made in the same style as her gloves and head band currently tucked into her belt with red and gold flame stitching. Lastly, she pulled on a brown leather jacket to conceal her lethality.

"Tonight," Harvest began, "we are here to track down the goblins that may have constructed the blade that was used against Kol's father. If it's found, we will call each other and meet at a designated spot." He reached into his left bottom pocket. He pulled from inside four small silver phones with wireless microphones to put into their ears and tossed them to Kol, Wilhelmina, Iris, and Lloyd. "The phones already have our numbers preprogrammed and the line is secure. There is an option for a group call, which we will use when something is found. Goblins may be weak, but they are treacherous. One will do nothing to us, but if we come upon a horde, we may be up against far worse odds. Goblins fight in numbers and will laugh when they play with you with hot knives and pokers." He looked up into the clouded sky with his eyes closed. For a moment he said nothing before looking back at them. "I've been hunting monsters all my life and have a sixth sense about it. Something will happen tonight."

Kol quietly closed the passenger door of Harvest's car as he dropped them off on a small hill looking over the town. Lloyd was not so cautious as he slammed the back door he came from. Kol could hear Harvest yelling angrily from within his car as Lloyd laughed to himself. Harvest must have let it go because he accelerated the car at a slow rate and was rolling down the hill. Kol looked at the truck that was following close behind and nodded to Iris. Kol watched the vehicles as they made their way down the main street. They would need to stop at the only traffic light in town.

Selma Pine was such a small town that Kol could take it in its entirety along with the forest that surrounded it and the sea it was built upon. Several broken roads flowed in between time caressed and poorly built buildings. There was no true organization to the town with a house uncommonly placed next to a bait and tackle shop. Kol could see a small steeple of a church near the south of the town and a school house toward the north. The cluster of buildings couldn't hold more than two hundred students. Dirty street lights illuminated the cracked sidewalks and aged roads in a pale aura. Kol couldn't make out any details of the distant docks, but he did see many fishing boats lined the wooden planks. The place was run down, that couldn't be denied, but Kol was glad that the townspeople tried their best for Christmas.

Many of the street lights had white Christmas lights twined around their stands. Kol knew a number of businesses and homes just by the arrangement of their of Christmas lights. Houses had them hanging from the roof and the other buildings had them taped around the display windows. In a few yards decorations would sit, twinkling along or moving in their slow animations. Kol would not be surprised to see a few wreaths on doors and Christmas trees peeking through windows. The town had only decorated what they could, so a few lamp posts gave only their light from above and buildings stood dark in the night, but the little bit was enough. Anything was enough when it came to December 25th, even a simple "Happy Holidays" to your neighbor.

Lloyd took the lead, starting first down the road, his head turned down and his hands in his pockets. He walked in a fashion to brace himself against the cold wind that rolled from the darkened sea. Of course, it did not have the same effect on Kol, but they were to blend in so he made himself hunker down as well. The first couple of buildings were empty: a clothing store, laundromat, and flower shop. The town was mostly small businesses holding families. As they moved further toward the center they started to find parked cars along the road, both old and new. They found their first individual coming along the sidewalk in front of them, an older man with stringy grey hair and mustache to match. He was tucked deep into his faded green jacket with a small grey cap for a roof.

"Evenin," the grey-haired man said in a rough voice as they neared him.

"I think you may be off by a few hours." Kol perked up and glanced around for whoever had said that. It too was a rough sounding voice, yet slightly lighter. He glanced to the roof, looking but found no one. He felt the need to draw his sword, but Lloyd spoke in a pleasant tone, "Where is everyone at this time of night?" The voice had come from him.

The old man paused and scratched his chin. "Mostly in bed, I believe, same as me here shortly." He gave a light cough. "But if you're looking for a place to lose yourself, no better place than Brandon's, a few blocks down the street."

"'Preciate it," Lloyd said in that same rough voice before stepping around the man.

The man's gaze followed him, confused. "Don't mention it."

Kol stepped past to follow after Lloyd. "Merry Christmas," he said to the man who nodded as he continued on his way, smelling thickly of alcohol. "What was that back there?" Kol asked Lloyd once back beside him.

Lloyd looked around at him confused. "What was what?" His voice was back to normal, well, as far as normal was to Lloyd.

"You changing your voice."

"You're stupid," he replied and sped up, looking suspiciously over his shoulder at Kol. He quickened his own pace and Lloyd did the same, trying to keep away from Kol like he was being chased. They were almost to the point of running when they came to the place the old man had told them to come.

Brandon's was a rather large bar and diner located on the main road with a view of the boat docks a little under a kilometer away. Light spilled into the street from the windows and the faint sound of music seeped from the walls. The building was made by what looked like hundreds of pieces of old driftwood nailed together. Two stories tall, the upper floor was smaller and dark, possibly the owner's apartments. The bottom was fairly large with the same old wood constructed into a front porch. Christmas lights wrapped the railing, and a red berry wreath hung on the front door beneath the bar's name in red neon lights. An older woman sat in one of the four rocking chairs on the porch wrapped in a thick blanket, holding a red cup steaming with something hot. Lloyd stepped up the few steps and greeted her with a nod. "Ma'am," he said with a heavy southern American accent Kol was getting used to hearing. She smiled at him and nodded back as the two of them pushed the front door opened and entered the building.

The room inside filled the front part of the building from wall to wall. On the left side were several pool tables along with high top tables and stools. Surprisingly, the place was extremely clean. Anything made of wood was well polished to shine from the floor to high ceiling. The right side had dark polished tables for dining, with a small section in the corner for the large flat screen television mounted to the hearth and lounging sofas surrounding it. A loaded bar was built on the far left next to the pool tables with doors leading into the back of the building. One of his dad's favorite's, "Little Saint Nick" by the Beach Boys, wafted from an old-fashioned jukebox. The back right corner was the home of the Christmas tree.

The place was filled with people both young and old. Most of the older man who had the touch of the sea about them crowded the pool table and bar. Booms of laughter came from them as they missed shots or told tales from when they were younger. Most of the dining tables were filled with families or groups of friends, waiting on seasonally dressed servers to take orders or bring meals. Children gathered behind the sofas to sit at small tables and play games of checkers or chess while their parents took the chance to talk amongst themselves in their respective areas.

A waitress from a nearby table caught their eye after delivering drinks to the small family there. Smoothing down her black work clothes and readjusting her blond hair, she stepped to the small wooden podium they were standing by. "Welcome to Brandon's, will you be dining in tonight?" Her voice was high pitched and sounded slightly nervous with the same accent as the rough man from outside with a slight slur and draw to the sound.

"Yes," Lloyd replied in his own drawn out slurred voice, "A small table towards the back please."

"All right," she said, smiling. "Right this way." She waved them to follow her towards the back.

She left them to a medium height round table with menus. Kol waited until she was out of earshot before venting his frustrations. "Why are we here?" He had to talk a little louder to be heard over the jukebox. "We are supposed to be looking for goblins."

Lloyd tilted his head while listening. When Kol had finished, he glared at Kol through his glasses. "Yell at me one more time." With that he flipped up his menu and disappeared behind it.

Kol shook his head and let it go. He sat back in his chair and began to watch the people around him. He had to trust Lloyd in whatever plan he was coming up with.

"What can I get you boys to drink?" Their waitress was the same age as the other, red headed and green eyes settled above slightly blushing cheeks. She spoke quickly, as if to imply a polite rush.

Lloyd snapped the menu closed, "Yes ma'am, I'd like a root beer and my friend...?" He opened his arms towards Kol and gave a questioning expression.

"Hot chocolate," Kol told her.

"All right, will you be ordering food as well?" Despite the slight urgency, her voice also sounded hopeful, which was odd for someone at their job.

"No, we won't be here that long," Lloyd said with a charming smile.

The waitress nodded to herself closing her serving booklet. "I'll have them right out. Feel free to join the tables or game: you can bring them back to your table if you want." She hesitated a few seconds, and Lloyd turned and nodded to her politely as she stepped away from them.

"What do you know about goblins?" Lloyd had not even waited for their waitress to be gone before asking, and even worse he did not attempt any form of discretion.

Kol kept his eyes forward, not wanting anyone who might have heard to find more interest in them. He waited a few moments searching his mind for any information. "Nothing, truthfully." This made him feel slightly ashamed. He should have looked in Iris's library for research before they left.

"Well," Lloyd began with a smile. He interlocked his fingers on top of the table and changed to a matter-of-fact tone, similar to Wilhelmina's but without any touch of arrogance, "They can be selfish little beasts. Constantly craving wealth, or anything shiny for that matter, and not caring how they acquire it. Creatures for hire on just about anything, so long as the price is more than fair. Crafting of any sort, including magic, and any other form of work they think will pay well, especially thievery, which means, if the item they are after is valuable, they may just toss the contract all together. Besides employment, they will also partake in their own endeavors to acquire anything they like, and in the easiest way they can do it as well."

"Murder?" Kol asked.

Lloyd nodded. "A favorite of theirs. They usually don't care what the things they create are intended to be used for, but if they had their preference they would rather do the killing themselves."

"So, evil all around?" Kol implied.

Lloyd made a strained face. "Well," he parted his hands and lifted one in a balancing gesture, "They hunger for shinies and rare items, which they will steal if they have a chance to; they can practically smell valuables. But if they believe stealing to be life threatening, they will barter or attempt to offer a service. Individually they are weak creatures and enjoy living their greedy little lives. They lie, cheat, and manipulate. Evil, yes, if you think selfishness is evil. Remember, then, goblins are not the only selfish thing out there. "

Kol nodded and leaned back in his chair, understanding. "Just because something is your nature, does not mean you are imprisoned by it." Lloyd nodded, possibly glad to see Kol knew that answer. Selfishness itself was not evil, if that were true then looking out for yourself was evil. The answer depended simply on who you are inside. "Here you go." The waitress set their drinks down in front of them. Kol was impressed with his large mug thickly topped with whipped cream and the handle of a spoon leaning on the rim.

Lloyd reached into his jacket and pulled out a fifty-dollar bill and placed it gently into the nervous hands of the waitress. "Why, thank you, ma'am." The accent sounded so natural from Lloyd. "Whatever is left is yours, okay?" He turned his head and beamed up at her.

"It is too much," she began.

"Keep it now," Lloyd reached up and squeezed her hand shut. "I ain't no friend of rudeness. Now, back to your other tables before they become distraught."

The waitress looked as if her words evaded her tongue. "Thank you. If you need..."

"Go on now." Lloyd spun her hand gently and urged her on. She hesitated a moment longer, possibly debating what to do next, then stepped away. "Cute thing," Lloyd said, turning back to Kol.

"Must have been a lot of practice to sound that way." Kol spooned his hot beverage on top of the whipped cream to melt it down slightly.

"Sound like what?" Lloyd put on an expression of being appalled before his smile returned. This one appeared less sane than the expression he showed outside. Lloyd took a swig of his bottle then started again. "Keep in mind that they like dark quiet places to live, but close enough to sources of profit."

"So we will find it here?" Kol expressed some disbelief.

"Take that kiddy drink and go play checkers or something." Lloyd snatched up his bottle and started in the direction of the bar and pool tables. Kol glared after him then shrugged. He thought about following after Lloyd but thought it better to just leave and check outside himself. He took a sip of his drink and remembered it had been some time since he had hot chocolate. Kol decided to finish his cup first then start on the rest of the town. He was not going to play board games when he should be busy; the drink was enough. He did not want to continue sitting at the table either, lest the nervous waitress returned. He lifted his cup and made his way to the lounge area anyway.

A few dads set on the couches discussing the sports game on the television. American football from the look of it: Kol did not have much interest in that. The wood burning in the fireplace smelled of pine and had low flames so as to not overheat the room. A bookshelf was nestled under the window, which Kol knelt in front of to examine.

"You cheated," a small boy's shout came over the top of the couch.

"No, I didn't! You're lying!" another shouted back.

"Dad, Jake stole my piece from the board."

One of the fathers did not look away from the screen. "Hush, or you can put the games up."

"I'm not going to play again anyways." Pieces clattered to the floor as a blond-haired boy darted into view and then vanished into the forest of chairs, legs, and people. Kol smiled to himself and went back to the books. Classic novels covered in a thick layer of dust. Kol could not blame anyone; he figured it would be difficult to read with all the commotion.

"Dad, will you play with me?" the boy Jack asked one of the men behind Kol.

"Later, son, after the game."

Kol did not recognize a title, so he reached for it when a light tug at his sleeve stopped him. "Will you play a game with me?"

Kol turned and found Jake smiling at him with two teeth missing from the top and one from the bottom. He was a small thing, lanky and pale under a mess of brown hair. His brown eyes watched him hopefully. He wore a red button up shirt with brown dress pants, one knee smudged with dirt. His white sneakers pointed inward behind a premade checkers board. He looked to the men whose focus stayed riveted to the TV and then back to the kid. "Sure." Kol sat with his legs crossed and placed his hot chocolate carefully on the carpet. "My name is Kol."

"I'm Jake," the boy said gleefully. "Red or black?" The boy set the board down in front of them, scattering the pieces with his haste. "Sorry," he told Kol sheepishly.

"That's all right," Kol said helping him gather and set the pieces. "I'll take black. No cheating now." He gave a light laugh.

"I don't cheat," Jake said, missing the tease. He moved his first piece into play. "Your turn."

Kol took his turn. "So, here with your dad?"

"Yeah, and my brother." A second move. "Mom's at work."

"Where does she work?" Kol defended a piece.

"She's the dispatcher for the sheriff's department," Jake told him proudly.

Kol laughed. "All right." He pointed at Jakes last move. "Be sure you move a piece behind him so he can't be captured." Jake nodded, concentrating on the board. "Are you ready for Santa?"

"Uh huh. I sent in my letter last week." Kol moved another of his forward.

Jake jumped the piece and took it. "Yes!"

Kol felt his own parental pride rise up again. "What was it you asked for? A new brother?" He couldn't resist.

"No, I want to keep Sam," he said as he took another of Kol's pieces. Kol smiled and took another gulp of the cooling chocolate. "I want a new robot. Someone stole my old one."

"Was it Sam?" Kol glanced over the board, making his next move quickly.

Jake bit his thumb in concentration. "No," he took another of Kol's chips. "I left him outside near the tree line."

"I see." Kol waited for Jake's next move before going on. "Don't move that one. I'll double jump you." Kol showed him what he meant, then pointed at another of Jake's pieces. "That one would be better. I'm sure Santa will bring you another. What did it look like?"

"Oh, it was red and had a big gun and talked all cool when you pressed the buttons on his chest." The innocent excitement made Kol smile. "I asked Santa to bring me my coin back, too. My robot had a compartment in the back. I put my uncle's old coin in. He gave it to me for luck before he was shipped out. It was silver and had a large eagle on one side and flames on the other."

"You just be sure to stay good and he will," Kol smiled at the boy. Jake nodded excitedly.

The game was nearly done by then so they made the last moves in silence. Another capture and Jake threw his hands in the air. "I won!"

Kol smiled behind his cup. "You sure did."

"Jake, food's here." A man's voice yelled from the tables. Kol saw one of the men had left his spot on the couch.

"That's my dad. I gotta go eat dinner now." The boy leaped to his feet. "Thanks for playing." And he vanished just like his brother into the jungle of tables and chairs.

Kol folded the checker board and placed it next to the bookshelf with the checker pieces stacked on top. He then stood and stretched before reaching back down for his cup and finishing his beverage. He looked out over the dinner guests, bar, and pool table looking for Lloyd. The Crazy was not even back at their table, and their waitress was busy with a large table, so that was also ruled out. A group of men burst into laughter around the bar, drawing his attention, but Lloyd was not the one who told the joke. Kol decided to return to his original plan and search on alone. The game had only taken twenty minutes, so he had not wasted too much time. Kol placed his cup on a table near the hostess lectern. Well, it was not truly a waste.

The cold greeted him like an old friend. The old woman from earlier was gone, leaving the porch less welcoming. If not for the warm glow of the windows and soft music, people would stay well away from the place at their first glance. He flexed his fingers and pondered on where to begin. Kol had night to use and the others had an hour on him already. The door opened behind him, and a middle-aged sailor with a large belly stepped out with his hat low and checkered jacket bundled tight for the wind. Kol watched him curiously. "Excuse me," the man spoke softly with a rough voice. The man held in an exposed hand a dark glass bottle, but did not smell like alcohol. He had a small limp to his right foot, and using his elbow, he balanced himself down the steps. He stopped a few feet into the road and looked back at Kol with Lloyd's face, "Well, are you coming?" He smiled around the wind from his lips, his speech back to normal.

"How long have you been doing that?" Kol asked Lloyd with a small grin. It was impressive.

"Long," was his answer, and this one sounded completely honest. Lloyd removed the patched jacket and hat and laid them neatly on the porch railing. He then pulled his own coat from under his shirt and his glasses from his pants pocket. Placing them on his face while securing himself within his coat, Lloyd was back to his usual appearance and posture. Kol caught a glimpse of something hanging inside Lloyd's coat, but he thought it better not to ask.

"So you were by the bar?" Kol now remembered seeing the red and black jacket. "Where did you get the clothes?"

Lloyd started walking. "Lost and found." Kol stepped along beside him. "So what did that minion say?" Lloyd's head gave a slight twitch, then a soft laugh seemed to escape from him.

Kol watched him carefully. "Why is that important?"

"Huh?" he looked at Kol, confused, and then gave another laugh.

Kol did not see how it would hurt, but Lloyd was acting odder. "He wanted someone to play checkers with him because his brother does not like to lose." Kol decided to add, "He asked for another robot for Christmas."

Lloyd nodded. "Another?"

"He lost his original one."

"Was that all he lost?"

Kol shook his head. "Said his Uncle's coin was inside of it."

"There it is." Lloyd gave a light skip.

"There what is?"

Lloyd turned sharply in between two buildings, making Kol misstep. "Goblins have an excellent nose for metals, especially the rare ones."

Kol caught on, "So we were looking for clues in there to narrow the search. Did you find anything useful at the bar?"

"Plenty." He made a left on the next street. "There have been a lot of theft reports over the past few months. This month there seems to be a decrease from the thievery, though. The off-duty Sheriff in there considered it a Christmas blessing."

"I suspect jewelry and the like?"

Lloyd agreed gleefully. "Now, where was this little robot stolen?"

"Near the forest." Kol confirmed his thoughts.

"Same as the others. Goblins need to be sought after for contracts and bargaining. They love living and humans generally prefer them dead. Sneaky creatures are just fine with probing along and picking what they like, so they stay near the woods for a quick escape they can disappear into with a cackle." He started to bob his head and increase his pace.

"I'll inform the others." Lloyd simply continued to bob his head as Kol placed the ear bud into his ear and called one of the others.

"Go ahead," Wilhelmina's voice told him.

"We picked up on thievery along..." Kol looked to the ocean and Lloyd's path for his bearing, "the southern forest line. We are heading that way now."

"Confirmed." She sounded slightly winded. "I will inform Harvest and we will locate Iris, then be on our way."

Kol started to reply but did not waste his energy after the dial tone hit his ear. His next action was to pull out his list and look up both Jake and his brother. He added his own special comments then closed it. Lloyd had made his way several meters ahead so Kol jogged lightly to catch back up.

What Lloyd had done in the diner was impressive to Kol. Where he was able to simply disappear and move unnoticed, Lloyd could simply become a part of his environment. He had not been lying when he said he had people skills. He had located the town gathering point quickly, ordered a drink that resembled the choice of most bar attendants, and simply asked questions. He did that without seeming out of place, which eliminated the avoidance that came along with drifters. He had even thought to send Kol to the opposite side of the diner with his "kiddy drink" to do his own form of knowledge gathering. All masks like the wooden green one he had. So who wore them?

There was no doubt that there was something wrong with Lloyd when he acted himself, though. With his eyes looking crazed and laughs where no humor was found, it was enough to put anyone on edge. Kol believed he glimpsed him speaking to things that were not there when at the Encampment. Perhaps he would truly know the reasoning one day. Kol wondered then which hid more, Harvest's silence or Lloyd's laughter. In some respects, they both hid the same.

They were no longer among the shops and services provide by the good people of the town. Instead they walked among their homes. No cars drove past so they remained unnoticed. The moonlight reflected off of a dead-end sign in front of them, beyond which laid the forest. Kol stopped at the sign wanting to wait on the others before proceeding. The sign vibrated loudly as Lloyd ran into it and continued on into the woods. Dogs began to bark loudly from the nearby houses so Kol followed after, grimacing at him. Lloyd did not even seem to realize he had struck it so hard or that he had given away their presence. His walk was one of desperation and Kol worried, following to check for his reasoning.

The start of the wood line was rough to get through. The bonelike fingers of the plants reached to hold him from entering, but he pushed on through to the easier spots. He found Lloyd sitting next to a very old tree. "Has something happened to you? Are you hurt?" Lloyd simply waved his hands at Kol and continued to sit still, his face resting calmly. Kol let him stay and decided to remove his first layer of pants now that they were isolated from anyone else. After a few minutes, Lloyd got to his feet and they continued on into the woods together. They reached a dirt road in the trees and Kol wanted to wait there. Lloyd continued on, and Kol finally decided to stop him. After the road were a few more trees before they stepped into a large open clearing. "Hold on, Lloyd." Kol gripped Lloyd's arm. That stopped him. "We have to wait for the others."

Lloyd nodded. "That's fine. I like it here."

"What happened back there?" The question was a demand. Kol checked him over, looking for any signs of harm.

"Fresh air," Lloyd snickered with a slight sound of fatigue. He gently pulled from Kol's grasp and started to wander the clearing. Kol let him do so but kept him in his vision. He went to check his phone for the others' locations. Harvest had showed them how they each appeared on the map so grouping would be easy. Kol tapped their location to tell the others that's where they planned to wait. He could see the others bunched together and not far off. Something cold touched his thumb as he looked at the screen and Kol started to smile.

Replacing the phone, he looked to the sky. The moon had illuminated the surrounding clouds that drifted closer to one another. Specks danced in the air and began to fall along the ground surrounding the two of them. Snow in its quiet grace had decided to bless their quest as the woods brightened. Kol's inner child grew excited. While he was enjoying the sky, the moon's light became overpowered by artificial light. He had not noticed the sound of an engine, but recognized it as Harvest the moment he did. Iris followed in her truck as they snaked closer through the trees. Rounding the nearest curve, Harvest's lights spotted Kol, and the two vehicles pulled to the side and joined the woods in its darkened silence.

The other three crunched their way through the twigs and speckles of white to silently greet him. "So what did you find?" Harvest asked, oddly in his human form. The three of them looked wind struck, but other than that fine.

"Lloyd and I," Kol turned and found him hugging a tree, "well, more Lloyd than I, asked some of the people at the town bar and diner if anything had been strange lately. An off-duty sheriff told him they had an increase in robberies. Reports of jewelry, coins, and others of the like near this particular wood line."

"He asked and found this out without raising any suspicion?" Wilhelmina was completely in disbelief, looking over at the odd creature.

Iris smiled and Harvest remained looking bored. "It's a start," Harvest said, agreeing with their assumptions. He looked to the sky with a grimace of his own.

"Well, then, they must be buried in somewhere around here." Wilhelmina glanced at the ground as if suspecting footprints.

"We could set a trap for them knowing where they travel," Iris suggested.

Kol shook his head. "Traps take time, and we don't have much to spare."

"Trees are sleeping." Lloyd was back to his old self, stumbling in and providing his own comment that naturally made no sense.

Harvest gave him a glance before kneeling to the ground himself. "Kol is right; we have to find their home faster than a trap can permit. We will have to track them."

"I'll get my armor." Wilhelmina began to turn.

"It's not needed," Harvest told her, standing.

"Then how are we going to track them? All vampires are good for are tracking blood, and I don't think we will find any around here."

"They can also hear very well," Iris said softly.

Wilhelmina ignored her. "It will only take a moment to prepare." She started for the truck.

Harvest stepped further into the clearing. "Bring my clothes and follow my sound." Kol nodded, knowing he would understand in a few moments.

Wilhelmina stopped and looked back to them. "What do you mean?"

Of course, Harvest did not respond. He was looking skyward towards the moon, which was in its first quarter. "Harvest?" Iris said, sounding slightly scared. Harvest took something from the pocket opposite where he kept his fang, then removed his jacket. Next were his shoes and pants until he stood naked under the light. Kol noticed him shiver violently from the cold before slapping his forearm with whatever he took from his pocket. Lloyd gave a joyful laugh as change came over Harvest once more. His skin did not turn pale, but black from the point his hand touched. The blackness crawled over his hand and up his arm in a process to consume the rest of his body. Harvest gave a hollow yell as his body tore itself apart. Kol watched his muscles grow and harden, the ones in his legs breaking the bones in his calves and forcing them backwards while also increasing his height. He raked his hands and clawed over the back of his head and across his face. Ears stretched and stood pointed. The creature buckled and hit the ground before him.

"Harvest?" This time it was Wilhelmina with a voice barely a whisper. She stepped toward Harvest, but Kol put up an arm to stop her. The change was complete, and the monster stood on his back legs and turned towards them. With a face that was no longer Harvest, a snout now stretched upward, sniffing the air with teeth flashing like silver. The black of his skin was fur as dark as the new moon sky. Harvest glanced at them for a moment, eyes of wild gold, before leaping away running on all fours, a haunting howl echoing from the trees.

Efforts of an Envoy

"**W**ell, despite your soreness, your run time is getting better." Mia reached a hand down to Holly who sat on the training room floor, panting.

Holly mixed her smile with a glare as she accepted Mia's offer to pull her up. "The only time we would ever need to run is if we don't know how to use our drums. Which I believe you still need to work on." Holly swiped the end of Mia's nose with her index finger as she finished her snipe.

"Yeah, yeah, we can't all be musically blessed like you, chica." Mia stretched her arms upward. "Okay, let's get cleaned up and get some food. I could eat a whole wizard."

"I'm sure that's not good for you," Holly smirked.

"How so?"

Holly gave her a knowing look, "Magic gives you indigestion."

Mia laughed softly, "Ah, I thought it would be more of a cleanser."

The two of them made their way across the Cadence training facility. It was a large gymnasium that offered a plethora of opportunities to hone the body for the potential work the Cadence might have to do. There were two running tracks, one bare of obstacles and the other abundant with them, consisting of several trampolines and spring boards so that the Cadence could learn to maneuver midair with their drums. A ranged target area for throwing enchanted drumsticks fused with stunning magic was nearby, with sparring grounds, ice rinks, and an area to practice drum rhythms completing the gymnasium. Originally the building mainly held individuals working towards being a full-fledged drummer. Now every single member of the corps rotated into the training room in shifts. The Drum Major said this was to keep everyone at the top of their skill, but Holly just thought she wanted to keep them busy and tired. Either way she did not mind; she trusted the Major and loved training and competing with or against Mia.

Exiting the facility, the two of them found their locker room to change from their green physical training gear, shower, and dress back in their red uniform before grabbing food. Holly winced as she pulled her jacket over her right shoulder. She told Mia without looking at her that she was going on ahead. Holly did not wait for a response before exiting and continuing down the hall. Her troubles were trying to catch up to her again and food was the best kind of distraction from them.

The cafeteria smelled wonderful. The Cadence always ate the best of selections. Then again, the entire North Pole ate the best of selections. She piled a bowl with a fantastically crafted stew of perfectly cooked chuck roast, bright carrots, golden potatoes, and onions. This of course could not be devoured without one of the small golden loaves of bread. Holly grabbed three. Juggling her selection, Holly was thankful to find one of the many round wooden tables empty of anyone else. The cafeteria was packed full of changing shifts and the general conversation was easy to guess before even stepping into the room.

"So wait," someone said somewhere behind Holly, "that makes five attacks now?" Holly decided to call the owner of this voice Fred. Of course, that was not his real name. She had no idea what his real name was. Mia had created a fun game to play with Holly, where they gave the owners of voices they overheard names to provide more character to a conversation. It helped pass the time, and Holly even believed it helped her remember people's real names better after she was told them.

"Yeah, five attacks after the last two days ago." That was Susan, of course. That deep masculine voice said as much. "The

Halls have no idea how they are getting in and out of the city."
Holly dipped her first loaf of bread into her stew and started the
digestion process.

Fred followed that with another question. "And how many
people have been hurt? Four now?"

"Seven." Paul decided to add to the conversation with a
lighter voice. "And the last attack was on a patrolling squad."

"No!" Of course Fred had no idea it had been a squad. It was
Fred, after all.

"Yeah, the Snow People are getting confident," Paul stated.
"At least no one has died." Holly rolled her right shoulder.

"Yet," added Susan.

"Yet," agreed Fred. Holly double-scooped her stew with
a metal spoon in one hand and a baked one in the other. She
wished her stew had something crunchy in it. Crunchy food
made it easy to ignore others talking because it was loud.

"It's defensive testing," Susan said more to themself than to
the of the others. "If they can get one in. They can get others. This
is a build-up to a full-on attack." Holly gathered her things and
moved to another table that had just emptied, out of earshot of
the previous conversation.

Holly sat in her new spot, disheartened. The food before
her wondered why she was no longer enjoying it. Holly's mind
drifted. The squad she had been assigned to that day had marched
in complete professional form. No uniforms undone or slouch-
ing on building walls. The Drum Major had brought the entire
corps together and had explained that they had a responsibility
as defenders to show bravery in the time of uncertainty the city
was wrapped in. Holly completely believed in this resolve and
committed to it utterly. No more wandering eyes or distracting
lists of things. But it was hard. Even though Holly now knew
what Kol was up to, trying to not be afraid felt like it was starting
to overflow within her and she could not stop it from going over
the top and down the other side.

They had been walking the border between the Hearth and Reciprocity District. A sleep shift, they called it, because distinguishing shifts by the sun was a little difficult to do. The other attacks kept the patrolling squads on constant edge. Every report had stated that the Snow People would appear almost instantly, lacking any armor or weapons, and use their might to try to attack buildings. They would then vanish before any retaliation could be mustered. There was no difference when Holly and her squad had been targeted. It had been the squad mate in front of Holly, an elf named Astra, who had looked up and seen the large ice projectile hurdling towards them. Holly had a choice of either moving or warning them. She had taken the former action and pushed Astra to safety as the other scattered. The projectile had grazed Holly's shoulder.

The fight ended in minutes. The Snow Person formed quickly and started randomly striking at the scattered patrol. By the time the squad was able to form ranks the Snow Person had dispersed itself back into the wind, leaving all of them in a state of shock. The Drum Major had made sure they all knew how valiantly they stood, but that bandage was slowly falling away. Holly's right hand started to shake slightly, and she dropped her hair to either side of her face. The anxiety crept around inside her like a spider, feeding off her withering spirit. The hand that gripped her shaking one surprised the sickening creature and caused it to flee back down to its home in Holly's mind. The reassurance of that grip offered to reinforce what Holly was just about to lose.

Mia sat down next to her. "Hey, it's going to be okay." So simple and standard, but Holly listened to her confidence and was thankful for it.

"Just seems like all this animosity will be erupting soon."

"I know," Mia said. "A lot of unanswered question can do that. But we will push through. This city stands for far too much for it not to."

Holly considered this, "Yeah. The truth will come out exactly when it needs to. It's just getting to that point that's hard."

"You're right. I'm sorry I wasn't there when you guys got attacked." The expression on Mia's face showed that she was grieved by that.

Holly shook her head. "Now don't you hold onto that. You were assigned elsewhere. Nothing to do with you."

"Can't help it." Mia wanted to change the discussion slightly. "So I think we are getting truths a little quicker than you expect."

Holly swallowed a bite of the stew she had started back on. "Why is that?"

"There is an envoy from the Flakes on the way to the city. The Drum Major plans to meet them right outside the wall."

"How many Snow People are in this envoy?"

"Just one."

"Wait," Holly gave Mia a sidelong look, "how do you know?"

"Notice just came down after you left the locker room. The Drum Major wants the word spreading about it. So that she can ease tensions. The fact that it's just one is also supposed to help."

"Well, this is great! They can investigate about the rogue Snowmen in these attacks! Provide insight and even help us stop them. It's not their entire tribe making these attacks. That's unreasonable. They could also…" Holly trailed off.

"Could also what, Holly?" Mia inquired.

"Nothing, I was about to repeat myself," Holly lied to Mia's acceptance. She had already said too much. Holly had been sworn to secrecy, after all, by Kol's mother who had shown her the letter Kol had left behind before leaving the city. It pacified her paranoia that Kol had not vanished at the Flakes. Mrs. Claus had then told Holly that Master Renshu used the information about the cursed blades inside the letter to try to end the curse early. So far there had been no luck. Regardless, the Halls were working sleepless days to find any magical loophole they could exploit. If they could not, Kol, wherever he had gone, was their only hope. Holly admired Mrs. Claus. Her demeaner was so steadfast about everything. Her husband in a coma and her son had vanished, yet she still did her part in the city with no hesitation, and she did it well. The mission of the city was still on its way to being fulfilled. People labored hard to complete the Christmas present quota and distracts themselves the best that they could. Now with this envoy coming, things could really be set back on the right track. Something nagged at her mind, and she needed to know one more thing from Mia. "So who is coming on the envoy from the Flakes?"

Mia swallowed her own food before answering. "OH! That's kind of important to the whole desolation. It's Frostein himself. The statement he sent stated that sending anyone else did not embody the level of seriousness of the situation. Or something like that."

Holly let out a long sigh of relief. *Hurry back, Kol. We have it handled...for now.*

CHAPTER TWENTY

Forge Grown Cold

The howl shook them as it pierced the snowy night. Willa and Iris both jumped, one in disbelief the other with possibly a hint of fear. Lloyd laughed hollowly while Kol began to move in the direction Harvest had gone. Reaching into his bag he found his sword and pulled it free. "What are you doing?" Iris asked, concerned, running up to Kol, the other two following after. Kol handed her Harvest's clothes as another howl erupted from deeper among the trees. Kol started towards them.

"Following his sound," Kol told her simply.

Lloyd bounced up beside him. "He's on the scent!"

Iris remained in her serious state, and she grabbed Kol's arm in an attempt to stop him. "Kol, he's never transformed into that in front of me, has he you?" Her tone was definitely that of concern. Kol shook his head in answer. "He could be more dangerous now than in his other form, Kol. That was not him who just looked at us. We should not follow after."

"Don't fret, my armor would be better protection, but this is all I need to remove the werewolf's head." Willa had pulled her sword and shield from her bag and held them in each hand at the ready.

"There will be no need of that. I do not think Harvest would put us in harm's way." Kol's tone was firm, but for an instant he wondered if he had just told them a lie.

"A werewolf is in the same class of monster with a vampire; the only difference is one has strength and the other speed. What makes the werewolf more dangerous is how wild they can be."

A third howl came from the left of their current course. "He has moved towards the coast." Kol started in that direction with the others following by their own means. The townspeople must have cleared the woods during the summer because it was clear of any snagging bushes or dead tree limbs.

"Exactly my thoughts." Willa gave her sword a quick swing.

"Oh, was it?" Lloyd teased.

"Kol," Iris was trying to keep pace with him so he could see her expression. "Have you ever dealt with werewolves before?"

"Once, but they were dying when we found them." Who would not be after running through the arctic wasteland? The Cadence had asked his father to come to the city wall to look over the situation while the Major was at the Island. The werewolves were unconscious because of the Cadence, and the creatures were frail, clearly having not eaten anything for weeks. They looked just as Harvest did except for having their own variety of colors in pelts. His father had sent them to the Island for questioning when they had turned back, and once they had, none of them remembered why they had been driven so far north knowing there was no food. They had all been new born. "Tell me more about them, though."

"Vampires take time to create more of themselves, as you already know." As Iris explained she sounded calmer with every word. "Werewolves are far simpler. It only takes one bite from a mature werewolf and the individual will change at the next full moon phase."

"Why is that?" Kol grabbed Iris as she stumbled over some old roots.

"We have been told it takes concentration to make a simple bite. They are so strong they could take away an entire limb if they bit someone. That is the primary danger. It takes years for a werewolf to learn to control himself when changed. Those bitten can become emotionally unbalanced and will change when feeling extreme levels of sorrow, anger, even happiness."

"So the moon has little to do with it?" A fourth howl that told them they were gaining on his location.

"Of course it does," Willa told him, annoyed. "All of them must change during the three nights the moon hangs most full. It is also when they are at the height of their power and hardest to kill."

Iris nodded. "The ones I have spoken with have all said there is no way to hide or fight from it. The pull is too strong, and if they do not accept the change, they will be snatched into it. They would then completely lose their humanity and become the true beasts. Those newly bitten usually have a pack that keeps them in check, and it takes all of them, but if not they are nothing more than animals. Their only purpose is to survive," she took a moment to judge Kol's face, "by eating," she finished.

"What is he?" Willa asked them, thinking she would finally gain information.

"Shapeshifter," Lloyd told her.

"Shapeshifting has to be either natural or done by magic. Strong magic that only fully trained witches and wizards are capable of. Faeries are able to cast glamour, but nothing like what he does." Willa gripped her sword more firmly, as though expecting Harvest to leap at them from the shadows. "There is nothing that can do what he does. Curse himself, then remove it just as easily. No cure exists for vampirism or lycanthropy once it is set in, yet he does it so easily." Kol loosened his own blade from its sheath as they crunched through the snow scattered forest.

Kol smelled it moments before they arrived: salt on the wind and sounds of crashing waves. The four of them emerged from the forest onto a cliffside rising well above the ebbing swell. Iris yanked both Lloyd and him away from the edge as they went to look over the side. They were easily ten meters up, and the cliffside was nothing but jagged, razor sharp rocks. The town was visible to their left, and to the right the land rose and fell to the ocean as they fought one another for existence. This sea was not as harsh as the one he was used to. There were no cascades of glaciers grinding one another into a gleam, yet still it was treacherous, for no one should forget that the ocean was all the same.

"I wonder where he is?" Willa asked no one in particular. It was true Harvest had given them no more signals since they arrived at the ocean. "Looks like he was just running around." Lloyd started to respond but he stopped as the brush behind them started to rustle. The werewolf stepped easily from the trees, teeth bared and eyes glowing. Willa raised her shield and rested her sword above it so that she could easily stab from safety. The beast glared at her and rose onto his hind legs to display his mass in a form of intimidation.

"How cute," Lloyd said, wanting to scratch his abdomen. Teeth flashed as Lloyd leaped away, grinning. Willa stepped forward daring him to strike, which caused the werewolf to release an ear-piercing roar.

Kol had seen enough of this mistreatment and pulled himself from Iris's cautious pulls. Stepping around Willa's defenses, he asked, "Find them?"

Harvest gave him a sniff then glanced towards Iris. Understanding, Kol walked back to Iris and collected the bundle she was carrying and sat it in front of Harvest. He gave them another sniff before tearing away a piece of his fur on his right arm.

The reaction was the reverse of what they had witnessed before but no less amazing. The fur began to fall from his body as he jerked about, bones snapping and realigning. The werewolf added to the noise with his own snarls and snaps that slowly started to sound human once the snout shrunk and ears as well. The enlarged muscles lost mass as the height of the creature lowered to theirs. Harvest stood before them as the fur became dust in the air. "Damn, it's cold," he told them, starting to shiver. He quickly put his clothes back on.

"I have a better reason to kill you now." Willa stepped toward the dressing Harvest. "What right do you have to put us at such a risk?"

Iris nodded in agreement. "That was dangerous for us, Harvest. You never told me you could also become a werewolf."

"I never told you I could become a vampire, either," he told her, placing the piece of fur safely in his pocket and stepping around Willa's point. "You were never in danger."

"And we should just take your word on that?" Willa was almost shouting as Lloyd passed her.

"So vicious," Lloyd laughed. Kol did not know which of the two he meant.

"So?" Kol pressed.

"Yeah, definitely goblins," Harvest said, rotating his arms to get used to them again. "Followed several trails but they all led to the same place. There is a cave further down the coastline we will need to investigate."

"I told you," Willa said. She had sheathed her sword and place them both on her back.

Iris nodded at this. "How many?"

"Enough," Lloyd answered.

Harvest gave Lloyd an odd look. "I'm not sure; the scents are faint but definitely there. And before you ask, Willa, the cave entrance is too small for your armor."

"Then let us be on our way," Kol said, and they followed Harvest's lead.

The distance over the hill was further than Kol expected, but they made it quickly enough. The first part of the stretch was spent with Iris attempting to talk urgently with Harvest and Willa about her own views of the situation. Lloyd made sure to stay close enough to add his own instigating comments. Harvest said nothing, giving Kol a significant look. Kol nodded and told the others to keep quiet because they were coming close to the destination.

The cave was a small entrance a few meters over the side of the cliff. They would have to crouch slightly to enter it one at a time. There was a small edge that the goblins probably used to get to the entrance they themselves could reach if they walked a little further down the descending cliff.

"I'll go first," Kol told them.

"Absolutely not." Iris planted her foot.

"It's my father they attacked, so it should be me."

"Lot of good you will do him if you slip on that freshly fallen snow," Willa said.

"Dead," Lloyd nodded with a slowly fading whistle. "Tree." He pointed to the trees behind him.

Harvest looked to where Lloyd was pointing. "How much rope do you have, Iris?"

"About thirty feet," she said as they all understood. "But I don't have any climbing gear."

Kol peered over the cliff side again. "That's more than enough. We can tie knots in it so that the climb is easier."

"Exactly," Harvest said. Iris agreed to this and pulled a small roll of rope from the back of her belt. Unsurprisingly it was enchanted, for when Harvest unraveled it, it grew longer. He moved to the tree line and began shaking each of them to test their strength. He then wrapped the middle of the rope securely. Half the rope he tied in several knots, and the other half he tied into a slip knot to go around their waists as they climbed down to catch them if they fell. Satisfied, he gave the knotted rope to Lloyd so that he could throw it over the side. "Now we can each watch the other climb down." Harvest then reached into his pocket and pulled his fang free.

"Right." Lloyd nodded seriously then sprinted for the edge. None of them could move quickly enough to stop him before he leaped into the open air.

"Lloyd!" Kol yelled as the laughter replied to him. They heard it until the rope went stiff in Lloyd's hands and he swung out of sight. They made it to the edge and looked for him falling to the rocks below. His body was not there when the waves retreated. The rope flapped freely off the rock.

"So worried," Lloyd said, sticking his head out from the cave entrance to look up at them. He waved at them then vanished back inside.

"Crazy," Iris breathed.

"Stupid," was all Willa managed.

Kol took the slip knot from the now vampiric Harvest. "I'll go next." Grabbing the knotted end he slowly made his way over. Kol had no fear of heights; you could not ride a reindeer with such a phobia. Still, he was careful as he slowly descended downward. The rock shelf was indeed slippery, but his boots gripped easily each time. Finally reaching beside the entrance, Kol stepped over and clasped forearms with a waiting Lloyd. "Took you long enough."

Kol tossed the rope back out to be pulled back to the top. Laughing, he said, "Can't be as crazy as you. I figure that is far more complex than others would believe. Have you been any deeper?"

Lloyd nodded his head. "No, but it does start to slant down a few meters behind us."

Kol shook his head, grinning, and he looked back outside and to see Iris making her way swiftly down. She did so naturally and with better ease than himself. When she was near the cave, Kol reached out and wrapped her in an arm. She gasped as she was pulled inside, but smiled all the same. "That was fun," she said breathlessly. Kol nodded and released her. Peering down into the dark tunnel, Kol pulled free his sword again. There would be no swinging in here, but the point would hold most at bay. The darkness he stared into was threatening.

Next came Willa and Harvest at the same time. Willa looked nervous as she made her way down, much slower than Iris or Kol. Harvest climbed down right beside her, his claws piecing the rock to make finger holes. Twice Harvest had to place his hand on Willa's back to steady her, and she scowled at him in thanks. Iris grabbed Willa once she was at the mouth. Harvest's head appeared in from atop the cave door upside down. His eyes peered at each of them then into the darkness beyond. "Have you gone any further?"

"Waiting on you," Kol told Harvest as he flipped right side up then swung in to land beside Willa.

Lloyd squinted into the tunnel. "Can't see."

"There used to be an old ward here," Iris told them, running one of her gloved hands along the wall. The leather band was in place along her forehead. "Used to hide this place, but it lost its power."

"Faded? Looks like they don't care if they are found anymore," Willa stated.

"This feels rather strong for anything a goblin could muster. Which means whoever crafted it no longer wished to have it enabled," Iris spoke faintly in fear. She had not told them everything.

"Blindly forward," Lloyd said louder, then started downward into the rock.

"Or," Kol retorted, pulling a lantern from his bag. Battery powered, the LED light shone off the slick walls around them. He knew it was better to keep the element of surprise, but Harvest was the only one who could see in the dark. Besides, he was sure whatever could be below heard them at the entrance. After two minutes of walking, Kol's opinion on that matter changed as even the sound of the ocean was lost. The path twisted and cracked in several different directions as they descended. The silence was demanded from the pressing rocks. They could move, but with difficulty. Roots lined parts of the rock and gave an eerie feel whenever one brushed their cheeks. Willa had the most trouble with her shield. Lloyd glided the easiest and made it quickly up a rock that blocked their path. Kol followed after and heard the sound of sliding as Lloyd reached the bottom of the other side. "Made it," he said, turning to look up at Kol. His vision dismissed Lloyd and looked at what was behind him.

It was off-putting how the roughness of rock melded into the dark shine of the door. Kol handed the lantern to Iris then fol-

lowed Lloyd's style, except staying on his feet as he slid. The area
had enough room now for them to stand comfortably, Kol noted,
before stepping past Lloyd and kneeling in front of the structure.
The others slid down after, Harvest landing first and speaking
next to Kol, "What do you think?"

"A crude thing," was all Kol could give him right then.
Crouching, Kol was as tall as the door and it was only centimeters
wider. The only way he could even say it was a door was because
it looked like one with a square bottom and rounded top. No
other door-like features were present, like a handle. It was simply
a solid piece of metal with scattered hammer dents in it.

"What is it made of, Kol?" Iris asked him.

"Metal," Lloyd answered her in a logical tone.

"It looks like just plain iron," Kol said, "but quickly placed.
They just heated large scraps and hammered them into one
piece." The lines in the metal told him that.

"How do we open it?" Willa asked, annoyed.

Kol took his sword and tapped the metal, making a soft clang.
"It's thick, so also heavy. Either magic or a counterweight somewhere on the other side."

Iris stepped close and brushed her hand along the door. "No,
there isn't any magic on it."

Kol nodded. "So either we need to find a switch or a plasma
cutter."

"Don't have one in your bag?" Lloyd asked him.

"Had to choose between that and a welder, so no," Kol replied
sardonically.

Though the rock allowed them more room, it took only seconds for them to check every space that could be hiding a switch.
"If I had the armor, I could open it," Willa sniffed.

"After we carried it down here piece by piece," Lloyd chortled.

"You can kill him later." Harvest spoke without looking from
the wall.

Several more minutes passed before the thought of retrieving
the armor was given more consideration. Kol and Willa could

not scratch it with their weapons, and neither Iris nor Harvest had the strength to move it, even if he was vampiric. "Do you have any ideas, Lloyd?" Kol asked him.

Lloyd smiled at Kol, but then felt the weight of everyone watching him. His face slipping into a serious expression, he nodded and walked over to the door. Perhaps now was a chance everyone could see just what Lloyd could do besides his physical talents. None of them could see what he was doing as he kneeled before the door. After a moment Lloyd knocked three times on the metal.

"Oh for the love of..." Willa did not finished as they heard a snapping sound and the door slid crudely into the floor.

"How did you know that would work?" Iris asked him, astonished. Lloyd merely laughed at her and darted inside. They all crouched and followed after him. Kol looked around the inside and found nothing out of the ordinary, just several old roots lining the door frame like the rest of the tunnel. Answers would have to wait as the others were further inside the dark passage.

The five of them carefully stepped into a large cavern. Thanks to the light of the lantern, they found easy footing and could see the majority of the room. The top of the cave was easily ten meters high once past the stalagmites, and the width was bigger than the Encampment outside of Selma Pine. The floor had been mined and polished smoother for an even floor. Across from them they could see another tunnel leading back into the dark. "We have found the forge," Kol said softly to anyone who wished to hear.

Kol had known immediately what the place was, though it was completely unorganized. Kol counted several work stations that held the basic assortment of tools. Crudely made hammers and clamps to hold the material. Anvils in a place of their own, one of them fairly large. At least, he assumed they were anvils, for the flat surface held a hunk of cooled iron. The forge itself was to their right and was simply a large pit carved out of the ground, charcoal lying cool and white in the bottom. The unused fuel sat in two mounds with several shovels sticking out of it. A metal tube was mounted to the side of it that connected to a bellows that sat dusty next to the flame. Goblins must not have needed oxygen for there was no place for fumes to exit. That, or something else moved them away.

"It doesn't look like anyone has used the place in a while," Iris examined. She pointed out the dust that had settled on the nearby table, and Kol knew the fire was long gone.

"Something's been here, though." Willa said, pointing to the floor. "Look."

Kol followed her gesture and found what she meant. A clear path lacking dust had been made from where they stood to the tunnel opposite of them. The path had been walked over so many times that a single footprint could not be distinguished. Kol stepped deeper into the cavern in search of some. The print he found was like a child's but instead of toes, four scratch marks of claws held their place. "Goblin indeed," Harvest said beside him.

"Can be, nasty little things," Lloyd chirped, sniffing at a nearby table.

"That's what they prefer," Harvest stated.

They started to check the place over looking for any clues. Kol fought off the thought of a dead end. Iris picked up a large hammer. "Some of these tools are enchanted."

"With what?" Willa asked, with her back turned.

"I can't figure that out just yet. We should probably go deeper into the cave. Perhaps that is where their living quarters are."

"In a moment. I'd rather not leave any stone unturned." Kol started for the pit.

"We are wasting time," Willa told him. Kol noticed then the walls still did not echo but absorbed the sound.

"He is right," Harvest told her, searching through another warped wooden work station.

The forge was too deep for Kol's liking. He saw an iron poker leaning on the inside against several layers of caked soot. "It feels...wrong." Iris had decided to join him.

"What do you mean?" Kol asked her. When she had mentioned it he had picked up on a dark vibe.

Iris looked confused. "I just feel a wickedness here. It became stronger the closer to the pit I came." She walked around the right side of the pit. "Magic most crude." Wanting to get away from the main focal point of the noxious enchantments, she went to another work table further back.

"Lloyd?" Harvest asked him.

"No hocus pocus here," Lloyd stated.

"Kol, come here." Iris had found a hidden scroll and had begun to unravel it.

The others joined them, Lloyd bringing the lantern so they could see what was on the yellowed paper. Kol's adrenalin spiked as he viewed it. Drawn identically to the blade in his pouch, the *Clauditis* Blades were displayed in charcoal. The twin items centered the page while forging instructions written in an unclear language decorated both sides. "Can anyone read this?" Kol asked.

"No, but I may have a translation back at the southern encampment," Iris said, handing it to him. "So it would seem that blades are in fact identical."

Kol nodded as he continued to scan it. He briefly had a thought that this page could hold a means for undoing the curse without needing the other blade. Should he return home and send this to the Halls for investigation? The whistling brought all considerations to a halt.

They all froze after all their heads snapped in the direction of the other tunnel. It was soft at first, and they could not recognize the tune. A few seconds of concentration told them it was "Deck the Halls" in a mocking tone. A faint light began to illuminate the tunnel, someone was climbing up. "Lloyd, douse the light." Harvest whispered.

Lloyd immediately reached for a hammer and held it high before Iris snatched the lantern and clicked it off. A clatter bounced off the far wall as something slammed into it. Kol tensed,

waiting for the whistling to stop, but it only grew lou
coming light gained strength. He placed his hands on th
ders where he knew Iris and Willa stood and slowly pulle
down so that whoever was coming would not see them. Ha
who could see them in the dark, did the same with Lloyd, t
darted to an area across from them.

The goblin had finally entered the work area as Kol watched
through a rack of scrap metal. In the dim light of the candle the
creature held, the goblin stood at about half their average height.
His skin was a sickly green beneath a ragged pair of brown pants
and shirt. No shoes or gloves, his feet ended in claws that made
a tacking noise as he stepped. His ears were pointed and jutted
well over his head of patchy black hair. A beak of a nose helped
to hide his razor sharp teeth. The goblin's eyes were a spoiled
yellow. Since Kol was the closest to the main walkway, he waited
for him to get closer before trying to grab him. They had no idea
what was further below. It could be a straight shot to the rest of
the goblins or a maze work of passages like his uncle's home had,
but the goblin stopped well before Kol could reach him.

The whistling had stopped as the creature began to sniff the
air, each whiff sounding more alarmed. Kol reached back for his
bell: the last thing he wanted was an alarm to be sounded. If Harvest did not appear, he would use it to catch him. The goblin
gave one final sniff and dropped his candle in a hurried retreat.
Harvest landed in front of the goblin, hunched and teeth bared
as Kol stepped up to him from behind. The goblin tripped backward and started to slowly shuffle away from Harvest. He looked
up to Kol's face looking down at him. "What's down there?" Kol
asked him calmly.

"Please don!" the goblins voice was raspy and his English
broken. It was not his common tongue.

"No one here will hurt you," Iris said clicking the lantern
back on and stepping beside Kol.

Willa, on the other hand, snapped, "I will."

`'"Tricksy thingy," Lloyd said, picking up the goblin's extin-.ished lantern.

"How many more are down there?" Harvest demanded, picking him up to his feet.

"Ho many?" the goblin asked falling back to his knees.

"Goblins." Harvest snatched him up again.

The goblin shook his head, "None....only me, I promi."

Willa pulled her sword free. "He cannot be trusted."

"We don't know that yet," Iris told her.

"Lloyd," Kol called.

"Sir!" Lloyd saluted Kol.

"Take Willa and search further down. Bring back anyone you find and use whatever force is needed."

"Sir." He nodded and started to laugh as he exited.

Willa did not move. "Go," Harvest said, and she did so with a scowl after Lloyd.

"Any force?" Iris rounded on Kol angrily.

"He said it was only him." Kol said. He had to converse with the goblin as equals because any form of intimidation had wavered because Iris's comforting words. Now he would try reason as Harvest kept up whatever was left in intimidation. "What is your name?"

He was right in his assumption for the goblin had been watching them closely and now held a bit of mischief in his eyes, "Willom."

"That smells like a lie. Try again or I'll remove the fingers from your hand." Harvest gripped the goblins shoulder with his claws turned inward.

"Ah..." the goblin sounded interested and examined Harvest closer. "Shoval," he said, nodding to himself.

It was most likely another lie. That was not what was important. "We are here to have some questions answered."

"Ah," he said again growing in confidence, "I have the anses." He stepped a little further away from them. "Any anses you lik.

Now true anses," the goblin said again with a mock bow, "Those a little harden to give."

The goblin is wanting a bargain, yet he told them the truth about being alone. Kol drew his own sword and swung it at the goblin. The goblin's knees buckled again and a cry of shock escaped him. "Kol, no," Iris told him.

"Yes, Kol, no," Shoval said standing up. "I'd ratha been dead than live withent payment." With Iris protecting him he began to show increasingly more of his arrogant self.

Harvest, sadly, had the same thought. "Here," he held out a closed hand. "I will torture you still if it is needed." He pointed to the goblin's chest.

The goblin caught several nuggets of gold that Harvest had provided and shrunk away from his hand. Kol wondered where they were from. "This is fine idid....uhm, Ask away."

Kol handed him the yellowed paper. "Where is the other blade?"

The goblin examined the sheet. "I neva seen this before."

Kol felt the urge to hit him, but Harvest moved quicker. Lifting the goblin, he slammed him hard against the wall. After the goblin's yelp, Harvest whispered, "I do not allow someone to take my payment and break from the agreement."

"I told you truth," the goblin pleaded. "I know nothin of it."

Harvest reared back a fist, but Kol stopped him. A work place like this was used by many and not a single person. "Shoval, how long have you been living here?"

The goblin struggled in Harvest's clutch and glared at Kol. "I'd say bout a month."

"Did you work in this forge?"

"No I dint."

"Tell us why you chose to come here." Kol would need to hear it all.

Harvest lowered him back down for an easier explanation. "I came lookin' for my brothee," the goblin sneered.

"You are not going to believe all the junk he has down there." Willa had returned with Lloyd.

"Sneaky graspy little creature," Lloyd added.

Shoval flinched at their return. Kol waved them to silence. "Shoval, what did you find when you came looking for your brother? Tell us the whole story."

Shoval searched the ground, possibly for a way out. Despite his boast of dying poor, Kol figured he still did not want to die at all. "'E owe me money," Shovel began, wringing his hands, "A ver' large sum. 'E bin runnin' from me for some time and it was diff'cult to tack 'im down. A friend of ours final gave 'im up after some.....persayes. 'E takin a job here in this forge," He smirked. "Time for me to get what's mine but when I come 'ere everyones was dead."

Kol felt unease cross them. Willa looked around with hostility and Iris with caution. Lloyd's eyes flickered to the stalactites hanging above with excitement. Harvest was, of course, unaffected. What Shoval said explained his unease and slight fear because he shook lightly. "I am sorry for your loss," Iris said, looking back.

"Ah...I cared not for 'im, onlin what he owed me. So I tooks this place as payment along with the junk. Nice little spot with plenty to gain." He gave a soft cackled softly.

"Why would you stay here," Willa demanded. "Wouldn't you think whatever killed your brother would return?"

"It was a chance yea, but they were killed fer knowin' somethin'. I don't know so I got no reason to be harmed."

Was he that stupid, or did greed sway him? Kol believed the second, with whatever was in here. "What did you do with all of them?"

"Burned 'em there." He pointed to the furnace, "Then toseed his bones in oceen. Dint take as long as I thought. Ther was no blod to clean up, that a blessin."

Kol believed all of their hearts stopped together, despite Harvest's being always stopped. "So they were killed by vampires?"

"Vampires wouldn't feast on goblins and their twisted blood tasting of rusted coin," Willa told them, "Especially with a village near by full of humans."

"They would if they had become ghouls," Harvest argued.

Kol turned to Harvest slowly. "What?"

Harvest locked eyes with him and knew instantly, but Iris explained, "It's what happens when someone newly bit is close to gaining the full transformation but lacks the remaining blood to complete it. They slowly degenerate into ghouls. First the body wilts, then the mind. They will eat anything warm-blooded both out of hunger and desperation to finish the transformation. They would be completely obedient as well until they lost their minds, clinging to any last shred of hope that their master will give them blood. Nothing can sustain them by then, and they rot away because the body eats itself."

"Did your creeping fingers grasp anything else, something as to why they died?" Lloyd picked up a pair of pliers and examined them while asking.

"Actaly," Shoval edged past them and went to another work station along the wall. Harvest and Willa followed him. He picked out a small hammer and struck a jutting rock with a downward strike. The work fell away easily, revealing a small compartment behind it. Inside was a small dirty notebook missing several pages from it and part of the front cover gone. Shoval took it and tossed it to Willa, "It was my brothas, 'e always kept notes on tings. Daily events and who 'e owed money. I was honored to have three pages to meself."

"What does this have to do with anything?" Willa spat at him.

Iris joined them and took the book from Willa. She flipped through the pages, holding her hands to catch the most light from the lantern. "Wenn," she said, her voice taut.

Kol was beside her the next second. "What is it?"

Iris glanced at the paper. "It's written in broken English."

Shoval nodded, "'e did it so no goblin could read. Rare to kno that spech besid our own."

Iris waited for him to finish then lowered her eyes and began to read, translating the broken English so that it was easier to understand, "*We had not had any work lately, everything had become quiet in the east. We found a nice little town here, great places for our little band to cause some mischief and find some self-gain. Chief would not let us do it though, said we did not need the attention. We were growing tired of him, always demanding and we wanted to find him sleeping and pull his teeth from his mouth and then hammering them back into his oil big forehead. That was until the vampire showed up. Scared all of us at first but when the chief talked with him comfortably the rest of us got curious. He said he liked the crew and gave us each a large bag of gold, for that I would kill my own mother. We had been hired to smith somethings for him, so we did in a nice little cave full of everything we needed. Don't know what and I don't care either. Turns out the vampire was not the employer though, only another hired to organize their little work. I heard him say the name to the chief, Benjamin Wendom was his name, but that was it.*"

"Anything else about what happened?" Harvest glanced at the pages.

"No." She turned the pages "Only them working. Wait...*A man came by today, poking in here all prideful and demanding what we was doing. Chief gave word and the forge became a stove that night.*" Iris looked like she had just become very sick. She took a breath and said while flipping to the back, "There's nothing else; he never had a chance to add more."

"I'll tell the Reverend once we head back."

"Roasted with garlic," Lloyd lifted a wedge of a garlic bulb. "Tasty." He scowled as he tossed the bulb back down.

"We have what we came for. It's time to head back," Harvest told them, taking the little book from Iris and putting it in his back pocket.

"Agreed," Kol said putting the blueprint into his back pocket. Only Harvest had picked up on how rigid he had become.

"What about him?" Iris asked for the goblin.

Willa of course offered, "We have all we need. I can end him now so he doesn't steal anything."

"No," Iris said, and Willa glared at her again.

"We leave him," Harvest said, but he clasped a hand around the goblin's neck and lifted him to eye level. "But he should know that once our goal is reached, nothing would stop someone from coming back and hunting him down with none of us to stop her. He should pack light and go now while he can."

Shoval had started to shake uncontrollably now and nodded after Harvest was done. "Yeah that be best 'bout it."

"One more thing." Kol said, and started down Shoval's tunnel.

CHAPTER TWENTY-ONE

Dance in the Forest Clearing

The grounds lay under a complete blanket of snow, which still fell from the sky in heavy waves. Three large burlap sacks were piled together next to Kol, who flipped a large silver coin in the air and caught it. He looked over the ledge at Iris who was coming up last. Shoval had already waddled into the woods, tripping over himself to get away. Willa had watched him go with a look of a hunter memorizing its prey's path. Lloyd was busy making snow angels as Harvest started lifting the rope with Iris attached. Kol tucked away the coin with the robot in his bag and reached out for her hand to help her up. "Thanks," she said, smiling, and started to roll up her rope and untie it from the tree.

"Everything set?" Kol asked.

"Yeah, we need to go ahead and leave the area now." She tied the rope around itself then buckled it onto her belt.

Kol, Lloyd, and Iris grabbed a bag each as they started back towards the vehicles. "Lloyd," Kol said. Lloyd hopped out of laying on his back and landed, leaving his creation perfect. He was the last through the trees as they retraced their steps. "All right." Iris pulled out a small device as big as her hand. "Ready," she said, then placed the bottom of the gadget in her left palm and pressed the red button on top. Seconds later the ground gave a quick shudder along with a muffled boom, and Kol knew the tunnel was no more. Harvest led the way in front of Kol, his eyes looking through the dark for any danger. Kol wanted them to hurry out, unsure to where because they had no goal set, but he felt like he was closer still.

Why did he not tell Harvest and Iris that it had been ghouls who had attacked the city? That would have connected the vampire who hired the goblins with the one in the city giving out his blood. Unless there were two vampires starving their newly bitten, but the coincidence was too strong for it not to be. Then there was Benjamin Wendon. Now that Kol had a full name, he could look up the person in his List as soon as they were in the car. The fact that the vampire worked for Wendon meant that both the others and his problem were one and the same. The vampire could possibly have the other blade. If the List turned up nothing, they would have to find the vampire to either get the key or find Wendon. Kol patted his bag and thought he would make a quick stop in town before they left, though. They cleared the wood line faster than the first time, and Kol could see the vehicles still parked past the large meadow.

The snow here was thick enough to cover their feet completely. Harvest came to a halt three steps into it. Kol saw that his back was tense, which immediately put Kol on high alert. He quickly made his way to stand next to Harvest so that he could follow his gaze. It was not on the sky, trees, or most importantly his car. No, Harvest's gaze was focused on the fallen snow. It was moving in small portions away from where they stood to gather together in the center of the meadow. A quick glance showed Kol it was not just the snow at their feet but the entire clearing that was mounding. The speed at which this event was occurring matched Kol's immediate horrific realization. The snowfall grew worse as if to solidify the creeping fear. "Why are you here?" Kol demanded of the forming mounds. He stepped forward, dropping his bag and pulling his sword free, the blade whistling its warning on deaf ears.

"What is this?" Iris asked, and he heard the worry in her voice. The others had quickly gathered next to Harvest and Kol to gain their own understanding of the danger.

Kol had no time to explain. "Snowmen," was all he managed. As Kol had witnessed many times before, twelve hands reached into existence from the living ice, an aid for the Snow People to pull themselves upright and into their humanoid form. Each of them stood in equal height, which was almost twice as tall as the average of Kol's group. Once again none of the Snowmen had two pieces of coal for eyes or a visible article of clothing. Just that same object spread across where their mouths would be should Snow People have any. As one their heads turned in the direction of Kol and his companions, their vacant focus more than enough to chill the soul.

Harvest flexed his hands and bared his teeth at the threat before saying angrily, "Looks like my feelings were right."

"I need to get my armor," Willa said, dropping her book bag and holding sword and shield in hand. "I will need one of you to help me into it quickly." The runes on her skin began to softly glow, her eyes doing so last. The same soft light glimmered in response just past the Snow People in the back of the truck.

"I will." Iris tightened her headband. "We will make for it at the first chance." She still sounded shaky, same as Willa, and Kol could not blame them. None of them had ever seen these snow behemoths before.

"Fire?" Lloyd pulled his coat from around him and tossed it to the ground along with his glasses. Just like Kol and Iris, Lloyd too had a utility belt. Two primary items hung from it: a sheath for a dagger and a holster for a revolver. The metal of both weapons matched in a dark green hue and the handles were oak. The wood on both looked alive, as odd as that was, with branches growing from the grips along the blade and barrel. The several other pouches on his belt must have been for ammunition. Kol felt mild panic seeing a gun in Lloyd's hands.

Remembering Lloyd's one-word question, Kol answered, "Fire is the best option. Just be careful, they can rebuild themselves, and with the rate of this snow, they won't be lacking in material." At the mention of their weakness Iris pulled out a small red canister from her belt. Thankful to always find her prepared, Kol asked, "How many do you have?"

"Just three," Iris said. "I'll use them to break through with Willa."

Nodding Kol said, "Good. We will hold them after you break through. They are slow but extremely strong. They can also shoot compact ice from their bodies, but it will diminish their mass. Also, just because they are made of snow does not mean they will be easy to harm. They have packed themselves to a density close to steel." Kol patted the container on his belt that held his bell. Despite the harm it did to his body, Kol still found comfort in it. Motion from the Snow People brought Kol's gaze around and he prepared a fighting stance. "Well, here they come."

The two center Snowmen started forward to engage them with fists up, ready to strike. The remaining enemy followed a few moments after one another to create a wedge formation, and Kol's group responded with their own forward movement. Harvest and Lloyd were on either side of him while Iris and Willa followed right behind. Seconds away from collision, Kol spotted the front two Snowmen's arms begin to flex. "Dodge!" Kol yelled, jumping, and Harvest and Lloyd did the same. Two jets of ice obliterated the ground where the three of them had just been. Kol took an opportunity from the missed attack and cut the outstretched arm off one of the Snowmen. It wasted no time in regrowing itself from the storm as the three of them landed. Willa and Iris then collided hard with the distracted Snowmen to stagger them long enough to allow Harvest, Lloyd, and Kol to regroup. With both enemies within fighting range, the field was nothing short of chaos.

The Snowman surrounding Kol started to throw punches down on him, which he dodged and attempted to cut away at limbs, only getting chunks at a time. Harvest flanked one of Kol's attackers and leaped onto its side, pulling free a large clump of ice hardened like iron. The Snowman swung backward and knocked him out of its range. Lloyd was only dodging his attacker, perhaps waiting for an opening. Kol had no idea what bullets would do here. Would they cause any damage from their heat or would they simply pass right through? Kol blocked a swipe that sent him to a knee as the lost arm fell like the other. The other hand came, but Iris slid beneath the Snowman and her fist collided with the location a knee cap should have been. She then sprung from her knelt position and slammed her other fist into the Snowman's belly, causing more pieces to fall. The Snowman tried to take a step forward but crumbled upon itself.

Willa had gone to Lloyd's aid, using her shield to block for Lloyd who had been finally hit and turned away from the Snowman in front of him. Lloyd pivoted, pulling his gun free over Willa's shoulder, and fired into the featureless face with an eruption of thunder. From the neck up the Snowman exploded. Stunned seconds followed and the Snowman fell. Nothing tried to reform unlike the Snowman Iris had just stopped, which was pulling in snow. Kol did not understand: the only weakness of a snowman was its article of clothing or fire. These were different, though, and since there was no clothing, the head was the next best thing. The remaining Snowmen had reached them now, moving at full speed with fist raised. Kol took a few more seconds and finally understood as he looked up at them, "The weakness is the paper in their mouths. We have to destroy them." He glanced back up to see Iris pull something from one of her pouches and yelled, "Move!" Iris hit the reforming Snowman with her grenade and green flame erupted from the spot melting the creature. She barely missed the shots of ice aimed at her, dropping to her stomach and rolling away. Kol did not have time to worry about her or the others because two more enemies were barreling towards him.

From what Kol could gather in between enemy attacks was that the Snowmen were trying to separate them, and it was slowly working. He had no opening to find an attack; every move was to evade the assault. He broke away and began to sprint back across the field further from his allies. To his left Lloyd had his dagger, slashing where he could with his pistol ready to fire. The three Snowmen he fought off had learned from their ally's mistake, and did not give Lloyd any chance to fire as they slowly herded him backwards. When he did an arm would block his shot, the ice exploding then quickly reforming. To his right, Harvest struck where he could, then dodged from retaliation of his own two. Iris and Willa still held together on the other side of Lloyd, trying to push their way through the remaining three Snowmen. Iris danced easily under the strikes while Willa cleaved them away. Tired of the stalemate, one Snowman simply collapsed onto Willa's shield. When she held firm, one of the others did the same to pin her down. Iris darted to her side, but was picked up by the last who saw the opportunity. Iris was struck by a fist that engulfed her and lifted her into the air, readying to slam her into the ground.

Kol listened for the bell now in his hand and grasped the Sound, leaving his own two Snowmen behind. He was just able to make it to the backside of the enemy holding Iris before time continued. Two cuts and the titan collapsed on itself, releasing Iris. She landed on her feet then back into the air onto the two suffocating Willa. With one hand she placed a device, then with the other she punched it deep into a Snowman's icy skin. With a graceful flip she was clear of the blast zone and the green flame once more erupted over the living ice. The beast recoiled as an enraged Willa appeared and stabbed one of them in the face. Two more destroyed while the one who had grappled Iris regained its strength. "Get to the truck," Kol gasped, readying himself.

"Okay," Iris panted, and she sprinted through the clearing, pulling Willa behind. Willa did not want to leave the field in her fury, but knew she could express it better once fully empowered.

Kol brought his sword to guard in front of him, waiting for their next move. Lloyd had caused two of his Snowmen to collide with one another and was fighting his third. One of the Snowmen Kol had left was pulling a tree free from the ground. Harvest saw the tree well before it flew at him and angled himself so that the oak crumpled his original two foes. Kol quickly scanned the field looking for the other Snowman he had left, but did not see it. There was no way he had miscounted. The one in front of him began to swing so he reacted in a leap backward, which his legs could not obey. Kol had found his other Snowman as two hands reached from the fallen snow and gripped his legs. The attack struck true and Kol was slammed into the ground. The pain was intense and blinded his vision, and it took a moment for Kol to regain who he was. He had not lost his sword, though, and he brought it up again as he lay, wanting to prepare for the next attacks. In his confusion the second Snowman had released his legs and was pulled up by his siblings. They were above him before any Kol could react. Raising their fists, they began to pummel him against the ground. He reached for the Sound but could not grasp it as each hit struck right after the other.

The punches stopped after several landed and both Snow-men above him smothered his face with hardened snow, cutting off any chance of breathing. He tried to cut his way free but they snatched away his sword and pinned his arms down after. He could feel it slowly creeping over him, and his thoughts were fall-ing to pieces, his sight beginning to darken. He willed himself to keep awake, but he was slowly losing. Gunfire and the sound of steam erupted above him. The snow holding him down soft-ened and Kol filled his lungs in desperation. Iris's face appeared above him, full of panic. Harvest appeared next and together they lifted Kol to his feet. Lloyd handed him his sword while Iris tried to look him over. She was pulling him away from where the Snowmen had almost killed him as they made a grouped retreat. Willa, once more in her true skin, held her giant shield between the two foes, daring them to move against her. They did not as the six walked to where Kol had almost died and waited for the two to regain themselves.

Kol pushed away from Iris to regain his feet. "You can't…"

He shook her off. "I'm fine. Nothing broken, just bruised. Just let me catch my breath." He was thankful for his clothes, protecting him as they could. Gripping his sword, he stepped up beside Harvest. The fallen Snowmen had reformed now and they bunched together in a defensive stance. They were waiting for their next move. "We have to defeat them. They won't let us leave otherwise."

"They will now," Willa's metallic voice grated from the armor. She gave her sword a taunting swing before hitting it against her enlarged shield. Kol was glad that this time she was fighting with them and not against.

Harvest cracked his neck. "I prefer it that way. I won't risk them damaging the car." He licked his fangs in agitation.

Lloyd slid new bullets into his revolver and slammed it shut. "Stupid kangaroos."

"Let's finish it." Kol had become rather calm.

"Stay together," Iris said.

"On your movement, Willa," Kol spoke stepping behind her.

With a cry that shook the trees, Willa stormed forward, causing the snow beneath to melt as steam erupted from her joints. Kol stayed just behind her, followed by Iris and Harvest on flank with Lloyd bringing up the rear. The eight remaining snowmen hunkered closer together, the front raising hands to strike. Willa powered forward at full force and slammed her shield into the center enemy. It braced itself but was overcome by the metallic strength and fell under the billowing steam into the ground. She did not stop until reaching the back, where they all followed in. The Snowmen that had managed to move began to circle them.

Willa stepped forward and swung hard at two frozen torsos, one of which stepped back and the other grabbed its waist so not to fall over. Kol went for the ones to her left, dodging a punch. Taking his sword, Kol cut upward, his blade cutting the snowman in two. He aimed for the mouth, but the head moved backwards out of his cut. Lloyd spun away from an attack, under Kol's upright sword arm, and fired into the evading face, destroying the paper. The Snowman fell as another had already flanked them and swung. Harvest was there, leaping over Kol and Lloyd and into the chest of the Snowman, ripping a giant hole with his claws. He jumped away before a jet of ice blasted through his created hole by another giant right behind the first. Iris ducked under Harvest and tossed her last fire grenade after the jet of ice passed, through the hole, and hit the other Snowman in the chest, causing green flames to engulf it. It perished in silent anguish.

"Look out!" Willa yelled, holding off four Snowman. One had broken off, pulled a large fallen log from the ground near the forest edge, and had hurled it at them. The log hit the ground before them and bounced erratically. Kol reached for the Sound and vanished, the tree frozen in front of him along with the others trying to find a way to dodge. Kol moved to the log and cut it quickly five times before the Sound left him, and the pieces rolled to a stop before the others behind him. His muscles cringed at the Sound, but just as quickly the feeling passed.

"Amazing," Iris breathed. The Snowmen assaulting Willa halted their attack and slowly made their own retreat to the one that threw the log. The last two who had kept a distance did the same as Kol counted six.

"What are they doing?" Willa said, making a step to start the next confrontation. Small puffs of steam came from her joints. "Are they afraid?" Kol heard the smirk.

One of the Snowmen kneeled into the snow and brought up a hand full of fresh powder. He packed it into a large ball, polishing it to a dark shine. Kol understood beneath his calm, "Snowball fight." All of their heads snapped at him, even Willa behind her shining helmet. Kol smiled faintly as he raised his sword and readied himself.

The Snowman reared back his arm and threw his boulder-sized snowball at them. The others watched its ascension so that when it began to fall they would know where it would hit. The single boulder exploded and became many, and the five of them watched the trajectories before moving out of the way and letting the dark colored objects hit the ground with such a force that mounds of dirt and snow erupted. All but Willa, who let three of the smaller spheres hit her shield. The first gave a hard thunk, the second made her arm bend, and the third almost knocked her shield away. Kol added to their new considerations of danger, "They put a bit of their existence in the missiles. Somehow they are able to increase their attack's lethality by pushing it." He wanted to say more, but the other Snowmen were not going to allow him any time.

The other Snowmen had collected snow into their own hands, but instead of picking up the snow from the ground, they simple fed it from their bodies, then collected replacement from the blizzard around them. Each released a snowball in turn, then reloaded and threw again. Many of the snowballs would shatter into smaller ones like the first, or they would remain firm and create large craters in their landing. Those would easily stop anyone of them with only one hit. Trees shattered and splintered, the sound like thunder around them. They were in a hailstorm.

Kol darted where he could and cut what came too close. He watched every snowball to see if it would spread like a firework or fall like a meteor. Harvest was also dodging, and even caught a few of the smaller ones and threw them at the next coming to slow its descent. Lloyd somersaulted one way then flipped another way, firing his gun at many of them without seeming to need to reload, much to Kol's surprise. Willa was the safest, though the snowballs continued to knock her about. She seemed unharmed, but irritated by the striking and used her shield to slowly push forward. Kol was thankful her armor was too strong and his sword too sharp for these projectiles. It was Iris he was making his way toward, for she was having the hardest struggle.

It was not that she could not handle the issue, she was doing that well enough. She was striking at the snowballs she could not manage to move away from, giving a light grunt each time then gracefully turned away from other snowballs seconds later. Some moves made Kol cringe because there was no way anyone could see it coming, and yet she managed to barely miss the hit. One did make contact, striking Iris's left hip, which caused Kol to dart for her. Her gasp of pain was quickly pushed away, but Kol wouldn't chance it. Another struck her right shoulder from behind as she shifted over which spun her around to face Kol. She looked up at him knowing already he was coming and glared as Kol embraced the Sound.

Kol sliced through several of the incoming missiles as he came closer to Iris, her frozen face still glaring at Kol's previous location. The instant the Sound left him, Kol wrapped his arms around her waist, spun, and tossed her back behind Willa's armor. Iris quickly used the momentum and tumbled back to her feet. With his side exposed, Kol could see in his peripheral vision a large snowball hurling towards him. Harvest rocketed another slightly smaller into it. Lloyd rolled up next to him and fired three shots from one knee into the remaining missiles. Seeing an opportunity, Kol darted forward with Harvest on his heels and Lloyd following. The gun continued to sound like thunder as Lloyd continued the barrage to clear the way, and the ground shook from Willa stampeding after with Iris. It was time they ended this.

Kol reached for the Sound as the Snowmen turned their aim from the sky and directly at them. He darted through the field of frozen missiles towards the snow monsters. The Sound left him as he cut the legs of the Snowmen before him. Lloyd slid in beside them and fired a shot at one of the Snowmen who fell backward. Willa passed them then, the armor moving at its top speed because the lack of objects to collide with. Iris was right behind her as Willa laid her sword, point forward, over the top of her raised shield and slammed into two Snowmen, steam rising in her wake. Iris leaped onto a third and then rolled away as one of her small explosive devices went off, this one destroying the paper and leaving two standing and two pulling himself back together. Kol, Harvest, and Lloyd came the next second, each finding the last two standing enemies and decimating them.

With all six remaining snowmen collapsed, the five of them circled up and readied themselves, knowing they would soon stand again. Kol could not see any of the papers, but the moment one emerged from the thick blanket of snow he would strike. The ground was still, long enough to make them question the reasoning. The blizzard around them thickened and landed the heaviest Kol had ever seen. Lloyd reloaded his gun and the moment he closed the revolver the white erupted around them. Arms of ice reached for them from the ground. Kol started cutting them, multiples at a time, but like the fabled hydra, every one that fell two came after. With only four remaining beneath them there should only be eight arms reaching for them, but they had no such luck, for far more grasped for them. One clasped Harvest's wrist and started to yank before Kol cut it away. Lloyd freed Willa from several around her legs, and Willa passed on the help to Iris who had one around her throat. The blizzard seemed focused on only them as the snow rose with each hand, almost to their knees. If the hands did not capture them Kol knew the snowfall would.

They fought with all they had, every second dedicated to themselves and each other to stay above the cold. Iris was able to dodge most and deflect others with impressive arm blocks, Willa smashed with both shield and sword cursing with every strike. Harvest clawed in furious swipes and Lloyd never lost humor with each shot and cut of his dagger followed by insane laughter. The snow was up to past their knees now; they could not do this much longer. "We need to move!" Iris yelled, but when one of them tried to cut away free for them the hands would only appear quicker. They had crashed into a trap, and the only way to escape that would be to find its weakness.

Kol parried another strike and listened for the Sound, freezing the hands in place. He could get free but he would not leave the others there, and his time with the Sound started growing shorter, so he could not move them. He made one circuit around them, holding his bell's Song as long as possible and cutting away every reaching arm to give them even the tiniest moment's rest. The moment he knew his friends could hear him again, he said,

"Aim for the ground." He coughed hard. "Find the paper beneath the snow." The hands came again.

His friends quickly overcame the shock of his actions, except Harvest who was never perturbed, and listened to his words. Lloyd's eyes were full of hysteria as he unloaded his gun once more into the ground in front of him, Kol guarding his flank on one side and Harvest the other as he did so. Willa's helmet glanced towards Iris, who understood and came closer to protect Willa as she lifted her sword high and slammed her blade downward in an overcharged eruption of first steam and then snow. The change was instant: Willa must have found one because the hands erupting began to slow. Harvest's and Kol's priority switched to the Knight so she had time to pull her sword free. Lloyd simply reloaded and continued to spatter the snow before him.

Willa grunted as her sword came free from its cut in the earth; the blade had stopped at the hilt. With a yell she put her arm into overdrive again and struck another area to her left, reaching over Iris. This too erupted but with less luck. Three more times they managed this and they once again destroyed another, leaving two. The snow moved around them, trying to recover the exposed ground and swallow them, but Willa would not allow it as she swung over and over again. Knowing the trap had failed, the snow ceased all movement completely. Kol breathed heavily with the chance of rest they had and so did the rest of them. He just barely glanced movement beneath the snow, as the remaining Snowmen scurried to a safe place to recover. Lloyd saw too and shot one but missed. The two rebuilt themselves near the tree line. Willa went to step after them but her armor locked in place, making a horrid grinding noise. "Overheated," she said, her voice lightly fatigued.

The Snowmen began to turn, making a retreat. Lloyd fired at them but had no target. Harvest started after them. "We can't let them escape."

"Kol," Iris said. He glanced at her and caught the small jar she had tossed him. He nodded and turned for the Snowmen as well. The Snowmen were falling apart, this time on their own. They would vanish beneath them again and would be impossible to find in the forest. He decided the Sound was the only way. One ring and he caught up to Harvest, a second ring he was meters from the trees, a third ring and he made three quick cuts to supposed necks, and with a final ring he snagged the two slips of paper and sealed them within the bottle. The moment the rune of sealing appeared on the top of the jar, Kol fell against a tree and used his sword to stay upright. He was quickly joined by Harvest then the others. "Got 'em," Kol said, handing the jar to Iris. She took it from him and then embraced him in a tight hug. "Easy," he coughed, tasting blood.

Willa's armor had cooled quickly in the now-dying storm. There was no mistaking it was connected to the Snowmen. "What where they, Kol?" Willa questioned Kol sharply. Iris released him but stayed close to make sure he did not fall.

"Snowmen," he told them again.

The helmet leered down at him. "What do you mean, 'Snowmen'? I have never heard of any 'Snowmen' like that." Harvest reached forward and collected the jar from Iris and held the paper close to his eyes. The papers were still inside and made no attempts to conjure the snow around them. Anyone seeing them would only think they were paper in a canning jar. "And just how do you know of such things."

"Leprechaun," Lloyd suggested. Kol looked at the helmet and did not answer.

Harvest handed the jar back to Iris. "Not Snowmen," he said to them. "I think it's something that's been lost for a long time." Ignoring Willa's further questioning, Iris's worried look, Lloyd's sarcastic agreement, and Kol's confused expression, he walked back to his car and cranked it, waiting for them to join.

CHAPTER TWENTY-TWO

Gathering Around the Fire

T hey stumbled mindlessly into the camp, each dragging their own pains. The ride had been in silence, except for the two stops they made on the way back to the Encampment. The first was to the local police department, where they dropped off the stolen items. The second was to the young boy's house from the diner, who had lost his favorite coin. It now sat in the boy's mailbox, along with his toy robot, and a small hand-written letter warning him to be more careful with his things. By the time they made it to the campfire, the sun had decided to join them.

Kol wanted to pester Harvest about his statement on what the ice monsters were if they were not Snowmen. After attempting to do so on the ride home, all Kol could gather was that Harvest wanted to speak with his employer first and collect all the facts before discussing it with everyone else. Kol then wanted to bring up on how their stories were connected, but he seemed to only have the strength for one question. As alarming and enlightening as this information was, it could still wait until the next day.

In the Encampment, Kol could see that the snow had fallen here as well, but only in a light blanket and not in mounds of threatening ice. As a group they handed out late night snacks and built up the warming fire before Willa, Harvest, and Lloyd climbed into their tents. Lloyd did not stay inside his tent, but instead pulled his sleeping bag out so that he could sleep under the stars. Looking up into the sky, Kol could understand his logic, at least this time. Once the storm had passed the stars above were able to shine brightly in the dark. Kol decided to stand by the fire for a few minutes more before finding rest inside his own sleeping bag.

"How are you holding up?" Iris asked him, squeezing his arm then stirring up the fire.

Kol moved to help her. "I'm fine, just bruised and battered like the rest of us."

"If you say so." With the flame now burning evenly she searched his face. "Don't stay up too late."

Kol nodded, which did not convince her, but she went to her tent anyway. Finding a nice spot for his blanket, Kol sat down and pulled out his List. He searched for "Benjamin Wendon" and was greeted with both good and bad news. The good was that only four results appeared on his screen. The bad was that each one was scattered across the entire continent and none of them were inside the city they had come from. Knowing what they did from the departed goblin's journal, they had three options in front of them. They would have to go together after Wendon for information on the vampire and the location of the other blade, stay in the city looking for the vampire, or split up to cover more ground faster.

Nothing was certain yet, and Kol fought his impulse to head out at that moment to wait for his companions. They had helped him this far, and he wanted their advice on possible next moves. Patience was the strongest part of the game now. They knew who the enemy was behind both of their problems, and the enemy did not know that they knew, which gave them the element of surprise. Now they would find out the best way to use it. Nodding to himself, Kol stood, stretched his tired body, and then found comfort in his sleeping bag. Iris woke everyone a few hours later so that they could pack up the camp and head back south. Kol decided to switch places with Willa for this trip and quickly found sleep again leaning against the door of her truck.

A finger pressed gently against Kol's cheek, bringing him to open his eyes. He watched Iris move her hand back and smile at him. "We're almost back, sleepy."

"I wasn't asleep," he told her softly. He had resurfaced back to consciousness a few minutes before. The glass his head was against was pleasant and helped ward off the oven that Iris kept the truck in. The sun did not help the few chances its rays broke through the Trail. Still, he did not want her uncomfortable on his account. "How much further?"

"You've been coming in and out this whole ride." She glanced at him and smiled. "About twenty minutes."

He nodded; that was good because they were making quicker time than the first. "So why do you use horses instead of vehicles all the time?"

"Exhaust isn't good for the trees, so in emergencies only." She looked at him, playfully hurt. "You don't like the wagons or horses?"

"I didn't say that," he smiled back. "Worried about them?"

"Yes, I don't like to be away from them. I'm just relieved we did not stay for long," Iris replied. "I left them enough food for four days, but still."

Kol watched the sway of the road. "They seem able to care for themselves."

She nodded. "Yeah, but still. Do you have any animal companions?"

He nodded again. "I do."

A few seconds of silence passed between them. "Well?"

Kol returned his head back to the window to watch the forest speed past. "He's a reindeer."

"A reindeer?" There was no hiding her curiosity. Kol knew that his answer was unusual. He only nodded again and closed his eyes.

"Iris," he paused a moment to collect his words, "I have new leads after we discovered Wen's full name."

"Using that little device of yours?" She kept her eyes forward.

Kol did not want her thoughts to linger on that, "Yes, but the thing is these leads are far from here, and..."

"Kol," she did not give him a chance to finish, "Will you wait until we find out the connection of Wendon's with the vampires? I wouldn't usually say this, but we need you with us."

"I don't have plans on going anywhere unless we decide to. Both our problems are the same now," Kol replied, and he could see Iris relax slightly. Even if Kol wanted to leave he still couldn't. His father would not want him to abandon his friends for his sake. Were they friends? He caught sight of Harvest's car lurking in their shadow, knowing Willa and Lloyd were riding along. After what they had been through, Kol could find no other way to describe Harvest and Iris. Lloyd and Willa were still new to the assortment of oddness, but if they continued this path together the only two options were to either become friends or enemies. Yet did the others see it the same way, or were they all simply a means to an end? He would not have come this far if it were not for them.

Iris poked his cheek gently again. "You're doing that thousand-yard stare again."

Kol turned back to look at her. "Can't be helped."

"We'll save him, Kol," Iris said softly.

"I believe you." Kol wanted to change the subject from the serious topic. "Can I ask you a few questions about these Trails and Encampments?"

"Sure, but there is only so much I can say." Iris gave him a quick smile. "What all would you like to know?"

"All the answers you can give me."

Iris gave a small laugh. "All right. Let's see. We don't know exactly how they were created; we just know how to use them. The song you hear me play has been passed down in my family for generations. The song allows me to enter the Trails, make Encampments my temporary home, and allow others to come and go. The whistles I gave to you and Harvest are only to alert me you are outside the protective barrier, and I can then either allow you in or deny you a haven. Nothing can force its way into the Encampment or Trails that we know of. Finally, if you have a musical ear, and you mimic my song perfectly, it still will not work for you. It has to be willingly taught." She then stopped abruptly, turning slightly red. "And that is all I can tell you. I've actually told you a little too much."

Kol reached over and squeezed the top of her hand before quickly letting it go. "Your secret is safe."

"Good. Or I will kill you." She smiled at him while applying the truck's brakes. "We're here."

Iris shut off the engine as Kol opened his door and slid out, his feet hitting the moist ground. No snow had fallen here, only rain. At least he made the assumption it was rain; he had yet to witness it himself. They had left the snow hours ago. Harvest came pulling up beside the truck and he too shut his engine off. The back door opened, followed by Lloyd tumbling out of it and shrieking, "It just keeps going." He dug his hands into the dirt and began to crawl away from the car.

Kol looked at him with amusement as Lloyd stopped crawling and began to twitch and make soft whimpering noises. Kol turned back to Harvest getting out of the car and gave him a questioning look. "Wilhelmina likes to talk," Harvest said under his breath, making Kol smile.

"What about?"

Harvest shrugged, "I don't know." Harvest turned for his trunk, and Kol caught sight of an ear bud in his ear.

Willa stepped out of the passenger side door and glanced at Kol. "What's so funny?" She came around the car and witnessed Lloyd's dramatization. "I do not talk too much."

Kol shook his head, stifling his grin. "Nothing."

Willa must have been lying or simply did not know the power she possessed when it came to speech. As they unpacked the vehicles, she constantly worried about her armor and took it upon herself to give out commands for where everything should go. Kol looked at Iris, who did not seem to mind. It even looked like it amused her as the small girl gave orders. Harvest and Kol simply ignored Willa, which caused her to focus on Lloyd, who would start making strange noises and jump into a martial arts stance every time she came near. Kol liked to see this coming from her, though; it meant she was becoming more comfortable around the rest of them. Perhaps she felt closer to them after going into the cave and the fight in the meadow.

Everything was as they had left it with the colorful wagons still curving around the darkened fire pit. The ground was dry here as expected. The horses neighed in their direction and Iris went to them immediately, Temperance trotting to meet her with Diligence right behind. Temperance nudged her with her nose, which Iris stroked. She laughed as Diligence tugged at her hair. Kol watched Iris for a moment as he set a cooler of food by the kitchen wagon then started back to the car.

"I'm going to go fix lunch," Iris said once all the tents and supplies were put away and the fire set was reconstructed. Kol made sure to place all of the pot, pans, and tools in their proper place. "Anything in particular you would like?"

Kol thought for a moment. "Your library."

"What?" she looked at him, "You can't eat my books."

"I could with the right type of sauce," Kol told her smiling.

"It has to be a cookbook, then." She grabbed his forearm and pulled him along. Wilhelmina was placing her armor on a folded-out quilt on the grass. In front of her was a small box that looked like it had tools inside of it. Harvest was heading towards Willa to possibly help her, or, more to his character, discover more about the armor. Lloyd could be heard laughing near the woods as the two horses seemed to be trampling him. Puffs of dirt came from Diligence pushing Lloyd with his foot. Kol shook his head and followed Iris up the stairs and into the middle wagon. Iris pulled him along inside where her books were. "Read anything you would like. I'm going to fix us all some sandwiches."

"Thanks, Iris." Kol kicked off his boots then walked past her to the comfy carpet in the back. The shelves were packed tight with both new and old text, many of which were even in different languages, Latin more frequently other than English. Kol

collected a few books that caught his interest and found himself
a comfy spot on the floor. Laying on his stomach, he pulled free
the first book of dark red and began to read about vampires. "So
how long does it take vampires to turn into ghouls?"

Iris gave him a swift glance before cutting slices of turkey.
"The longer they go without the vampire's blood, the quicker it
happens. Only after they drank too much of the donor."

"How much is too much?"

"All depends on the person, we believe. Weight, height, and
metabolism too."

"Interesting." He placed the book to the side for further reading later and grabbed the blue one that had an illustration of a
full moon on the cover. The author was apparently a werewolf
himself, and sometime during the American Civil War he took
the time to construct his work. Iris left to deliver everyone's plate.
When she returned Kol asked, "So, with a werewolf, all that it
takes is a bite and the next full moon. So why are there not large
numbers of werewolves running the streets?"

"Territory, for one. Having a large number of werewolves
would cause constant fights for leadership. So the alphas usually
keep a firm grip on those he allows to get bitten. A pack usually keeps any of their recruits in check while they are changed.
Those who work alone, however, are the ones who cause more
trouble." Iris lifted her own plate and the one she made for Kol
and set it in front of him. It smelled amazing: turkey and pepper
jack cheese on a loaf of wheat with a mixed sauce spread across
it. Though it was cut in halves, the sandwich was a foot long.
"Interesting fact, no one truly knows where they or any of the
others have come from."

"These books don't say?" Kol did find that interesting. Iris
shook her head. "Someone must have taken note of it."

"My family's work is old, and so are the people Willa comes
from. Both have always said that they simply always have been."

Kol picked up a half and tore a large chunk away with his
teeth. The sandwich had been toasted after being made, and he

had to pull a piece of warm cheese from his face as he crunched the bread. He heard Iris laugh softly while chewing her own piece. He showed her his food before swallowing it. He thought better of himself afterward but Iris still laughed. "Still, seems like there can be more than that." They finished their food in silence and comfort of one another's company. "That was delicious," he told her after a deep sigh.

"You're welcome." Iris reached for his plate, but Kol pulled it away. "Kol..." she warned, and then without any form of warning, lunged for it. Kol was no stranger when it came to grappling; his years playing with the Snow Children could attest to that. Unfortunately, Iris was a whole new level. She had mounted him by the time he reacted. Kol slid the plate away and with both hands he pushed her hips up and slid his legs from underneath to prepare a guard. He could not manage to make one before Iris pushed his legs aside with hard strikes into his thigh with her elbow before attempting to reach over him for the plate. Pushing past the pain put directly into his nerves, Kol tried to stop Iris by locking his legs around one of hers. He was successful, and her posture collapsed on top of him.

After a few more moments of struggle, Kol had Iris locked around the waist and supported himself on one arm away from her reach. "I can get it," Kol told her, slightly out of breath, which he knew was not from fatigue.

Iris' hand was only just out of reach of the white dish. She even tried to grip the carpet to get closer. She looked back at him after he spoke and glared. "It's no problem." Like lightening her right leg came out in a kick to his supported arm and he collapsed to the ground. Kol did not lose his hold of her, but she managed to snag the plate. She then flipped around to hover over him. "You may be good with a sword, but I believe I have you beat at this particular skill." She touched his face lightly.

Kol lifted his leg into the air and slammed it into the ground using its force mixed with his own to push up and flip Iris over.

Iris squealed in surprise, and her face was cast in shadow from Kol's body now over hers. "Or maybe equals."

Kol felt a light squeeze around his waist from the guard Iris locked as he flipped her. "I won't accept that." She smiled softly and released him. Kol understood and helped her onto to her feet. He grabbed at the plate, but she spun away from him gracefully. "Go ahead and continue reading." She was also out of breath. "We're going to the city later to find out anything we can." She cleaned off the plate and then turned to leave for everyone else's. Kol watched her go and then returned to the books.

✶✶✶✶✶✶

Kol opened his eyes with a start, and in an instant willed them to focus on where he lay. He blinked a few times before seeing the lines of ink script trailing from where his head rested. Lifting it, he felt the pages of the werewolf book come along with his cheek. They released him shortly after, and Kol sat, rubbing his head. He had only planned to close his eyes for a moment. The wagon was dark inside, the only light flickering faintly on the kitchen floor near the open door, which meant that a fire had been lit outside. The others must have been out there enjoying it. Knowing Iris, she had found him asleep and decided to wait until he woke before they went to the city. Closing the book, Kol collected the others and placed them back on the shelf before heading outside.

The fire was burning slowly, and Kol could see the dozing horses barely painted by the glow. They were the only things with a beating heart inside the meadow from what he saw. The other two wagons were dark and still, no beam of light beneath their closed doors. The blankets around the fire were bare, and so was Harvest's bed. "Iris?" he called, but only the burning logs answered back. "Harvest, Willa, Lloyd?" Willa's armor was still laying on its quilt, reflecting the flickering glow of the campfire.

A feeling of danger slowly rose in Kol. He darted back inside, grabbing his boots and putting them on. He then quickly pulled his sword free from his bag. What had happened? Where did they go? Were they attacked? Kol knew he was not dreaming. He sprinted out of the meadow and down to where the cars were parked. To his slight relief, Harvest's car was gone. That meant they were safe, just not currently in the Encampment. Harvest would see his car destroyed before he died to keep anyone else from having it. Placing his sword back in his bag, Kol made his way back to the fire.

Sitting on his blanket, Kol felt his panic and worry slip away with the slight relief he found down where they parked. It was being replaced with annoyance. Annoyance that they would willingly leave him. Sure, Iris would do that, wanting him to rest, and Willa along with Lloyd probably did not give it two thoughts. But for Harvest to also agree? The betrayal was almost too much to bear. The only conclusion was that they went to the city to find information on Benjamin Wendon. He was far more important to him than to the others. A few vampires were nothing compared to what would happen if his father did not ride in the days to come. This thought made Kol feel guilty right after he had it. Finding those monsters was just as important as finding the weapon's twin.

Iris was only looking out for him, and possibly the others were too. Maybe under everything they were truly creating bonds. Wouldn't that be something his father would say? Making friendships can be important this time of the year. Kol had another thought cross his mind, one that took his mood from the darkened ice and made it feel like freshly fallen snow. Kol got to his feet and grabbed the axe from the cooking set.

It did not take him long to find what he needed. A tree that was just the right size sprouted from the ground just outside the meadow's tree line. Placing his flashlight on the ground, Kol was careful not to step from the Encampment. He may have had the whistle, but with Iris away, he might be locked out for good. Checking the axe head for any faults in its edge, Kol made several crisp swings and gripped the tree with his free hand. The weight took only a little effort as he hoisted the tree onto his shoulder and started back to the wagons. Kol finished his goal back in the Encampment before making his way next to the storage wagon.

This was the part he had to have faith in. What he needed may not be among this storage, but he placed his luck on the idea of miracles known to be common these days. He remembered the door that held an avalanche just behind it so he tried the other. Gripping the handle, he stood as far away as he could, ready to move at the first sign of danger. He turned the knob and winced, but nothing tumbled over him. Only the dark was inside which Kol cut through with the power of his silver flashlight. Inside he found plastic storage boxes stacked tightly along the walls, random objects and fabrics stuffed in extra spaces, and one large pile of other miscellaneous items that was the cause of the avalanche from the other side. He did not think anything dangerous was inside here, but Kol still used caution.

The boxes he could see were labeled, which made his job easier. He passed over boxes named *fishing, clothes pins,* and even *water purifier* before he found a box full of Christmas decorations. This box had been difficult to retrieve, because firstly it was hidden behind other cases, and secondly it was at the very bottom of a stack. With a few minutes of restacking, reorganizing, and again the worry of being crushed, Kol pulled the rather large box free. The sight of it made him happy: Iris truly did prepare for everything. Kol was proved wrong when he opened the tub because a note was attached to an ornament centered on top of everything else.

Remember the holidays - Eliza

This, of course, was Iris's sister, the one who had painted the wagons so beautifully. A topic for later on. Kol had work to do and did not know how much time he had left. Replacing the lid, Kol went back to the newly planted tree. The large tub contained far more decorations than Kol had realized, and a large abundance of lights as well. The thing that truly impressed him was that he only had to untangle one roll of them. Kol quickly undid the knot and continued.

The quiet of the woods faded back as the sound of an engine came through the trees. That made only a few hours for Kol to have completed the work, so naturally he had time to kill. Kol had let the fire die low, nothing but the embers casting light, and that was only across the surrounding ashes. There was a faint light displaying sides of the trees, but it vanished when the engine went quiet. Next was the closing of doors, then the combination of soft voices and rustling leaves. Kol took the position he had selected while setting everything up. Cloaked in the dark, he did not think any of them would find him, except for Harvest if he was showing his fangs. The soft talking died away as the rustle grew louder, the Encampment within their sights. "Kol?" Iris called for him. He did not reply.

"He's probably still asleep," Willa said, annoyed.

"Okay," Iris agreed as they came closer to the wagons. Kol could see them now, barely silhouetted by the moon and stars.

"It's so chilly," Lloyd spoke in a strange voice.

"Well, build the fire back up," Willa suggested strongly.

"What?" he replied and laughed.

"Just move, Lloyd." Willa pushed by him and went to pick up a few of the freshly split logs.

"Not a single word," Kol spoke. He saw Iris jump and Lloyd gasped mockingly. Willa looked around for him suspiciously and Harvest looked directly at his location.

"Kol, I'm sorry," Iris started, "you were sleeping so deeply."

"I don't think any of you truly understand how important this is to me."

"Oh, and like it's not important to us?" Willa asked him, tossing a few logs in the fire in hopes of more light. Their eyes were coming closer to where he lurked.

Lloyd seemed to be listening more than looking for where he was. "Pesky air and its noise."

"I fully understand how important it is to you." Kol was smiling now. He nodded at Harvest and stood from his crouched position atop the center wagon. "That's why I didn't worry about it." He took the two objects in his hands and connected them together as Willa, Lloyd, and Iris looked to him.

The slowly growing fire was no match for the illumination that leaped to life between Kol and the others. The tree that Kol had relocated emitted a magnificence of twinkling blue, and the glass ornaments that lingered on its branches made it look like a frozen life. Each piece had been hand blown from what Kol could tell as he hung them all. Kol made sure to catch everyone's expressions before they had a chance to hide them once realization came over them. Iris had taken a step back and placed her hand over her mouth in amazement. Willa's body language read an immediate defense, but a smile crept into the open. Lloyd laughed, but by now that was expected. Harvest's never changed. Iris lowed her hand and found Kol standing over them. "What are you doing!" she demanded.

Kol reached down to set the electric plug and picked up the small item. He then took a step and rang his bell, appearing in front of her once the sound passed. "Remembering," he said, as she gave a small jump. He reached for her hand and placed the last ornament into her palm with her sister's note.

She read the short script to herself then smiled at him. She gave him a knowing look then stepped around him to place the ornament atop the tree. "Remembering what, exactly?" Willa asked him.

"That we should always remember why we are fighting, and take time to ourselves to be a part of what exactly we are fighting for." Harvest had been the one to answer her, a surprise to them all.

"And we are doing this by putting up Christmas decorations?" she asked him, crossing her arms.

Kol would have said that is exactly what he was fighting for, and in a way so were they. "If we spend all our time running after our goals and none being a part of what we stand before, what is to stop us from losing heart when we need it most?"

"That's right," Iris told her with a smile. "Come help me make up some food." Kol looked over her shoulder and saw the ivory carved angel resting on the tallest perch, looking over them in a motherly posture, wings nestled close and hair flowing down her dress. Kol returned the ornament's smile with his own.

"I just think great discipline will stop you from losing 'heart." Willa laughed slightly and walked with Iris.

"So did you find anything out?" Kol turned to Harvest.

"We actually did."

"So you chopped him down just to relocate him and place burdens on his arms?" Lloyd said, softly stepping between them and Kol examined his face as he did. No smile or delight in his eyes accompanied the crazed. This expression was unnerving, because Lloyd was sad.

"Well…yeah?" Kol could only manage.

"Maybe it's not too late," Lloyd spoke again, barely loudly enough to catch. He stepped to the Christmas tree and knelt before it. Kol glanced at Harvest who gave a slight shrug. The two of them went to Lloyd and watched him with curiosity.

"Shush," he spoke. "Only a few moments more." Lloyd's look seemed to focus completely, and he began to hum softly, followed by soft whistles and clicks with his tongue. A new sound merged with his noises of sifting dirt, as if something moved beneath them. It was the tree responding to Lloyd's coos. Kol knelt beside Lloyd and searched in the darkened soil for the source. Roots pushed through the surface of dirt and then drove back beneath it. Several times he saw them split and grow larger in strength. The arms reached from the trunk in all directions. The sight was breathtaking; he simply never got used to things such as this. Unless, Kol thought, you were Harvest, where nothing seemed to faze him. Lloyd's song, the only title Kol could give it, seemed to grow slightly louder and the roots seemed to reach downward together with it, a choreography perfectly synchronized. And as Lloyd's voice slowly faded away, the tree became still again. "There we go," Lloyd said, standing and heading for the fire for warmth.

"Wait," Kol looked from the tree to Lloyd, "What was that?" Kol remembered yesterday Lloyd speaking about the trees sleeping. Was that not just more of his random behavior?

"What was what?" Lloyd asked him, and to add more confusion he tossed another split log in the flames.

"You sweet-talking the tree." Harvest seemed to know more than Kol, and yet could not believe it.

Lloyd laughed, and just like that he was once again falling from sanity. "Living." What did that mean, and why would he appear defensive of the tree Kol cut and then toss bits of other trees into the fire for consumption? Kol glanced back at the tree and took it in now that Lloyd had performed. The tree was alive, not with the illusion the decorations created, but actually alive. Kol thought he could actually feel the joy coming from it. It seemed to accept the challenge Kol had asked of it. "You simply had to ask," Lloyd said to himself and to Kol.

"Boys, set up the tables," Iris called from the wagon. Kol and Harvest turned to the wagon and stared in matching silence. "Please?" she added, without even seeing them.

✶✶✶✶✶✶

"You know these will drain the batteries, right?" Iris asked, sitting next to him at the table.

Kol swallowed a bite of his grilled cheese. "I know. Price for leaving me alone for too long. Shall I take it down?"

"No, I love it," Iris said, taking another sandwich from the pile she and Willa had constructed. "There is enough power for them during the night until we go to bed. I just need to turn on the generator during the day tomorrow to charge them back up."

Kol nodded to Iris. "It sounds like a fine enough price to pay."

"Then it's your task," Iris told him, as if giving him an epic quest to take. Kol smiled to himself. One at a time. Whenever this one was over maybe he would slay a dragon or two.

"So what did everyone ask Santa for Christmas?" Iris asked them after finishing a portion of the meal. Kol caught his breath and almost choked, but managed to regroup before anyone noticed.

"New strut bar," Harvest said first.

Lloyd chimed in next. "A golden radish," he said, "or another knife."

"Kol?" Iris turned to him.

Kol looked at Iris and her look went from pleasant to searching. He must be easy to read at that moment, "Um..." he thought quickly, "A new screwdriver. Mine back home bent a few weeks ago." It actually had. "What about you?"

"Hmmm. Perhaps a few fabrics. Mine are running low."

They looked to Willa next, who had glanced at both Harvest and Lloyd with disbelief. "What kind of question is that?"

"What do you mean?" Harvest asked.

"Asking something from someone who doesn't exist?"

"It was only to go along with the rest of the night," Iris said.

"Which I still find to be a distraction," Willa placed her half-eaten sandwich back on her napkin. "We should be making a plan for what to do next."

"Why can't we just enjoy the evening some more?" Harvest asked her in a hostile tone.

"Because every second we waste means another second someone out there can die!" And the cheer was gone.

"Did you ever believe?" Kol asked her.

"In what? Santa Claus? Why on earth would I ever do that? Lying to your children every year and give him credit for gifts you bought with your own hard-earned money? No, I was told from the beginning the truth." She looked around at them all, "Now if we do not go over the information from today I will step into my armor and march on the building TONIGHT." She meant it.

"I'd like to know what you found." Kol wanted to ease the growing tension. Harvest nodded, and he stepped away from the table to go sit by the fire. They all found a spot around the fire and settled in. Kol looked at Willa and went over how he felt when she had finished talking about his father. She truly had never believed in him, and he felt a deep sadness come over him because of it. He had no problem in believing in Santa, but then he had proof of his father's existence. Willa did not, and sometimes simply having faith wasn't enough, so he had no reason to be angry with her for what she said. Because of what she said he wanted to show her one day that sometimes you do not have to see something to know it is there. And sometimes it is far greater than one could ever imagine. "So, you found out who Benjamin Wendon is, then?"

Harvest nodded again towards him. "We did. He is a businessman, a very successful one in fact. Millions in assets."

"Built it himself?" Kol asked.

"No, it began mostly from inheritance, but after that with investments and consumer finances." Harvest sipped from his cup to clear his throat. "His main company takes advantage of the less fortunate. Providing them with loans attached to high interest rates that they can rarely get out of."

"It's a horrible thing," Iris said. "Helping people by making them think they are climbing out of a hole only by piling more dirt around the top to make the climb that much further."

Kol could only imagine. "So, where is he?"

"Out of the country." Lloyd said.

Out of the Country? "Just start from the beginning."

Willa nodded. "Better to cover it all. We went to the city and began to ask people if they knew the name. The first few did not but we eventually found a man who knew the name and told us it belonged to one of the only truly successful men in the region. It just so happens that everyone knew the company, but not its

CEO. Not uncommon, truthfully. After, Harvest drove us to the main office building of the company."

"Which would be the tallest one, wouldn't it?" Kol shook his head in a small form of disbelief. "Am I right?"

"You are," Willa said.

Kol organized this quickly. "So we locate him and go after him?"

"That was the better news we found." Harvest pulled a folded piece of paper from his pocket and tossed it to Kol. He quickly opened it and read the flyer. Surprisingly, he smiled, "He is coming to us."

The flyer was informing the employees of the annual Holiday Party two days from now, one of the biggest parties in the city. Not only did the employees attend, but so did anyone who was high on the social ladder. That was not what was most important. In small text at the bottom, the flyer said Mr. Wendon would personally be hosting the event. "We can capture him there." Kol felt a spike of excitement.

"Exactly," Harvest said. "It is on the twenty-third, which is four days from now. Plenty of time for us to come up with a plan of action."

"We just need to be careful," Iris stated.

"Careful isn't fun," Lloyd told her.

Willa snapped at him, "Fun creates more effort. Something we cannot continue to do."

"We also do not know the full extent of his power." Harvest pulled the small jar from inside his folded jacket nearby and set it in view of everyone. The pieces of old paper lay still inside.

"Power?" Willa asked.

"You finally know what those are?" Kol asked him.

"I do," Harvest said. "My employer called me this morning."

"And just why should we trust this person?" Willa asked him.

"Because he knows," Harvest returned shortly.

"So what was it we fought, Harvest?" Iris asked him.

"It's a rune magic, of course, but one so old that it was believed forgotten. These slips of paper are used to animate inorganic material. They create golems." Harvest waited for anyone to speak, then went on, "My employer said that the one thing golems have in common is a seal laid across the region where a mouth would be. A person that creates a golem has absolute control over them and the golems can be crafted from any form of solid, inorganic material. The danger is that those who can create golems have the potential to create armies in no large amount of time. The golems feel no pain, ask no questions, and grow neither tired nor disloyal. From our fight yesterday we can all agree to this."

Kol could more than they. The golem in the hospital was the exact same as the ones from the night before. They did not listen to reason or seemed to truly exist, only moved.

Lloyd lifted his head from the fire. "They are a false life...a wicked thing." Iris agreed. "They are at that. The sight of them is terrifying."

They were terrifying in both their appearance and action. What added more was that his people thought they were something that they were not. Someone knew this, and sent the golem to the North Pole to create fear amongst its races. Benjamin Wendon must be stopped. "So they just create runes on these pieces of paper, and that's it."

"No, the spell is far more complex than that. For instance," he lifted the bottle to the light, "these are not pieces of paper; they are bits of flesh."

CHAPTER TWENTY-THREE

The Old Way

I t had taken the entire night to come up with the best plan of action for the coming party. The original ideas they had each offered clashed with the others so strongly that the likelihood they would find an agreement seemed impossible. Kol and Harvest's were the only two that were similar: they thought using stealth was the best means. Iris preferred using only a few of them to find him so they were less likely to bring attention to themselves. Willa, of course, wanted to just wait for the party to be in full life, then simply storm the room and collect Wendon. What almost brought Willa to blows was Lloyd, who made small comments during Willa's presentation and fabricated a strange idea that consisted of using aliens and giant spiders to get the job done. Willa had become so angry that she pulled a half-burned log from the fire and began to chase Lloyd through the camp. It took some time to bring her rage down, partly because she could not catch Lloyd who had leaped into the branches of the trees, but it eventually happened after Lloyd started throwing pieces of bark at her and screeching like a monkey. Whenever an emotion overcame Willa it really grew exponentially, and that included the laughter they heard that night when the storm finally broke.

Kol thought hard about the strategy they should pursue as Willa lumbered after Lloyd and decided to share a new one with them once the two had returned to the fire. Each one of them had brought a good point to the matter with each of their plans, even Lloyd. So Kol used the parts that were important from each of them and shared his new idea. They all listened quietly and asked questions when they believed they found a flaw, which cropped up occasionally. Once he was done he brought up things that they would need to truly construct and solidify their next action. The most important thing would be to acquire plans for the building. That way they could determine the best paths for entry and multiple paths of escape if necessary. They then each took on different tasks to get completed before the twenty-third. With decided steps to take the next few days, Kol slumped into his hammock, and surprisingly, fell asleep.

"Rise and shine." Kol had only seconds to twist his body so that he landed crouched on his feet with one hand to balance. He glared up to find Willa with his hammock's edge in her hands. "We have work to do."

"So you thought it best to snatch my hammock from under me?" he asked coldly, standing and brushing the leaves from his hands.

"That's not the point. We have to get going." Willa turned and started for the path leading to the vehicles. Kol already knew why she was not in a good mood today. She did not find their job necessary. Kol saw Harvest and Lloyd still asleep in their respective places: the bed, and this time, atop a wagon. Iris was probably still in her wagon or taking a shower, yet a sniff of the air told him otherwise. The sun was barely shining on the morning frost. Kol gave it a slight glare then shook it off. They did have to start early, as their task was of the utmost importance. Kol changed from his shorts and shirt into clothes for the day.

Pulling on his jacket, Kol headed toward the path himself. "Kol!" Iris called, dressed in pajamas from the kitchen door. She started towards him and they met halfway to each other. "For the road." She handed him a brown bag.

"Thanks," Kol told her, smiling, then turned back.

"Be careful," Iris said to his back. Kol waved over his shoulder.

The truck engine was running with Willa sitting behind the wheel irritably. Kol opened the door and seated himself on the passenger side. "Don't want to take your bike today?"

"Not with the cold front that is coming through," she said angrily, "And I would rather not have someone hanging on."

"I wouldn't mind driving it." He started unfolding the paper bag.

The truck now idled in front of the exit slowly opening for them. "That is even more unlikely."

Kol pulled out two cloth-wrapped breakfast sandwiches. He handed Willa one of them and then started undoing his own. "It is a beautiful bike."

"Of course. It is mine, after all." She took a bite as the truck started forward and gave a hearty grunt. "This is amazing."

Kol saw that the sandwiches were a stack of bacon, fried egg, and pepper jack cheese between lightly toasted wheat bread. He gave an agreeing grunt as he bit a large chunk free.

"We might not agree on issues, but that girl really knows how to cook." She took another bite, then added, "I've been around many great cooks, and she is definitely one of the top."

Kol nodded. "I know of only one other great cook and I can't decide..."

"There was this one place back in Northern Europe I went to..." Most of the drive to the city was spent in this way. Lloyd had been right about her talking a lot, but Kol did not mind, though he could understand what it must have been like on a long road trip. Willa went on about how the food back home was amazing and all the diverse types of food they made. Whenever the topic would change, Kol would add a short line or two to send her on her next topic. She would do so whether Kol talked or not regardless, but this way Kol could learn more about her. He knew he could just continue talking when she interrupted, making the next word louder as he went on. Kol simply listened and watched the tree line as she continued to talk about the weather, her bike, and other things they glimpsed on the way.

Deep within the city, Kol focused more on his surroundings. The large tower stood only a few blocks from them. Kol could glimpse the top over the parking deck they were pulling into. Willa passed the few cars that covered each floor until they made it to the top. Putting the truck in park, Willa made known another one of her opinions. "I don't see why we can't find blueprints instead."

"I went over that last night," Kol said as they got out of the truck. "The prints are probably at the courthouse, and we would have to go through some process to get them."

"Just go and get them tonight," Willa snapped.

Kol shook his head. "Not needed, and we can't take the chance that Wendon would hear of it and become suspicious. Besides, we don't need to know the plans of the whole building, just a few things."

"Then why send me in now and not just look the night of the party?" She was going to fight every step of the way.

Kol did agree with that, but only if he was working alone. "Better to have complete evidence and go with something planned than simply make it up as we go along. There is too much at stake, Willa." Kol knew that they could not plan for everything, but they could try. "And it's best to not send any of us in because we will be going inside the night of the party."

That was probably the worst thing to say, and Willa showed it. "Fine!" she said loudly. "Let's hurry up then." Kol followed in the wake of the storm as they descended back down to the street.

They were only a building away now and could see the tower in full. Kol reached into his pouch and brought out a simple blue cap. "Just see what all you can learn inside, while I look around outside."

"Whatever." And she was off. Kol hoped she lost the anger while inside. He placed the cap on his head and followed after Willa who now walked several meters in front of him. He watched her climb the steps and disappear into the front revolving door as he started to circle around.

The tower had an entrance on every side. The one Willa entered and opposite her seemed to go into a lobby. The other sides both went into a bank and restaurant. The bank created more trouble. Any security would be greater than he thought. He found that a corner of the building had a ramp going down to a loading dock and service door. That was a good sign, he remembered, from the hospital back home. What he found towards the back of the tower was the most promising. On either side were a set of ramps that drove down into a small parking garage. The chain gates were both opened and rolled to the ceiling. Kol glanced around to make sure no one would see, the road completely empty, before he casually walked down inside. About twenty cars could fit in the garage, and all but two were filled. He didn't worry about those; he looked for something else and was relieved to find it. A single elevator door was painted with the same off-white as the walls it sat within. There was no button on the outside, only a small round opening for a key. Kol turned and walked back out to the street to wait for Willa where they had agreed.

Willa's reconnaissance took a little longer than his did, but Kol did not mind. He saw her come out from the same door she went through and he believed her to be in better spirits. She did not acknowledge him as she passed, and he simply followed her. Her silence did seem strange, but he waited to ask when they were back in the truck. "So what did you find out?"

"That people with my color hair stand out," she stated coolly.

Kol knew that it would, "They won't see it..."

"I know that." She started the engine and shifted into reverse. While looking over her shoulder, she said, "Really, there wasn't much to be found on the bottom floor. The entrance I went in goes into a lobby that is open completely across to the other side. A round desk sits in the middle with a guard stationed at it where he can see all of his surroundings and the display of camera monitors on his desk. Doors lead into the bank and restaurant on either side, and there is also a small supply shop for the employees in there. The only way up are four lifts in the center walkway."

"Only accessible from the lobby, I would guess."

She nodded as they pulled onto the street. "Yes, and I managed to get into one. The building is more than just one business, just office space to rent out. So many people must come and go, and the guard didn't really care. Three of the floors I checked on all looked the same."

"And the top?"

"Didn't get a chance to look. Another security guard got in at my last stop and started questioning me. He didn't tell me to leave, but I decided it would be best. I did try the top floor first, but you can't go there by the lift without a special key."

"Thanks, Willa," Kol told her before going over this additional information.

"You're welcome." Unbelievably, they rode without speaking through the city. On the interstate, however, Willa piped up. "I still question why I'm involved with all of you, regardless of what has happened." Kol turned to look at her questioningly. "I know we have a common goal, but that still doesn't mean that any of you can be trusted. I have no idea where any of you are from or exactly why you're doing this. You're from the north and Iris from the west. I asked Lloyd after saying that, and he laughed at me and said he was from the south. He looks nothing like someone from South America would look."

"And Harvest?"

"He is the main reason that I'm wary. My purpose is to slay monsters and he is possibly the greatest form of it, with his ability to change into two of them then walk in the skin of a human. He won't say, but my guess is that he is from Europe like myself."

Kol spoke while she gathered her next words. "I don't know where you come from and why you are here."

Willa turned to him and looked shocked. "You don't? The others haven't told you?" He just looked at her. "Well, you must be from a secluded place if you know of monsters and not of Knights." Kol could taste the arrogance filling the cab. Of course, he knew of Knights, he just didn't know that they still existed. "Ever since the beginning of the monsters roaming, the Knights took an oath to protect the people and struck against them. Our purpose has never faltered and so long as the darkness hunts, we will stand with sword and shield ready. Everyone should know this and respect the authority we hold."

Authority on whose opinion, he wondered. "So you exist to slay monsters. Even if they are good?" Kol knew already from the others, he just needed the clarification.

"They will all turn wrong eventually. Stop them before it happens." She waited for Kol's argument. Kol tactfully gave none.

They arrived back at the Encampment around mid-afternoon, and Kol saw that Harvest and Lloyd were gone. That was a hopeful sign; their job had been difficult compared to theirs. Kol was glad because Willa had begun to ask questions about his past again. With each one he had to remain silent or give short answers to satisfy her. Iris had told her of Kol's father as they had ridden north together, and that had only created a deeper curiosity rather than making Willa content. He was ignoring her now, and felt a slight guilt as he realized he had slid from the truck and closed it while she was mid-sentence. Willa, of course, was unfazed and increased her voice while opening her own door to finish her question.

"Willa, I can't and won't tell you anything else about who I am and where it is I'm from," was his final answer. She tried to respond, but he cut her off. "I'm here to find a weapon responsible for my father's coma and stop whatever is happening in the city."

"Whatever you say, Kol." They stepped into the meadow when she finished.

"How did it go?" Iris asked them from beside the fire pit. She had a large amount of red cloth in one hand that spread before her and atop her crossed legs. In the other she held a threaded needle and moved it expertly into the fabric to touch up small pieces missed by her machine.

"It went well," Kol told her, looking over her work.

Willa gave him a sidelong glance. "All we got was the lobby and a few other floors. So not a success."

Iris stopped her motion. "Well, we can work with that, couldn't we?"

Kol nodded. "The rest won't be so difficult."

"We should go back tomorrow and gather more," Willa told him. Kol shook his head and started towards the woods. He wanted to take a shower before the others came back. He knew Willa would fill Iris in on what all she found and ask more questions on his origin. He just wanted a little quiet.

When Kol returned to the meadow he was in sweat pants and short sleeved shirt, his belt loosely secured on his waist. The soft grass was always a comfort on his bare feet. He was glad to find that both Harvest and Lloyd had just entered from the passage to the vehicles. "Went well?"

"I start training in the morning," Lloyd groaned, collapsing on the grass.

Kol looked up at Harvest questioningly. "He does," Harvest told him with a shrug. "Apparently they were understaffed and desperate for someone. What about you two?"

Willa and Iris were gone, probably in Iris's bedroom wagon. "We gained a lot. Willa couldn't get to the top, but we have a good idea of the lobby and the parking garage beneath it."

"We will be heading back tomorrow." Willa stepped from Iris's wagon with Iris behind her.

Kol turned to her. "We can't risk any form of suspicion."

Iris ignored them. "So did you get it?" she asked Harvest.

"He got something," Harvest told her. "What about the costume, Iris?"

Iris nodded. "I'll have it done by tomorrow afternoon. I ran out of fabric, so I will need to go to town for more tomorrow." She hesitated a moment. "I could take Willa there while I am at it."

Kol saw what was happening. "If you do they will notice her this time, and we can't risk it."

"I'm trying to understand why you think you have any authority here?" Willa glared up at him.

Kol stared back at her. "Because this may be the only chance I have to capture the weapon my father needs to wake from his curse. If we give a warning, I may lose my only chance of saving him in time."

"Why by a certain time? If he is asleep, then why the rush if he is not dying?" Willa's voice had begun to rise. "None of you are willing to tell me anything, and I am sick of it."

"I can't let you go, Willa," Kol said.

"Let me?" Willa's eyes became wild. She spun and strode towards her armor. "I believe I remember someone unable to stop me. Who would be dead if not for the crazy person in the grass." Lloyd gave a small laugh at that. Willa reached down and pulled her sword free of her shield. Spinning, she pointed it at Kol. She continued, her voice growing louder, "If you think you can stop me, then try. I will go and do as I please."

Iris stepped up beside Kol. "Willa, that's not..." Kol placed a hand on her arm and lightly pushed her to the side.

Kol understood what she was insisting here. His father told him of such times long ago where respect was not given but earned. Earned not by your words but with action crafted from daring and ability. Willa watched him, still glaring, that storm raging inside her. Kol, who had his own form of storm brewing, reached into his bag and pulled from it his sheathed sword then handed his belt to Iris. Gripping the hilt, he pulled his sword free and lay the sheath gently on the ground. "Until yield?" he asked her calmly.

"Or first blood," she told him. Kol nodded in agreement.

"You can't be serious, at a time like this!" Iris told them. Harvest then placed his own hand on her arm. She looked back at him and grew silent. Lloyd had sat up and was watching them intently, his craze slowly being replaced by a serious expression.

Kol admitted that he had been wondering what it would be like to cross swords with Willa. Truly cross swords, no bell or armor, just their bodies. Which, of course, included their weapons. Kol nodded towards the shield. "Use your shield."

"Oh, you think I'll need it?" Willa spat.

"No," Kol told her. "I just want to fight your best form. It would be the same as me fighting with half a sword."

"Only half a sword is needed with you." But she picked it up regardless. Kol knew it was out of honor and not suggestion. Kol stepped away from the others out into the open. The sky was of evening now, and the cold calm inside Kol met the fading heat of the sun.

The moment the shield was firmly latched she charged Kol with a shout of fury and sword raised high behind a guarding shield. Kol stepped into a defensive stance with sword held above him also. She swung the sword vertically which collided with Kol's raised blade. He had not underestimated her without her armor. If he had, her blade would have contacted his head. She held great strength in her small body, and their blades shouted at one another as they connected. It was not a dance they stepped, nor was there any beauty within it. It was the work of savages and the old ways of the blade.

Willa took the offensive, which was odd for someone with a shield. She used it as a weapon. Her blade continued to come at Kol, and he parried some and blocked the rest. He had to constantly switch from holding his blade with either one hand or both. Both hands were needed to stop her direct strikes and one hand to deflect strikes made to glance or put him off balance. When Willa thrust her shield forward, Kol had no other choice but to step away and watch for her sword point hidden behind it. She would either lung forward in hopes of stabbing him or swing across with more force. Kol found little time to strike in return but whenever he did the shield was always there followed by her sword wanting his blood. This too he had to either step away from or to the side.

Willa made another strike, which Kol ducked beneath. Planting his hand, he kicked out his foot, but her foot collided with it in her own hard kick, halting his motion. He used her kick to help him spin back away and moved his leg before her sword contacted the ground he had kicked from. Regaining his feet, Kol swung for her arm, but once again contacted the shield. She knocked it skyward and cut up from the ground. The blade missed him, but dirt spattered his face. Momentary blinded, Kol brushed the debris quickly and put his sword on guard. Willa, who was still being fueled by her rage, honorably waited for him to see clearly again. The moment his eyes locked with hers she continued. It was possible that Kol was slightly stronger than Willa because of his body type. Yet if the two of them were to be compared on strength alone, Willa would be the victor. Kol had always trained his body to move swiftly, whereas Willa knew how to use her strength with precision, which was far more dangerous. A wrong move and he would lose.

One overhead swing caused Kol's forward knee to buckle slightly, a motion Willa saw and immediately acted on. She hammered down again and again, wanting to force him to a knee. Kol had his free hand on the back of his blade to better take the attacks. She gave a shout for each, and Kol let her storm rage. He matched it with his own, she a catastrophic hurricane and he a hell-freezing blizzard. He watched her relentless form with each strike; she took a moment more on the next strike to gather her full strength. He chose his moment carefully and moved out of her attack. Believing his blade would still be there, Willa was surprised as her sword continued forward and pulled her off balance. Kol spun in and grabbed her foot, pulling it up, to continue her motion forward into the dirt. She was too well-trained to be a victim of this, as her shield hit the ground first followed by the rest of her rolling back into a standing guard facing Kol. He had followed her roll and turned with blade in both hands to assault her side. Needing to turn her body to stop him, his strike caused her to become off-balance once more. Willa had to replace her foot to catch herself, and Kol kicked her raised shield to force her back. Surprised, she backed into a tree and readied herself for his next move, placing the flat of her sword across the front of her shield.

Kol made none. She scanned him for any clue of his next assault. Kol simply stood there with sword beside him, "COME ON!" she yelled at him. Kol remained frozen. He knew where Willa was best, and it was not when she took the offensive. If he attacked the fight would end with the side of her shield colliding with his head. The sword would parry his own and her shield would have made for the opening. "ARE YOU AFRAID!" Still Kol stood and waited. Understanding hit Willa and she lunged from the tree at him, battle cries coming from her mouth. She made a thrust that Kol blocked and followed it with her planned move regardless. Kol barely had time to duck under the shield before attempting something dangerous. He stepped towards her between her sword and shield. She swung her sword inward as he stepped under that too and very lightly placed the edge of his blade on her arm the exact moment her sword grazed his. At both points of connection blood graced sharpened metal.

"First blood," Kol told her simply.

The rage shook Willa, her entire body and her face. She closed her eyes as if to stop them from showing it. Then she let out a long breath and began to calm. "Agreed," she said. "Kol, I understand that you want to be cautious, but we need to have more information."

Kol watched her for a moment. "It's difficult to explain the importance of helping my father." Harvest, Iris, and Lloyd had begun to approach them once they saw the duel was over. "It's not that I don't trust any of you, at least to an extent. We've been through too much already." He turned to look at all of them. "It is not for me to say why it is important, too much is a stake. Who knows if any of you would believe me? Each of us has hidden pasts, but we are here now with one combined cause. From that faith is needed." He looked to Willa. His father always taught him to have faith in others, for no one should carry burdens alone. "So I will have faith in you."

The next day they gathered to eat breakfast before preparing for the coming day. Harvest and he were eating while Iris fixed herself a plate. Lloyd was busy going through Iris' storage wagon after asking her permission. Willa was the last to join, coming from the shower station area. From an outsider's point of view, things would appear normal. But after they had fought there was a new aspect of closeness between Kol and Willa. The building aggravation with one another was gone, for now.

"Here." Lloyd had come from his search and handed Willa a camera. It was an older one but seemed advanced regardless. "You're taking pictures of the city at Christmas time for a calendar that shows different parts of the city at different parts of the year. Personal hobby that you came up with to help you get over your bad breakup almost a year ago." He then looked confused at his own words and sat down to eat. "Here is a nice hat to wear to better blend in."

Willa gave no argument as she took the items. "All right. I guess that will work."

"We need to go, or I'm going to be late for my first day," Lloyd pouted.

"We will, shortly. Finish your food before we do," Iris said, smiling at him. Lloyd grumbled and did as he was told. They finished their food and cleaned up. Once everyone came home, they would continue to go over the coming night's plan.

CHAPTER TWENTY-FOUR

Assault on the Tower

The building radiated Christmas colors, possibly the brightest Kol had seen them since coming to the city. Two sides were bathed in red and the other two in green, the filtered spotlights causing the window panes to shimmer under the clear starry night. The buildings surrounding it had no chance to draw attention to themselves. Only the moon attempted to challenge the building's magnificence, but even it found the challenge difficult as gleaming spotlights swayed across the sky, displaying to everyone that tonight everything that was important was occurring within.

Kol scanned the tower from his shadowed patio on a building across the street from the festivities. No lights were left on in any of the office spaces between the bottom floor and the top. Harvest crept up beside him to watch the action below as well. People had begun to approach the building from the surrounding parking decks and street openings. Hailing from a higher social class, the guests spared no expense in their decorated clothing and vehicles. Kol heard Harvest whistle softly several times as valets acquired the keys of expensive looking sport or luxury cars and drove them off for safe parking.

The people had a choice to spend some time around the entrance area to admire the decorations set in place there. A small band played Christmas tunes as some carolers caroled. Stands of candy were displayed, and the adults had to practically chain their children to them so that they did not band together and conquer the delicious ensemble. The rest of the stands were providing a selection of Christmas ornaments or cards to send in last minute gifts. "Ho ho ho!" came a happy bellow that sounded strained among the noise of a crowd. The two of them looked for the owner and found someone in a Santa costume walking up the street. The costume had all the original qualities, from the red coat, pants, hat, and black fabric boots. The white beard was massive, covering all but the eyes, which were shadowed by the hat, and reached to his leather belt. The person was rather large within the costume, but was difficult to tell as he was bent over carrying a large brown bag. "Merry Christmas!" he yelled before taking a seat on one of the park benches facing the building beneath them. Kol worried if the wooden bench would hold as they heard splintering sounds from where they hid several meters above the Santa. The actor inside the costume only laughed while placing the bag next to him. Thankfully law enforcement was directing traffic, because any attempt from the parents to stop their children from the siege on the candy stand was lost as they rushed the street to see Santa Claus.

Kol smiled, showing all his teeth. He pressed the small button under his shirt to switch on the microphone above it. "Doing great, Willa."

A few seconds passed as the Santa attempted to fight off the children. "I swear I will have your head for this, Kol." Her reply came through the small ear piece tucked into his ear, free of the external augmentation that made her voice sound masculine.

"I think you are very convincing," Iris chimed in, "though children can be difficult to fool. Good thing Harvest thought of the presents to distract them." Kol scanned the entrance yard for Iris. It did not take long for his eyes to find her. She approached from the left, looking absolutely stunning, wearing a strapless blue evening dress that exposed a good portion of her back with heels to match. All of it shone in the created light, including the silver netting covering the elegant bun of her hair. Iris was completely on form to play her part, just as Willa was below and Lloyd already above. Perhaps too well, as heads of coupled and single men followed her path, along with several women.

"The only reason you are saying that is because you created the costume," Willa replied, lifting another child from her lap.

"I don't see any other reason to believe it," Iris stated matter-of-factly.

Harvest looked to the four balconies above. "Any sign of the host yet, Lloyd?"

"Huh?" Lloyd sounded distracted.

"The host of the party. Has he made an appearance yet?"

A few moments passed. "Look, I have plates to fix right now. I don't have time for your grand mission and other games. I have a job now, responsibilities. I have to grow up and take charge of my life. Blood and death from your little vampire problem are nothing compared to what will occur if the turkey is not distributed just right." The radio went quiet after that.

"Thankfully we are using a secure channel through Willa's armor," Kol told Harvest.

Harvest yawned idly. "Once this is done, I will throw him from the top." He reached into his coat pocket and retrieved his fang. Opening his mouth, he inserted the tooth and began the familiar change. After it was over, he closed his eyes and sniffed. "Nothing vampiric near us at the moment. Hopefully that doesn't change."

"That would be unfortunate," Kol replied. The plan seemed to be going as planned so far; hopefully they could remain unnoticed.

"The crowd is beginning to head up to the party. I'm going to head up as well," Iris stated. Watching her, Kol saw her scan the crowd before finding a worthy target. She made her way over to a group of young people and began talking with them. After a few minutes, the group began to head towards the door, Iris locking her arms in one of the gentlemen there. At the opened doors, she pulled the invitation that the Reverend had acquired for her from a small purse and continued inside. Kol quickly disregarded the small stab of jealousy. This was not the time for such things. Iris knew what she was doing. If she had gone in alone, it would have drawn more attention to her.

"The demons are being summoned away," Willa reported. She reached for the bag and looked inside. "Bloodthirsty little things, almost had to give away Iris's and Lloyd's present."

"I don't think any of them are naughty enough for that," Lloyd stated. "Wait...catch one quickly and let him bring it up here to me."

"ABSOLUTELY NOT!" Kol grimaced from the speaker as Willa's raised voice attempted to rupture his ear drum.

"Lloyd, stop trying to get a rise out of her. Everyone on the elevator looked at me because they heard her." Iris was irritated. "And bring me something to drink."

Lloyd replied with his usual bird calls and chipmunk noises.

Only a few more people remained outside. "Shouldn't be too much longer." Kol tried to count and came up with twenty or so.

"As soon as Wendon shows himself, we will move out," Harvest confirmed again. Kol nodded and decided to go over the plan again to kill time. Iris was putting an eye inside the party as a guest along with Lloyd as a member of the catering company. They had both been the best choice when coming up with the plan. Iris knew how to talk to people and create a positive environment, regardless of whom she was with. Lloyd had showed Kol his ability to disguise himself, and Kol knew he would be able to do the same tonight. Originally he was supposed to steal a work uniform once they had found out who would be catering the party. Instead, he got a job working for them because they were shorthanded. These past few days either Iris or Harvest had to take him to work, and one day he had been sent to a wedding. Lloyd had brought back cake for all of them. He now waited tables, going unnoticed by his coworkers and the guests alike, which was the plan.

"Just so we're clear, don't expect me to sit here all night doing nothing. Keep me updated, or I will take matters into my own hands." Kol glanced down at Willa. She had wanted to attend the party, along with Iris, but the plan had a greater success rate with her being where she was. Willa was not the blending type; she was far more accustomed to crashing parties rather than partaking in them. More importantly, they had no idea if there would be any enemies they would have to deal with. The two inside would not be able to carry in their weapons or gear. If Willa had gone inside, she would have to leave her armor behind, which was their main defense. Once Harvest had explained this to her, she had no choice but to agree. That was also why she was the one who did reconnaissance inside the building a few days ago. She was the only one who could be seen since she would not be at the party. Having a watch stationed outside took care of a potentially hazardous blind spot once Harvest and Kol made their way inside. Willa might not see any action, but it was better to be prepared for anything.

They all knew the layout of the party above before even arriving. Willa's second trip back had indeed become very useful. Using the camera Lloyd had found for her, she was able to give them every detail of the two floors the party would take place on. The twenty-third floor had been the entranceway connected to several private rooms that would not be used for the party. Instead, guests would be urged to ascend the curved staircase wrapped in tinsel to the left of the elevator lobby, which would deliver them to the festivities above. The twenty-fourth floor opened into a large lounge area complete with bar. From there, the guests could go into the second room that was half-filled with round dining tables and the rest a tiled dance floor. The guests would be able to enjoy all of the seasonal decorations, complete with a large Christmas tree beside the tile. The kitchens and serving stations were located out of sight behind the lounge, and each room had a connection to the large balconies above.

"Everyone is taking their places at the tables. Still no sign of Wendon," Iris updated.

"That's not good," said Lloyd. "The red velvet cake is nowhere close to being done."

"It would be in your best interest to save me a piece. The one who brings me one will not have to be beaten like the others," Willa told them.

"Someone is coming onto the stage," Iris said. "He's welcoming everyone to the party. It must be Wendon."

"Lloyd?" Kol inquired.

"Boss man says it's him," Lloyd sounded breathless. "He started going on about how he had seen him as a kid before I placed a carrot into his mouth. Now, if you don't mind, I am going to quit talking to myself while passing out plates. People are starting to think I'm insane."

"Willa," Harvest said.

"Valets have gone inside to escape the cold." Her head turned up both streets. "Outside vacant and secure." Harvest nudged Kol's arm and they both stepped from their hiding place just as the street lights went dark below them as well as the lights along the entrance steps and front area. "Thirty seconds," Willa told them as they landed on either side of her. They bolted across the street and split to either side of the building, jumping over railings and bushes to do so. They landed at both entrances to the employee parking down below. Kol glanced across the cars along with Harvest and saw that they were alone.

"Lloyd, send it down," Kol heard Harvest say from across the parking lot and through the speaker. The two of them ran for the elevator door that was painted the same color as the rest of the supporting wall. Pressing their backs against the wall, they waited. Kol could hear the elevator coming. Only a few more seconds. From both the entrance ramps, Kol could see the street lights come back on. The elevator door slid open, a small beam of light across the dark cement opening wider before two shadows darted inside and pressed the top button. The door slid back closed, and they began to rise to the top. "We are inside the elevator," Kol said. This elevator was the one used by the employees and staff in order to keep the four main elevators customer friendly. Most people don't enjoy sharing a small space with a dirty mop bucket.

"He's still talking," Iris said. "Seems to be stretching it out a bit."

"Good, we need all the time we can get," Willa said.

"Iris, is that young man behind you finished with his plate already?" Lloyd was the one sounding irritated.

"Lloyd, this isn't...yes he is."

"Well, he will have to wait. Maybe that will teach him not to be a glutton." Kol could hear the up-turned look of Lloyd's face in his tone.

"I don't think we will be going to the top floor, like I said," Harvest told him, ignoring the others.

Kol glanced at the highlighted number in confusion. "Why is that?"

"Needs a key." He pointed to the small hole next to the number.

"We should've expected as much." Kol glanced up at the ceiling, "We will have to do something else. Lift me up." Harvest did not object but held out his hand for him to step on. Not a lot of strength was needed for him to do so in that form. Kol ran his fingers along the tiles until he found the right one. Lifting it, he moved it to the side, exposing a hatch to the top of the elevator.

Kol tried to turn the knob but it would not budge. "Locked from the outside. That's weird: shouldn't it be unlocked for emergencies?"

Harvest lowered Kol back down, "Maybe so that no one could try and climb out of it in order to get into a room they shouldn't. One second." Harvest eased Kol back before leaping to the ceiling of the elevator. His claws pierced through the thin metal and with a grunt the door crunched in his grasp. Harvest then bent it outward and pulled himself up. Smiling, Kol jumped up after him.

While Harvest activated a flashlight so Kol could see, Kol replaced the ceiling tile so no one would see the bent door.

"Hope we won't be crushed." Kol examined the lifting cables then watched the walls slowly pass around them. They were two-thirds of the way up.

"Unlikely: there is a workman's space at the very top." Harvest glanced above as if to check. Kol gave him a sarcastic look of panic.

The walls began to slow around them as the elevator door lowered in front of them. They had to move quickly before someone called for the elevator to go down. Harvest was able to stick his claws into the split of the door and slowly forced it open. Turning off his flashlight, Kol waited until he had enough room before ducking under his arms and stepping into the darkened area beyond. Harvest did the same after he saw Kol was through, then closed the doors behind them. Kol had to give himself time to adjust to the darkness, but the adjustment never came because the room was void of all light. Kol had to place his faith in Harvest, whose eyes were far greater in the dark than his own. Harvest took in the area making sure there was no one near to cause an alarm before telling the others, "We've made it to the top."

"He's sitting at the main table eating along with some highly pristine guest," Iris said.

"Keep us posted," Kol told her, then turned to Harvest. "Let's hurry and locate it if it's here before moving on to the next plan. Hopefully there wasn't an alarm on the service door." The next plan was when they would go from stealth to a more direct approach. If the blade was not here, then they would ask Wendon personally. Either they would capture him discreetly or have Willa knock on the door. Harvest nodded before they started forward cautiously. The elevator was for the cleaning staff, so of course it was hidden away from the rest of the office area. Harvest gripped a door handle somewhere in front of them and opened it outwards. The hallway beyond was also dark, but a small window at the end of the hall allowed a little city and moonlight. The elevator had deposited them into a small washroom full of mops, brooms, and other cleaning supplies. The hallway they now explored stretched in front of them. Two small doors on the left were bathrooms, and a pair of double doors on the right led to the main elevator lobby on this floor. He had been correct in his assumption when he and Harvest quietly opened them and passed through. The four main elevator doors gleamed dully under dimmed lights from above the lobby. They passed them in search of what was beyond the second pair of doors opposite of the ones behind them. Kol tried the doors and was thankful they were not locked as the two of them once again vanished beyond.

They were in an entrance hall now, illuminated by the moonlight beyond within a larger room. They crept along the shadows slowly, watching for anything that would impede them in their mission. They stopped at the end of the hall and took in the new surroundings. Harvest would have made it known if anything was near, either with a heartbeat or without. The only things that would have to rely on their eyesight were cameras, and, thankfully, none were in this room.

The wall across from them and the one two their left was made completely of glass, allowing Kol to see what else was there. Beyond them was the small balcony that ran the top of the building above the larger ones surrounding the party below. A large glass top conference table was centered in the room surrounded by several large leather office chairs. The wall along their right had a small door built into it and a dark color cabinet beside it. The place was simple, professional, and unused. There was no sense of personal touch or familiarity within the room. Looking back left, Kol could see another set of double doors. Kol made another assumption that behind those doors was Wendon's main office and possibly where he would keep the *Clauditis* blade.

They had two ways to search the area: start from here and cover everything, or go to the most likely place first to save time. Kol preferred the latter and started towards the doors, only to be stopped when Harvest reached out and gripped his arm. Turning, he looked for the alarm, but found Harvest staring at the wall cabinet next to the small door. He could only see a part of it because Harvest blocking his view, so he stepped out to see what had gotten his attention. Realization hit him and they both moved to the cabinet. Placed beneath it was a safe standing a meter tall with a similar width. It was a simple thing with a number pad and silver handle next to it. Excitement rose within Kol, but petered out when he considered how they could get inside of it. "We found a safe," Kol reported quietly into his microphone.

"Any way of getting it open?" asked Willa.

Harvest looked along the side. "No, my claws can't dig into this much reinforced metal. And moving it may be out of the question, too. Far too big to move without being seen or heard."

"I can come and grab it," Willa said proudly. Kol did not have to look off the balcony to see her begin to rise from the bench.

Harvest knew it too. "We'll save that as a final effort."

"What kind of safe is it?" Lloyd's tone was rarely serious, but his question sounded genuine.

"I have no idea." Kol checked the sides and top looking for any name brand. "It's completely blank. No brand name or anything."

Lloyd responded immediately, "What does it look like?"

"A meter in measurements. Solid black with a simple key pad and handle, both silver. No other description on it." Harvest continued to examine.

"I'll be up there shortly. See what else you can find." They stood to continue their search after the radio went silent. Kol walked around the table searching for anything else that seemed significant, while Harvest looked through the cabinet above the safe hoping to find the code or anything else of use.

"He's stepping away from the table, taking a phone call," Iris broke the silence, "Leaving my line of sight."

Kol's alertness went up. "Lloyd?"

A moment passed before, "Nothing. He's nowhere to be found. I'm going down to the floor below, but unlikely he's there."

A soft bell rang from the elevator lobby as one of the doors opened to allow a passenger to exit. The two of them froze as they heard the conference room doors open at the end of the hall. "How long before he arrives?" His voice was deep, a tone that was to the point and haughty. Kol dropped to the ground behind the table as Harvest crouched beside the safe and cabinet, blocking his vision from the hallway. "I believe we had a set time." Kol wondered who was on the other line. Wendon stepped into view. Kol could see him from a small spot behind the table. He was relatively young, but Kol could see that age had begun to win the battle against youth among his face. He had blond hair with a beard to match, both trimmed short. His eyes were blue, and though Kol could not see them clearly, he felt they carried a coldness to them. He wore a black suit and tie, his vest beneath his jacket a dark green. His very posture was cut for business, matching his demanding tone. Benjamin Wendon was a man of action and wasted no time with pleasantries. His goals were his only drive. "I should have had it in my hands long ago. Prepare them for shipment and leave once he has left me and returned to you." There was no goodbye or any form of ending in the conversation as Wendon walked to the doors at the end of the table.

Beyond the door were more windows and an object Kol knew was a desk that centered the room. Both Harvest and he rose from their spot as Wendon stepped inside. They made no sound, two shadows amongst darkness as they moved to stand on either side of the office door. "Nothing down here. Anyone else?" Lloyd radioed. Kol felt a slight panic, hoping that Wenn would not be able to hear him.

"He hasn't returned to his table, either," Iris reported.

"Kol?" Willa's alert was at its highest point, "Harvest, is he up there with you?"

Kol met Harvest's eyes who understood. Kol reached for the wire on his ear and pressed a small button there twice. A soft beep would be heard over everyone else's radio: signal for silence, which the others thankfully kept to, even Willa, who only needed the slightest excuse to set her on a rampage through the building. They all had to trust Kol and Harvest and await information.

Wendon could be heard inside pacing around the room. He had not turned on a light, so the small one they saw come on across the floor in front of them must have been from his phone.

Kol listened hard but could not miss Harvest's tension in his stance. His eyes went wide and his head turned to listen for something Kol could not hear. Carefully, Kol reached into his bag and pulled his weapon from within. Whatever had Harvest alarmed, a person who showed no emotion, was something worth being ready for. To his surprise, Harvest reached into his mouth and pulled free his fang and transforming back into his human body. Kol gave him a confused look, and Harvest shook his head and mouthed the words "wings." A few seconds later Kol could hear it too.

They struck hard against the sky. Kol could hear even though the windows buffered noise from outside. Wings, powerful ones, grew louder as they approached the tower. Wendon had also heard the buffeting wings. "Finally," he said, bored, and could be heard moving away from the desk.

Kol and Harvest took a chance to peer inside and witnessed Wendon opening glass doors out into the balcony. He stepped into the night just as the winged creature landed before him, a darkness against the lighted sky. Kol saw no detail, only an outline. Massive wings protruding from its back, spanning the entire view of the office windows. Horrifyingly, they curved wickedly over the balcony before beginning to fold behind the creature they were connected to. Two horns protruded from its head, which Kol realized were ears when they began to move and listen to the air. Kol strained to examine closer to what it was but the wings and ears began to absorb into its body along with what Kol briefly saw as elongated claws on its hands. "It seems like the party is coming along nicely." The creature had receded within itself and took the silhouette of a man. Kol remembered the voice: it was the vampire who had sent his descendants on him at the river what felt like an eternity ago. The only reason why the vampire could not sense them there was the amount of people down below at the party, throwing the vampire off. Kol tried to still his heart anyway.

"Sickening," Wendon told the vampire. "I hadn't planned on coming back here. I left it for a reason. There are more important matters to attend to." Wendon turned to gaze off the balcony. "The only reason I had it arranged was so I didn't raise any suspicion. I can't go anywhere in this city without someone knowing who I am."

"So why choose this city for me to recruit from? You were correct in stating that I would find plenty who were more than willing to be turned." The vampire sounded mildly curious.

"I wasn't the only one who wished to escape this place. We all knew it growing up, the rest of those at the school I went to. It crept on us slowly as we moved on each year, that unspoken knowledge that we would never escape from this condemned place. I was able to figure out my own way, but the others did not. As I left, I was able to realize that it was not only we who had this creeping feeling, but every generation to come after and those who went before. Of course, you could have found another place in this world where everyone had the same failing ideals, but I knew this place was guaranteed. With the young becoming obsessed with the supernatural these days and the old desperate to have another chance at the life they wasted, I'm proud enough to say you couldn't find a better spot."

The vampire gave a soft chuckle. "Well, you couldn't have been more right. I have thirty prepared from when we last spoke; they are on their way to meet with her at the river." Harvest became tense again as they listened. Kol watched as he slowly peered around the corner to see if the two outside were looking within. When he confirmed they were not, he pulled his phone from his pocket and hid it inside his jacket as he sent a message to Willa. "I would have had more, but with a Knight in the city along with whomever attacked us at the docks, I felt it would have been best to relocate them. They obeyed me perfectly, their cravings made sure of that, yet others still took notice of them.

I had them locked away in a freight well outside the city. Only drawback is that they have all become ghouls: the lack of human blood hastened the effects along despite what I could bring to feed them. They are in the final stages from being completely turned, so they will still obey me but no longer remember who they are. Only feeding and following my orders." Kol remembered the ghouls who had attacked the Lake of Frost had human speech and a form of intellect.

Wendon nodded acceptingly. "It doesn't matter. The ghouls will serve their purpose as a distraction along with the goblins you enlisted and others who have joined us. As long as you lead them properly, you should find the job easy. The Cadence will be predominately focused elsewhere, and by then the barrier protecting the city will be down. The two forces will be weakened, fighting between one another. You will have no trouble claiming the city." Kol's heart froze. He saw Harvest's face grow slightly in concern, but Kol gave nothing away. His body was of ice so cold it would quench the strongest of fires. It was true: they knew of the North Pole existence. Soon they would see its anger within Kol. "Do you have it, Andrew? Our Master had messaged me saying you would bring it for me to add to the other for safekeeping."

"Ah, yes, that is why I am here, is it not?" Andrew agreed: the vampire had finally been given a name. "He also gave me a message to tell you upon delivery. 'Separate them immediately.' Strange thing he wanted with the blade." A moment passed as Andrew handed off whatever he had. "I prefer a bowler myself." Kol did not care if he was seen he had to make sure that his assumption was wrong. How could it be true? But they knew of the North, so knowing of this would be of little surprise. The two of them faced away from the office. Andrew looked over the railing while Wendon examined the slightly larger black top hat in his hands. The hat worn by the leader of the Snow People, lord of the Flakes, and his uncle. No, that hat *was* his uncle, and without snow he could not exist.

"I'll have them both sent to my private holds the moment this meeting is concluded." Wendon laughed, the sort of laugh made when making fun of another. The sort of laugh that saw others beneath the owner of the sound. "Fascinating how easily the North fell into a civil war without their leaders present."

"Yes." Andrew stepped onto the railing. "The assault begins." He stepped from the balcony and their sight.

CHAPTER TWENTY-FIVE

If the Way is Not True

Kol moved the instant the sound of Andrew's wings vanished from his ears. The North Pole was at war, or close to it, and he had wasted enough time. He would take the hat, then make Wendon tell him where the blade was. Bringing back his uncle and waking his father was the only way to stop the two groups from destroying one another. He began to step around the door to confront Wendon outside, but Harvest placed a hand on his shoulder to stop him. Kol turned to him with ice in his eyes cold enough to shatter bones. Harvest understood and released him while taking stride beside Kol. Harvest placed his fang within his mouth as Kol pulled free his sword, both of them separating at Wenn's desk and making for the glass. The time for walking in shadows was over; Kol wanted Wendon to understand.

The door was his least preferred option at the moment. Kol would need to alter his path to use it, and he did not want to give Wendon a chance to dart one way off the balcony or the other. Bringing forth his blade, he brought both hands to the grip and cut diagonally across the glass window, turning his blade mid cut to cause the pane to shatter. Harvest simply slammed both his fists into the opposite side to create the same effect. He watched as Wendon spun in surprise, looking from Harvest in his feral appearance of fangs, claws, and the start of his trademark screech to Kol landing in silence with sword wrapped in moonlight. Wendon darted for the door in between them but did not make it far as Harvest stepped into his path. Grabbing a fistful of his jacket, Harvest lifted Wendon from his feet, and Kol stepped closer, pulling his uncle's hat from Wendon's grasp. Harvest then slammed him into the balcony floor. Wendon grunted from the pain and gasped for the air that had escaped him. When he refilled his lungs he was able to ask in a panic, "What are you doing?"

Kol was next to Harvest and swung his blade towards Wenn's face, who flinched as the blade stopped centimeters from his left eye. "Move and I will take your eye, continue to do so and I will take the other." Kol moved his blade slightly to show he could do so with nothing more than a muscle tensing. "Where is the key to the *Clauditis* blades?" His voice remained calm, but he saw Wendon become crushed by it.

Wendon did not answer immediately, which angered Kol further. He moved the blade closer still and only when Wendon's eyelashes grazed the tip of Kol's sword did Wendon find his ability to talk. "It's inside my safe."

Kol quenched the relief he felt. Wendon could be lying, and there were still other answers he needed. He brought the top hat into Wendon's view. "How did Andrew get possession of this, and how is it that you and your friend know of the North?" Kol remembered that Harvest was there, but knew he had no time to construct lies when the truth was present regardless.

"I can't tell you that." Kol made a swift shallow cut down Wenn's face from his eye. The strong, powerfully willed personality broke and showed the weakness beneath "I'm not sure," his story changed. "It was given to him to bring to me for safekeeping. I don't know who gave it to him." Kol searched his words for any false claims. Harvest must have found them within the man's heartbeat because he lifted Wendon from the ground. He could have been pulling him to Kol's blade, but he moved it out of the way as Harvest lifted him even higher and threw him into the balcony railing, cracking one of its supporting columns.

"If you do not speak truthfully, I'll keep my promise of blinding you, and then you will only have your other senses to tell you how far you have fallen before the ground catches you."

They moved closer and Wendon lurched upright, shocked, as if trying to escape, yet knowing he could not.

"It was a business deal for me. I would be given the North if I provide resources and funding. I was told Andrew was new to this world and would need aid in arranging the coming attack."

Harvest broke his silence. "New to this world?"

"I didn't understand it, either," Wendon told him. "But then, I had just been told that the monsters were real. I eventually stopped being surprised. I'd asked him but he never answered. I was to give him a place to recruit followers and any funding he may need."

"The blades?" Kol asked.

Wendon nodded. "Yes, I helped find the goblins and supplied the materials needed so they could forge the blades. Andrew handled the transactions through me."

Harvest wanted another answer. "Who has he gone to meet with? Who was the person on the phone?"

Wendon gave a small smile. "Another interesting individual. She was something I didn't expect."

Kol waited for Harvest to further question him, but when he did not, Kol asked his own. "Why is it that you want the North?"

"Running a business is like ruling a nation. You create an army and conquer those around you to grow in power. Yet no matter how ambitious you may be, there are always higher powers placing regulations and policies on you. So much time and effort into developing your empire, and yet the greater you grow, the thicker the chains that are placed on you." Wendon's voice began to change, the fear they had created in their sudden appearance slowly becoming the arrogant tone they had heard while he spoke to Andrew. "In return for my aid I was promised the North, a place known only in myth. No notice from outside nations would notice if someone were to usurp the current power. A hidden kingdom."

"No one would follow you," Kol told him.

"That's true, but new loyal followers can be found and replace those who currently reside. My employer is a man of great power, and he assured that he could make them obey me."

"Who is it that the three of you work for?" It was the person behind it all, the one that was truly after his father.

Wendon stood at his full height now, back in his proper form. He looked to Harvest then to Kol, preparing whatever it was he believed he could say to fend them off. He opened his mouth to begin but stopped. The building arrogance in his eyes drained and began to fill with fear. Not the fear that they had put in him coming through the window, but a new fear one that spoke of the inevitable. "No!" he yelled and looked to his feet, "I would tell them nothing of you." Kol followed his gaze and saw the shadow Wendon stood in. Created by no carving of the moonlight, it grew beneath Wendon unnaturally. It was not night: he stood in a void. Nothing existed within something so dark, and yet existence manifested in creeping hands reaching from the shadow much like the golems they had fought in the forest. There was no cutting down this onslaught as Kol moved to save Wendon. His blade simply passed through the limbs as they firmed their grasp on Wenn's arms, legs, torso, and around his throat. Wenn tried to scream out to them, but it was muffled as he began to lower into the void. The last they saw of him was eyes pleading until he was gone, along with the void.

"What...?" Kol could only manage in disbelief.

"I have never seen magic like that," Harvest said. "We need to get into the safe and get to the river. The others have already gone ahead." He reached for his microphone as they started back inside, "Willa, have you arrived yet?" Nothing came back through their ear piece, "Willa, Iris....Lloyd?"

"Yes?" Lloyd said from beside the safe.

Kol felt a little surprise followed by the thought that he should have known. "Where are the others?"

"River," Lloyd told them while tinkering with the safe. "Figured I was needed here." He had the electric key panel off and was fumbling with the wires.

"How much longer before it is opened?" Harvest asked him.

"I'm not a physicist," Lloyd said dreamily. "You have to consider air resistance, terminal velocity, and acceleration. I believe the three of us can move it."

Kol realized what he meant to do. "You think that will get it open?"

"We'll see," he said, laughing softly to himself.

"We don't have enough time to drag it over to the balcony," Harvest told him, sounding like an older brother telling his smaller sibling to quit playing around.

Lloyd finished messing with the wires behind the electric panel. "This is why I question the company I keep around me." He grabbed the little handle and turned it. The soft click came next, followed by the opening of the safe. "Here you go."

Kol nodded and knelt to peer inside.

The only item inside the nearly unused safe was a weapon in the form of a dagger. Its blade was a sickly green and curved for wickedness, an exact twin to the one that had been plunged into his father by a man cursed by its very touch. Kol finally let the relief flow through him visibly, making him shake. It was the item at the end of a quest. A quest he felt like he had been on for ages, and now finally finding the blade he felt the exhaustion that had been building from the moment his father had been attacked. Kol realized he still held his sword, and he sheathed it to pull a small cloth from his bag. He carefully picked up the blade and wrapped it in the soft white. He now held in his hands the two items that could save the destruction of his home.

Lloyd investigated the safe as well. "No money?" he said sadly, as if his work on opening the safe was for nothing when everything was held in Kol's hands. "What's with the hat?" Lloyd asked, turning back to Kol.

Kol placed them both into his Bag of Depths. "Let's get to the river."

It took little time for the three of them to travel down into the staff parking, out onto the street, and into Harvest's parked car. Iris's truck was gone, of course. Harvest wasted no time driving to the waterfront, breaking every traffic law within the city, but surprisingly, they did not attract any attention. The streets were completely bare at this time of night. The three of them sat in silence as they rode, which was strange, of course, for Lloyd. He knew that now was no time for games.

Kol went over what Wendon had told them on top of the tower. Someone had organized the attack on the North Pole. The ghouls, the blades, and the inevitable civil war. None of this was by chance, which means that someone understood the city and the life within and around it. The attack came from within the city, a betrayer. To what purpose? This person offered the king-dom to Wendon. Was it a lie he gave him, or was there some-thing more being constructed that was bigger than the North Pole or his father? Worry best left for after he revived his father and uncle. Perhaps they had answers he could not find.

Kol glanced at Harvest, who kept his eyes on the road. What had Wendon meant by Andrew being from another world and why had it created a rise from Harvest? He wanted to ask him but figured that questions of the North would only be presented back. He had heard far too much on top of the tower to not deduce that Kol was from somewhere more than a simple town in Canada. Harvest had not asked either, so Kol thought they stood on a bal-anced ground. Kol would ask no questions about Andrew, and in return, Harvest would ask none of his home. As usual between them they had a silent understanding. Lloyd laughed quietly as if to suggest he too was a part of the understanding.

The entrance to the riverfront was not a simple road to the shore, but a tunnel made for people to walk beneath moving traf-fic. Harvest ignored the barrier chains and drove through them, breaking the links. The car's engine echoed within the tunnel, which was lit in green light. Seconds later the car exited the tunnel and Harvest drove her over the cobblestone. The three of them searched the area desperately as Harvest started over grass to keep close to the river. They kept the course between the river and what Kol believed to be railroad tracks to their right. Kol had been looking out of his rolled down window when Harvest snatched his wheel right and began to slide across the damp grass, tearing it free from the earth. Kol glanced to see what the problem was and found it when Iris's truck came into view.

The truck was damaged as the three of them got out of the car to inspect it closer. The tailgate was gone, and metal had been ripped above the cab. Two groups of claw marks, Kol deduced, after climbing into the bed to look. Beneath them was another large gaping hole, which Kol also knew Willa's sword had created. "Andrew attacked them, but Willa must have fended him off."

"Not completely: both left tires are completely gone," Harvest responded. "Iris must have continued driving on rims until she made it to this point."

"She came from another entrance further down the river ahead of us. You can see where the rims dug into the earth," Lloyd also added.

Kol stepped from the truck and started for the river bank several yards away. "They must be down this way."

The crossed the ground quickly at a jogging pace, the river stretching before them in a dark mass. "Iris...Willa!" Kol shouted.

"Over here," Iris sounded back. Relief flooded Kol at the sound of her voice. The three of them quickened their pace as two figures came into sight. Iris had small cuts along her arm where it looked like Andrew had grazed her, and the bottom of her gear she had changed into from the party was covered in dirt. Other than that she was fine and only looked slightly winded. Willa, on the other hand, looked completely fine standing in her armor, except there was also dirt from her knees down. She had her helmet off, which she had placed on top of her sword stuck into the ground next to her shield. Her arms were crossed and the expression on her face was the purest fury Kol had ever witnessed on her.

Lloyd was the craziest one, so he asked, "So what happened?"

Iris started to explain but was stormed over by Willa. "First, we get a text to go to the river from him," she jabbed at Harvest, "who forgot to mention that there was an ELDER VAMPIRE in the area and there was a high possibility that he would be heading in our direction! It would have lessened the surprise of a giant winged creature descending on us from above. Of course, I was able to fight it off. I even think I wounded him enough to need future medical care, but not before he sliced our tires and grazed Iris. Because of that our paced slowed and we were unable to make it down here in time. The river boat, which is indeed filled with ghouls and who knows what else, had just vanished into a storm cloud. Yes, a literal storm cloud complete with lighting and thunder."

Harvest took the time to speak as she caught her breath. "There was no time to explain. I thought they trained you to be ready for everything."

This may have been a mistake because Willa now had a focus for her anger. "Train me? TRAIN ME?" Willa took her helmet in one hand and the sword in the other to point at Harvest. "They do train me to be ready for anything. They also train me on how to COMMUNICATE with my team. Doing this fundamental tactic increases chances of living during an enemy confrontation. It also increases the chance of gaining victory in battle. Without it we are nothing more than highly skilled individuals acting randomly, something that the enemy can exploit if they had enough experience. All of us keep so many secrets that how could we trust each other to the point of no longer needing explanations?"

"Our secrets are not ours to tell; each one of us shares these secrets with others that we protect." Kol stated. "We simply have to trust without it. That is the only way we can survive."

"Trust?" Willa seemed to become slightly more unstable. "How can I trust someone who is close to the enemy, Harvest?"

"What do you mean?" Harvest asked.

Iris stepped forward to speak. "When we arrived, we were not the only ones here. Someone else was on the shore. We eventually realized that she was the one who was conjuring the storm cloud the boat vanished into. She was using a wand, so a witch, and by the skill used in weaving her magic, a powerful one. We tried to question her, but she only ignored us. Willa decided to make her pay attention and started for the witch but she snared us with earth at a simple gesture of her off hand." Iris nodded to a spot nearby where it looked like someone had indeed been digging a hole. "Only after the boat had vanished did she turn her attention on us, well, more on Willa." Iris glanced at Willa who was walking back towards them. "She told Willa that..."

"She told me that Harvest always had the potential to do better than me. She then asked us to tell you that 'Jen misses you dearly.'" Kol barely heard it and thought he imagined it, but Willa sounded hurt. "Who was she, Harvest?"

Harvest remained quiet when asked this. His expression was blank, but his eyes were sad and distant. Kol knew he was not going to say who she was, not at this moment. The person here had to be the person Wendon had been talking to on the phone earlier. Harvest must have suspected whoever this person was all along. That did not mean he was helping the enemy, however. Kol could see it in his eyes that whoever she was he did not want her to be a part of it. "I know where the boat is going," Kol said to draw attention away from Harvest.

"You do?" Willa asked, turning on him.

Kol nodded. "It is heading towards my home. Those creatures on board are meant to attack my home, which is currently in a weakened state. What they have planned will be achieved unless I can make it back there." Kol started reaching into his bag for the small present that Master Shane had given him. It was time for him to go back and save his father and his uncle.

"What makes a little village in Canada so important?" Willa pressed on.

Kol did not answer, but Lloyd did. "Shared secrets," he told her, laughing.

Finding the present, he pulled it free of the bag, and something silver fell out after it. "I'm sorry, but I truly can't tell you. I can tell you that once I save my father, the ghouls will be stopped. I just have to get home to do that."

"Home? Right now?" Iris looked concerned, "How do we get there?"

Kol did not meet her eyes. "There is no we. I must go back alone. I can't take any of you with me."

"What do you mean you can't take us with you? We have been doing this together! We should finish it together!" Willa did not like being told to stay.

Lloyd began to sing Jingle Bells softly to himself, changing a word frequently. Regardless it caused Kol to glance at him suspiciously. "I don't think I can even take you this way, and above that I truly can't do so." He would take the portal back to the Halls and then make his way to his father. He would then warn him of the coming attack and the defenses could be set in place while his uncle rallied his own forces on them. From what Andrew said, he had a considerable number, but it would be no match against the Snow Soldiers and Cadence together.

"How do you plan to return?" Harvest sounded normal and the sadness in his eyes had been buried deep along with the rest of his emotions.

Kol could at least answer this. "A wizard back home gave me this box and told me to unwrap it once I found the cure for my father."

"Kol, you can't expect us all to stay here while you go alone to fight our battle." Iris placed a hand on his shoulder.

"I won't be alone. My home can handle the situation." He opened the box and from within a tiny light hovered inside. They all gathered around him to look before the tiny light shot into the air above them and vanished with a flash. It must have been a signal of some sort to alert Shane that it was time. He did not know what would happen next. Would he travel as he did on the way here? He hoped to understand within the next few seconds.

They all waited in silence at his actions. The seconds became minutes, "Well, are you home?" Lloyd asked him.

Kol started to feel panic, "No. I don't understand what is taking so long."

"Maybe the wizard didn't get the message." Willa sounded sarcastic.

"No, his instructions were clear. When I was ready to return, I should open this box, and they could bring me back." What if he didn't get the message? Every moment passed was weighted. People could be dying in the North. He started to feel sick and angry.

Iris offered help. "We could take the Paths like before. It would take some time, but it could be done."

"No, your paths would not go that far."

"How far north is your village?" Willa demanded. This made Lloyd laugh, which once again made Kol look at him suspiciously.

A train horn sounded in the distance, and another louder after. "Too far to travel with the amount of time I have left." The train sounded again as it passed into view. One engine pulling only a dozen carts before it continued its way. He gritted his teeth. "People are going to die." He ended his sentence with a frustrating yell. The others became concerned that he had raised his voice. It was, after all, unlike him. "They are all counting on me to return and save them, both from the ghouls and as far as they know from themselves."

Harvest nudged Kol with his elbow to get his attention. "You dropped this," he said, and handed him the piece of silver from his bag. Kol took the piece of silver into his hands and examined it. It was a ribbon of northern fabric, an elegant design by an elf with simple words etched in black: "This is if the way is not true." Kol did not know where the fabric had come from for the first few seconds, but it eventually came to him how he came across it. It was the man in the diner he had spoken with before departing to this city. He had handed him this and told him this very phrase. The train sounded again in the distance, and Kol knew what he had to do next.

He started walking towards the tracks, the others following. Willa had retrieved her shield and had placed them both on her back, keeping her helmet under her shoulder. Iris brushed the rest of the dirt from her gear and Harvest and Lloyd both watched within their own character. He had remembered his father telling him about this fabric. It was made to look like a simple ribbon to keep any suspicion down when the Scribes ventured from the city. He had explained to him how they left the city and returned on Christmas Eve, which was today as of a few minutes ago. What luck would he have if there was one near to could carry him home? The tracks lay cold, three sets of them awaiting trains to use them in their daily jobs. Kol took the fabric and smoothed it out on top of one of them. The effect was exactly as it had been described so many years ago on his father's lap. The fabric dissolved into the train tracks, and the set of tracks began to frost and turn into ice. An ice forged in the fires of the Snow People and set by the people of the North Pole to help continue his father's dream. If only the two factions could see it how Kol did, how his uncle and father did. He heard Iris' light gasp from behind him and Lloyd's cry of amazement.

"Kol," Iris asked, "who are you?"

Always a simple question to ask, but with an answer too complex to say. Kol turned and looked at his friends while the rails gleamed white behind him, the ones who had been helping him this entire time. They had separate goals at first, but when they realized that the situation was all the same, they had increased motivation to stop the enemy at hand, whoever the enemy was. Even now they wanted to continue fighting, even for what they believed was a simple little village. Kol's plan of being transported back to his father's side were no longer available. He would have to enter the city from the outside now and possibly have to fight his way through the army of ghouls. There was a possibility he could do it alone; he would always think that way. Yet he could also think that having them along would help his situation. Each of them was something special and had showed countless times how they were capable of handling any task given to them. Kol decided that they could come along despite the rule. Harvest already knew enough to piece it together, but the others had no idea. At least, Kol believe Lloyd didn't, despite his frequent hints. He had broken one by leaving the city, so why not break a few more on his return.

Taking a breath, Kol told them. "My true name is Nicholas, named after my father who holds the title of Saint and resides as king of a nation known as the North Pole. Of course, you know him better as Santa Claus, same as the rest of the world who believes in the myth. My troubles started when a group of ghouls attacked an inn back home. After I caught them they destroyed themselves, but not before leaving three of those cursed blades somewhere in my city. While I looked for the weapons, one of those snow golems we fought attacked a hospital. I, along with the rest of the city, believed it was one of the Snow People. Though because I know more on the matter, I thought it was a rogue one. The rest of the city didn't, and thought he was sent by the rest of his kind. The Snow People are sentient beings that look like the golems with a few differences. They live not too far from my city and are led by their chief, Frostien. You would know him as Frosty the Snowman, and not only is he their chief, he is also a sworn brother to my father and uncle to me.

"On the first of December, my father was attacked by a civilian who was being controlled by the blade. The blade made him yell 'for the glory of the Snow People!' before stabbing my father. I attempted to stop it but was unable to. Thanks to the curse, a seed of internal destruction had been placed. You see, people often fear what they did not understand, and they did not truly understand the Snow People. In fact, there is a fear in the city of them, seeing them like monsters compared with other creatures that dwell beneath our beds. A fear slowly being removed by the combined effort of both my father and uncle. But with my father gone in the way that it happened, and the attack on the hospital, my people had no choice but to start to panic with fault turned towards the Snow People.

"I spoke with my uncle, who in his metal and spell working mastery, told me what the sickly blades were made for. He sent me to find the twin of the weapon and promised me that no hostility would come towards the city." Kol reached into his bag and pulled from it his uncle's top hat. "Yet he too was apparently taken from his people and resides inside this very hat. Without the two factions having their leader, a civil war is bound to occur. Whoever is behind all of this has put a lot of thought and effort into this plan. The people of my kingdom will war with one another, and once all the resources have been spent and the people fatigued, the small army of ghouls will finish the job that was started. For what reasons I truly cannot say, besides Wendon's promise of land, but it is more than enough for me to act."

Silence blanketed their faces, followed by disbelief. "Wait." Willa, of course, was the first to speak, "Are you trying to tell us that you are the son of Santa Claus and Frosty the Snowman is your uncle?" Kol merely watched her. "How do you expect us to accept any of that, Kol!?"

"I don't expect any of you to, but it's the truth, and that is where I'm going." The rails behind him began to vibrate. "Regardless, I need your help now that I can't return directly to my father."

"Kol," Iris said softly, "It's difficult to understand. They are just stories told to children around Christmas."

"So are vampires, werewolves, and knights," Harvest pointed out.

"Yes, but this is far above any of that. Those are things of legend, this is mythic." Willa still held her disbelief.

A whistle blew in the distance, one Kol used to peer out his window to find as a small child. "In the end, despite doubt and suspicion, all I ask is for you to believe." An icy mist bellowed out around them, causing all line of sight to be reduced to only a few feet. The whistle came again as a light pieced its way through the mist, one that sat on the front of a train. The train flew past them as the brakes squealed with work. A sleek silver engine pulling silver carriages with windows filled with light appeared. Once stopped, a door opened downward toward them, creating steps for them to go inside. Kol turned and started up the stairs, looking back at the top to his friends below. "Let's finish this." Despite the disbelief, lack of understanding, and shock in different volumes on their faces, Harvest followed, then so did Lloyd, Iris, and after a brief hesitation, Willa.

CHAPTER TWENTY-SIX

A Ride of Lore

When Kol was old enough to understand his surroundings, his father had taken him on a tour of the city. On this venture he showed Kol every aspect of the city, both from high above in the sleigh and inside the different areas. They had walked inside the post office and hospitals and had journeyed throughout the factory beneath the city and inside the buildings that grew their food. All of it had been fascinating, and Kol had soaked in all of it. Their day had gone on long for the two of them, and his father had stated it was time to return home in order to keep them both out of trouble with his mother. Yet before the sleigh turned for the plaza, Kol heard the faint sound of a train whistle. His interest piqued, and he asked his father if they could see the train. With a chuckle, he'd agreed, and the two of them soared off to meet the shining machine as it halted at its station.

That had been a while ago, but Kol's memory did not fail him as he entered the carriage. At first the light from the ceiling blinded him both from above and reflecting from below. Once his eyesight adjusted, he instantly felt like he was home. The carriage was made for passengers like a majority of the other carriages this time of the year. The remaining ones were used for cargo, but there was also a kitchen, two full bathrooms, and private quarters for the crew. Though the outside was coated in snow-forged steel, the inside was a brightly polished hardwood running along the floor and halfway up the wall. From the point where the wood ended white marble stretched upward and curved into the ceiling, breaking only at two parallel lines a foot between one another. Here the interior light bathed the room, stretching from both compartment doors at either end of the carriage. Green carpet protected the wood beneath it as it divided the room between the rows of seats. The seats were cushioned red with the chance of a passenger losing him or herself if they were to sit down. They could comfortably look out into the winter night and enjoy the scenery, or what they could witness, as the train sped along at a pace far swifter than any normal train could manage. Kol felt a hand on his back urging him forward which he did, momentarily forgetting that others were waiting to get on.

Kol walked inside and then turned back to his friends when enough room was available for the others to stand comfortably. Harvest came into the view first, his expression completely blank in his usual expression. He did glance at one of the seats before deciding it was worthy for him to sit on, and he sighed once relaxed. Lloyd showed both rows of teeth as he examined the room, making soft noises, poking the fabric, and then feeling the texture of the wood. Iris was the one looking astonished as she also examined the room, but with her eyes only. Finally, Willa stepped inside, the weight of her armor causing the carriage to tilt once she stood on the carpet. To enter she had to board sideways to fit into the door. She was unable to stand completely upright due to the hunched position she was in, fully taking up the amount of space offered. Kol read disbelief on her face as she viewed the surroundings curiously, perhaps with even a touch of innocence.

"I don't think I want to stand like this the entire ride," Willa said rather calmly. Looking behind her, she nodded and backed towards the rear of the carriage because she could not turn around. There she took a seat in the middle of the floor and propped her arms on the seats on either side and stretched her legs out before her, the carriage creaking slightly as it settled in position. "This will be better, I think." She put her helmet on instead of setting it on one of the seats.

Kol smiled at her and started to ask if she wanted to get out of the armor for now when the door behind him slid open. "Be thankful ya signaled us when ya did. We were close to passing the area. If we had, yer wait would have been much longer." Kol turned to see who the owner of the deep voice was that he knew would eventually come to inspect them. The voice belonged to the same gentleman that had spoken to him in the diner before Master Shane had sent him south.

"The way was not true," Kol said, "so I used your gift, hoping that this one would be."

The man laughed in a voice that boomed amongst the room. "Well, it appears to be, or ya would still be out in the chilly air." The man stood tall and broad shouldered with dark skin beneath a well-pressed suit of red matching the tie laying over his white dress shirt. His shoes were polished black leather that seemed to be made from the same material of the hat upon his head. The hat was accented with a sliver band, along with his wrist which sported a watch gleaming the same silver. He looked to be in his mid-thirties and looked with brown warm eyes at each one of them in turn, only giving Willa a few seconds more before lifting his watch to his ear and tapping its face, which began to glow blue. "ALL ABOARD! Train's clear for departure."

A voice that belonged to the engineer replied, "Yes sir." The man in the suit lowered his watch as a whistle blew from the front of the train. The staircase that had let them on closed upwards, and the stairs tilted to become flush with the wall. Another sound of the whistle, and the train shuddered into motion and quickly gained speed. A flash of bright light ran along the window. Kol knew this was the signal that the train had left physics behind and rushed into the tunnel of magic, which greatly increased their travel time.

"It is good to see ya again, Prince Nicholas," the conductor said, walking towards Kol.

Kol felt his face begin to turn red. "Just Kol, please, helps keep my peace. Did you know who I was in the diner?"

The man nodded. "Indeed I did, but that was not the first time I met ya." He allowed Kol a moment to look confused before giving the answer. "I was on the train when ya first came to visit as a little boy. I was beginning my training around that time and remember the energy ya showed when ya took your first ride."

"I see. Well, I'm sorry to say I don't remember you or your name," Kol admitted to him.

"My name is Logan, and I am..."

"Excuse me," Willa interrupted before he could speak. "So you also believe that Kol is the son of Santa Claus?"

Logan peered over Kol at the suit of armor sitting in the back, giving her a half smile before looking back at Kol. Kol nodded and stepped aside. "So, there is someone within that armor. How fascinating. I wanted to ask about it, but figured all would be revealed along the trip back. Yet before I continue the introduction, where is it that ya believe ya are headed, Miss...?"

"Wilhelmina," she told Logan. "According to him, we are going to the North Pole, which I am still finding difficult to believe."

Kol watched the man as he began to frown. "There is trouble in the city and I need their help. Don't worry about the rule; I will deal with that once we get there."

"What rule?" Iris asked.

"I'll explain shortly," Kol told her softly.

Logan gave her an apologetic smile before saying to Kol, "So ya heard about the Snow People attacking, then?"

"Yes, and I know how to stop it, but we must get there quickly. There is a small army of ghouls heading there now, and with the Cadence distracted I fear they will get to my father. Have the Snow People started on the city, then, or is it something else?"

"Yeah, that is the reason we are heading back to the station. The attack has not started, but they have marched within the city's territory dressed for battle. If the worst were to occur, we have to evacuate as many people as we can. That means we have to arrive and connect as many passenger carriages available and drop the cargo. Let me inform the engineers of the situation so that we get there as quickly as possible."

"Wait. If you can receive messages from the city, is there any way I can send back to them a warning of the ghouls?"

Logan looked ashamed. "I'm afraid we can't. After we got the message, I attempted to ask further questions, but there is nothing but static on the other side. It's been that way ever since. We are still going back because the people need us, too."

"I understand. Thank you, Logan." The man nodded and started for the door. At least he was going back.

"Wait, you never told us where the train is going," Willa called after.

"The North Pole!" Logan laughed and was gone.

Willa still seemed in disbelief, and decided she wanted to focus on something else. "Well, then. Guess I should relax for a moment." The chest piece of the armor hissed as the interlocking parts released outward. Willa removed her helmet and set it to the side before climbing out of her second skin. Kol found it always interesting to watch.

"Kol, I think it would be best if you told us the whole story so we know how best to help," Harvest said without looking up from his phone.

"Yeah, I thought the North Pole was a tiny place full of little elves wandering around with a deep natural urge to make toys," Lloyd pondered while helping Willa out of the armor.

Kol began to realize how complex this was for everyone to understand. Iris looked up at him and suggested, "Just start from the beginning, and we will listen."

"Yes, I think that would be best," Willa added.

Taking a seat facing them, Kol took a moment to gather his thoughts. It was true, the best way was simply to start from the beginning, not of his father's attack, but from his start. "The North Pole was once like you think it was, Lloyd. Besides the tiny elves thing. They have the same variant of height as humans do. Originally when my father traveled there, he encountered a large group of elves. These elves had been driven from their home years before, and had spent their time moving on top of the ice, believing it was a place no form of monster would find them. My father knew who they were, and understood that they held great skill in what they like to refer to as the art of tinkering. He already had his mission in mind and believed that they were the perfect race that could help him achieve it. He explained his plan to them, and after considering, the elders agreed to help him. After that, they settled and began to build a small village at the North Pole, thus taking the location as the appropriate name."

"His mission? You mean making toys." Iris wanted to confirm.

"Well, it holds more depth than that, but yes, in essence, to make toys." Kol scratched the back of his head. "During this time, the ages had become dark, and it seemed that humanity was destined to become composed of nothing more than shadow. Monsters ran in great numbers, and if Willa agrees, the Knights' battle with them could have gone either way. So my father left humanity in order to find a way to save it. He eventually understood that the children where the only ones who could save the world. It began just as the stories say: each child would be rewarded for being good throughout the year."

"And punish those who did not, right?" Willa scuffed. "As if any child is completely naughty or nice."

"That's correct, Willa, and he understood that. So yes, he would leave coal in order to urge the children to do better, but he never left them giftless. All children get a gift from him in one form or another."

"Only one?" Lloyd laughed.

Kol nodded. "Yes, leaving an abundance would usually cause a lot of questions, and that was not what my father wanted. One special gift for each child to have. Naughty or nice."

"Still, parents don't notice this one gift?" Lloyd tried again.

"Hard to when the toys are enchanted. You see, during the process of building the toys, the elves and my father placed enchantments on them. When they began the spells were made of protection, this halted any form of monster getting close to them. They were also enchanted to go unnoticed by adults, causing them to usually think a relative got it or another simple excuse. He did not want fame, only to let the children know someone was watching over them, and expected them to help progress the world towards something better. Sadly, when parents participate in my father's work, some can put forth more of their own money than others. It causes a strain of belief from those that are less fortunate when it seems like someone is always getting more than you. Of course, that's not anyone's fault, but my father needs their belief to complete his work."

"How is that?" Iris took her chance to ask, "And how is it he knows who's been naughty or nice?"

"My father told me he uses an extraordinarily advanced form of divination magic to gather the names of all the children in the world, where they live, and places them within his vast mind. It's easy to do that when the children believe in you. The divination magic requires that. When he visits their home, he can read their auras while they sleep. Everybody has them, and the older you are the more solid they become. Now, a child's is always shifting back and forth between positive vibes and negative. My father will consider this when leaving a gift behind for them. One that can help them in their current struggles of growing in our world."

Harvest was peering out the window while listening. "So when did a city begin to form?"

"During the end of the time of monsters, a band of them accidentally came across the North Pole, wanting to escape from their destruction. They lay siege to the village and were close to victory until my father entered the battle and rallied the elves against the monsters. By this time my father had grown powerful in the arts of magic, having the elves as his teacher. Adding this to his ability with a sword, and the monsters had no power to stop him. Many elves died that day, and the village was completely ruined except for a few houses and the workshop at the center.

Afterwards they rebuilt, but still, the fear began to grow from then. As time went on, the world grew, and so did the demand of toys to the point there were not enough hands to continue work. My father suggested to the elf elders that he go out into the rest of the world and recruit. It took some time, but the elders accepted his idea. Once they did, he went out and found humans who were willing to join in his cause. This is what I was referring to with the rule."

"Shhhhh," Lloyd hissed, with a finger to his lips.

"That's right," Kol agreed, "the North Pole must remain a secret. He walked among the sick, poor, homeless, and orphans and offered them a second chance. Come with him to the North and join him in his mission, and in return they would have a place to sleep beneath a shelter near a fire. They would be taught a skill, some who were able would learn magic, and together they would continue to fight to make the world a better place. The only thing they would have to agree to is to keep it a secret. This means that whoever comes to the now growing city could not leave unless they gave up their memory of the place."

"That seems like a tyrant," Willa said, now free from her armor and sitting behind Harvest.

"A tyrant wouldn't give you a choice, would he?" Kol heard his anger clearly. "People can come and go as they wish, but the secret must be kept. If not, then someone may try to return to the city and destroy it." He let them understand that this very situation was why it was necessary. "There have been a few who left and always in good spirits. Yet most of them stay to start families, and eventually it grew into what it is today."

"And you are expecting us to allow someone to wipe our memories?" Willa demanded.

"I did not expect you to come. If you want to leave now, feel welcome to step off the end of the train. That is not the main concern right now."

Iris moved to cool the conversation. "The fear?"

Kol's eyes lingered on Willa, daring her to say more of tyranny. "When humans began to come to the North, they discovered the existence of elves, who in return confirmed that the old nightmares of the world were indeed true, and that the city was a place of sanctuary from them. With this paranoia planted, my father began to see what would become of it. When he found my uncle, he thought that things would change. On the last days of winter, he discovered Frostien slowly succumbing to the heat. He gave him the same offer as everyone else, promising to also move him to a place of colder temperatures. Excited by this, my uncle agreed and journeyed back."

Kol took a moment to breath a new lungful of air. "When he arrived, the citizens feared him because of how large he was and his level of intellect. He did not know of his origin; his memory began when children placed this hat on his head." Kol motioned to the hat still in his hand, then placed it safely in his bag. "Just as the story says. He also didn't know much of the world, and with my father's help he began to learn. After a time, he found meaning and something he could both enjoy and help give strength to the city.

"During his time in the city there were many misunderstandings. Things being broken from his clumsiness or lack of communication. He is a quiet person. After studying books on the magic arts, he eventually discovered something amazing. You see, Frostien was the only Snow Man ever to exist. This caused him to feel lonely. With the people of the city treating him as an outcast despite their leader's wishes, Frostien discovered how to make another like himself, and thus created a wife by creating a new form of clothing. He was able to place a piece of his soul into a cloth ribbon and nurture it into a new soul. This was difficult to do with just himself, and almost killed him, but he did it."

"It's exactly what flora and fauna do," Lloyd said in a professional manner, then snickered to himself.

"This was amazing and brought joy to my father and uncle's hearts, but the others saw it differently. Remember our fight with the Snow Golems in the woods? How powerful they were? Think of what an entire army of them could do in your city. That was what the people of the North Pole imagined what would occur should the Snow Man and his wife wish to continue procreation. They attempted to mob against them, but instead of striking back, my uncle went to my father and told him that they would leave to colonize another part of the North, and from there they would work on the citizens accepting the Snow People, which was working, up until recently."

"So, someone knows of the fear of Snow People, and decided to use it to start a civil war between the two factions." Harvest glanced out the window, and Kol saw snow drifting by. "While they fought, the ghouls would enter the city and attack from within."

Kol nodded. "My thoughts exactly."

"Which means the attack was created from someone inside the city," Harvest said, as if to drag the idea from out of the place Kol had hid it.

It was true; this appeared to be the only logical answer. No one, besides himself, could leave the city without being enchanted. So someone must have found a way to travel outside the city, or at least communicate, without the Halls knowing. A feat thought impossible, but how else had the ghouls managed to enter without raising alarm or people in the outside world knowing of his home? "If that is the case, we will seek him out and hold him accountable for his crimes."

"So there is crime?" Iris seems glad to find a place for her question. "How does the North Pole do this? Do they have a military or police?"

"The Cadence Corps is an elite group of individuals who keep the peace within the city. They act as both military and law enforcement." Kol glanced at Willa in warning. "The North Pole is a small city, smaller than the one we left, but where there are living creatures, there is bound to be mischief. So, yes, there is crime within the city, but it is held to a reasonable level. The

Cadence Corps are masters of combat, both in hand, weapons, and magic based on sound waves. They use drums to maintain order, and if needed, to fight. If the Snow People are moving on the city, they will respond accordingly in order to protect it."

"There is no one else who could become temporary leaders?" Lloyd asked while drawing tiny woodland creatures on the window dancing among flowers.

"For the Snow People, yes. His wife would do so. But it's complicated. Once Frostien could create another like him, they both found a child could be made with less stress if they placed parts of their own soul together. Whenever a new child is born everyone gathers to help; everyone carries the burden. Besides Frostien and his wife, all Snow people after had to grow from a small form. The older they become the larger they can possibly grow. Frostien is the reason they exist, and they have absolute devotion to him. With the idea of him being captured, it's hard to imagine any of them trying to calm the situation.

"As for the North Pole, there is a council made up of heads from both races along with the Drum Major of the Cadence Corps and High Wizard of the *Ve'rema,* the Halls of magical teachings in the city. It is called the Crafted Council. Not only that, but my mother always stands in for my father whenever he is gone." Kol let all the information soak into his friends.

Willa glared. "Could you not have also taken command, prince?" Of course, the "prince" was in a sarcastic tone.

"I could, but I also had the only clue for how to help my father, and I was the only one who could leave the city during this time. Of course, I did so illegally. I figured by the time the Council had decided on someone to continue the investigation I had started, the trail would have gone cold. And I could not trust anyone else to do it. The Council are more than capable to hold power, but with the Snow People on the assault, there is little that can be stopped unless both leaders are revived."

"Kol, the engineers have been informed. They tell me we should be there within the next few hours." Logan had returned through the door he left. "If ya would like ya can go to the kitchen and get some food while we continue."

"Thank you Logan, we shall." Logan nodded and disappeared again. "I'm going to get food if you'd like to come with me." They did, and the five of them started after Logan.

"What's the reason for the train if no one can leave?" Iris asked.

"Every year people actually leave the city. You've probably seen them yourselves."

"Oh?"

"Yes, in department stores and malls. There are a lot of Santa that sits in those chairs come from the North Pole. We call them Scribes, and they help determine what a child would like. Then my father reads them with more of that divination magic I told you about. They also help keep the story continuing."

"Fascinating." Kol could not tell if Lloyd was talking about the Scribes or something else.

They entered the kitchen, which of course was a marvel to behold. The ceiling, floors, and walls remained the same, but instead of comfy seats, there were countertops with barstools running along either side, high enough for people eating to look out the window if they liked. The middle was an island with counters, the same as the ones lining the walls. Inside food was stored, either refrigerated or not, in drawers along with whatever else was needed. In the middle of the island was a stove for cooking and a variety of pots and pans hanging above it. They decided on something light and found everything needed to make sandwiches.

Once done, they all ate in silence, thinking over what Kol had told them. Kol pondered what was to come. Stopping the ghouls was the second most important thing: the main objective would be to awaken his father. His uncle's hat was damaged and might not work when placed in snow. His father was the only one that he believed could fix it.

"So how does he do it, then?"

Kol turned to Iris. "Do what?"

"How does one man deliver toys to every child around the world in one night?"

This question made him finally smile. He rather enjoyed telling the secret, though he shouldn't. "Well, first, there is the idea of all those toys. He places them in his bag. My own is made from a small piece of his." Kol patted the small white pouch on his belt. "It is able to hold all those gifts inside of it because of the magic woven into the fabric. As for the reindeer, they are a special breed we raise. When they are born and mature, they have shoes that are now made by my uncle himself that enables them to step on air. At first they were enchanted, but once my uncle discovered an easier way was to enchant the shoes and not the animals themselves, the reindeer became faster and could pull a heavier load if needed. The sleigh was crafted by my father and can also ride on air with the same metal for the runners."

"And the single night?"

Kol reached into the leather box on his right hip and pulled the tiny silver bell from it. "With these. My father has the rest of these on the sleigh, reindeer, and suit. Where they come from I still don't know; he said they themselves were a gift on Christmas when he first began his work. When they ring," Kol shook his and felt the vibration pass over him without using it, "they emit a special sound that he can used to step outside of time. With each ring he can continue to do so. So when he begins, he doesn't take up any time at all, and only emerges back in our time to let the sun move further to maintain the tradition. He is also able to bring the reindeer and sleigh with him."

"You can't do it like him though, can you?" Harvest asked beside him, facing the window.

"No, I cannot hold onto it like he can or use the bell to its full power." His sadness was easily masked from years of practice. "The Sound won't accept me for very long, with one bell or even with all of them. He gave me this one in order to practice. So far

I have a limit, and going past it is too painful. I have come a long way, though. Originally I could not use it at all."

Kol remembered the first flight he took with his father. They never guessed that the sound would reject Kol like it did. The reindeer could do it and so could anyone else his father was touching, including Kol, which is why they thought it was safe. They had been flying high above when he had let go of Kol to stabilize the deer, and that was when Kol fell from the sky. His father had been able to catch him, but it was on that day Kol began to see he could never be like his father. It was because of that day that he had started to look towards another career path. When he could not perform magic, it had only been a minor upset that he would train to get over. He could control the sleigh and craft things with his hands: it was simply the Teachings of magic that held him back. Once he had fallen and afterward when the Sound would not let him stay did he truly begin to lose hope.

"So you are destined to carry on the title?" Willa asked. "Become the next Santa Claus?"

Kol turned to her slowly. "No, I don't possess the abilities my father does. So I plan on joining the Cadence once all of this is finished."

"Kol," Willa started again slowly and calmly. Kol expected her to continue, but when she did not, he swallowed the bite of sandwich in his mouth and turned to face her. Softly, she went on, "It is still difficult to believe all of this."

"You will see soon enough."

"No, it's not the city that I find hard to believe. I am also from a place hidden from the rest of the world, and though the actual North Pole can be difficult to understand, it's not entirely outside of being real. It's the history of the city that bothers me. You spoke as if your father was the one who started all of it. Are you sure Santa Claus is not some form of title passed down through generations and referring to the one who started it as your father isn't just a figure of speech?"

Kol felt his heart tighten. What Willa spoke of was very close to Kol, because he could never be his father. "No, Willa, it is him."

"Kol, you were speaking of the Middle Ages, when the knights first began to fight the plague of monsters that killed millions almost a thousand years ago. There is no way your father could have lived back then. No human has ever been able to achieve it. Vampires, fairies, and the like can, but always at a hard price. Humans never have been. Kingdoms have fallen at the very idea, and people made into legends in their attempts to gain it." The next words from Willa's mouth were the ones everyone thought were true yet found the most impossible to believe: "He would have to be immortal, Kol."

Kol looked at her for a long time while the others awaited his reply. There was no true way he could explain, because he truly did not know. When he had finally asked his father, all he was able to say that his life was also a gift from the same person who gave him the bells. Kol turned back to his sandwich and watched outside as thousands of trees passed. Every time he had asked his father afterward had been met with the same answer. This was the final piece that caused Kol to give up becoming like his father and continuing his work, instead becoming a vigilante when his father forbade his entry into the Corps. He wanted to protect the city in his own way because no amount of training would prepare him to take on his father's role. Kol would one day grow old and die, and his father would carry on. There had never been any other siblings; he was the only one that ever came from Saint Nicholas. As Kol grew, he understood the simple fact more each day. His father had lifetimes dedicated to his abilities: Kol only had one. "He is," was all he managed to say.

Beat to the Same Drum

The uniform had tedious parts. The mesh green undershirt had to be snug to the body so that heat was not able to escape. It must be tucked neatly into the into the uniform's red pants. The pants had the buttons to hold it closed around the waist and three more at the bottom of each leg that had to be fastened after the boots were slipped on. The boots were tightened with silver buckles and did not take long to form to the wearer's feet. The bottom of the boots was enchanted to hold firm to any surface, which included ice. The jacket, made from the same material as the pants, had several shining polished buttons on the sleeves and in two rows up the center front to hold it closed. Two slits in the side of the jacket could be unzipped so that the person wearing it could reach inside to the several pockets lining the inside of the jacket. They could hold drumsticks, rations, a tool kit for the drum, the uniform's gloves, and even an incident reporting booklet. The back of the jacket had the Cadence crest, a wreath of silver musical notes crossed on top by two drum sticks. The notes were reflective so that they could be easily spotted at night.

The drum itself was just as tedious. A red casing with a solid white head was clamped on top by a silver metal rigging with the Cadence crest printed on the top. It could be carried by its standard silver strap. The strap was only needed when the drum was not in full use. It was cumbersome, not for anything physical about it, but for the magical properties it had. It reacted to set rhythms to bolster resolve, calm erratic emotions, and even frighten those who wished to mistreat others. It could manipulate pressure to use as a deterrent, lighten its user should they ever fall, and a whole list of other things. Whenever its full power had to be used, the drum would float before its owner and allowed its handler to move it where ever they wanted it to be, so long as it stayed close to the Cadence member. Holly considered each of these things before donning both uniform and drum. It was just another distraction.

The locker room was quiet. It was not a standard quiet, but the kind created by an inevitability. A void of impending ruination. The entire Cadence prepared for battle. The Chief of the Snow people had never made it to the city, and all attempts to contact the Flakes after that date have been met with silence. No one dared to venture to the Flakes themselves; there was too much unknown to factor the risk in the North Pole's favor. It was whispered that the Drum Major had still planned to go but changed her mind after the scouts had returned with their message. They had seen that the Snow People were preparing for a march.

Several large devices had been discovered close to the Flakes—siege machines of some kind that were packed for travel. The Snow People who guarded them had started throwing their projectiles the moment they noticed the scouts in their aerial reconnaissance vehicles, destroying one of them in the process and causing the Cadence member to ride back with a squad mate. Now new reports gained from a safe distance stated that the Snow People were on the move to attack the city. So now the city was evacuating to below ground, and the Cadence and Halls had been ordered to prepare for battle: the first at the North Pole in centuries. The first for everyone on both sides of the battlefield.

With uniform in place and drum hanging from her hurt shoulder, Holly shut her locker with a grim face. "I'm still in a state of disbelief, Mia," Holly whispered.

Mia was finishing up the front buttons on her jacket while she whispered back, "You're not the only one, querida." Mia scanned the rest of the room. Everyone else was close to being fully dressed as well.

"I can't help but think if we can just wait a bit longer that we could find a way to stop all of this." Holly gave her head a light shake.

"I know, Hol," Mia tried to be as soothing as she could with her words. "But we have to protect the city."

Holly, who had just fitted her gloves on, slammed her fist into her locker door. "I know." She held her fist there for a moment and Mia did not say anything more. When she pulled her hand away, the locker had a small dent in it.

As much as the North Pole had tried to stay their hand after the attack on Saint Nicholas, the march of the Snow People had breached the final restraint. The North Pole could not fall. The Crafted Council may try one more time to reason with the Snow People, but Holly had little hope in that. A single drum began to beat the Cadence march somewhere down the hall. Holly inhaled deeply and cleared her mind, focusing it on what she must now do with the rest of her corps. No more distractions. Her thoughts became like steel now. Holly would not fail. This was her home. Holly looked at Mia one last time, seeing her resolve was the same, before they both marched forth.

They exited the large doors of the Cadence Corps' headquarters in the North Pole. Once outside they formed ranks in the large, vacant area in front of the white stone building, totalling four companies. The standard Cadence Corps was nowhere near this large. These numbers were capable because of all the trainees in the rear guard and the substantial number of retired members who had pulled their old uniform from out of their closets. At first, the Drum Major had tried to send the trainees and retired party underground with everyone else, but the veterans only laughed at her. They said they could either go under the Major's command or under their own. Holly was sure that the Major could not help but feel inspired by this. So here they all were, marching together through the Reciprocity District, towards the city walls. The Snow People had decided to use a full-on attack as opposed to invading the city individually like they had been. The Drum Major and her officers decided it was because they could not transport their weapons and armor in the same form.

They drummed as one, their feet in sync, their sound perfect. They were a rolling thunder that echoed among the abandoned buildings that intensified their noise. If the Snow People were close enough, Holly believed they would start feeling a bit of hesitation after hearing the Cadence Corp march. They were a force. A call to defend. Holly's drumsticks slammed hard with each beat, as if to focus her ferocity through her hands and into their icy souls. Somewhere ahead the Major blew a whistle four times. This was the signal for the four companies to split and take separate routes to separate gates on the other side of the Hearth District.

Their beats continued. Each company reaching out to the other, letting them know that they were all still there. No distance would change that. Holly and Mia kept their faces forward to avoid any thought on how empty the Hearth district was. The city walls no longer felt like a comforting structure as they marched closer to it. The white stone loomed down, as if to foreshadow the dreaded sight on the other side. Atop the wall a row of gold objects could be counted. They were the golden cloaks of the Learned of *Ve'rema*. A light wind billowed them about, and the elves and humans who wore them attempted to keep them closed. The Learned were not warriors by any means. Their studies were more focused on the pursuit of knowledge in all magical things, living their lives with full bellies and full minds inside their halls. Their fight was better focused in clashes of words, not armies. When the message of the Snow People on the march had reached Master Renshu, he had not hesitated in calling a conference of his mages. They had agreed unanimously to help defend the city. Once again the Major had been stunned by the level of devotion, so she formed a plan to place them above the wall to keep the barrier strong and projectiles out of the sky.

On that note, the Drum Major had grounded all aerial vehicles. One of the Snow People's strengths was to fire forceful amounts of ice high into the air. Their aerial vehicles had never been designed for the purposes of battle, so they would be like fish in a barrel to the enemy. Only the swift moving snowmobiles would be used. The Major had prepared them in twos and assigned to the Cadence Corps top riders so that they could drag heavy cable and take out the Snow Peoples' legs that strayed too far from the opposing army. Holly's company stopped in front of one of the North Pole's gates—gates that had never been opened since their construction. They were pointed at the top, made of course by a magical alloy, and had one large snow flake engraved into it. They were large enough for ten people to walk through side by side. Two of the Learned on the wall made gestures with their hands, a staff in each, focusing on the enchantment that controlled the doors. There was a deep thump and the doors slowly began to swing outward. The true northern air rushed in and snared itself within the Cadence Corps' uniforms despite the warmth of their drums. Its fingers carved deep, and Holly felt like her heart was just barely grazed by its grasp.

"Holly, remember the protection," Mia whispered sideways.

"Oh, right." Holly felt embarrassed as she reached up to the sleeve of her jacket and pinched one of the metal buttons there. A burst of warmth ignited from the threads of her uniform. The frigid cold had no choice but to release her from its dangers. She had forgotten about this function since she had never been outside the walls before except when traveling to the Island in one of their larger transports. The company leader sounded of a new rhythm once the door was fully open and the rest of the group joined on its second repeat. The beat dedicated to battle. It was finally happening.

The four companies marched out of their respective gates and then joined once more. They formed into their trained positions. After one more round of the beat, all noise halted. Holly spotted the Drum Major stepping up onto a raised platform. She kept her back to the corps and surveyed the icy field before them. Holly's eyes widened as she too looked at what was to come. Making sure that none of her superiors were looking, Holly pulled out a pair of binoculars and peered at the distant army.

Hundreds of Snow People trudged with no rank or form. Their movements were lumbering and slow. A glacier on a rogue path. From her readings, Holly knew that the Snow People froze any water in their path the moment they stepped on it, so traversing the shifting ice was an easy feat for them. The mass of behemoth fighters carried weapons on their shoulder, dragged them in their wake, or began to give practice swings before them. They had brought large spiked maces, double sided axes, and swords. Those at the front carried spears and tower shields decorated with some of the Snow People's developed written language. Their armor was white laced with glowing blue veins, crafted to form around their chest and more importantly their legs. They did not wear gauntlets so that their ranged ability was not hindered. Their helms incased their entire head in a solid piece, the short crest starting at the front and reaching towards the back. It also glowed blue with their magic. The sight was terrifying, and Holly pulled the binoculars away from her eyes. Her cheek was cold, so she reached to see why and found a tear had frozen there despite the magical warmth of her uniform. Another joined it right after. The steel of her mind slowly weakening.

Mia reached out her hand and took Holly's from the top of her drum and held it. The warmth once again bolstered Holly's resolve. Holly reach up and pulled the ice from her cheek, gripping Mia's hand tighter in return. Something began to slowly return to her body that she had not felt in weeks. It was a mix of hope, joy, and comfort. It was belief. She could not determine how but it was there like a fire in a hearth filled with fresh logs, the smell of a dinner after crossing a threshold, or a distant train horn that was arriving to carry her home. This was not going to be the end, no matter how the scene had been painted.

The Drum Major turned on her heels to face the rest of them. Touching a button on her collar, she spoke, and her voice was projected crisp and clear to all those waiting. "You who protect the North Pole stand ready to fight for its existence. Not an existence of just the people and the places they live within, but for the mission and reason why this city stands. Our king has fallen, and though we may never know exactly why or how we must still answer to his will. A will to stand as sentinels at these walls. Our sound will be heard. Our song will hold firm." The Drum Major raised her right hand high in the air, a drumstick prepared for her instrument. "On my lead!" The Drum Major shouted. She waited as everyone else prepared as she did. Holly released Mia's hand with one final squeeze of comfort and the two of them prepared. Satisfied, the Major pivoted on the spot and focused on the field. Right before she began to play, Holly heard a sound for the second time, not realizing she had already heard it once in the silence just before. It was the whistle of a train somewhere in the night. "BEGIN!" shouted the Drum Major, and their thunder rolled forth once more.

CHAPTER TWENTY-SEVEN

Tide of Shadow

Kol walked back into the passenger carriage where he had asked his friends to wait after he had finished eating. Under his arm was a map of the North Pole that Kol had taken the time to draw while the others had finished their meals. Each of them gave Kol their full attention as he came closer, eyes on the rolled piece of paper in his hand. Willing to pacify their curiosity, Kol unrolled the paper and showed them what was inside. "I'm not the greatest artist, but this is the general layout of the city." They continued to look at the paper with a deeper concentration. It was nothing overly complicated, just one circle within another to represent the two districts and the plaza.

"What adorable looking snowmen," Lloyd snickered. Logan had said the attack was coming in from the opposite side of the train station, so Kol had drawn cartoon Snow People holding clubs and stick figures with drums marching against them.

"I know." Kol continued onward, "Focus, Lloyd. The station is here, and that is our current destination. I have to get to the center of the city where my father is. I don't know where the ghouls will be coming from, so I believe our best plan of action would be to head straight for the center and revive my father: he can help us find the ghouls and stop them. After that he can fix my uncle's hat and we can stop the North Pole and Snow People from tearing each other apart."

"I'm a fan of it," Willa nodded to herself. "The plan is simple and allows for change."

Harvest sat up straighter when he glanced out the window. "Kol." Placing the map down, Kol looked for what Harvest had seen. Trees no longer laid scattered before them. Now only the ice stretched into the distance, but this was not what Harvest wanted to see. Even at this speed they could see sitting on top of the ice several meters away what he counted to be six types of vessels. He recognized a yacht, a ferry, and others made to carry many passengers. The one that truly grabbed his attention was the river boat from the city. "This would seem as far as the witch could send them. They must be on foot the rest of the way."

"So there were other locations where vampires had been recruiting." Kol started to calculate just how many those boats could carry.

"No need to hunt them all down now. We know where they all are." Lloyd knocked several times on the window with anticipation. "This is very exciting."

"I wonder how long they have been here," Willa inquired.

"I'd say the moment they entered that dark portal the witch conjured or shortly after. Too bad ghouls are unaffected by the cold." Iris stiffened from her own window. "Looks like it's close to time."

"I'd say so, we just passed the arctic circle. We will arrive in about half an hour." Logan entered, a grim smile on his face. "Is there anything that ya need?"

Kol shook his head, "No, just get us there in one piece and we'll do the rest." Logan nodded with his professional style once more before leaving them alone.

The five of them began preparations for the coming battle. Willa inspected her armor, finding all readouts to be satisfactory before the chest of her armor opened magically and allowed her to be closed inside. Kol felt as though the armor held excitement for what was to come, and as Willa put it on, another feeling of strength and ferocity emitted from her just as it did the night they met her at the club. Iris tied her hair back with the leather fire-sewn headband and checked the compartments of her belt to make sure all her tools were prepared before fitting her gloves and chest armor. Lloyd checked his ammunition and slid his dagger free of its sheath and then back in, making sure it was loose. Harvest reached into his jacket and chose his favorite form of becoming terror incarnate. "Won't Iris and Lloyd freeze in the city?" Willa's voice was wrapped in her usual metallic distortion, but was unable to disguise the strain of anxiety in her words.

"Yeah, I'd rather not shatter from the cold. I work very hard to retain my image, you know." Lloyd tapped on the window again with his gun.

Kol spoke before Iris could, seeing her eyes holding a little worry. "Inside the city there is a protective barrier that keeps the climate at a comfortable cold. Outside the city, yes. If you leave the city, you are embracing the harshness of the wasteland."

Willa found another question to ask, "If there is a protective barrier, then how do the ghouls get in?

"Same way they did the first time. Which is still a mystery." Kol stopped to consider, but before he could continue his thought, a shriek of metal on metal came from beneath them as the train jerked to a slower pace, causing them to grab hold of the seats to remain upright. The train continued to slow, and the sound of brakes grew louder. There was a familiar flash of light outside the train window as it left the swift safety of magic. Another shudder ripped through the car, and Kol believed that any more would tear the walls apart around them. The lights above flickered as if displaying the train's desperate cling to life. "The tracks!" Kol managed to yell to the others before the final tremor flung them to the left wall, and the carriage turned over on itself and began to slide beneath where they lay across the ice. The windows shattered, and Iris had to snatch Kol away from the windows.

Iris braced herself over Kol before shouting, "Everyone hold onto something!" Lloyd was the only other one to make a sound. He was laughing, and every breath pleaded for his sanity as he held himself above the window. Harvest had not been thrown like the others and knelt safely next to Willa. The carriage rocked back and forth as they slid, bouncing off chunks of upturned ice, before finally coming to an abrupt halt, allowing silence to creep from them as the sound of the other cars around them also came to a stop.

"Is everyone all right?" Kol asked as Iris helped him to his feet on the wall that was now the floor.

"I didn't know that the train could travel on all sides," Lloyd assured him of his health.

Iris stood up next to him. "We're all fine, Kol."

"What kind of welcome is this, Kol?" Willa asked.

"Such poor hospitality. My people know better than this. We need a way out, Willa, if you don't mind." Kol pointed at the ceiling next to him.

"My pleasure," Willa said, without pulling her weapon free. Instead, she punched hard with her right hand, then again with her left. The strength was always impressive as Willa placed both hands into the small impact hole she created and ripped it wider, allowing the frigid air to sweep in like a thousand knives.

These knives were welcoming to Kol despite the danger, but Iris and Lloyd would be freezing. "Here." He reached into one of the seats where a small compartment was attached. From it he pulled several thick blankets from them to wrap around themselves. "This will have to do for now." Despite the enchantment on his clothes, Kol wrapped himself in one to protect his face and slow his own freezing.

"It will be fine," Iris assured him, wrapping the blanket around herself.

"Let's find out what happened." Kol moved to the open hole and stepped out into the ice with Willa following, then the others.

The ice stretched out for kilometers before them in every direction, racing the darkened shy into the distance with the stars watching it go. Kol turned and jumped onto the outside of their carriage to inspect the scar of the wrecked train. To the left he could see the assortment of cars destroyed in one form or another and piled either next to or on to of each other. There were not that many: only ten or so that were behind them and five in front. Some cars were still connected to one another, except theirs, which seemed to have completely separated and slid further than the others. He spotted the engine further away to the right. Pointing so the others can see, he called, "We have to get to the engine to check on Logan and the engineers." Kol leaped from the wreckage and sprinted across the ice.

Kol made it there before the others, but only by a meter or so. Logan met him coming out of the back of the engine, which was still standing on the right side. Behind him two older gentlemen emerged, one a human of average height with pale skin and a mustache of silver to match the curling hair beneath his hat. The other was an elf with golden hair cut short, revealing his pointed ears. Both wore matching blue jean coveralls striped in white with thick green coats over them. All three of them were either scratched or bruised from the train wreck. "Are you okay?"

"Yea, we managed to not tip over, and I'm glad the five of ya are okay after yours did," Logan said.

"I'm glad you are all fine as well. What happened?" The others joined Kol to listen.

"Well I'll be. We carryin' a tank on board with us," The engineer said, looking at Willa approaching. The old man's voice was scratchy, mixed with excitement and fatigue that only the elderly seemed to master. Kol made a gesture with his hands asking silently for the answer he wanted. "Dang rails where destroyed. There we were just a'tutten along at far faster speeds than I feel safe about, mind you. When Gen here done shouted to me and says dat the rails were gone. So, I pulled on the brakes in hopes of slowin' the old bullet down, after I saw for meself because Gen enjoys his laughs. Should'a listened, cause we may have had a safer stop. Anyway, we was able to slow down enough that when we left the tracks we didn't cause total damage."

"Total damage?" Willa made her own motion to the piles of cars behind them.

"Well, miss, we saved the engine at least?"

"Look at your little ears!" Lloyd had been inching closer to Gen while the old man talked. He now poked at the top of his ears with his finger.

"Stop that!" Gen said and swatted Lloyds hand away.

"You really are an elf?" Iris asked him.

"'Course I am. Do the four of you honestly still find it hard to believe? Humans! Have to throw it in front of them and they still ask question. No problem with asking questions, but when you place doubt in it the fun's all ruined."

"How far from the city are we?" They had come too far for Kol and the others to stop now.

"About five more minutes, s'long as the engine can do it," the old man said to him. "Name's Wose. Climb aboard and we can carry on. Good thing there are more carts to hook to at the station."

"You expect this thing to go with no tracks?" Willa asked, surprised.

"See!" Gen threw up his hands and followed after Wose while talking to Logan. "Gotta throw it in front of 'em. Stay here and freeze for all I care."

"All aboard?" Logan asked, smiling. Kol did not hesitate and mentally pulled the others along. They all climbed into the large engine room, Willa clumsily bringing up the rear.

Inside was a mass of gizmos, gadgets, and levers to behold and the temptation to see what they did urged at Kol. With this thought, Kol grabbed Lloyd to stop him from going through with his own thought process as the engineers began to work. Logan stood toward the rear and shut the door once Willa climbed awkwardly through. The control room was rather large for just three people, but with five more added, plus the large suit of armor, they had to stand very close to one another.

Wose pressed several buttons while Gen pulled levers. The two of them moved so fast that Kol could barely keep up with their movements. The engine roared back to life, and within a few seconds they were moving. Sliding may have been a better word at the start, but through methods of magic and machine the train sped, at a slower, controlled pace, into the direction of the city. "We arn't gonna do no rushin' in this state. Once we arrive, we'll get more engineers and supplies to fix the track so we can get out of the city safely." Wose laughed after his statement and handed a rope hanging from the ceiling to Lloyd, who was close to exploding from standing still. Knowing instantly what it was for, he pulled the rope and sounded the whistle.

"Must have been whatever came on those boats that destroyed the tracks," Harvest said, standing next to Kol. The others were busy looking out the window or talking with the working trains-men.

"That's what I figured. Whoever is leading them must have suspected an evacuation was going to be ordered. Which provides more evidence that whoever is attacking the city is doing so from within it." Kol glanced out the window when something in the sky caught his eye. "Look, everyone, it's the Northern Lights. We are almost there." The others moved to look at the colors dancing in the sky, a sign that showed them the way to go while shadows creeped around them. Kol strained for the next image he knew would come, the one that told him he was home. He turned to Willa. "Prepare to believe." She, surprisingly, remained quiet.

Finally, Kol saw it: the top of the tallest building climbing from the horizon. Glacial peaks at first glance soon allowed the realization that instead of ice, the mountains were made from handcrafted stone topped with glass domes. He heard Iris gasp beside him as the buildings continued to climb into the sky. More time passed as the village houses circling the towers appeared before them. The city was alight with shining lights and warm windows. Yet even still he saw something was wrong. Though the light appeared warm to the heart, his eyes showed him a different form of cold had truly settled in the city.

"Look there!" Woze yelled as they began to move around the city. They all looked and found the source of Woze's cry when an explosion of ice erupted in the distance. Others followed as Kol looked for the source of the explosion and found them in the sky as spheres the size of boulders flew into the air and exploded, followed by battlecries. The Snow People were several kilometers from the North Pole and marched in thousands, roaring battle cries, clasped in white armor and weapons of the same metal. They beat the ground before them with maces, swords, axes, polearms, and other melee weapons. Behind them they pulled deconstructed siege engines on massive carts meant to batter the protective barrier of the city and the opposing army that stood before it.

The Cadence stood between them and the city. It was difficult to pick out individuals in the red fabric of the uniform, but with the entire Corps present, they stood distinct against the marble city walls. They drummed in unison a melody of battle. The Learned of the Halls had to be amongst them preparing spells, which seemed to be the reason Master Shane or any of the others were not able to summon Kol back. He knew Holly was out there as well; no force in the two armies could stop her from helping. The Cadence waited for the Snow People to march into their range. Kol did not think he had enough time to get to his father before the fighting began. Every second counted.

"Where are all the people during this?" Willa sounded deeply concerned.

Kol made himself speak. "Hopefully below ground in safe bunkers. There is a rather large tunnel system underground, and if ever an emergency arose everyone is to move into the designated areas until evacuation can be made."

"Which means us," Gen said from the controls. "We need to get back on the tracks, Woze."

"Uh huh," Woze said, and the train turned towards the city. Gen pressed another button, and the engine gave a small jolt as the train hopped onto the tracks and made for the station.

The armies vanished from their sight as the train continued around the city. The details in the walls became clear as the train moved centimeters from it. "There's the station," Logan announced, and the engineers began to apply the brakes. The track before them split into thirds and continued to split into fifteen different rail systems laying parallel as they moved into the station. The huge, curved roof seemed to be made of gold, the columns holding it upright were crafted beautifully to appear like the Nordic wind. How easily everyone forgot it was the Snow People who crafted these masterful works. The walls were a bright red brick once they were inside. Extra carriages were lined to the right of the station and the engineers had the train take the tracks to the far left to stop at the platform. The train finally came to a halt in the center of the station, placing them in front of the raised platform.

While the door slid open Logan said, "Good luck out there. We are going to quickly assemble a new train."

"Thank you for everything, Logan, and for both of you also. We will fix this." Kol nodded to him and stepped from the train. "Let's hurry to the center plaza." The five of them crossed the platform and exited through the passenger entrance that took them into the wall and brought them to the start of a street.

Everything appeared to Kol to be perfectly in order in the Hearth District. Houses were lit with interior lighting from normal sources and Christmas decoration. A tree was visible inside every home, with wreaths on many doors. The house's roofs, windows, doors, and anything else they could decorate were outlined in Christmas lights, and the oil lamps lighting the road were wrapped in tinsel and boughs of holly. Kol moved between them, knowing the quickest path. He realized he travelled alone, and turned to his friends, who had not moved since they saw the village houses. Even during so much turmoil and chaos Kol smiled at them. They stood in complete wonder, and even Harvest held a soft smile. Kol could see them as the children they once were and knew that they had all once truly believed in this place. Even Willa, who was able to hide behind her armor, showed her awe by reaching out to the first lamp post and gently touching the decoration. "Now do you believe?" They all stared at him, speechless. "Help me save it."

In response, Willa pulled her shield from her back and freed her massive sword. "Lead the way, Kol."

They moved between the buildings swiftly but cautiously. This place, though an embodiment of magic, now felt cursed with the absence of people. They were all aware that the dreams that once constructed the city were now haunted by nightmares they had not yet found. There had not been any sign of their presence here, yet the feeling was strong around them: they could be using stealth to reach the city plaza or to flank the Cadence and Snow People. Anything was possible. The group passed a tunnel entry that had been sealed shut, which meant that enemies were still above ground or, less likely, had found another way in. Thankfully Kol knew the shelters would hold for a time until the Cadence could return for the true threat. All the same, they should position themselves better. "Lloyd and Harvest, jump to the roofs of either building to watch our flank while I take point on the ground. Iris will be ready center to support. And Willa protect our weakest point from the rear."

Lloyd laughed and hopped onto a nearby porch before climbing up, pulling his weapons free from their homes. Harvest did the same on the right, and Kol was thankful his senses should warn them long before they closed in on any enemy. Iris and Willa also stepped into formation, and they started a brisk jog as Kol planned, sacrificing stealth for speed, but the price seemed appropriate. They continued onward through the ghostly streets.

As they drew closer, Kol began to hear the sound of the fighting. The drum style was the sound meant for attacking, a cadence rarely heard in such power here in the North. Shouting clung weakly to the air as it reached them along with the sound of structures being destroyed or damaged. Kol picked up his pace, and the others felt his drive and carried along with him. It was true that he could possibly outrun all of them by both knowing the city and using his bell, but should the hidden army corner him, he would have no chance. The five of them together may not even stand a chance, but their odds were better together than apart. It was why he agreed to finally bring them along.

Harvest gave a light whistle and they halted in a guarded stance. Kol held his sword in a forward guard to protect the point as his position dictated, and Willa did the same, turning to face the way they had come. Harvest was crouched in the shadow of a chimney, and Lloyd took the silent advice and did the same on his own roof. They waited as Harvest surveyed whatever had caused the alarm to be raised. Kol took a brief chance to look up at him and saw Harvest motion for Kol to join him. Checking the spaces between the homes, Kol jumped up to Harvest's position as Iris stepped forward to watch his post. "What do you see?" he spoke in the smallest of whispers, knowing Harvest's ears could hear him.

"They are close to us. Watch the shadows." Harvest nodded to the street beside them, and Kol did as asked. At first there was nothing to find, merely shadows born from where the homes and lamps stole the moonlight from meeting the ground. The image was wrong, and Kol figured why the next moment. All the homes were dark, as well as the lanterns, all embraced now in the haunting cold. Lloyd gave his own soft whistle, and Kol and Harvest glanced over. The power on the road next to him was shutting off and the lanterns were dying out. From on the roof, Kol swept his gaze over their surroundings and found the same thing happening all around them. The only light now was the area they now stood in. "We are surrounded," Harvest said so calmly that the situation seemed unreal for a moment.

Kol then saw the shadows begin to move around them, coming from every alley, porch, and roof, each stepping into the moonlight. The way they all moved was like they were standing in the middle of an ant bed and they were intruding. Kol slid from the roof and dropped down next to Iris and nudged her back. "What did you see?" Willa called. The feel of the coming fight was on her without her knowing because she discarded the silence to make sure she was heard.

Next came Iris, concerned: "Kol?"

"We are surrounded. Prepare: we're going to have to fight our way through." His voice was calm and determined. It was only a matter of time before the journey became difficult once more.

A familiar shriek came from high above them. The beat of wings swelled around it as Lord Andrew flew unseen from above. The screech grew louder as the vampire descended on them. They all looked up, and for the briefest of moment they saw black wings beat once, then a gust of wind hit them strong enough to unbalance them. The lanterns around them went out, and sparks crackled as the lights in the houses vanished. With the party unbalanced and partially blind, the ghouls made their attack.

They leaped from every space a building did not occupy, their rotting flesh gleaming in the moon. Kol could even see their sharp, rotting teeth as they lunged, but he cut them down swiftly, and they dissolved beneath their rags just as the ones had that first came to the city. Gunshots rang from Lloyd as he took the heads of every ghoul that joined him on the roof. Harvest was ripping his foes apart before casting them away from the team. Iris had moved closer to Kol and the two began to fight together. Iris would disable a ghoul with a swift kick or punch and Kol would end them with his blade. Willa, of course, needed no support and appeared to be fighting the majority. A few clung to her back trying to pry her armor off while others danced beneath her. They had no luck, and once Willa found room to breathe around her, she ripped the monsters from her back and tossed them into the houses where the impact crushed their insides.

"Look out!" Iris yelled to him over the gnarling and hissing of the creatures. Kol spun and caught a sickly-looking mace before it could connect to his head. Behind the mace was a goblin, or that was the name that first came to mind, that stood waist high and was clad in dark crude armor. Iris spun beneath the mace and kicked the goblin hard in the chest where he soared back into more like him and exploded with a hidden treat Iris had placed in his armor.

"Willa, there are goblins here too!" Kol shouted back to her.

Turning to check on Willa, Kol ducked just as a goblin flew over him. "You don't bloody say."

The fight went on as the goblins and ghouls became evenly balanced. Lloyd continued to fire into the enemy from above, no shot missing its mark. When one came too close, the dagger made quieter work of them. Harvest's roof was nowhere to be found, save from where he stood in the sea of armor and rotting flesh around him. "Iris, he needs your help."

Turning, Iris saw Harvest's trouble and started running for Willa. "Harvest!" she yelled as Willa caught her mid-leap and tossed her onto the roof. Iris landed on a goblin and proceed to fight her way to Harvest. They made progress and quickly cleared the roof. It could not go unnoticed that their surrounding was slowly growing thicker in potential death.

"We have to push onward; we can't fight them all."

"I do need to reload soon," Lloyd yelled down to him.

Kol looked down the end of the street to where it split both left and right and a house blocked their straight forward momentum. "Willa, we need you to make a path."

"GLADLY!" Willa roared, pulling a goblin from her back and tossing it hard into one of its allies. She then unleashed a strong horizontal cut to clear the area in front of her. Next, she planted her foot in a defensive stance and raised her shield above her. Kol pointed to the house, and Willa nodded back curtly. The suit seemed to expand, and Kol felt that the suit of armor was taking a deep breath before the steam began to slowly billow out with a whistle. "KEEP UP!" she yelled to them and thundered ahead.

Kol stepped aside and sprinted after her, and the other three jumped down quickly to follow. The action surprised the surrounding force and many them stood still as Willa moved, paying dearly for it. She ran them over and stomped them beneath her boots, and those who tried to move went flying upward to greet Kol's blade or backward where they were trampled still despite their efforts. Willa aimed for the front door of the home and crashed through it. They stayed close to miss the debris, moving too fast for it to hinder their path. Willa emitted steam again and yelled as she crashed through two walls and then through the next house. They erupted into a new street, and Kol could see the start of the Reciprocity District. "We can't stop now!" Kol said, and the motivation empowered Willa onward.

Willa made it a few meters up the street when Lord Andrew's ear-splitting screech came directly to left of them. The vampire came into full view, and Kol finally understood what form had possessed those horrifying wings on top of Wenn's tower. The monster was a personified nightmare. The giant leathery wings protruded from its back and created torments of wind with every push. The body was pale, just like the weaker vampires, but all human facial features were gone. Instead the ears jutted upwards from the head, the nose had become no more than slits, the crimson eyes were enlarged, and the mouth gaped unnaturally wide with rows of fanged teeth. The instant Kol witnessed all of this, Andrew's onyx clawed hands and feet collided with Willa, lifted her into the air and tossed her several streets over.

"WILLA!" they all yelled together as Andrew flew into the distance. Howls muffled their cry in response from her location.

"Werewolves," Harvest said, pulling his fang free of his mouth. He kept the fang in his left hand and with his right pulled out the werewolf fur he carried. Tearing free of his jacket and shirt, he slapped it to his arm and began to spasm. "Can't take on a pack in that form. Too fast." He then began to change violently as ghouls jumped towards him, his remaining clothes and shoes ripping.

"Defend him!" Kol told the other two, and they instantly surrounded him and fought while he finished changing. Kol witnessed Lloyd pull a small brown seed from his bag and eat it. The next instant his energy seemed to surpass what his body could hold. He moved faster than Kol could see as he reloaded his weapon and fired it in a rapid succession. Iris tossed more explosives into the crowd, scattering them. Harvest finished just as the pack of werewolves came over a roof, howling as they soared into the group. Harvest snarled back and leaped into them taking two in his paws and smashing them together. Lloyd turned and fired on the massive pelts as Kol and Iris moved out of the way. The ghouls and goblins moved back from the foaming mouths that snapped obedience. The two Harvest had slammed regained their posture and turned to Harvest, now standing on the roof.

The two leaped into Harvest, and the other four pounced on the rest of the group. Lloyd fired at the three around them, but they seemed to ignore the shots. Iris used powders, however, that shimmered and seemed more effective as the werewolves shied away from it. Kol caught a werewolf in the mouth with his blade, but the beast only bit down on his sword and attempted to snatch it away. Snarling back at the wolf for its audacity, Kol drew back his off-hand and punched the werewolf in the nose, causing it to release the blade and whimper. Kol checked on the others to see Lloyd loading something new into his gun while Iris guarded him. He understood and continued to distract his own werewolf. Harvest had ripped one werewolf in half and now had his muzzle buried in the neck of the other. Lloyd had enough time and commenced firing into the werewolves, who instead of ignoring these shots cried out in pain. Silver was deadly to them, after all.

The werewolves decided they wanted to live instead and began to flee from Lloyd's fire. Harvest leaped in front of Kol and began to growl, facing away from him. Kol looked to the city as well and saw a completely new threat. A hundred men were walking towards them, but once Kol could truly see them, he knew that they were not men, but the golems made of ice. The rune paper-like skin on their mouths seemed as blank as their faces as they marched out of the city towards them. "You can't continue." Andrew was back and landed in front of the golems, who stopped abruptly. "Lay down your weapons now, and we will chain you." It was odd to watch that terrible mouth twist words.

"I don't think so," came Willa's metallic voice, and the building beside Andrew crumpled as she flew from it. Andrew attempted to flee, but Willa was able to grab one of the vampire's wings. "Throw me over a building!" She swung Andrew around like a flail and destroyed the first row of snow golems. "As if I could be so easily stopped!" She then swung him over her head and into the paved ground. "I AM A KNIGHT OF THE CAELESTIBUS! YOU WILL RESPECT OUR MIGHT, OUR DETERMINATION, AND OUR FURY!" Willa picked him from the ground and swung him back into it a second time. The Snow golems focused on her then while her back was turned, causing her to release Andrew. The vampire regained his footing and attempt to flee again, but this time Harvest stopped him.

With a snarl, Harvest leaped onto Andrew as he began to fly and sank his teeth into his back. The vampire screeched and broke free, but he left behind one of his wings. Harvest spat it from his mouth and then watched Andrew crash into another house. The ghouls and goblins began to attack again at the sight of their fallen leader causing a rally point, but they were now in a frenzy of panic. Kol, Iris, and Lloyd turned on them, leaving Harvest to his kill. Reaching to his arm Harvest pulled the black fur free and changed back into a human. "Wendon would not answer, so maybe you will. Who are you working for, and who was the witch on the river bank?"

Andrew screeched again as he attempted to stand, but the loss of his wing had left him unbalanced. "I'll tell you nothing. Death by you will be easier than life through him."

"Your choice." Harvest placed his fang in its rightful place and became the pale demon once more. The two vampires met in the middle of the street and began to fight. The two thrashed and slammed one another into the lamps, which left the street, the houses, which cracked, and into the pavement making an impression like Willa had when she slammed Andrew into it. At this point the goblins had stopped, and so had the ghouls. The snow golems continued marching towards Willa but at a very slow pace, allowing her to keep them cut down. Andrew slashed at Harvest's chest leaving deep, dark marks, but his talons were too short because they missed his heart. Harvest then struck forward into Andrew's exposed chest and pulled the cold dead stone from it. The motion was so quick that Andrew did not realize what had happened until Harvest held his heart before him and squeezed.

Andrew then began to thrash about as his body eroded into dust. Harvest tossed aside the heart and grabbed the vampire lord's head tight. He then reached into Andrew's mouth and pulled free one of his fangs before the head vanished into the dust. The snow golems had stopped now as if to witness what had occurred. Kol had the feeling that whoever controlled them could see through them and wanted to experience what came next.

Harvest reached into his own mouth and pulled free his tooth, placing it into a jean pocket that still held. "You came to this place in worship or fear of him. Now you will flee from this place in fear of me and worshiping whoever you please next to protect you." He then placed Andrew's fang into his mouth and showed them all the potential within. His back ripped open as wings shot from it. His hands and feet also changed into larger sickled clawed forms. His face contorted into the same visage that Lord Andrew had. The transformation seemed to cause Harvest the most pain, but when it was done, he stood and spread his wings wide. "Come at me if you wish to avenge your master. My blood will sustain you now if you can kill me. Or flee if you value what you have left." The ghouls responded as expected and lunged at Harvest with savage intent while the goblins turned and ran. Harvest took to the sky and slammed down amongst them, using his wings along with his new claws to strike out around him.

"Kol, now's your chance; get to your father. We'll stay here and push them back!" Iris told him in his ear.

"You're right." Lloyd had begun to join the fray as well, and Iris followed. "Need your help getting over the remaining golems, Willa," Kol said, beginning to run towards her.

"Yes." Willa said turning towards him, placing her shield on her back, and lowing her now free hand. Kol jumped into it, braced himself, and felt the full force of Willa's armor as it catapulted him over the remaining golems. Kol arched over them and his boots slowed his fall. He landed a few seconds later and sprinted towards the Reciprocity District without looking back.

CHAPTER TWENTY-EIGHT

A New Face to an Old Problem

His boots echoed off the buildings, a new sound in a familiar place. The North Pole was perhaps the only city that slept, but even then there had been no echo. The place was usually full of life with the occasional night owl could be seen gliding by. Despite the buildings being vacant when office hours ended, they still felt warm through their illusory ice. Kol hated the city being cold and still like it was now and found more motivation to push harder as he neared his home and his awaiting father. The thought occurred to him that his father might not be there, perhaps moved into the bunkers below, but searching each one would take hours. It would be best to start in his room where Kol had left him before his departure.

Just ahead was Tannenbaum Plaza. The small ring of lantern lit trees that was the beginning of the plaza embraced him. His feet next touched the colored stone of the open plaza. The trunk of the central tree stood strong as always with its magnificent branches reaching over the colored stones. It was still lit with the light of Christmas, and every single one of its ornaments shimmered in the enchanted light. As Kol ran past hit he ran a hand along its bark to make sure it was real. The workshop waited for him in all its majesty on the other side of the plaza. Kol quickly gripped the door handle to his home and darting inside.

The lights within were not lit, though, but Kol did not care; he knew the way without using his sight. He moved up the stairs until he was on the fourth floor and ran swiftly down the hall.

The door to his parents' room was at the very end and of course matched the rest of the house. Kol moved inside and turned on the light. The circular room was exactly how it was supposed to be. The walls were draped in red curtains from the marble dome down to the brown shaggy carpet. A dresser sat on either side, and naturally one of the largest fireplace built within a home burned cheerfully. The sleigh bed was magnificent, pleasing his mother when she got it, but at this time it only made his heart sink. His father was not in it.

Thinking quickly, Kol darted back out the door and down the stairs. He would search the tunnels below as it was his only option. He entered the vacant workshop, but was met with grief once more. Each of the four large tunnels had been sealed shut from within, and there was no way to contact anyone inside. Kol now had to make his final move, which was to run to the Cadence and find out where his father had been taken. Starting to feel a creeping fatigue, he made his way back out into the plaza. The fight would be taking place at the city walls almost directly behind the house. Kol opened the front door and froze.

The place was draped in night. The great tree no longer stood lit, nor did the lanterns around it within the forest ring. It was impossible to believe because the tree was lit by his father's magic. Had something happened to him? Kol quickly shook his head and fought the thought that would easily destroy him. His father was still alive somewhere. Kol stepped down into the plaza, being cautious of each of his steps. He did not want what ever was happening to slow him down any further. His eyes caught movement beneath the great tree. When he realized what was there, his veins ran cold.

Beneath the tree his father lay in his curse presented in the form of slumber. He was laying on a grey platform that had not been there when Kol had passed it mere moments before. The platform seemed to grow from the plaza floor instead of sitting on top of it. His father had been dressed in his traditional clothing, complete with the red hat with the white ball on the end. He looked so peaceful laying there beneath the branches. Kol began to move toward him when a figure wearing black turned around.

The hooded cloak the man wore was not of any fabric Kol knew. It seemed to be made from shadows themselves and moved less than it should have, which was why Kol had not seen him at first. He stood taller than Kol, who was already above average, and was terribly thin. The only thing Kol could see was the white mask the man peered at him through. Two dark holes replaced his eyes, and where some form of mouth should be was a blood streaked rune that matched every golem Kol had fought.

"So, you're the one that constructed all of this," Kol motioned at the chaotic world around him as he moved closer to the tree.

The figure remained silent for a moment as if considering if he should respond or not. In Kol's opinion the man decided right as he spoke, "You had put forth so much effort in discovering me that I could not let you go without at least one meeting. Consider it an early gift." There was no mocking in his tone, but Kol felt it nonetheless. His voice was deep, but not in sound, as it felt hollower. A depth where darkness is born from. Yet youth mixed in the foundation: he could have been the same age as Kol.

"You sent the ghouls, had a person brainwashed to attack my father, and started a civil war."

"A plan thought out for the last couple of ages. The only factor I did not expect was you." The figure snapped open his cloak and swung forward a black staff. The darkness reached out for Kol and snared him in place. The very same darkness that had pulled Wendon away from Harvest and Kol back at the tower. "As I said, once I realized you had become involved, I wondered if you would be able to get in my way. At that point I decided that the time to stop me had long passed and that you would not cause any trouble. I was wrong." He did not sound hurt at this, nor was his pride slighted. He simply stated a fact.

"When did you know I was on your trail?" Kol wanted to both buy time to think and was truly curious.

"The moment you confronted the ghouls I sent into the city. Thankfully, they had finished their job."

Kol pushed on, trying not to show his struggle. He did not want what happened to Wendon to occur to him as well. "What is your reason?"

"Kol, if I must explain that, then I truly can't understand how you got so far." He gestured towards his father. "He has something that I have coveted for a long time. Now I will have it." He turned his back on Kol and began to feel along the tree.

Kol did not understand. "The tree?"

"No, this tree is vast in magical power, but not where my passion lies." His voice was becoming bored. With his back turned, Kol began to struggle and found he could move his hand slightly. "Has your father ever explained to you his immortality, Kol?"

"Yes," Kol said, using every bit of strength in his arm to move it towards the box on his belt.

Kol heard a small sigh. "You lie; I expected more honesty from the Son of Winter."

"Then tell me." The cloaked man did not reply. He no longer wished to acknowledge Kol. That was fine, for Kol had just opened his box and pull his bell free. It rang softly, causing the man to turn back to him. Before he could make another motion with his staff, Kol shook it and embraced the Sound.

Kol was instantly free from the shadow's restraints. The magic could no longer restrict his movements, so he snatched his limbs free and ran for the tree. The Sound released him, and Kol appeared meters in front of the man. The staff lashed out with the same spell, but Kol had once again embraced the Sound. Pulling his sword from his side, Kol lunged it forward over his father to finally finish everything. His blade ran true and Kol was released from the Sound. When it did, the cloaked man was gone. "That truly is magnificent to witness."

Kol spun to the man's voice now behind him, and found him standing there, no longer wearing his cloak. Beneath it he wore black pants with darker boots and a white embroidered shirt tucked into them. He wore a silver chain from shoulder to hip that was attached to something Kol could not see. His skin was extremely tan, and his hair was short and black behind the white mask. The staff moved again, and Kol moved a fraction to escape the shadows. "That won't work anymore."

"Understood," the white mask said, slamming his staff into the ground before him where it remained standing. He then pulled the other object from behind him and opened it. It was an immense tome bound in yellowish leather. Inside the paper were different shades of tan, which Kol sickeningly realized were skin. The man bellowed an enchantment into it, and the words vibrated beneath where Kol stood. A few pieces of paper then flew from the book and shredded before circling the man. Pulling a pin from his book, the enemy cut across his wrist and let his blood flow free. Reaching out, each piece of paper ran across his hand before darting at Kol. He raised his sword, but the paper did not aim for him directly but the plaza beneath him. Kol could not count the amount of skin that circled him. The only thing he did know was that he could no longer stand still.

Hands of stone reached from the plaza and pulled the now stone golems free. This left the mosaic ruined as the golems mixed the stone and assorted colors they held. Kol did not truly fear them, as his sword was able to cut through stone, but it took more effort and slowed his form. He strategized and began to cut at the mouths of the golems emerging around him. The effect was rewarding as they crumpled back, but by the time Kol had cut a few the others had become fully upright. Kol looked for the masked man, but he was gone. Kol could still see his father and saw the golems were not focused on him. As the golems reached for him, Kol stepped into the Sound.

Kol made quick work just has he did in the forest, destroying the source of their artificial life. When the sound released him again, he jumped onto one of the golems and leaped into the air. There was still no sign of the masked man, so he shook his bell once he descended back into the small force. Kol expected to touch the ground safely, but the staff swung towards him, caus-ing Kol to react and meet it with his blade. Surprise hit Kol, then the strongest form of panic. The masked man stood beneath him within the Sound.

They both emerged from the fold, and the man used Kol's surprise to continue his assault. His staff spun expertly in his hands, and the ends held with it the sharpness of death. The golems reached for him as he fought off the strikes, but it was too much. He stepped back into the Sound where he was once again followed. At least here Kol could fight one on one amongst statues. Kol felt dread creep over him, knowing that he could not keep it up. His limit had created a delay of the inevitable. Back and forth they went, except where Kol could not land a strike, the man could, and slammed the staff hard into Kol's side, leg, and arm. The pain from the points of contact were blinding, and Kol felt bones starting to break. Another strong strike came around his guard and sent him flying in a burst of purple out of the swarming golems and away from the tree.

"You thought only you and your father could step away from time?" The masked man sounded slightly winded. He stepped from around his golems, who continued to move to where Kol lay, gasping for breath. "You simply need to know how to listen."

Kol picked himself up and readied himself for the next strike. When the staff began to move, he stepped back into the Sound and met him. At the sound of the winded voice Kol had gained a realization. Every moment Kol shook the bell and stepped back out of time, he felt the stress placed on his body, and so did his adversary. That thought was hope to Kol while his insides burned, and nausea rose within him. Kol grew tired with each step and took strikes whenever he was not fast enough. The dif-ference now was that Kol's strikes also found their mark and left gashes in the man's body, the blood providing the evidence that Kol had been right. Kol made sure to watch his footing on the ruined stone. He and his adversary had moved far enough away from the golems now. After another successful strike from both, Kol went to a knee and coughed blood onto the plaza floor.

"How pathetic, and yet still you believe yourself able to save him." The man stopped abruptly, reaching for his stomach as if something inside was harming him.

Kol laughed though a mouthful of blood, standing and wiping his mouth. "I can tell that you did not expect that to happen. The Sound only accepts one person, and he is the one laying upon your table. Your body is rejecting it, just as mine is. If you wish to kill me, then you must carry the same pain that I do."

"That's insane. We both would die." The man now let emotion escape from behind the mask. It was disbelief that he had been rejected, which meant that he had never stepped from time before.

Kol nodded, raising his sword. "I would gladly die to save this city and my father."

"Fine." Back to the simple term and nothing more. Then the staff spun faster and Kol continued to use the Sound to slowly kill them both. They had begun to step among the golems again and Kol found he had an advantage here. Not that he could barely land a strike, but he did seem to outpace the masked man, most likely from being used to the torment that was so fresh to his enemy. Whenever he struck, he also tried to destroy another statue, thinning the area for them both. The man noticed this and struck out to stop Kol, but the reaction caused him to spasm.

Kol never stopped the motion of distracting the man with stopping the golems. When he was close enough, Kol feinted an attack towards one of the golems, but when the masked man started to reach out, Kol raised his foot and kicked him hard in the chest. In that moment Kol turned and sprinted towards his father, reaching into his bag and pulling the *Clauditis* blade from inside. Kol quickly unfolded it and gripped the hilt in the fabric. Ducking beneath stone arms, he stood over his father and stabbed him with it. He hoped that this would awaken him and not finish what was started. The blade vanished just as the one before it did inside of his father. Yet there was no immediate reaction.

Kol began to worry that it had not worked, but the worry left him when the staff went through his body. He did not feel anything at first and looked down at the blunt weapon now sticking through him in disbelief. He reached to grab it, but before his fingers touched it, the staff slid back through and out of him. Blood drenched his shirt jacket and pants and he spun to look at the masked man. Kol collapsed against the raised platform. "You may have saved him this time, but next time you will not be around."

"Kol?" That voice he had heard all his life asked softly from behind him. There was an explosion of brilliant light and the masked man was sent flying. Kol raised his hand to weakly point but shadows began to emerge from the ground, the man landing deftly in them and vanishing. "Kol!" His father's face filled his vision now, and his hands lifted Kol up onto the place where he had been resting.

"He was here." Kol could not fully think; he must have been going into shock.

"I know, Kol. I am proud of you." His father moved around him quickly and Kol began to see the faint glow of magic. "Hold still," he said to him. Kol agreed, and then was gone.

******

Kol opened his eyes and slowly looked around him. Everything was bright, which could only mean he was in the afterlife. There was no pain in his stomach and he felt completely rested from the ordeal of the last month. In fact, he felt better than he had in a while. "Kol, you can sit up now."

"Why?" he asked in a soft voice.

"Because your friends are here."

Kol focused on his father's voice and cleared his mind of the fog. The light did not come from the afterlife, but from the life he always knew. The tree once again shone in its brilliance and reflected off the buildings surrounding the plaza. Kol bolted upright and reached for the hole that should have been in his stomach. His shirt was shredded and covered with blood along with his pants, but his body was physically fine. The parts where the staff had contacted his skin where no longer darkened and bruised, and the bones beneath them no longer felt fractured. "How?"

'Ho ho ho," his father laughed. "Magic." He stood there next to Kol and gave him a helping hand when Kol tried to get off the dais. It was astonishing how well he felt. Of course, he barely felt the staff go through him out of shock, but he at least thought he would feel something. No, he felt completely whole and renewed.

"Kol!" The voice belonged to Iris, yelling from across the broken plaza. Kol spun toward it and saw his friends running toward him. Harvest was human and wearing his shirt and jacket now, walking with Lloyd, and Willa still wore her armor. They had the look of battle about them, as did Kol, but at least they were all still alive.

His father chuckled. Iris jogged straight to him and embraced him as the others came closer. "I'm fine, Iris."

"You don't look fine." She checked him over just to make sure.

He pulled back from her. "The monsters?"

"They retreated out into the waste," Harvest told him.

Lloyd stepped close and poked Kol's stomach through the large hole in his clothes. "Where is the ow?"

"My dad saved me." Kol stepped toward his father. "Everyone, this my father, Nicholas, or better to say, Santa Claus."

Any doubt they may have had vanished in the shining light beneath the tree and what radiated off of his father. Kol realized that his own doubt was gone as well as he saw his father standing there. After all their arduous work, he had saved his father. "Well, it is wonderful to meet all of you. But the time for proper introductions will have to come later." Another explosion came in the distance.

Kol's heart sank. How could he have forgotten about the armies? Reaching into his bag, Kol brought out Frostien's hat and handed it to his father. "It was damaged. I figured you alone could fix this."

"Excuse me, sir? Do you know what is going on?" Willa sounded extraordinarily passive asking.

"Ho ho ho." Santa Claus took the hat from Kol and quickly examined it. "I put it together when I woke while healing Kol. This confirms that someone wanted to start a war between the Snow People and the North Pole. Now stand back, everyone, while I concentrate. Fixing this is no mere hatter job; old magic is woven within." The hat began to glow blue in his hands and then float softly in place. His father began to chant a forgotten language while weaving more colors into it, colors of mending and crafting; Kol had seen it performed in his father workshop when he was creating something truly magnificent. A light hum began to harmonize with his father from within the hat, and everyone watching could see the tears in the fabric begin to slowly close themselves like Kol imaged his healing wounds had. While keeping his right hand working charms and spells into the hat, Saint Nicholas leveled his left hand out beside him and began to rotate it towards the ground.

Flakes of snow began to fall on them then faintly, and then at a heavier pace. Yet the snow did not lie still and sleep: it was alive and swirling beneath his father's hand. Holding his right hand still with the hat, he then motioned with his left hand upward into the hat, and the snow followed. At that point the hat moved from its floating spot and toward an untouched part of the plaza with a whirlwind of snow following. The powder mixed thicker and became harder. A rough body began to form and polish out to a shining white. Nowhere near his full height, the Snowman stood level with Santa Claus. As the snow finally died down, Frostien, Chief of the Snow People, once again stood in his own strength. He looked at his hands, then at Kol's father: "Thank you, my brother, for bringing me back to life."

"Any time, but if not for Kol, we would have lost you completely."

Frostien walked towards the group. "What has happened?"

"Nothing too far gone we cannot fix," Saint Nicholas said, bringing his fingers to his mouth. He expelled a high, compelling whistle. When it faded, a new sound came in a commotion of hoof beats. From behind the workshop where the stables were kept, the reindeer shot into the sky, all eight of them. His father's magnificent sleigh followed behind as reins and harnesses manifested on the flying reindeer in a shimmer of magic. Next the front doors of the mansion burst forward as hundreds of silver bells greeted the coming sleigh and settled among the deer and reins. Kol felt each ring of the bells pass over him as the reindeer descended. They quickly landed before them, all eight snorting in the cold and dancing from excitement, antlers thrashing as muscles became loose. "Everyone climb on," Santa Claus said and stepped into his sleigh, grabbing hold of the brown leather straps. Frostien did so next and sat next to his brother. "Everyone," he said with a demanding cheer, looking at Kol and his friends.

"I would climb up if I were you," Kol said to them.

"My armor?" Willa asked.

"These strong brutes could carry a semi-truck if need be. I think they have, once upon a time. Ho ho ho. Hurry!" Saint Nicholas finished, and the others climbed up to find a comfortable seat. "There are more blankets for you in the back. Put them on to keep warm."

"You don't have to twist my arm," Harvest said, pulling a giggling Iris up after him followed by Willa taking the place where the large bag was usually placed.

All except for Lloyd, though Kol tried to get his attention once already.

"Lloyd, we have to go." Kol turned to him and saw that Lloyd had not been looking at the sleigh or anything else that had just happened. Instead he gazed up into the tree with eyes full of rapture. "Lloyd!"

Snapping to his senses, Lloyd looked around and laughed. "Oh, a sleigh." He too climbed up after them.

"Kol?" his father asked.

Kol shook his head, and as if waiting for this cue, Soar came down and landed beside him. While his companion nuzzled his arm, Kol said, "I'll keep up." He then climbed into his reindeer's saddle.

His father laughed and snapped the straps, causing the reindeer to pull. Swiftly they moved, regardless of the weight, and went from pulling on the broken stone to pulling in the open air. Kol urged Soar to chase after, and he did so fast enough for Kol to see his friend's faces. Harvest showed all his teeth in a smile while Iris smiled and gripped both a spastic Lloyd and tense Willa. Within the next few moments, they were high above the buildings and flying towards the battlefield.

Because Soar was not pulling the amount of resistance as the other eight were, Kol pushed him into a faster gallop, which his friend gladly did after being cooped up for so long. Together they descended towards the fighting, and Kol was able to see everything from his seat. The two armies had broken into combat by now. Large weapons clashed with sound waves sent by drums. Shards of ice shot towards pillars of fire launched from the golden cloaked Learned stationed on the wall. The siege equipment had mostly been destroyed, but that did not stop the Snow People from using the remaining two. Kol watched with horror as several Cadence were sent flying from a swing of a hammer, and felt sickened observing a Snowman falling to pieces as a group focused on him alone. What they did not see was the third force of creatures creeping towards the fight. Ghouls, goblins, and other things that Kol did not recognize moved closer, waiting for a chance to engage. Kol sensed they would once both sides had fatigued themselves.

"Here, take the reins," Kol heard his father yell once they had caught up. Looking over, Kol saw he was speaking to Harvest. "Frostien, we have to get down there now!" Nodding, the Snowman stood and readied to exit the sleigh on either side.

Waiting for Harvest to guide the deer to the best location, Kol watched his father begin to weave magic once more. A small portal opened before him, and from it his father pulled his sword, Jolly. The claymore was familiar to Kol from his time sparring with his father. It too had been made by his uncle, the blade gleaming white with guard of dark green. Red leather had been wrapped around the hilt tightly, and the blade shown like a beacon. His father wanted everyone to stop and look to the sky.

Frostien also reached into the portal and brought from it the gift his brother had given him in return for the great sword. Also a strong symbol of winter, the great club was made from an oak log that emitted a ruddy orange glow along the carved patterns from eternal embers embattled into it and was wrapped at the smaller end in white fur. Saint Nicholas had both carved and enchanted it himself to never burn the wielder. Its name was Cinder. These weapons had been what finished the ritual common in the North Pole and declared them sworn brothers.

Gripping the sword tightly in his right hand, Saint Nicholas motioned toward the deer with his other and the bells attached to the leather straps flew to him and surrounded Saint Nicholas. "Let us stop this terror." The two of them stepped from the sleigh and plunged towards the ground. Neither of them seemed to be affected by the height. The bells rang as they fell, and his father held his sword before him, showing their presence. Near the ground the two changed from diving head first into feet first. His father sent a burst of magic beneath them that slowed their fall just enough for their landing to create a crater and shower of ice.

"ENOUGH!" both Frostien and Saint Nicholas shouted together, facing their respective people. Kol did not know if their vocals had been enchanted to be louder, or if it was simply the force of their presence. The soldiers on both sides instantly halted their assaults upon each other. "Look at what has become of you!" Everyone heard his father speak. "You lay siege to one another seeing monsters that only your fear has created, when the true monsters are at our back." Kol and the others guided their respective transportation to the ground just behind the two leaders.

Raising Cinder high so that it was displayed, Frostien spoke after his brother. "Soon, another force that attacked the city opposite of here is now waiting just beyond in the shadow of the wall for both factions to finish one another off so that they can destroy what is left." Frostien's voice was also carried well over the now-silent field. The others must have filled both the leaders in on the story as they flew from the plaza. "They would have the city if not for the heroes landing here before you." The tired faces all looked to Kol and his friends, then back to their leaders as his father spoke again.

"Cadence and Snow Soldiers, ready yourself for the true battle and fight beside those you are ready to defend. You move to kill one another for your leadership: now let us guide you."

Frostien nodded his agreement by slamming Cinder into the ground before him. "Nicholas and I swore an oath to always protect each other. On these weapons we gave our word to always come to the other's aid. We expect those who follow us to do the same."

"We move to engage the true enemy. Follow us if you truly believe." They turned and strode toward the coming enemy they had seen from above. No one denied them, and both armies followed and slowly became one single army of the North Pole. Kol followed, and so did his friends. "Have the medics collect any wounded along with any Snow People who can help and move them into the city," his father told one of the higher officers. The officer ran to give the order.

"Sir." Drum Major Smithson stepped in stride with Saint Nicholas and Frostien. Next to her, the High Wizard Renshu sat on his giant blue cushion enchanted to fly. "We only meant..."

"I know exactly what you meant, as Frostien knows exactly what his people meant by what they did. With he and I out of the picture both of you were moved like pieces on a board. You did what you believed was right. Ready your troops, Eileen." Nodding, she took her whistle and blew it four times. The Cadence heard and began to reorder themselves in marching lines. Kol watched as they did and was able to see Holly among them. She did not wave or act like her hyper self. She was a soldier now, and acted like one. Kol nodded at her, and she gave a small smile, nodding back. Then Kol caught the eye of the person standing next to Holly. She too gave a smile and nod.

The wizards and witches from the Hall moved to supporting positions for the three columns that formed. The Snow People had no concrete rank or file to move into, just loosely assigned positions. After Frostien spoke with one of them, the Snowmen intermingled with the Cadence corps, an even number balanced between the now established columns. Kol remained at the front with the others behind Frostien and Saint Nicholas. Once they had left the original battlefield, his father called, "Renshu, provide us with light in the area before us."

"Yes, your Highness," the old Master said, then pointed his staff forward, as did his personal guard around him with staff and wand alike. Bright flares shot from them and arched over the ice ahead. Nothing happened at first, but eventually the monsters lost their sanctuary of the shadow of the wall. The force remaining was insignificant compared to the combined forces watching them. Not even a hundred creatures stood against almost five hundred of the combined northern forces. The light caused them to stir and roar in frustration. Kol figured they would flee at the sight of the combined armies, but they did not. Instead they began to charge at their foe.

Saint Nicholas reached out and gripped Frostien's arm. The bells hovering behind him rang, and Kol refrained from stepping away into the Sound like his father and uncle did. The two of them vanished and appeared at the front line of the opposing army. Their weapons clashed with the ghouls closest to them as the army of the North Pole erupted in a battle cry from the Snow People and the drum beats of the Cadence, both groups storming after their leaders. Frostien swung Cinder into the ground, and a shock wave knocked those around them to the ground as Jolly sang its song. With Saint Nicholas' full control of the Sound, he could destroy the entire invading force with only Frostien and himself, but Kol knew that it was more important for the people of the North Pole to see them fighting together. It had to be seen that it could be done. Two groups of people once parted by fear were now united by belief.

Kol remained out in front charging with his own elite force as he watched his father and uncle fight. Screeches came from above as more vampires like Andrew flew. From the flares, Kol could see four of them circling. That was how so many ghouls had been created: there was more than one elder vampire employed by the masked man. They became the instant target of the Learned as spells shot forth. Kol looked at Harvest, who shook his head. He would not transform into one of them in case the spells also turned on him. Harvest placed in his first fang and became a regular vampire, throwing his blanket to the side. Kol made sure to stay with him so no one would confuse him for an enemy there, either. By now they had reached the monsters, and Kol gave the first strike before the remaining force powered through.

The army of the North Pole divided along the center column and flanked either side of the hundreds of monsters. The pincer movement collapsed on the force as Snow Soldiers sent ghouls flying, along with everything else that formed their force. The Lord Vampires realized that there was no hope and took higher into the air to escape the coming defeat. The force did not last long, and minutes after the fight began, it was finished, as ghouls fell to dust and any creatures with a logical understanding surrendered to the Corps. Kol turned to his friends. "It's finally over."

Saint Nicholas heard him and walked over. "Not yet."

CHAPTER TWENTY-NINE

'Twas the Night Before Christmas

Once the threat had been eliminated, Nicholas had called for the people to come out from hiding, as had Frostien to the youths of his clan and those not trained in combat. They ordered that the armies begin the standard cleanup while the army of civilians mobilized for Christmas Eve that would begin in the next eight hours. The elves and humans were overwhelmed at the sight of their king awake and listened carefully to his instructions after they realized the Snow People were on their side. After speaking loving words to her husband, Kol's mother turned on him with joyful tears. Santa Claus established that the gifts that everyone had continued making without him would not be in vain and would be delivered on time. He gave a brief explanation about what had occurred and promised to explain more tonight at the ceremony. All they needed to know was that the Snow People were there to help, so the workers began to pull the resources together as Kol and his friends were ushered inside the workshop. Kol watched, mesmerized, as the Snow People and the people of the North Pole worked together, the previous aura of fear dissipating rapidly with the return of the leaders.

After the group had taken showers and removed their field gear, they gathered in his father's office to tell the story that had occurred while he slept. It was mainly Willa and Kol who spoke as Harvest listened, and Iris nodded in agreement, adding her own comments when needed. Lloyd had asked to omit himself from the story and go examine the tree further. Kol started from the night the ghouls had attacked and continued until he had met Harvest and Iris, then the other two, and Willa began to add her side of the story when Kol took a breath. Frostien arrived part of the way through and continued to listen, standing behind Saint Nicholas, who sat quietly at his desk, smiling and nodding along occasionally, writing something down. When they got to the part where Kol found his uncle's damaged hat, Frostien was able to explain how they had gained it.

"It shames me to admit this, but I was on my way to the city to speak with the council. I was deeply concerned for you," Frostien placed a hand on Saint Nicholas's shoulder, "and wished to check on you myself. After Kol had spoken with me, I held a great guilt that I was not there to protect you."

"It's fine, my old friend."

"Even so, I journeyed to see you. I went alone so that my alarm to the city would not be too great. Halfway through my walk there, I was attacked by a witch and those other elder vampires you saw. I managed to kill one of them, but they eventually overpowered me and harmed my hat." He tipped it forward. "That is the last I remember. I imagine that with my clan knowing the city was my destination and that I never returned, they feared the absolute worst. Then my wife sent our First Sons to look for me and ask if I was here. The guards at the gate told them that I had never arrived. They feared betrayal, and thus reacted."

"Thankfully, we may not have to worry on that matter any longer." Santa Claus patted his brother, "How's the cleanup?"

"Well, once the field is cleared, I will have them start in the city and begin the rebuilding the homes lost," Frostien rumbled.

"No, they may start that after Christmas. Let them rejoice together, and we shall start the next day. Those who were affected are currently being provided residence by others who are willing to share their homes." His father smiled at the caring involved and felt pride there. "Now, Kol and your sweet friend here carry on."

And so they did, continuing with what occurred at the river, and Kol made them aware that the witch that attacked his uncle could have been the same one. Once this was considered, he went on, and Willa let him finish the rest of the tale. Lloyd had returned and was playing with the wooden train set on the floor while Iris had curled into a ball and fallen fast asleep. Harvest had also decided to sit down in one of the chairs that one of the workshop workers placed for them.

Once Kol finished his tale, his father took a long moment to gather his thoughts. "Well," his voice woke Iris, who sat up to listen, "It would seem that the five of you have gone on quite an adventure, and thankfully the end result will help all of your goals. It is amazing how people can be pulled together by some unknown force for a common cause. I deeply thank each of you for helping my son wake me from the curse, and I in return am very proud of him for setting his own cause aside to help you all. I must say that each one of you is remarkable in your own ways. I hope you can finally believe in me, Wilhelmina, since you stopped at such an early age, as I recall." Kol believed Willa actually turned a faint shed of red. "The North Pole has all of you in its deepest debt."

"Do you have any idea who was behind all of this?" Willa and the others had heard about the masked man just now once Kol had told them of it.

His father took another moment. "That I can't answer, but I agree that it must have been someone within the city who knew exactly what was occurring amongst the people. Once everything is set right, I will have the Cadence check the registry and see if anyone is missing. If no one is, well, then it would be best to keep the enemy close. I believe that it will take some time before anything like this can be constructed again, especially with the people of the Flakes and North Pole fully believing in the coming alliance. I can say this to you all before you go: it is not over. I fear so long as something dark exists out there, our fight will continue. For now, go forth and have some food, and maybe get some much needed rest. We will begin as the evening comes along."

"And after?" Willa's worry could now be heard. "Will we have to stay here, or be enchanted before we leave?"

Saint Nicholas looked deeply into Willa, those eyes boring through her own and into her soul. Willa even took a step back at the intensity he showed. "This place is more than just a city or a sanctuary for the desperate. It is a symbol of hope and wonder to all the children of the world that we hope continues into their adulthood. You see what can occur when others outside of the city learn of it. Either to conquer unknown land, destroy the people within, and stop the primary reason this place was built." He let everyone absorb this before making his final statement. "This city owes you, and you risked your life to protect it. Those vampires that escaped know of it, and so does the witch, and whoever the masked man was. No, I will not hold you here, nor enchant you unless you ask us to. When you are ready, you are free to go. Simply ask someone to guide you to one of our own wizards or witches here. I will send word to Master Renshu and tell him so."

The five of them left after that and decided what they wanted to do. Lloyd went back to the tree, and the girls decided to go up to their provided rooms. Kol went to the kitchen with Harvest for some much-needed nutrients. "Well, you finally came back with very little time to spare. Thought you cared more than that," said the little familiar voice from behind him.

"I did not see you coming with me, Slee," Kol joked.

The elf cackled, "Indeed. Thank you, Kol."

Kol patted him on the back. "Of course." Slee then scurried off to help with the preparations.

Kol helped Harvest decide what would be best to eat, a full festival plate, and the two of them each gripped a mug of tea before setting off to eat on the front steps. The stage was under construction, and they sat and watched. There were also Snowmen and Snow women helping the elves fix the plaza.

"So," Kol started after finishing a roll, "You were okay with leaving your car behind?"

"What kind of question is that?" Harvest was annoyed. "The moment you summoned that train, I texted the Reverend and had his men come and pick it up, along with Iris's truck."

"You actually had someone else drive it?"

Harvest pulled his keys from his pocket and jingled them. "Nope. They brought a truck and loaded it up, placing them both in a private holding area. Rest assured, any damage will come out of the Rev's bank, and then some. Like the heart of one of his workers." Kol was not sure if that was a joke or not. "So this is where the original village was?"

Kol nodded while drinking his tea. "Yeah, the Tannenbaum Plaza is a memorial to it."

"And the tree that Lloyd is sleeping in?" Harvest nodded, and they both saw Lloyd slumped on his belly, splitting a branch half way up.

"My father planted the sapling when the village was first being built. It is grown ever since."

"Interesting."

Because he was communicating verbally, Kol decided it was worth a chance to ask. "So, you can take on the form of monsters so long as you have a piece of them?"

Harvest considered not answering; Kol read it plainly on his face. "For the most part, yeah, after I have killed them, but it's not simple." Kol did not ask why, but remained silent for whatever Harvest was willing to say. "Sometimes I can't control the monster." Kol nodded and ate a piece of turkey. That was more than enough.

"Take all the time you need, Kol," Holly quipped, approaching them. She was out of her uniform and drum, and back in her blue jeans and hoodie. "Hi, the name's Holly."

Harvest silently looked at her standing there. Kol supplied, "He doesn't talk very much. Yeah, but it really was as quickly as I could go. Thank you for the clue, Holly; we would have never been able to find the other one unless you had given it to me." He had given the remaining blade to Master Renshu, who immediately took it to the vaults in the Halls.

Holly nodded, smiling. "If you run off again without sending me a note I will kill you. You were just in time: we almost hit a point of no turning back."

"What do you mean?"

"None of the Cadence or Snow People were killed in the fighting. There were about a dozen who came close, and are currently in intensive care within the hospital, but they are expected to make full recoveries. If someone had died, then many might have believed that only blood would justify blood." She sounded so tired. So much energy drained; she must have been up for days. "Those other ice creatures had attacked the city several more times after you left. One even attacked a squad I was assigned to."

Kol became alarmed, "You weren't hurt too badly, were you?"

"Nah, just my shoulder. They kept attacking then fleeing."

"Causing as much fear as they could," Harvest said nodding to himself.

"He speaks!" Holly said in declaration, pointing her finger at Harvest.

Kol felt relief wash over him again, "I'm glad you are okay is all. And everyone else for that matter." Holly gave him a hard look. "As in no one died. That worry can now pass."

"For now," Harvest spoke, and Holly turned to him questioningly. Kol already knew what he was about to say. "This is not over yet, and in time it can only get worse." Kol did not reply because he agreed with him completely.

"You may be right. If so, we will be ready. Now that the Flakes and the North Pole are combining forces, I feel sorry for any other enemies to come." Holly sounded like she too agreed. "I'll see you later, Kol, and thank you too, creepy man."

"Harvest," Kol supplied.

"Yeah, thank you, and it was nice to meet you, Harvest." She smiled again and turned back to walk across the plaza. She met the same Cadence member Kol had seen her next to in the battle on the edge of the ring of trees. He made a mental note to ask Holly about the individual later. The black-haired person reached out and grabbed Holly's hand before the two of them walked off together, and Kol smiled.

******

The crowd was restless as they packed into the plaza around the giant Christmas Tree. There was a mix of excitement, joy, relief, and many others that could be associated with what occurred within the city. Unease remained as well, for among the citizens of the North Pole the Snow People also stood in small forms, many leaving their armor outside of the city and wearing their enchanted articles of clothing among the other fabrics they wore. Kol laughed quietly when he saw one Snowman wearing a red hat complete with a fuzzy white ball. Another fantastic sight was a child sitting on the shoulders of another Snowman. They all waited for Frostien and Santa Claus to address them on the raised stage erected out from beneath the hanging limbs of the tree. The eight reindeer stood harnessed and completely decorated for the event. His father's red sleigh had been outfitted for the journey as well, with the trim white sleigh polished to a shine, and white bag nestled in the back, tied tightly with gifts inside ready to be delivered.

Kol stood close to the stage wearing the new clothes he had been given after the battle. Everyone else had also been given new clothes to wear, sewn freshly by elves who would not stand for the heroes who saved the city to attend the event without fine clothing. Kol had been placed in the usual royal wear, which he did not approve of, but after the harsh assault his mother launched at him for making her worry, Kol had little choice. Harvest made sure he had black dress clothes made, and Lloyd had asked for green. Iris had chosen a gold dress that she stood beautifully in. Willa also wore a dress of her own decorated in purple.

Kol noticed that she was indeed rather pretty when not scolding or wearing her armor, though quickly remembered to never underestimate her, regardless of attire, as she grinned fiercely at him, seeming to sense his thoughts.

The clock above the workshop struck midnight, and as the deep bells tolled, the crowd erupted into pent up excitement. It was more than that: a joyous release that after all the hardship, the year ended like it should. Perhaps the darkest Christmas Eve yet, but beneath the beaming tree all feelings of shadows could easily be chased away. At the final ring, the doors of the workshop opened, and Kol's father came out in his traditional attire. Next to him Frostien stood in a green trench coat with his black top hat, of course. They raised their arms in celebration as the crowd continued to cheer. The reindeer also jumped in exultation: they would soon be able to fly again. The bells were attached to them and the sleigh sung in the emotions.

Together, the two of them walked down into the crowd along the open path the parting people made. Both stood proudly as equals, the exact message the people needed to see. As they approached the stairs and climbed, the noise went up with them, which seemed impossible. In front of the sleigh they walked and then stopped to let the crowd quiet back down. When it did not, Frostien raised his arms and eased the noise down. The effect on the crowd was as expected. Saint Nicholas began:

"Once again, the time has come for me to take to the skies and deliver to the children of the world all your hard work and dedication. No matter the faith or belief, each child is presented with a gift in one form or another. All in the hope that someone is looking after them, and through that we pray they grow into someone to make the world a better place. All of this is possible because of you. All of you." He let the crowd understand his speech was becoming something more before continuing, "All the metal used comes from the Snow People, from the rails of my sleigh to the cogs within the tiny robots. It is with the combined effort of everyone this night can truly exist. That your homes truly hold a gathered meaning among the nation. One nation, not two."

Frostien took his cue and spoke out. "When first I came to this place, I was rightfully feared by those who lived here. I understood why, so I departed the city to show from a distance how my people also believed in the mission. Overcoming fear takes time, and my brother and I believed that we had plenty of time to show everyone the truth. Yet someone understood this fear, and he decided it was the perfect weapon to destroy everything we hold dear to our hearts. This person who we have yet to discover may live among you and feed from that which you did not truly understand. It was he who attacked Santa and it was he who ordered the attack on me. He knew that the balance was only kept by the two of us alone. That is not how it should be. There may be a day when the two of us can no longer be here to lead all of you, just like it was days before. It cannot be that with us gone everything we have worked so hard to achieve can be so easily torn apart."

"The Snow People are nothing to fear."

"And neither are the people within these very walls."

"If we do not stand united," Santa Claus went on, "then the enemy can truly move against us again and with the same amount of ease as before. So, from this day forward, we have a common enemy, and because of that the bond between the two factions can stand stronger, and in time become something that no other force on earth can stand against, so long as their intent is evil. From now on, we will ask everyone to experience one another. Snow People will be able to join the Cadence and Hall."

"Just as elves and humans will be able to learn our art with metal forging and cloth making. We can all learn from one another, and we hope that you can all learn from us. Protect one another; we are all one family united by one cause. The evil that once consumed the earth so long ago will never sleep and we must be ready." Frostien ended their speech, and the crowd was quiet.

So much time had allowed the paranoia to grow between the two people it might be hard for them all to truly accept this. From the back of the crowd, the small child sitting on the shoulder of one of the Snowmen yelled his belief in their speech, and from his innocence the crowd began to cheer together until another uproar had been created. Kol's heart soared with his own pride in the people, his people.

"Now, I would like to acknowledge the individuals who made this possible." None of them, even Kol, had expected this, but the time to turn back had passed. Kol climbed onto the stage at his father's beckoning and the others followed. Kol went and stood by his father, then Harvest, Willa, Iris, and Lloyd. "My son Nicholas," he used his true name, "along with his friends Harvest, Wilhelmina, Irisalyn, and Lloydric, all dedicated their lives to bring my brother and I back. If complete strangers can do that, then so can the people of the North Pole and those of the Flakes." Kol was not surprised that his father knew their true names when they had told no one. Iris, however, was certainly surprised—and Willa shifted awkwardly. Kol smiled to the crowd while Harvest remained himself. Willa gave a small bow and Iris turned bright red. Lloyd laughed widely and waved. "Now," the crowd calmed again, "We shall be off. My brother and I have much to discuss on my trip." He turned once more to them. "Thank you for everything, truly." He took his rightful seat in the sled and so did Frostien beside him.

"Dad," Kol called, as the Cadence in the crowd began their roll.

"Yes?" he asked, turning to speak with him.

Kol pulled a note he had written the hour before from his pocket. "There are people, children mostly, on this list who also helped me. The one at the bottom being the most important. You'll understand."

"Indeed I will..." Santa Claus spoke the phrase that everyone had truly been waiting for at this moment. "Now, Dasher, now Dancer, now Prancer, and Vixen! ON Comet, on Cupid, on

Donner and Blitzen!" Each name caused the reindeer to begin his pull, and on the final name the eight were off the stage and once more into the air. "To the top of the porch! To the top of the wall!" The sled came next, and his father was off into the sky. "Now dash away, dash away, dash away ALL!" Kol heard the bells ring, and his father accepted their Sound. Kol did the same and was able to watch his father slightly longer than the rest of the crowd. When he let the Sound go, the swift silence away from time was once again filled with noise.

Forward unto Dawn

Kol made his way through the village houses dressed now in common clothes with his hood pulled up tightly. The last thing he wanted was for anyone to recognize him. Because of his father's display the following night, he and the others could not go a breath without being praised by anyone close. Gifts of gratitude in forms of food, clothes, and even jewelry quickly arrived, but they accepted none. Thanks to Holly and a few other Cadence members, they had finally been given space to breath. Next came the festival, where tables were conjured into the area and the food was transported there just like on the first of the month. There was even flavored ice that the Snow Men used as a food source for themselves, more for the simple pleasure of taste than sustenance. Everyone took their place, and together they all sat and became merry.

Once the food was gone, the crowd dispersed to head home after the long day. After all, how else would Santa come if no one was asleep on his final stop? The five of them climbed up into the workshop and told each other their good nights. Before she could leave, Kol asked Iris for a moment of her time. "Yes?" she asked him, sleepily.

"Iris, now that we accomplished our goals, I'd like to spend some time with you."

She looked at him slyly. "And why, Kol, is that?"

Kol hesitated. Someone who feared little and always spoke easily found it difficult to do so now. "I would like to take you to a special place of mine tomorrow."

"Like a date?" She looked up at him blankly, completely unreadable to Kol.

Kol was physically nervous. "Yes, if you find that to be all right." He handed her a piece of paper. "Ask one of the carriages to bring you there tomorrow at that time."

Iris looked at him for a moment longer. Slowly she reached out and took the piece of paper in her hand, keeping it on his. Then she completely caught him off guard by reaching with her other hand and pulling him down so that his lips met hers. The fire from her lips surged through his body, and he felt as though his strength would leave him. He was able to regain his composure long enough to pull her closer and kiss her back deeply. Kol had once again stepped from time, thinking this moment lasted forever. Yet too quickly she pulled away. "We'll see," she said, and vanished upstairs.

✶✶✶✶✶✶

The Lake of Frost came into view just before him. Thankfully the place was in a part of town the monsters had not been. The Cadence had had checked everyone's home for any monsters hiding there and had found a few. They had been arrested and sent to the Island for interrogations. The front door jingled as he stepped inside. "KOL!" Kol was pulled off the ground as Mr. Mugsteeve swept him up in a bone-breaking embrace. "Why didn't you tell me you were the King's son?"

"Shhhhhhh," Kol whispered in a strangled tone from within the painful hug.

Mr. Mugsteeve set him down. "Oh, guess you would like to have your privacy. Luckily no one heard me."

Kol knew he was right. A bard sat on the small stage playing Christmas songs, and every table but two were full of laughter, jokes, and games of different sorts. There was even a Snowman sitting at a table telling a story that the made gentlemen around him laugh at the end. "So I see."

"We owe you so much. Whatever you need, just say it."

"You owe me nothing. But maybe my own table; I have a lady on the way."

"Ha, I knew you would find you a lucky lady. I'll have my wife cook you something special and get you some of my best seasonal drink." He turned and was gone before Kol could say otherwise. Kol found his table next to the one Shane frequented. A few minutes later Mr. Mugsteeve brought over two mugs of golden liquid and was off again. Kol barely touched it; he had become too nervous. Minutes passed, and he waited, his heart jumping slightly whenever the door opened. Eventually Kol pulled out his list and checked the time; he had asked her to meet him a little over half an hour ago.

"This for me?" Kol looked up to Master Shane standing before him in his golden robes.

"No, it's for a lady I asked to meet me here, but you are welcome to sit." Shane did so.

"This lady of yours. She one of the ones who helped the city? The one without the armor?" Shane reached into his coat.

Kol looked at him suspiciously. "Yes, why do you ask?"

"She wanted me to give you this." Master Shane pulled out a brown letter for him sealed in red wax. On it was an imprint of a flame and across the other side was his name in Iris' handwriting. Without saying another world, Kol opened it and began to read.

Dear Kol,

I am deeply sorry to tell you like this, but it is one of my flaws to not be able to do so in person. You see, I hate goodbyes, and to do so in person would have been painful to endure. This past month with you has been truly amazing. We accomplished so much in such little time. That, along with learning that the North Pole exists, has led me to believe in miracles far more than I ever had before. Unfortunately, I must return to my wagons as quickly as possible. My horses must be worried, and I must write to my sister back home and tell her the mission is complete. I must continue my trial so that I can return to her and the rest of my family.

I am sorry to also tell you that for right now the two of us cannot be, no matter how much each of us wishes. I hope you never felt as if I led you on. You will be in my thought as this world continues, and perhaps once more we can fight alongside one another.

Iris

When he finished, Master Shane was taking a long swallow of her drink. "When did she give this to you?"

The old wizard looked sad when he replied, "This morning. She and that armored lady came to me and my colleagues asking for a portal back home. Before I made one, she asked me if I knew where the Lake of Frost was. Then she asked me to deliver the letter. She didn't know I knew who you were."

"I see. And the armored one," Kol was avoiding any more talk about Iris, "did she leave or say anything?"

"No, just something odd." Shane took another long swig. "The first ones that can leave without the safety spell we use, and she asked for it anyway."

"Truly?" Always surprising Kol, Willa was.

"Yeah, them both. I of course, in my curious old age asked why. She said that if anyone ever tried to get the information from them, they would not be able to tell."

Kol's respect for Willa intensified, as did his for Iris, but he didn't want to think about that. "Thank you for bringing this here." Kol stood and placed several coins on the table. "Tell Mr. Mugsteeve I'm sorry, but I had to go."

"Don't want to stay for a quick game?" He eyed his chess board next to them.

"No, not today, Master Shane. Another time." Kol turned to leave. "Were you in the battle?"

"'Course I was. They kept me towards the back, 'fraid I might break something by tripping and falling into the ice." He laughed, and Kol smiled as he made his way out.

Kol reread the letter a few more times as he made his way back. He understood every word, but he could not deny the sinking feeling that came along with it. This was not his first rejection. Holly and he had had their bumpy stage, but Kol thought that this would be different. Especially after they had kissed last night. Folding the letter neatly, he placed it in his pocket until he could find a safe place for it.

He made it back to the workshop easily without drawing any more attention to himself. Lloyd was once again up in the tree, and Kol saw Harvest standing beneath it asking him to come down. "Did you know that Willa and Iris left?"

"I did. She came and woke me up to say goodbye. Not Iris, she was already gone to the Hall. She said they needed to get back."

"I see." Kol watched Lloyd sitting above. "Coming down any time soon?"

"No!" Lloyd yelled down.

Harvest yelled back, "Well, you need to; I have someone I'd like you two to meet." Kol looked at Harvest questioningly but he said no more.

Curiosity was strong enough to pull Lloyd back down to the ground. "And who might this be?"

"He's speaking to your father now," Harvest told Kol, and together they started for workshop.

"I didn't expect my dad to be up," Kol said. "Guess he decided he had slept enough."

The workshop was completely empty when they passed through it. Everyone was at home spending time with their family. Kol thought of Iris being alone, but then remembered that Willa would be with her so it was not so bad. They walked up the steps, and Kol pulled both doors wide for them to step into his father's office. His father was in his chair with very tired eyes but a pleasant smile on his face. He had been talking to the other man in the room when they had entered. The stranger was a little shorter than Kol and held a very small amount of extra weight. His stance was pleasant yet formal, and he was dressed in a white suit with a blue dress shirt and black tie. His skin was dark, and his eyes almost seemed black behind square framed glasses. "Ah," the new individual said. His voice was light. "This must be Nicholas."

"Kol is fine," Kol told the guest, continuing to examine him.

"Hmm." His face was pleasant, and his expression was of someone with a deep interest and an old understanding. "I'm well aware. I simply, as I have told your father, love the name Nicholas. My teacher was also named Nicholas. Of course, this other young gentleman is Lloydric, or Lloyd, as he chooses." Lloyd bowed in an exaggerated gesture. "Good to see you whole as always, Harvest."

"As you should always expect." Harvest sounded rather amused. "This is my employer, Weldon Greerson."

Kol shocked to finally gain a little more information on Harvest than expected. "Well, it's very nice to meet you, Mr. Greerson. Can I ask why you're here?"

"Professor," Harvest corrected him.

"I knew his teacher very well, and as such came to know his protégé," his father stated, indicating the professor, his voice only a pitch above exhaustion. "Weldon, if you would like to explain…"

"Certainly. Kol, Lloyd: I have a proposition for the both of you." Professor Greerson moved from around the desk to examine them closer. "Harvest here has told me about the two of you and how you helped him with his trivial problem in the States. You see," he patted Harvest on the shoulder, "I no longer have the amount of youth needed for the things I like to accomplish. So I hire individuals of superior skill to fully investigate matters that come to my attention. Yes, part of the proposed employment is to either help or detain the normal and supernatural beings of the world that are either seeking sanctuary or prefer acting the part of monsters that like to cause a stir among those who think of them as only bedtime stories in October. Of course, there are others that do these things as well; the Knights and the gypsy girl, but I am not often fond of their methods completely, and groups so large cannot be trusted with the deeper reasoning for the existence of this proposed group. You see, I, along with your father, come from an old order that helped keep the world safe.

"Your employment will be to not only help protect the innocent from the harms of the powerful, but also to investigate more extreme information that pertains to the safety of the world on a global level. Something deeper is happening in this world; the attack on the North Pole is testament to that. Your father agrees that you should be made more aware of it. I would like for the two of you to come back with Harvest and me, and from there I will send you on your missions, and perhaps show you parts of the world you have never truly heard of, like this place."

"I thought you may be interested in this, Kol," his father urged. "On my trip tonight, I spoke with my brother about what is to become of you. Though I have my hopes, I can't make you do anything that your heart truly does not desire. I also do not expect you to carry such a burden for a world you have seen so little of. Once I convince your mother of the same, I am sure she will approve. Weldon will explain more once you arrive at his home."

"Indeed I shall: I can't tell you everything until you agree to join us," Professor Greerson reassured him with a smile.

Kol looked to him then back to his father. It was true, Kol knew very little about the world that had interested him in books. He truly wanted to see all of it and share it with his people once he had returned. It was an adventure he could never pass up. Kol looked at Lloyd, who was nodding his head and bouncing on his feet. Kol reached out his hand to Professor Greerson. "You have me."

About the Author

Kahner C. Calloway has spent the entirety of his life in Alabama, where he grew up first in its capitol city, then in the city's surrounding area. Much of his primary education was spent in the way most people experience it: trying to find himself in the ocean of uncertainty that is adolescence. As a kid, Kahner could be found often with his nose in a book or with his hands holding a video game controller. During the summer he would spend the days with his loving grandparents, and the rest of the year it was not unheard of for Kahner and his brother Kayne to be packed tightly in a car to head off on another excursion to somewhere in the United States with their adventurous mother.

After graduating from high school, Kahner attended Auburn University at Montgomery, where he graduated with a history degree, hoping to become a teacher. Life has a way of causing the cards to fall where they may, and not where you wish. As such, Kahner was unable to become a teacher just yet, but has devoted his time to completing his book while working in-between jobs.

Kahner wrote his first book during the free time he had while attending college. He was inspired by his mother after she had read a short story Kahner had written explaining how the magic of Christmas worked. "There is something more to this. So, don't show anyone else about it yet," she said, encouraging him to develop his short story further. After that, it was normal to find Kahner at his computer at two in morning, tapping away at the keys. Once the book was complete, Kahner had to find someone who could help him edit it. A lack of funds hindered that process for a year.

Thankfully, marriage is an acceptable exchange for editing a book. Kahner met his wife Miranda on the day of their shared graduation—Kahner with his undergraduate, and Miranda with her Masters in English. While they were dating, Miranda decided to take on the daunting task of arranging Kahner's abstract conglomeration into something more enjoyable for all. This, and the fact that Kahner was madly in love with her, helped sealed the deal. They live happily together in Alabama with their three pets.

When Kahner isn't obsessing over his notebooks, he enjoys woodworking in his garage, playing Dungeons and Dragons with his friends as their Dungeon Master, or traveling as far and wide as he can.

Made in the USA
Middletown, DE
11 December 2018